# My Lucky Star

## Love Istanbul ✴ Book 1

## Enni Amanda

1st edition, 2023

Lumi Publishing

Edited by Rachel Collins / Do It Write

Proofread by Roxana Coumans



ISBN 978-1-99-116502-2 (paperback)

ISBN 978-1-99-116501-5 (ebook)

Designed by Yummy Book Covers
Typeset in Droid Serif, 10.5pt

*To all the dreamers
who've lost their way*

# Note to reader

While this book takes place in real locations of Napier (New Zealand) and Istanbul (Turkey), it is a work of fiction. I've bodly made up some local businesses, such as cafes and hotels, inspired by real ones but altered to suit my story.

I wrote this book before the earthquake that hit Turkey and Syria, and the flood that ravaged Napier in 2023, so these events are not referenced.

However, if reading this book leads you to fall in love with these amazing locations, please consider donating to disaster relief.

# The Glossary

This book features some Turkish words. The meaning of each should be clear enough from the context, but in case you're a fellow language geek, here's a quick glossary:

*Türk dizileri* (dizi) - Turkish TV series. Longer format than your usual Netflix shows, often highly emotional, romantic, and more chaste than the Hollywood variety.

*Hoşgeldiniz* - *Welcome*

*Teşekkürler* - Thank you

*Görüşürüz* - See you later

*Merhaba* - Hello

*Aşkta şanslı* - Lucky in love

*Aşkım* - My love

*Annem* - Mother

*Evet* - Yes

*Yok* - No

*Bey* - Mr. (a formal title used with the first name, i.e. *Cem bey*)

*Çok güzel* – Very good

# Prounciation Guide

**Turkish names can be difficult to pronounce. Here's a quick guide to the main characters:**

**Cem:** Pronounced like "jem" with a soft "j" sound, similar to the "s" sound in the word "measure."

**Emir:** Pronounced like "eh-meer" with the stress on the first syllable. The "e" sound is pronounced like the "e" in the word "pet," and the "i" sound is pronounced like the "ee" in the word "see."

**Burcu:** Pronounced like "boor-joo" with the stress on the second syllable. The "u" sound is pronounced like the "oo" in the word "boot," and the "c" is pronounced like the "j" sound in "jeans."

# My Lucky Star

# CHAPTER 1

I love Turkish.

The food, I mean. It's the perfect takeaway – not full of sugar like Chinese or greasy like pizza. Yet, it's always tasty, unlike those spiritually aware bowls of sprouts.

"Thank you!" I grinned from ear to ear as the stocky middle-aged Turk handed me my trusted chicken kebab.

Kerim smiled back, a glimpse of his handsome youth showing through the cracks.

"How do you say delicious?"

"*Lezzetli*." He drew out each syllable with passion.

I repeated the word, and he insisted on high fiving me.

"You have a good ear! And you're very beautiful today."

I chuckled. He told me that every time, and every time, I

instinctively glanced at my outfit. This time, I'd tucked a loose T-shirt into denim shorts and was using my ballet flats as slip-ons, completely destroying their structural integrity. They had some sparkle, though. I'm not a cavewoman.

"You laugh. I'm serious." Kerim threw up his hands, mock offended. "You remind me of a movie star. I'm not remembering the name..." He tapped his forehead in frustration. "It will come later. Old age."

My long, dark hair had always been shiny and thick, which usually saved me from looking like I'd slept in a car, even if I lacked in every other aspect of put-togetherness. I smiled obligingly at Kerim's praise, my mood elevating with each word. Getting my lunch with an ego boost was definitely one of the upsides of being back in my old hometown. That, and not having to worry about appearances.

I inhaled the rich scent of frying meat and spices. Since moving back to Napier a couple of months ago, I'd already decided that Kerim's Kebab deserved to become a famous movie location. A place where every traveler had to stop and photograph themselves next to those pretentious, airbrushed actor headshots adorning the walls.

I would make that happen, I promised myself. After all, it was my job to attract international film productions and channel money into the region; a brand-new job I was still figuring out, but figure it out I would, because it was a real job with a real salary, not a pipe dream. I was done with those.

Someone tapped their foot behind me, and I moved along,

waving my foil-covered roll in goodbye. In December, the seasonal tourist activity had already started, limiting our lunch and dinner chats. Still, everything in Napier happened at a leisurely pace.

With the burn of midday sun on my skin, I strolled down the street toward my car, browsing the cream, pale pink and minty green stucco buildings with golden zigzags and sunbursts, proud and polished like artisan cakes. Hailed as the Art Deco capital of New Zealand, residents of Napier had discovered gold paint and geometric detailing in the 1930s while rebuilding after an earthquake. I found it unsettling that it had taken total destruction to birth something so beautiful and unique.

What had once been fashionable was now historical, a money pit of constant restoration. Still, nowhere else in New Zealand could you time travel to the 1930s like in Napier. That was one of the lines I now recited, a friendly smile splitting my face, as I spent my time selling the town and its surroundings to discerning location scouts, directors and producers.

I reached my car, a cheap hybrid in an unassuming grey I'd bought based on the specs and nothing else. The vehicle was part of my new life plan of lowered expectations and practicality. It added little to my personality but did its job and didn't leave me on the side of the road.

I'd get used to this new version of me, I promised myself. The always-broke dreamer I'd been in my twenties would soon be an anecdote I told witty, wildly exaggerated stories about at parties. That was one part of me I couldn't shut down. I'd always be the inappropriate one with stupid jokes.

My phone rang. I knew it was Mom before I even found the device in my pocket. Ever since I'd moved back, she'd taken it on herself to fill my calendar with family obligations, possibly to distract me from the fact that I had nothing else going on. Also, nobody else I knew used their phone as a phone.

"Are you free for dinner on Thursday?" Mom chirped. "We're having fajitas to thank Felix for his help with the lawns and the pergola."

My stomach tightened. Felix, my old friend who now lived next door to my parents, ran a one-person carpet cleaning business and clearly looked after my parents better than I did. I should have been grateful, and I was, but he was also the reason I couldn't move back into my old bedroom in my parents' house, not even in the short term. Living next door to a guy your parents were eyeing up as a future son-in-law would have taken the small-town suffocation to a whole new level.

To make matters worse, I really liked Felix as a friend. We'd always had an easy-going relationship that included the occasional poking-fun-of and laughing-until-our-lungs-hurt, but never the wonder-what-he-thinks-of me or other weird crap. I'd carefully avoided giving out any 'I want to be Mrs. Carpet Blast' vibes, hoping I didn't lose his friendship. The only friend I had in this town, apart from my colleagues.

"Um... I don't know. I haven't really been part of this."

By this, I meant the garden makeover my parents had orchestrated with the help of Felix, the world's best neighbor.

"Maybe you can think of yourself as part of this family as we show gratitude to an exceptionally helpful neighbor." Mom's voice had a tired edge.

I swallowed. "Yeah, of course. He's been amazing."

"Maybe Felix can help you feel more at home. He loves Napier, and he's well connected."

God, she was good. So diplomatic. I had no reason to diss my only friend, even if this fajitas gathering sounded an awful lot like a chaperoned dinner date.

When I thought about my newfound realism, I had to admit Mom was right about Felix. He wasn't a looker, but definitely husband material. Dependable, helpful, always around. Absolutely the kind of guy I should go for. See, I didn't say 'settle'. The trick to settling is that you should never call it that, because in the end, it's realism. The necessary process of giving up flighty dreams and facing the real world, something I was definitely working on – even if I wasn't ready for that next step. That lanky, baseball-cap wearing, carpet-cleaning step.

The phone line crackled. "Are you still on lunch break? I told Felix he might find you in town around this time, getting your kebab."

As if on cue, I heard an engine and Felix's trusty van pulled up behind me. Of course. Mom was working on all fronts. Lunch, dinner... what else had she planned? Moonlight walks?

"He's here," I muttered into the phone and ended the call, resigning myself to my fate.

Felix tumbled out of his van like an elk in loose denim, a faint chemical smell in his wake. "Hi there! How're you doing?"

He was so skinny. The poor guy couldn't stand solidly on two feet. He always swayed a little, like a young tree in a moderate breeze.

I cursed my mother's meddling. Before all the dating hints, I'd thought of Felix as a friend and never judged him like this.

"I'm good." I tried to smile, lifting my kebab. "I grabbed a quick lunch, but now I have to get back to the office."

"Will you get fired if you sit down for one coffee? There's a new place that opened and I swear they do triple shots without you asking. Gave me double vision." He crossed his eyes for emphasis.

Felix knew I liked my coffee strong.

"Let's go another time? I promise." I tightened my fingers around the car door handle, desperate to get away.

His face lit up. "Great! I'll text you."

I gave him a quick smile, slid behind the wheel and pulled into the traffic, mindlessly following a silver taxi as it circled the Masonic Hotel.

Guilty and confused, I unwrapped the kebab with my teeth and filled my senses with its spicy flavor. Surely, being more realistic didn't mean I had to date someone I didn't find attractive? I was allowed to have some dreams, I told myself. Small, doable, passable dreams. Like finding a man with an ounce of charisma. Or failing that, some amazing movie locations.

I loved gorgeous buildings, imagining the secrets, drama and love affairs they'd witnessed over the years. Entering a house that wasn't built for utmost functionality instantly elevated my spirit. The opulent, decorative, even the odd and visually disturbing, connected you to those who'd dared to live more courageously. Or rather, who could afford to live more courageously, chasing their dreams in a way that wasn't accessible to me. The lucky ones.

I drove mindlessly around town, eating my kebab. I didn't need to go back to the office, but I didn't want to risk running into Felix again.

My mind still on dreamy architecture, I swerved onto the beach road, away from the town center. I wanted to see the old hotel. The pink Art Deco building was one of my favorite pieces of architecture in Napier, and according to Trade Me, currently for sale.

Not that I had money to buy a house, let alone a hotel. I could barely cover the rent of my one-room apartment above the laundromat, but I'd heard my boss Janie talking to an American film producer who was looking for an Art Deco hotel. It might be a long shot, but I hadn't done any of these matchmaking deals yet and itched to get my hands dirty. If my favorite building got chosen because of me, I could say I'd brought business to my home town, to Kerim's kebab shop and to countless others. I'd prove my worth at the film office.

I parked on the street outside the pale pink stucco facade, admiring the maroon detailing above the entrance. As I got out to investigate closer, I spotted a white van in the driveway. A stocky, greying man in a T-shirt and baseball cap stepped out of the side door with a cardboard box. I waved at him, stepping into his line of sight. "Hey! I'm looking for the owner—"

"I'm only here for maintenance," the guy grumbled, pushing

past me. "It's for sale. Look it up on Trade Me."

"Yes, I know." I followed him to his dirty van. "I was hoping to find out what's happening in the meantime. Is it still working as a hotel, are they renovating...?"

The man opened his side door and slid the cardboard box between toolboxes. "I'm just here to change the lightbulbs." He turned around to face me, lips puckered.

I offered my full wattage smile. "I'm with the film office and this is such a beautiful location that I wanted to find out a bit more."

He seemed to assess my trustworthiness, his expression thawing a bit. "My wife's coming to prep the rooms later today. She's been cleaning here for the past six months, and this is the first time they only want two rooms done. Sounds like the whole place is booked for a very small group." He leaned in, lowering his voice. "I reckon it's someone pretty... um, precious. They asked me to change all those fine led lights to these..." He opened the box and held out an empty packet, squinting at it, "'rose-tinted' ones." His voice oozed contempt.

My curiosity climbed up several notches. "Is there anything else?"

"That's all I know, and I'm in a bit of a hurry, so if you'll excuse me..."

He disappeared around the vehicle, getting behind the wheel.

I waited for him to leave, then snapped a couple of photos of the exterior. A shiver of excitement ran up my spine. So, someone had booked out the entire hotel and requested new lightbulbs. Something was going on.

# CHAPTER 2

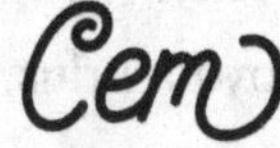

I was used to seeing my name on various boards, magazine covers, and of course, in massive letters on the big screen. I'd never seen it scribbled with a magic marker on a handmade cardboard sign, misspelled so grossly I dismissed it until we were the only people left in the small airport lounge. A shock of blond hair hung on his forehead and an oversized T-shirt on his slight frame.

Sam Larkham, the sign said.

"Cem Erkam," I said, pointing at the cardboard.

A relieved smile lit up the man's face.

I shook my head in disbelief and followed him out the double doors, into a small, mostly empty car park. No people? This place was already making me nervous. Not that I intended to stay long, if I could help it.

I'd suffered the eternal series of flights in relative silence, alone in my corner of first class. My brother Emir had abandoned me moments before my departure but assured me he'd join me later. When, he hadn't said.

They'd sure been in a hurry to get rid of me, sending me as far away as humanly possible. Emir insisted he'd chosen the location carefully, but I was fairly sure he'd called our cousins who lived in New Zealand and outsourced the entire job to them. I could imagine the assignment: Find an obscure small town where nobody will know a Turkish celebrity. Their answer: Napier.

I got into the silver Toyota Prius, which at least had working air-con, and tried to revive my phone. The driver chatted about something in a weird nasal accent I couldn't make much sense of.

In my twenties, I'd spent a couple of years in Los Angeles and was fluent in English, or so I thought. Based on this first encounter, New Zealand didn't speak the same English as the rest of the world.

My phone still searched for a network as we took a narrow, two-lane road through an endless display of rolling hills. I closed my eyes against the green brightness invading my vision. It seemed I'd landed on a completely uninhabited island, apart from sheep, but I knew better. I'd been promised a hotel to myself, with room service.

I know most people don't get a hotel to themselves. Back in Turkey, I didn't either, but I was here to hide, and they'd gotten a good deal, apparently.

I peeled off my designer jacket and folded it haphazardly over my satchel bag, which held the basics – toiletries and a change of underwear. I didn't enjoy dragging bags on airplanes. That's what the cargo hold was for.

I couldn't wait to get changed into something more comfortable. A couple of fashion houses had a vested interest in me, so I never ran out of designer gear. Thankfully, one of them also made fitness clothes. For the next couple of weeks, I would lounge in my gym clothes and train. Hopefully by then everyone would have forgotten about my blunder, and I'd be ready for the lead role in Ottoman Games, a new series by Epic Studios with all-star cast and international distribution.

To get ready, I needed to get back to my exercise regime. I'd been between jobs and cutting myself a bit of slack lately. Emir had given me a serious speech outside the airport about getting my act together. If I lost this next role, my career might never recover. Yada, yada. Something about being selfish and lazy and only thinking of myself. The economy was crashing and the whole family depended on my income. I felt a weight sitting on my chest just thinking about it.

I'd made a weak argument about wanting to stretch myself artistically. That maybe I didn't want to play another syrupy romantic lead. Maybe I was tired of gazing deep into the eyes of some pretty girl, thinking of kissing them, but nine times out of ten not actually kissing to appease the conservative viewer base. Each time, I perpetuated a myth, branding myself as the romantic hero I knew I wasn't.

But Emir was right about one thing, Ottoman Games was my only shot at real money.

I settled into the seat, watching the foreign, yet somehow familiar, sight of those green hills, a bit like driving to the mountains in my home country.

I tried to breathe against the tightness in my chest. I only had to make it through a couple of weeks, three at most. I'd secure that role and I'd nail it. Maybe then I'd be free.

The car came to a halt, and I opened my eyes. We'd stopped in front of a pink, plastered building with curved corners and geometrical detailing. Art Deco, maybe. Despite its off-the-map location, I immediately liked the house. It had character.

"This is it," the driver confirmed.

He didn't move, so I got out of the car. "Can you get my bags?"

"What bags?" he asked, his forearm hanging out of the open window, eyes on my shoulder bag.

"My luggage." I raised my brow, counting to ten in my mind. I'd come across some dim-witted staff during my career, but I prided myself on always controlling my temper. The day I took my frustration out on a servant, I'd become my own worst nightmare – the entitled asshole.

I was lucky, far luckier than most, and worked hard to keep that in mind.

The driver shook his head, his eyes widening almost comically. "I asked if you were ready to go and you nodded."

I must have nodded twenty times when he first spoke to me. I'd spent hours wandering through hallways and passport checks at airports, dogs sniffing me for drugs and apples, filling out forms about my stay using the one brief email from my brother. I'd done my part and assumed everything else was taken care of. That's how it usually worked.

Was I supposed to have done it myself? I hadn't been near a baggage carousel in years. An uneasy feeling turned my stomach. Did this mean that I was an entitled asshole?

I forced my face to neutral. "I'm sorry, but I don't know how things work around here. Can you go back and pick them up?"

He winced. "I would, but I have another job. Sorry, mate."

He continued with a detailed explanation I couldn't quite follow. Something about a film shoot, drinks and ice creams.

The sound of the front door of the hotel opening cut him off. The hinges cried out as a rotund female appeared on the steps, waving madly at us. "Welcome, welcome!"

Her voice bellowed across the sidewalk and distracted me from the fact that my driver was getting away, speeding down the deserted road. Were there any other people, anywhere? Across the street, a vast view of grass, sand and ocean greeted me with desert island vibes. Empty and quiet.

I shook my head in disbelief, mentally preparing myself for whatever was coming. Taking my satchel and jacket, I approached my new residence. The lady held the door for me, sucking in her stomach to let me pass. She smelled of sweat and disinfectant but smiled enthusiastically.

"You must be Sam. You've had a long journey! Let's get you settled." She herded me into a worn-out, empty reception with an uneven wood floor.

I didn't even have the energy to correct my name. I followed her up a curved, wooden staircase and along a carpeted hallway. The top note of the citrusy disinfectant emanating from both her and the house didn't fully cover the musty smell of abandonment.

"Has this place been empty for a long time?" I asked as she guided me into a room with a king-sized bed.

She shrugged noncommittally. "It's not peak season yet."

I took a tentative step forward, surveying the state of the room. It had been cleaned, but no cleaning could fix the bald spots on the carpet, or the peeling floral wallpaper. Dear God.

"There's some food in the kitchen for tonight, help yourself. I'll come around later in the week to restock. There's no microwave. It got rusted through and we had to toss it, but the oven works."

My jet-lagged brain tried to catch up with the situation, like an engine revving in neutral. "You're leaving? I'll be… alone?" I wish my voice hadn't wobbled in a very unmanly way.

"Bar the ghosts, I suppose." She cackled.

With that, she shuffled away, leaving me standing in the middle of the room, my heart racing.

I'm not a spoilt brat, I told myself. I don't need room service.

Emir had a lot to answer for, though.

The bang of the front door reverberated through the building, making the upturned glasses on the chrome-and-glass sideboard clatter. The sound woke me from my momentary paralysis. I sprinted down the stairs, desperate to catch her before she left, my mind forming questions I needed answers to.

Where was the nearest shop?

What was the wi-fi password?

How could I order a bottle of whiskey?

But as I reached the door, she was gone. I didn't even hear the sound of a car. How had she arrived and where had she gone? I closed the door, backing away into the room until my back hit the reception desk. Maybe *she* was the ghost. A cold sensation crept up my spine, and I shook myself to dispel the creepy vibe. Standing in a deserted hotel reception didn't help. It must have been late in the afternoon as the sun streamed in through the two small windows, exposing pillars of actively churning dust.

Chill, I told myself. Everything is fine.

Looking for a wi-fi password, I spotted something on the reception desk; a flyer featuring a heavily airbrushed shot of the hotel exterior. Price by negotiation. Was the building for sale? I pocketed the evidence. I'd definitely question Emir about his choice of accommodation.

I checked my phone again, but it kept complaining about not having a network connection.

I crossed the reception, which opened onto a musty sitting room with velvety, seashell-shaped chairs and heavy curtains in dirty shades of pink. What a time capsule.

On the other side of it, I spied a glimpse of stainless steel through an open doorway, and stepped into a commercial kitchen with a wide island. I rummaged through the fridge and found a couple of trays of something baked, possibly lasagna. There was also milk and juice, soft drinks, butter and cheese. After ten minutes of searching, I had to conclude the room wasn't hiding even an ounce of whiskey.

I settled for a soft drink. I knew I needed sleep, but I felt too wired. With no alcohol available, there was only one way to settle my nerves – a workout. I didn't have any exercise clothes, but since there was nobody around, it probably didn't matter. I unbuttoned my shirt and flung it on top of the reception desk, eyeing the floor area. I could modify my usual routine to fit the space.

After a moment's hesitation, I took off my pants. Suits had no give and the pants would rip during the first squat. The irony of getting undressed in a hotel reception didn't escape me. It was basically how I'd ended up here. But as long as I didn't get photographed, nobody had a reason to get upset with me. That's why I'd been sent so far away from the civilization, so I couldn't possibly cause any more scandals.

A bit chilly in my boxer shorts, I hobbled upstairs to grab the wireless headphones out of my bag. With my phone connected to an offline playlist of rage-y old-school rock, I felt some energy return to my core.

On the way back down, I checked the other rooms – all either smaller or identical to mine – and concluded the reception was the only one with enough floor space for burpees and mountain climbers. I would work up a good sweat, shower, sleep, and then figure out the rest.

# CHAPTER 3

"This could be it!" My boss, Janie, clapped her hands. "Why didn't you take photos of the interior?"

"I couldn't get in."

Janie cocked her head. "If we had a few more pics, I could send this away right now and strike a deal by tomorrow! I told you about this Hollywood production, right? It's medium budget but they're hailing the director as the next Lars von Trier; ambitious and motivated. The story has some local connections, which could be really good for us."

I took a deep breath to stop my heart rate from climbing. I couldn't help the reaction every time I heard the word 'Hollywood', even if I wasn't chasing that dream anymore. "I don't even know if the hotel's available for filming," I said. "It's for sale."

Janie beamed, flicking her strawberry blond hair over her shoulder. "That's perfect! If they're selling, they'll be receptive to other ways of making money off it. But first, we need to check the interior. The producers want authentic. Beds, chairs, bathrooms, mirrors… anything from the 1930s." She stared at my poorly framed photo for so long that even our part-time assistant, Pete, emerged from his desk to look over her shoulder.

"I know that place," he announced flatly. "It's on Trade Me."

"I know." I didn't mean to roll my eyes, but there may have been some upward movement. "I checked the listing, but there were only two photos of the interior, and nothing of the rooms. The janitor I saw leaving said his wife cleans there and she's coming back later today. I'll try to catch her, see if I can take a few more pics."

"Great. You do that and I'll…" Janie left, her attention on her phone as she sailed away to her next appointment.

Apart from the film office, she ran a small farm and looked after her two children, chickens and pigs, as well as gave occasional interviews on why she'd left her high profile TV presenter job and escaped to the country.

She was the one who'd made it, then happily given it all up, two things I'd never experience. I could still remember those uncomfortable silences during my job interview. I wanted to agree with her. After all, I needed the job, but I probably couldn't hide my pang of jealousy when she described her previous life in Auckland, the one she dismissed as meaningless.

I scanned her beautifully aged face and lithe body, looking for clues. Why would she want to give it up? She still had it – the looks and talent that had made her a household name. She could have continued for several years. What was so amazing about keeping piglets and composting feces?

"Don't work too hard!" Janie called from the door.

It was her motto – one that Pete had taken to heart. He'd appeared around 9:30 a.m. to do some admin, then disappeared for a two-hour lunch and had now spent the rest of the afternoon boxing T-shirts he sold online. They had nothing to do with the film office, but he said it was easier to do the packing in the office than in his flat. Janie didn't seem to mind, as long as he did his hours.

After a few minutes, I clicked 'send' on my last email and let out a deep sigh. "Okay, I'm off. See you tomorrow!"

Pete waved from the couch, his grey rat tail bobbing to the music in his headphones.

I found my car baking in the afternoon sun, boiling hot inside so I rolled down every window, groaning at the heat. What I really wanted was a long, breezy beach walk, but I had to sort out this hotel business first. This could be the one achievable dream I'd finally make true.

My hopes were dashed as I arrived at the hotel and found no cars in the driveway. The neighboring buildings seemed equally quiet – empty shop fronts advertised 'for rent'. With only the ocean on the other side, this pocket of Napier had a bit of a ghost town feel.

I left my car out front and snuck along the driveway to check behind the building.

As I reached the back door, I heard a faint sound. It seemed to be coming from inside the building – a steady thumping I couldn't identify. Was someone inside? Maybe they'd started renovations after all. I rushed back to the front entrance. The door remained closed, but I could still hear the thumping, and it was definitely coming from inside.

I inched closer to the door until my ear was pressed against it. I could have knocked like a normal person, but I'd become too invested in sneaking around. To be honest, my life hadn't contained a lot of excitement lately and maybe that's why the simple act of eavesdropping fired up my nerves like an imminent audition.

The thumping ceased and I heard footsteps. Spooked, I jerked back and knocked on the door.

I waited, then knocked a little harder, but since there was no answer, I finally turned the knob. Unlocked.

I pushed the door open and tiptoed in. "Hello!"

What I saw caught me so off guard I tumbled backwards, hitting my back on the heavy door as it closed behind me.

A man hung from what looked like an original Art Deco staircase, his fingers gripping the ledge, legs dangling in the air and muscles rippling as he moved up and down. Pull-ups. He was doing pull-ups in boxer shorts. The staircase wobbled, letting out a squeaky cry every time he moved. What if it all came down?

"Stop!" I cried.

It came out more alarmed than I'd intended, but it worked. He let go and landed on the original kauri floor with the grace of a cat, but with such solid weight that the old wooden planks transmitted the vibration all the way to my feet. As he pivoted on his heels, his glossy, dark curls caught the evening light. He removed his wireless earphones, blinking at me.

"Is there a problem?" He had a ridiculously gorgeous face, a dark beard and a foreign accent that made me think of Kerim.

"No... I'm concerned about the building. Actually, I'm interested in the building. We have a possible movie production looking for a space like this and I really wanted to check the interior." I cleared my throat, aware I was staring.

Small droplets of sweat glistened on his olive skin, backlit by the light streaming through a small window behind the reception desk. The lighting felt deliberate, as if he stood on a movie set, ready to film a scene millions of women would later leer at.

I'm not sure how long I stared at him with my mouth agape, but as my gaze finally returned to his face, I wasn't expecting him to stare at me. I mean, he was the one in his underwear, yet I caught his eyes roaming my body so shamelessly I instinctively crossed my arms, wondering if my T-shirt was see-through.

Eventually, he shifted his stance, swiping the back of his hand across his forehead. A trickle of sweat ran down his arm and he winced. "I'm sorry. I forgot to bring a towel. Do you mind if we continue this upstairs?"

Continue what? Ogling?

Not waiting for my answer, he headed to the stairs, light on his feet like a panther. Against my better judgment, I followed, leaving a respectful distance, but close enough not to lose sight of him. He leapt the last three stairs as if he'd mastered gravity, a force I felt very much bound by as I gripped the well-worn baluster for support.

When I made it to the top of the stairs, I saw him disappear into one of the rooms along the narrow hallway. Slowly, my brain made room for other visual input, such as the patterned Art Deco carpet. It was perfect. Worn, but original. How had this place survived? Most of Napier had been renovated many times since the 1930s, with the loss of much of the original decor.

"You can come closer."

His voice jolted me and I looked up from the carpet. "I was admiring the decor."

He stood at the doorway, a towel around his neck, waiting. I attempted to move, but somehow the brain–leg signal got intercepted and my feet did nothing.

He closed the distance, offering his hand. "I'm Cem. Nice to meet you."

"Gem?"

"Cem." He leaned in and patiently repeated the soft sound that definitely didn't exist in the English alphabet but had me completely enthralled.

"Cem," I said, mimicking the way his lips puckered and teeth nearly touched.

"Perfect!"

My chest filled with pride at my achievement. "I'm Aria."

His handshake was firm and sent a warm tingle up my arm.

"Where are you from?" I asked.

"Turkey." The way he said it sounded foreign, tur-key-ye. He looked at me pointedly. "So, what do you need? You said something earlier but I think I missed it."

Probably because of all the ogling, I thought, feeling a little hot. I filled my lungs with the smell of lemony soap and general mustiness lingering in the hallway and threw on a professional smile. "I was hoping to take some photos."

Cem held up his hand. "No! No photos." The change in him was so instant I took a step back, hovering on one foot.

The way he shielded his face made me think of paparazzi. He must have meant photos of himself. "Oh, no," I said. "I meant photos of the hotel. No people. Only the hotel."

He dropped his hand, but the suspicious look in his eyes remained. "Why would you take photos of the hotel? It's for sale. They have photos." He stepped back into his room and returned a few seconds later with a brochure. "Here. You can have this."

I turned the sales brochure in my hand. It had a couple of photos, the same ones I'd seen on Trade Me. "I'd rather take my own photos if possible. We have to email them to the location scouts."

"Location scouts?"

I nodded, my spirits lifting as I detected the curiosity in his voice. "We wouldn't bother you during your stay. I only want to talk to the owner about using this place as a movie location. It's a great opportunity."

His curiosity morphed into keen interest. "Movie location? What movie?"

I shrugged apologetically. "I don't know much about it. An American production. A historical drama or something. They're looking for an authentic Art Deco building. This would be perfect."

"So, you work in the movie business?" He leaned his head against the doorframe. I'd never seen anyone look so effortlessly self-assured wearing only boxers and a towel.

I dragged my gaze higher. "Not really. I organize locations, promote local businesses and landscape, trying to get some movie business in town."

"We're sort of in the same business then." A hint of a smile.

"What business are you in?"

He stared at me for a beat, then burst out laughing. "You don't know who I am? Of course not. For a moment there I felt like we knew each other. Sorry. It's been a crazy week and I haven't quite..." His eyes glazed. "I'm not used to this yet. I don't know where I am."

"You're in Napier." My confusion made it sound like a question. "In Napier," I repeated, forcing my voice to a lower register, wishing I hadn't opened my mouth at all.

"Yes, I know. New Zealand. I apologize. I haven't slept in a long time." He smiled, then yawned so widely I had to stop myself from yawning with him.

"Did you just arrive from Turkey? You must be exhausted."

He nodded, eyelids dipping. "I am. Sorry, it's hard to speak English when I'm tired."

"I can imagine."

His earlier words rang in my ears. Was he famous or something? It made sense, with him being so blindingly gorgeous.

"Are you travelling solo?" I asked, glancing around the empty hallway. It was a big place for one person.

"My brother will join me soon." He followed my gaze. "We don't usually book the entire hotel, but I guess it worked out that way."

"You guess?"

He shrugged. "My brother made the booking. He's my manager."

Manager? Okay, the guy was definitely someone famous. I looked at my hands, noting the remnants of pale pink polish I'd tried a few days ago to stop myself from biting my nails. I shuffled the brochure so that it covered my hands. "Must be nice, not to worry about that stuff. Hotel bookings, I mean."

He huffed, raking his fingers through his hair. "Except when he sends me into the middle of nowhere. There are no staff. I have no luggage. My phone doesn't work here…" He leaned in, his brown eyes widening. "Honestly, it's a little creepy. I thought I saw a ghost."

He was deadly serious, but I couldn't help the wayward laugh that bubbled out of me. "I'm sorry. Did you say a ghost?"

He pouted. "I mean it's a bit… spooky. Like in a horror film, you know?"

I looked around me, baffled. Sunlight streamed in through a small window, making everything glow in golden tones. "Horror? This would be a perfect location for historical romance. Look at that carpet!" I pointed at the intricate geometrical pattern.

"It's very old," he said matter-of-factly, staring at me like I'd lost my mind.

He wasn't wrong. The high-traffic areas sported several bald patches, but a good director of photography would choose the best angles and shoot around them.

"Where did we land on the photos?" I fished my phone from my pocket and held it up with a pleading smile.

He rubbed his beard. "Your internet works? Let me use it and I'll let you take pictures."

"Deal." I tapped on the phone to enable a hotspot as he strode to his room to fetch his own phone.

After a moment of tapping and password-spelling, Cem was online. With his focus on the screen, eyebrows drawn into a look of deep concentration, I snuck off to take some photos. I peeked into one of the rooms, then covered the hallway and staircase. I also needed some pics of downstairs but going that far would have probably cut off Cem's internet.

I returned to him, waving my phone. "I'm done with the upstairs. Are you… finished?"

He lifted his gaze from the screen. "No. I need more time. Can I buy your phone? I'll pay a good price."

My jaw dropped. "Buy? You mean like—"

"Pay money, change ownership." He frowned. "I don't have any cash on me… what is your currency?"

"New Zealand dollar," I said helpfully, rolling my eyes a little less helpfully.

He huffed. "Of course. I need to get hold of my brother. I need internet. Wait…"

He slipped back to his room and returned with a gold watch. "You can have this. It's worth twice as much, maybe more."

I had no reason to doubt him, but I couldn't hand over my

phone. "I'm sorry, but I can't give you my phone. I need it for work and it has…" I gestured with my hand, not wanting to say 'private stuff', but hoping he'd figure that out if he only stopped to think what he was asking.

His mouth stretched into a cheeky smile, and he held out his hand. "Come on. I won't read your emails or look at your cat photos. I only need the internet."

Irritation coiled in my chest and I held tighter onto the device, which was three years old and probably worth as much as a regular alarm clock. "I don't have a cat."

He shrugged, unbothered. "Well, whatever you keep on there. Your secrets. I'm not interested."

I arranged my expression to neutral, but the words 'not interested' felt like a tiny needle poking my gut. "It's not that," I argued. "I need those photos I took. I need to take more photos downstairs. And I need to call… people."

"Okay, call them, and email the photos. Then we make the sale." He gestured at my phone, which I held white-knuckled against my chest.

The way he spoke sounded magnanimous, as if he was being wonderfully accommodating and reasonable. He tried to rest his back against the door frame, but the bulky towel was in the way, so he flung it over his shoulder, then folded those muscled arms across his chest. The Calvin Klein underwear commercial only needed a tagline.

I allowed myself a second of ogling (what else was I going to get out of this?) but eventually found my voice. "I'm going home now. Have a good evening."

I spun on my heels and headed down the stairs. This visit had taken a weird turn. Why had I even considered it safe to follow a half-naked stranger into an empty hotel? This was the problem with small-town life. There was so little danger, especially from other humans, that you eventually let your guard down and did something shockingly unwise.

I made it to the heavy oak door, contemplating those pictures I should have taken downstairs, when I heard footsteps and a wall of tanned muscle blocked my way. "Wait!"

His presence sucked the air out of the room, turning my insides into jelly. He wasn't touching me or yanking the phone out of my hand, but he stood so close I was forced to inhale him instead of oxygen. Spice. Musk. Sweat. Potently male. He'd wrapped the towel around his waist. Did he still have the boxers underneath?

My head feeling light, I did the only thing I was capable of. I joked. "Um... Can I see that gold watch again? I forgot to bite into it, make sure it's genuine. You can bite my phone in return."

He smiled but didn't step back. "I'm sorry. I think I was out of line. I would have given you a fair price, but if you're not willing to sell the phone, maybe we can come to another arrangement? I'm a bit stuck here." He spoke casually, like it was okay to stand this close to another person you weren't presently having sex with.

"Can we discuss this outside? I need some air." My voice sounded strangled.

To my relief, he stepped back and opened the door. In the street, the afternoon sun peeked from behind the building, stretching the shadows across the pavement. The daylight settled my nerves.

I skipped down the steps and glanced at my car, wondering if I could make a run for it, but as I turned back to Cem, the sight of him held me captive. Standing in the doorway, further away, he didn't seem so imposing. In his towel outfit, he looked a little lost, like he'd escaped a burning building, or a backyard spa.

Despite the weird phone-buying episode, my heart went out to him – alone across the world with no luggage or a working phone. Maybe he was used to solving issues by throwing money at them. Wasn't that what wealthy people did?

"So, you're trying to reach your brother? Is he in Turkey?" I took a tiny step forward, smiling cautiously.

"Yes! He was supposed to come with me, but..." He rubbed his hand across his beard. "Something came up."

"And this is your first time in New Zealand?"

His eyebrows raised in a silent 'duh'.

"Quite an adventure."

"No. I..." He grimaced, glancing at the empty street. "I'm just... keeping my head down. No adventures."

My eyes narrowed. "How long are you keeping your head down for?"

He shrugged. "I was hoping a week or two. Until my brother lets me come back. I mean, when it's safe to come back."

"So, you were *banished* here?" I tried to smile but couldn't help the ill feeling. He stood at the door of my favorite building, in my beautiful hometown – a destination I promoted for living. Even if I struggled with living here, Napier was still gorgeous.

Cem sighed, raising his eyes heavenward. "I suppose."

I couldn't help the sarcasm pouring out. "What did you do to earn this horrible punishment?"

He didn't laugh at my exaggerated tone. Instead, he visibly recoiled, crossing his arms, eyes dark as thunder. "I don't want to talk about it."

What was he hiding from?

"Okay. We don't have to." I lifted my hand, edging back toward my car. Maybe it was best to end this odd visit before I learned something Interpol could use against me.

As I reached the car door, he leapt closer and cast me a pleading look. "There are some things I don't want to talk about, but I'll tell you anything else if it helps you trust me. I really need your help." He leaned on my car for balance, rubbing his forehead. "I'm desperate for sleep, but I'm scared."

"Scared?" I blinked, wondering if he'd meant to choose that word.

Here, in better light, I could see dark shadows under his eyes. Breathtaking eyes. He stifled a yawn and wobbled on his feet, leaning heavier against my car. What if he keeled over? I would have to call for help. There was no way I could move a gazillion pounds of muscle by myself.

"Not scared, but... um... what's the word? I don't usually sleep alone." He exhaled a long, deep sigh, his eyes floating like chocolate buttons in warm milk, trying to focus on mine.

I scoffed, almost involuntarily, imagining the women willing to warm his bed. All of them.

His eyes narrowed in confusion. "No, I mean… there're always people in my house. Cooks and cleaners and family. Friends. You're never alone in Istanbul unless you go into the forest or something." He groaned into his hands. "I can't… English. Sorry." Shifting his feet, he accidentally stepped off the curb, lodging his foot between the edge of the footpath and my car tire.

I reached out to steady him, almost as a reflex, and got my hand stuck between his shoulder and the car door. "Ouch!" I yanked it away and nudged him further from my car, back toward the hotel. "Let's get you to bed."

Firm muscles rippled under the warm olive skin and my stomach wobbled. In that moment, I recognized two things – my intense desire to keep touching him, and the danger of it. Satisfied that he could walk without falling over, I pulled my hand away.

We made it back to the front door, through the lobby, and up the stairs.

As he entered his room, he eyeballed the tidily wrapped white sheets for a split second, frowning, then fell like a tree trunk. I swear I saw a cloud of dust in the shape of a skull rise from the mattress. Maybe it *was* a little creepy in here.

"Please, don't go," he mumbled into the pillow.

I glanced at my phone. 6:34 p.m. Not knowing what to do, I sat on a squeaky chair by the bed. Maybe I could wait until he fell asleep and then sneak away.

As if sensing my thoughts, he rolled onto his side and cracked his eyelids. "Please stay. There are plenty of rooms. You choose." He wiggled his fingers in the direction of the hallway, looking at me under heavy lids. Bedroom eyes.

Holy shit.

I gave him my best Florence Nightingale smile. "How about this? I'll sit here until you fall asleep and then come and check on you first thing in the morning. I'll bring you a New Zealand SIM card so you can get online. I promise."

His eyelids dipped again, and the corner of his mouth tugged like caught by an invisible fishhook. "And tea."

"Tea?"

The fishhook tugged harder. "I love it when you bring me tea."

"When did I bring you tea?" I waited for an answer, but nothing came. After a while, his breathing got deeper, with a hint of a snore, and I took my exit, but not before I allowed myself a moment at his bedside, staring at his impossibly beautiful features. I even took a photo. One quick snap for myself. Who knew if he'd still be here in the morning?

CHAPTER 4

✳

I woke up to the sound of birdsong, as loud as the seagulls at home, but with such creative melodies that my ears immediately perked up. These birds weren't fighting over food. They were having a chat. As I rolled out of bed and cracked the window, the singing grew louder.

My window gave to the side of the building with a slice of overgrown garden. A tall palm tree grew in the middle, evidently a home to thousands of birds. Behind it, the sunrise had painted the sky peach and gold. Peeking to my left, I saw the street and the ocean behind it, all glowing in brilliant pastels.

I padded to the bathroom for the shower I'd failed to take the previous night. How had I even gotten to bed? I remembered the woman, Aria, standing in the doorway. Then, I must have fallen asleep. This jet lag was a dog.

The shower took a long time to heat, the old pipes coughing and rattling before they finally delivered the hot stream of water I desperately needed. What had I agreed on with that chick? She'd looked oddly familiar, but I'd been too tired to piece it together, connect the arch of her eyebrows, the way her lashes curled in the corners... That pointy, decisive chin and the curve of her mouth. It had taken me all night, the answer only arriving at the last second before sleep claimed me.

If you ignored her dark hair and funny accent, she was the spitting image of Burcu Yılmaz, my first co-star and the reason for my fame. As if she'd come back from hiding after three years, looking happy and healthy, no longer consumed by the demons that once stood between us.

We'd been amazing together. Phenomenal. That's what everyone said. I'd been a newbie, unsure of what to expect. I'd thought of our on-screen chemistry in that first series as normal, or at least *my* normal. How wrong I'd been.

The next two series after that tanked, and it took a lot of convincing from my agent to get me anything other than cologne commercials. Finally, I secured another romantic lead and did better, but with a lot of work. I had to learn those looks and glances as if I'd never done them before.

It all came so easily with Burcu. Something between us snapped into place like two interlocking pieces. The audience saw it. We felt it. It felt real and at the time, I thought it was real.

We decided to not sleep together to keep the tension on screen, and to keep her reputation intact. The agreement lasted for two agonizing seasons, almost, until one drunken night, only three episodes from wrapping up the show, we caved.

The next morning, I couldn't wait to see her again. I arrived at the set early, quite the feat with the 6 a.m. call time. Burcu never showed up. Her agent told us she was sick. Later, the media reported about a nervous breakdown. The showrunners wrote her out of the story with one hasty episode, after which the studio cancelled the series.

I kept asking myself, and occasionally my brother, if her breakdown, or whatever it was, had something to do with me. At first, Emir laughed at me, but eventually, to shut me up, he contacted her family. We didn't find out much; other than she didn't want to see anyone from work, including me.

I needed to hear it from her, but Emir convinced me to stand back. She had protective older brothers, and the paparazzi swarmed her house. So, I forced my attention on the next job, and let go.

I toweled myself and perused the tall, gilded mirror, fogged up from the shower. I wiped it with a hand towel and sucked in my stomach. I wasn't too far off my goal, but I shuddered as I thought of what I had to do to achieve it. I hated starving myself to coax out the eight pack that ensured higher ratings. Like my body wasn't mine. Like I wasn't good for anything else than those shirtless scenes.

Not that we ever had to worry about ratings with Burcu. Even with the show ending abruptly, it gradually became one of the most popular in syndication, sold to seven countries, cementing my place in the starry sky of Turkish TV, *Türk dizileri*. Eventually, those cancelled TV series', *dizis*, didn't matter. I had clout because of that first series, because of Burcu.

I hadn't thought about her in a long time, and the realization shook me out of my jet lag stupor, because after she left the show, I'd sworn not to forget her.

Not because of our relationship. I knew the *dizi* storyline had infiltrated our reality and merged with our love story, making it half-fictional. I'd been okay with that, like our millions of viewers were okay with believing in the romanticized on-screen version of me, never knowing the real me.

No. I swore to never forget Burcu, because if I did, I'd also forget that I hadn't earned any of my fame. I'd been in the right place at the right time, with the right person. I could work hard to create something similar, but I couldn't manufacture it. There was no formula, only a stroke of luck.

I tried to smile at my reflection, ignoring the spots of mirror rot framing the picture. Maybe it was the forgiving lighting and soft fog reappearing on the surface, but my skin looked better. I peeled the old, shower-soaked nicotine patch off my forearm and dropped it in the rubbish bin, grateful I had a packet of them in my satchel. It had only been a week. One week since my father's diagnosis. One week since I quit smoking.

One of the worst weeks of my life.

They'd ganged up on me, Emir and Dad, accusing me of shaming the whole family when those photos went public, but they didn't live in the spotlight, the paparazzi tracking their every move. They didn't understand how easy it was to slip up. I hadn't planned it. How could I have known? But I had to admit the timing was shit. My bare ass blurred or pixelated across mainstream media, then again in high definition in the darker corners of the internet, right after my wider family found out about Dad's cancer.

And that's how I finally stopped smoking. Not because Dad asked me to, but because he didn't. He had lung cancer, yet he didn't say anything when I lit up a cigarette. He didn't even ask me to cut down.

I didn't have to be like him. That sudden thought was the most freeing in that moment, and it carried me through the week, all the way to the plane with my hypnosis app, an e-book about reprogramming the brain, and four packets of nicotine patches.

I could have killed for a smoke, though. The urge was so strong I found my hand shaking as I searched my bag for a new patch. I peeled off the plastic backing, repeating my new mantra about how I wasn't a smoker. I had to reinforce the new identity, according to the book.

The knock on the door gave me a start, and I scrambled to wrap a towel around my waist. "Coming!"

I first thought of room service, wheeling in a tray of something delicious ordered by Emir, but as I opened the door, I laid eyes on Burcu… no, Aria. She looked so similar, yet different. Like someone new had jumped into Burcu's skin, inhabiting her body with an entirely different energy. She also had a dark spot below her left eye, an oversized freckle shaped like a broken heart.

Staring at her, the previous night's events fully rearranged themselves in my mind.

I'd asked her to return.

Apparently, I'd also asked her to bring me a mug of light brown liquid. I took the cup from her and gave it a sniff. It smelled vaguely of tea. "Thank you."

She raised her eyebrows as she smiled. "I made it downstairs. The kitchen's pretty well stocked."

I took a sip. Definitely tea – the British version that was both milky and weak, like dishwater, but I didn't want to be rude, so I took a deep breath and another, long slug.

I couldn't hide my grimace as I swallowed. "Thank you."

Aria stared at me, blinking a couple of times.

"Did you want sugar? I meant to offer this, sorry." She pulled a stack of single serve sugar packets from the pocket of her emerald-green dress. A cute, casual thing that concealed more than it revealed, but I still couldn't stop staring.

"It's okay." I placed the half empty cup on the nightstand.

Aria's eyes flicked up and down my half-naked torso. "Do you want me to find you some clothes?"

Lounging around this godforsaken hotel in my designer suit felt a little out of place. Maybe it wasn't the worst idea to find a casual outfit to tide me over until my bags arrived. I needed to get hold of Emir.

"Yeah, maybe." I gestured for her to come in.

She stopped in the middle of the room and slowly rotated around to study every inch of it. "Original." Her eyes grew wider, spellbound.

I bit back my smile. "Let me guess. You want to take more photos."

"Yes, please!" Her eyes shone with delight as she stuck her hand into her dress pocket.

I expected her to pull out her phone but instead, she handed me a small plastic-covered card. "Here's your SIM card."

Internet in exchange for photos, like yesterday.

"Thank you." I made sure our fingers brushed as I took the card from her. I wanted to make sure she was real, not a Burcu-like vision conjured up by my imagination.

She jerked almost imperceptibly, fumbled her phone out of her other pocket and crossed the floor to frame her first shot. "Can we cover that?" She asked, pointing at my bed.

"Sure."

Before I could set down the SIM card, she'd straightened the duvet. "Is there a bedspread?"

"I don't know. Probably not."

She opened a side cupboard and unearthed a huge roll of golden velvet.

It turned out to be a bedspread, and I helped her stretch it across the bed, feeling embarrassed. I shouldn't have let her in with my bed unmade. That was the kind of oversight my mom found horrifying. A lapse in both hospitality and cleanliness – the pillars of Turkish society.

Maybe Emir was right. I'd become a lazy, spoilt, self-centered jerk. I'd tried to buy her phone, my brain reminded, as if to offer more evidence. In my defense, that move would have been well received by a Turkish fan. I think. They were generally happy to give me anything. I didn't even have to ask.

Still, I found Aria's response stimulating. She presented a challenge I hadn't experienced in a while, not outside of acting. In the *dizis*, women played hard to get. In real life, they were anything but. Except in New Zealand, it seemed.

No one knew me here, and this is what it felt like to be a nobody. The woman in front of me was more interested in photographing the Art Deco furniture than my face and body.

I hopped across the floor, trying to stay behind her as she moved around with great purpose. Her green dress didn't hug her curves, but when she crouched down to get a low angle on the seashell-shaped chair, the fabric tightened around her bottom, revealing a delicious hourglass figure. It shouldn't have affected me at all, but my mind went rogue, flashing images of Burcu, digging up memories.

The chase. I remembered the chase. The obstacle course of working through a woman's defenses, layer by layer. The push and pull, the frustration and elation.

I adjusted the towel around my waist, trying to obscure the tent I was erecting.

I could have simply stopped staring at her ass. Instead, I circled to the other side, using my vantage point to peer into her cleavage, simultaneously enjoying the intensified throbbing in my groin and feeling like the biggest perv on the planet.

I'd had this problem on set with Burcu regularly and really appreciated the loose-fitting jeans and untucked shirts that dominated my character's artsy-casual wardrobe.

I'd travelled back in time, back to a romantic scene with my old co-star, surrounded by the crew, yet somehow in our own little bubble nobody else could enter. I'd find an excuse to touch her, and feel that electricity course between us, keeping us locked into the magic, knowing the scene would come out perfect.

Aria stood up without warning, her gaze gracing my visibly bulging towel. Her cheeks flushed and she reversed across the carpet, almost hitting the door. "I... I could get you some clothes now." She fumbled for the doorknob. "I told the office I'd be late this morning so I can swing by the shops..."

Great. I'd freaked her out. My only potential ally in a foreign country and I'd already introduced her to my penis. This was why Emir had shipped me away. I ran a hand across my face, wishing I could keep it there permanently and not catch the panicky flash behind those brown eyes before she neutralized her expression into something between polite and... wait... amused? Her mouth twitched unmistakably as she fought hard to not look me in the eye.

Emboldened by the giddy warmth that crinkled the corners of her eyes, I smiled back. "Apologies for the... um, distasteful display. You look a lot like someone I used to know. We were... intimate."

Her jaw dropped. The stunned silence seemed to stretch the moment from seconds to minutes. It probably wasn't that long, but enough time for my gaze to roam up and down her body, noticing her soft planes and hardened nipples, which only made my situation worse, but I was no longer trying to hide it, so I kept my stance. "I'm sorry. I'll take another shower. A cold one. But please don't leave. Please, Aria."

# CHAPTER 5

My eyes bulged, burning hot in my head. Every part of my body vibrated. Confusion, disbelief, amusement, arousal. It was all here, swirling under my skin like a torrent. I tore my eyes off his erection, stifling the laugh that rippled at the bottom of my belly. Focus.

His words re-played in my head. *Please, Aria.*

"You remember my name," I whispered. It was the only coherent sentence not featuring the word 'penis' I could think of.

His lips pulled into a lopsided smile. "Of course. You told me."

"And I look like someone you... used to know?" I asked before I could stop myself. At least I avoided repeating the word 'intimate', even though I couldn't help another glance at the prominent hard-on fighting its way out of his towel. He wasn't even trying to hide it, and the thought of him having this reaction to me was so unbelievable and unsettling I feared I might spontaneously burst into flames. My neck burned so hot it would probably be later identified as the starting point of the fire.

"An actress I worked with, a long time ago. Her name was Burcu." I caught the moment of sadness in his eyes before he reverted to that self-assured half-smile.

I wondered why he didn't say 'girlfriend', since he'd already alluded to sleeping with her, and had evidently been thinking about sex while I'd catalogued every significant Art Deco piece in the room.

"That's… wild." My eyes roamed the room. "Could I take a couple of pics of the bathroom if that's okay?"

His eyes lit up. "You're not leaving?" He closed the distance between us and took my shoulders, smiling. "Thank you! I was worried I freaked you out."

I laughed at his over-the-top reaction, simultaneously tense and hot from his sudden touch. "It's okay. I've seen an erection before. Maybe don't poke me with it."

I shifted to one side to avoid actual penis-to-hip contact and he released my shoulders, letting out a burst of laughter. "Yes, absolutely. I swear I'm not normally like this, but this week has been… I'll tell you later. Can you wait here while I get dressed? Then I'll let you photograph the bathroom, I promise."

"So, you have some clothes here?"

He gave me an odd look. "I didn't fly long haul in a towel, if that's what you mean."

He took a suit from his closet and disappeared into the bathroom.

I collapsed in the seashell chair, releasing a sigh. I couldn't think straight around him. I could easily imagine him on screen though, lighting up every scene with that intense presence, staring straight into the soul of his co-star. I wondered what that actress had been like, the one I apparently resembled. Probably two inches taller, several pounds lighter and nothing like me.

Still, I couldn't help imagining what it might have felt like to do a scene with him, to touch him, kiss him… I could imagine him being good. Very good. And I could imagine my throat closing and knees wobbling as I forgot my lines and lost myself in his touch.

The bathroom door flung open and Cem stepped out, buttoning a ridiculously shiny shirt. Even his dress pants had an unreal sheen to them.

I covered my eyes. "Oh, God! I can't even look directly at you!"

He glanced down at this outfit and threw his arms out. "You don't like my clothes? They're Sarar."

I didn't know what that meant, but the hurt in his voice gave me a pang of shame and I backtracked. "They're just so… shiny."

He shrugged, sauntered across the floor, skipping over my outstretched legs, snatched his phone off the nightstand and threw himself across the bed to change his SIM card. "It's either this or the towel, sorry. If it's too shiny for you, I have a pair of sunglasses in my bag."

My shoulders dropped in relief. He was playing along. A gentle buzz began in my gut, a low hum like I'd drunk very fizzy, very strong cider. I stared at the pale purple of that satin shirt reflecting the morning sun. It made me think of commercials of lavender-scented laundry liquid (I'd spent too much time near that laundromat), and I wondered if underneath unreal fabric was indeed a real person, not some kind of photoshopped vision come to life.

Gathering my wits, I stood to photograph the bathroom, which was also original, as well as pretty worn out.

"Shit! Shit!" Cem's voice drew me back to the bedroom.

"Bad news?"

"My brother hasn't been able to track down my bags. Apparently, all unclaimed baggage is shifted to a storage facility out of town. He's saying, in the meantime, I should order what I need and keep a low profile."

I cocked my head. "Do you usually keep a... high profile?"

Cem pulled a face. "I've been in the media lately, not in a good way, and they'd love to catch me again. But I can't stay indoors day and night. I'll go crazy." He groaned.

I studied his shiny outfit. I couldn't let him leave the building like that. He'd be a magnet for unwanted attention. There was no keeping a low profile in a shiny suit, not during off-season in sleepy Napier. He probably didn't know he'd landed on an island where even shoes were optional.

"Don't go anywhere yet. I'll find you some clothes. I have to make an appearance at the office first, but I'll sneak out during lunch."

Napier had some clothing shops, but my budget was limited. Could I borrow something? I thought about the only guy as tall as him in my immediate circle. Felix. Could I borrow his clothes without telling him why? Nope.

Something covered the phone I held in my hands. A credit card. A shiny, gold credit card. My heart stopped.

"Use this."

He rummaged through the nightstand drawers, found a ballpoint pen, took my left hand and scribbled on my palm. 6-5-5-4.

"Your pin?"

"Yes. Could you also find some Turkish tea? Maybe they sell it somewhere."

He followed me to the door, closing his hand around my arm. The jolt that travelled up to my chest could have restarted my heart.

My gaze fell on his half-finished teacup on the nightstand. "You hate English Breakfast, don't you?"

He followed my eyes. "Oh, the tea? It's different." He shrugged. "I'd love to make you a cup of Turkish tea. If I can find some Turkish tea and… equipment."

"Sounds complicated." I glanced at my arm, which he still held. "I really have to go."

"But you'll come back?"

He smiled at me with the kind of boyish excitement that made my stomach flip-flop. Combined with his touch and warm, spicy scent, even my knee joints felt oddly loose.

*He doesn't care about you. He's using you.*

"You'd better hope I come back, since you gave me your credit card." I slipped the card into my pocket with a bullish smile.

His eyes flashed with alert. "Wait. I need your phone number."

He offered me the pen he'd used, and his arm. For a split second, I could only focus on the cords of muscles under the olive skin, thinking I could swing like a monkey from that arm, and he could probably hold me. The thought excited me more than it should have.

Focus, Aria.

"We can find a piece of paper…" I scanned the room, trying to spot something good for writing on.

His eyes rolled. "It's not a tattoo. Just write your number."

My heart pounding, I wrote my number on his skin, thinking of how much I despised my handwriting, as well as my nails, then returned the pen. "I'll see you around lunchtime. Will you stay out of trouble until then?"

He grinned from ear to ear. "Well, I usually have a minder twenty-four-seven, so who knows?"

Despite the cheeky grin, I had a feeling he wasn't kidding.

# CHAPTER 6

Guilt stabbed my gut when I spotted Pete, already in conversation with Janie. I'd never arrived at work later than him.

I swung my bag onto my desk. "I'm sorry I'm late. I went by the hotel again and got some better photos." I thrust Janie my phone, displaying a photo of the original staircase I'd taken on my way out.

Janie browsed my pictures and her face brightened. "Oh, my God! This is perfect! Where is it? Is it vacant? Who do I call?"

So many questions.

I rubbed my temples. I could never quite match her speed. It must have been a TV presenter thing, thinking faster than us regular people. Moving faster, too.

"Wait, I'll Airdrop these first." Janie fetched her laptop and started sending the photos from one device to the other.

Grateful for the breather, I popped into the kitchenette. A half-full plunger of coffee sat on the counter. Not totally cold yet. Good enough.

When I re-joined my colleagues, I found Janie typing on her laptop. I went to fetch my phone from her desk, but she picked it up again. "Wait. Did you take any photos of the kitchen?" Her fingers already danced on the screen, swiping away. Dread shot through me like an icy breeze. She'd find—

"Who's *this*?"

Too late. She'd landed on the photo of sleeping Cem. The sudden change in her tone alerted Pete, who rose from his chair.

My hands jerked involuntarily toward the phone. "Yep. Funny story..." I attempted a sheepish smile. I hadn't planned on telling anyone about Cem. How much could I reveal without getting him in trouble?

"Aria?" Janie raised her perfectly shaped eyebrows as she handed my phone back to me.

My gaze landed on the photo of Cem, his sleeping face illuminated by the bedside lamp. Behind him, the headboard's golden detailing made it painfully obvious he was sleeping in the same room I'd presented to my boss as a potential filming location.

"This guy is staying at the hotel. He'd recently arrived from overseas and was really jet-lagged."

"So, he fell asleep while you were there, taking photos?" Pete summed up. "Jet lag sucks." He nodded absentmindedly and sat back at his desk, his mind clearly moving on to something else.

Janie rolled her eyes at him and flashed me a conspiratorial smile. "Let's get some coffees. Pete, do you want us to bring you anything?"

Not waiting for his answer, she linked arms with me. I discarded my cup of cold plunger coffee, my mind searching for the most palatable version of the truth as she marched me out the door.

Our office was located right by the water, which meant we had an excellent selection of cafes. Janie steered us to the nearest one. The morning queues had dissipated, so she walked straight to the barista and ordered – an espresso for her, a triple shot flat white for me.

"Oh, Pete. Bless his cotton socks." Janie shook her head as we sat at an outdoor table. "There's more to that story, right?"

It wasn't really a question, so I nodded.

Janie leaned in, rosy blots appearing on her cheeks. "You know I don't usually gossip, but it looks like this location is everything we've been looking for. So, anything that might stand in the way... You understand why I'm asking questions, right?"

"Of course." I felt my cheeks flame as I cleared my throat, suddenly desperate for that coffee. "I'm not sure why I took that photo. I never meant for anyone else to see it. I think he's sort of hiding in there. They've booked the entire hotel." I rubbed my forehead. "I feel horrible. He's so concerned about his privacy."

Janie patted my arm. "Oh, don't worry. Pete's already forgotten about it, and I won't discuss this with anyone else. You have the only copy of that photo, right?"

I smiled meekly, relaxing a little. "I'll delete it." I knew I wouldn't, but I felt better saying it.

Janie leaned in. "Before you delete it, can I have another look? I feel like I know him from somewhere."

"I think he's famous in his own country." I brought up the photo on my phone again. "In Turkey."

"Oh! Turkey has a huge film and TV industry!" Janie peered at the photo again. "So, you guys... hit it off?" Her sharp gaze made me squirm. "I'm only asking because it seems we need to negotiate with this guy and if you two already have a rapport, that's great."

"Well, he's lost his luggage and needed internet, so I'm... helping him out a bit."

"Fantastic! Anything you can do to make him feel like he owes you. Use your... charm." She winked.

If only she knew, I thought, my neck blazing like it had in that hotel room. I'd have to keep my charm, if I had any, well and truly locked away with this guy.

Our drinks arrived and I took a long, grateful sip, hiding my embarrassment behind the bowl of caffeine.

Janie drained her espresso in one go. Her phone buzzed and she picked it up. "It's the production company!"

My whole body tensed as she opened the message. Janie's face melted into an excited grin. "Yes. Yes. Yes! They want to come for a recce. Listen to this... 'this could be the missing piece and we're very excited to visit.' They're booking flights and want to stay at the hotel from Tuesday next week."

Blood drained from my face. "Did you tell them it's vacant?"

Janie's smile had a guilty glint to it. "Sometimes, you have to manufacture your own luck. I trust you. You're resourceful. You'll find a way to arrange things."

I swallowed a hard lump. "Okay…"

"Obviously, when I emailed them, I didn't know there was a Turkish celebrity sleeping in there." Janie gave me a meaningful look. "But we have a bit of budget. We can offer him a room at the County Hotel or a nice Airbnb if he's willing to relocate for four or five nights."

I took a deep breath. How could I possibly bargain with a guy who could book an entire hotel and hand out gold credit cards?

"I'll… do my best," I squeaked, pouring warm coffee down my throat, thinking of that gold credit card in my pocket. "I promised to go back and bring him some clothes."

"Great! That'll butter him up. Keep me posted," Janie smiled reassuringly, gathered her bag and stood up.

I finished my coffee and followed her outside, waving at her as she headed back to the office.

I ambled along the street toward the city center on wobbly legs. This was the weirdest job I'd ever had. As my gaze roamed the shop windows, aimlessly browsing the jeans, bags, and shoes, it hit me. I didn't know Cem's size and had no way of asking. I'd kept my phone at hand, checking it more often than I liked to admit, but he hadn't messaged me. I didn't have his number, and he must have only asked for mine as a precaution. In case the hotel caught fire or he thought of something else he needed. The man was clearly used to being served.

Did he see me as another staff member? Was that why I currently held his credit card as I stepped into a clothing store I only ever visited during a 70% sale?

"Just browsing," I told the shop assistant, hiding behind a rack of shirts.

After a long session of over thinking and second guessing, I managed to pick grey slacks, a dark hoodie and a black T-shirt with a Māori koru pattern surrounding the word 'mana'. It was probably akin to cultural appropriation by the fashion brand, but the word – the Māori concept of authority, influence and spiritual power – resonated with me.

Approaching the counter, my fingers curled around Cem's credit card, and my throat tightened. If I used it, I'd be like one of his staff, running an errand for their famous client. A touch of nausea swirled in my belly.

With my heart hammering and thoughts circling in a vortex of irrationality, I pulled out my own credit card, gingerly passing it across the counter. I winced as the digital numbers on the cash register climbed to new heights. But a week or two or five of living on noodles was a small price for my dignity, even if I couldn't quite articulate how buying a pile of expensive cotton for a stranger was linked to said dignity.

# CHAPTER 7

As I rummaged through the fridge, I heard the knock on the door. Aria. The thought of seeing her again gave me a jolt of excitement. I glanced at the tray of lasagna, thinking I could share it with her. Maybe she could help me figure out how the oven worked.

Approaching the door, I glanced at my outfit. I'd found the old, maroon velvet robe at the back of a cleaning cupboard and decided to try it on. I didn't want to hear more comments about the shininess of my shirt. She'd laughed at it like it was something embarrassing, too feminine or too opulent.

I shouldn't have cared. Millions of people thought I looked hot. Why did I care about her reaction? If anything, she was ultra-casual, hiding her beauty behind the plain and boring. She couldn't hide it though. She couldn't hide how much she resembled Burcu, either. It both perplexed and fascinated me.

The door creaked as it opened, and my jaw dropped.

Emir.

My brother held the door for a young man in a hoodie and board shorts, who hauled two suitcases over the threshold. I had to admit I was slightly more excited to see my luggage than my brother. Only slightly.

Emir guided the guy toward the stairs.

"First room on the left." I pointed upwards.

"No worries." The guy looked a little startled but took my bag and dragged it up the stairs with two hands.

Emir picked up his own luggage and followed him. I'd never understood his partiality for doing for himself what he paid others to do.

We looked alike but couldn't have been more different. He had the looks that could have put him on the silver screen. Too bad he hated cameras, smiling, and other people in general. Filming a doe-eyed, romantic scene with someone... I couldn't even imagine my brother in that scenario. He would have probably self-combusted. However, he was sharp and strategic, which made him a good manager. Excellent in negotiations, terrible at social gatherings, but those were in my arena anyway.

The bags dealt with, Emir returned downstairs, showing the driver out the door with a hefty tip.

He turned to me, his eyebrows raised. "Brother!"

"*Hoşgeldiniz.*" I pulled him into a hug, which he didn't fight too hard. "How was the flight?"

"Which one? This place is… far." Emir rubbed his three-day stubble, bleary-eyed.

I raised my brow in a silent 'duh'. "Was that a surprise to you? I thought you wanted to send me as far away as humanly possible."

Emir almost smiled. "And you're still alive. I'm impressed."

"I'm not a week-old puppy."

"No. Apparently, you're the Turkish Jeff Bridges." He gestured at my outfit.

I responded with a shit-eating grin, spreading my arms. "The Big Brown Lebowski."

We'd started watching American movies together as I'd prepped for my stay in L.A., back when stardom had only been a fun dream – one I'd shared with Emir and no one else. He'd believed in me. He'd fought Dad to get me to L.A. and I'd disappointed both of them by coming back as unsuccessful as I'd been before.

I'd developed a passion, though, which carried me all the way to my first big *dizi* role. Emir never stopped believing, even if he called me lazy and pushed me to try harder.

"Did you get my messages?" I asked, a little peeved that I hadn't known about his arrival.

Emir pulled out his phone. "No, sorry. My phone stopped working when I left Turkey."

"Fear not. I have a local SIM card. I can share my internet."

Emir's eyes flashed with suspicion. "How did you swing that? You haven't been out there, have you? I told you to keep a low profile. You know *Aşkta Şanslı* sold to India and Mexico. There are immigrants here. Someone might recognize you."

I threw him a tired look. "Chill. I haven't been anywhere. I only talked to one person who came to the door. A location scout. She definitely didn't recognize me. She wanted to take pictures of the hotel."

"Really?" Emir turned around, as if taking in the surroundings for the first time, his brow furrowing. "Weird."

"I know, but she was nice enough and let me use her internet and fetched me the SIM card. So, I let her take some pics. I stayed out of them, don't worry."

"Nice enough, huh?" Emir studied me for a moment. I could never hide anything from him. "She hot?"

I shrugged noncommittally. I hadn't done anything wrong, or scandalous, at least on record. My jaw twitched as we entered a brief staring contest until Emir gave up.

"Any food?" he asked, bumping my shoulder as he pushed past me and into the kitchen.

I followed him. "Sure. But you have to prepare it yourself."

Emir frowned over his shoulder. "I paid for that lady to cook for you."

"I saw her once when I arrived. She hasn't been back."

"Seriously?"

"Technically, she did cook for me. I just wasn't there when she did." I opened the fridge and pointed at the foil trays. "Should we put one in the oven?"

Emir yawned, stretching his neck. "I need some sleep, but the plane food was like… miniature portions. For miniature people."

An inch taller than my 6 feet, Emir wasn't one of the miniature people.

"First, I need to figure out how to turn on the oven." I fiddled with the knobs, looking back at Emir.

My brother scanned the kitchen, then flicked a small switch on the wall. The digital screen turned on and I sighed. I hadn't been near a kitchen in years, not since I'd had to do my own cooking in L.A. Even then, I'd mostly opted for takeaways, or fasting.

Emir chucked the lasagna in the oven and I boiled the kettle to make some tea. More of the weak English crap. "How's dad?" I asked, unwrapping the teabags.

"Still waiting for test results."

"So, it might not be that bad?"

Emir shrugged. "We'll see. Whatever it is, it'll cost a lot. Especially if it's treatable."

I waited for the water to boil, staring at the hot steam pearling droplets on the ceramic tiles. "We have the money, right?"

Emir's silence became deafening. I poured the boiling water into teacups and took the drinks to the kitchen island.

When I sat down across from my brother, he fixed his deathly serious gaze on me. "The studio called again. That lady who warned us earlier. She's some kind of PR person they've appointed to deal with you."

My stomach plummeted. "I've apologized. I'm out of the country. What more do they want?"

Emir winced. "It sounds like they're prepared to recast the role. I got the idea that one of the producers had fallen in love with you in *Aşkta Şanslı* and they wanted you based on that. Now they're aware of your recent publicity, they've started looking into your... lifestyle, that's the word they used, and they see you as a risk."

"Risk? It was a one-time thing! I don't drink that much. I don't do drugs. I don't even smoke anymore!" I couldn't help raising my voice and may have accidentally spat on my brother a little.

He calmly wiped his cheek with the side of his thumb, giving me a sharp look. "It's about perceptions. They want someone the moms would want their daughters to marry. Someone... family minded."

"But—"

Emir took out his phone. "Hotspot?"

I shared my internet and he opened Instagram, beckoning me closer. "I had some time to think about this on the flights. Look."

He placed his phone on the table, spun it with two fingers, and pushed it across the table like he was dealing cards. I found myself looking at my own Instagram, which I hadn't updated in two weeks, but Emir obviously had. There were two new posts – one of me leaning on a marble wall in a designer shirt. A shiny designer shirt, I noted begrudgingly. Another pic displayed me in a pair of aviators. Cool and unattached, the way I liked it.

"Thanks for posting," I said. I knew my sponsorship money would quickly run out if my account went quiet. I also knew Emir had fired the PR firm after they added fuel to the fire with my recent scandal by posting a phony apology with multiple errors. Seeing that, Emir had taken over my account again.

"I had to post something, but it's not the right stuff." Emir reached across the table to swipe my screen, travelling back in time. "This is what we need."

The glossy advertising shots whizzed past, gradually turning into something more candid – photos with other people, people from my past, pictures of my home, plates of food, the neighbor's cat... and Burcu.

There she was, smiling at me behind her fingers, slightly out of focus. We were on the set, my arm around her shoulder, my attention on her like nobody else existed. I hadn't even noticed Emir taking the photo as he visited us during the short lunch break. The days were long and grueling. I'd been permanently sleep deprived and delirious, but I'd never felt like I was working.

"What do you mean?" I frowned at him. "I can't go back in time."

Emir yawned again, rubbing his eyes. "We need to soften your image. There's too much sponsorship stuff, not enough... heart. Love, dating, family, all that stuff."

"You're one to talk," I mused. We were both single, and he didn't even date, or not to my knowledge.

My brother had been engaged once, then given up on relationships. To this day, I didn't know what exactly happened and never asked. I didn't like the way his face contorted when the subject came up. Like now.

I laughed to diffuse the tension. "Fine. If we go back right now, I can try to get some dates set up in Istanbul, make sure we're seen by the press?" Hope lit up in me at the thought of returning to the comfort of my home. Dating some opportunistic actress was a small price to pay.

Emir stared at his phone, his mouth twisting like it always did when he was thinking. I crossed my fingers under the table, holding my breath.

The knock on the door jolted us both off our seats.

# *Aria*

As the door swung open, a breath caught in my throat. A taller and meaner-looking version of Cem stared down at me. Behind him, the original Cem grinned in a tight, maroon velvety robe.

"There's two of you," I stammered.

"Burcu? Burcu Yilmaz?" the tall one said, still staring at me with unblinking eyes. His shirt wasn't shiny, but he looked like a businessman in crisp white and grey.

"No. Aria," Cem corrected, pushing him out of the way so I could step in. "This is my brother, Emir."

Cem gave him a playful slap on the arm and Emir extended it. "Nice to meet you."

We shook hands while he continued to stare at me in that intensely confused way, making me want to hide under a rug.

I offered Cem my paper bag. "Here you go."

I watched in anticipation as he pulled out each item of clothing, hanging them over the reception desk. I'd left his credit card on the bottom of the bag, and I noticed how quickly he pocketed it, not letting his brother see it.

"Do you think they'll fit?" I asked, anxious. "I got stretchy materials, to be safe."

Cem looked at the display of casual cotton and smiled. "I'm sure they're fine, but Emir brought my luggage, so I'm all good."

"Ah, okay." I tried to sound casual, but probably looked nothing but. Cem no longer needed me, yet I needed him. Disappointment twisted my gut.

Cem studied my face for a moment as if trying to read my mood. He picked up the T-shirt and held it against his chest. "Looks like a good fit, don't you think?" He cast a loaded look at Emir who manufactured the slightest of smiles.

"Absolutely. It looks very… um, tribal."

I didn't need their pity. I huffed, trying to replace my welling sadness with anger. "Mana is the Māori word for authority, spiritual power, many things… "

"That sounds amazing." Cem's appreciation sounded genuine, if laced with concern.

"I love Māori words," I babbled on. "They hold so much meaning. Like whakawhanaungatanga, it's—"

Emir cleared his throat. "Aria, was it? Will you join us for dinner? I think the lasagna will be ready soon." He gestured toward the kitchen without a hint of a smile.

I stared at him in confusion. "Dinner? I... haven't had lunch yet."

"Well, it's dinner time somewhere in the world." Emir rubbed his forehead. "I only arrived. Jet lag..."

His flustered embarrassment lifted my mood. "It's okay," I said. "And thank you, but I don't want to impose."

I shifted toward the door, but Cem grabbed my arm. "Oh, no. We insist."

"Do you now?" I muttered as the brothers joined forces in escorting me into the kitchen.

Emir seated me at the kitchen island and opened cupboards until he found plates. While he set the table, Cem fetched flavored soda water bottles from the fridge. He made a fuss about letting me choose a flavor and I picked a random one based on the color. On a closer look, it appeared to be raspberry.

Emir placed a foil tray of lasagna on the table and dished out huge portions, despite my protests. I liked lasagna, but would have never had such a heart-stopping amount for lunch. It was tasty, though, and for a moment, we all ate in silence.

"Where did you find the robe?" I asked Cem.

"In the cleaning cupboard. I think it's an original." He patted on the gold-embroidered logo on his chest.

I swallowed a lump with my lasagna. I'd emptied my bank account trying to buy him clothes, when he was happy to wear a 100-year-old bathrobe. Was there any limit to my stupidity?

"Good for that movie, maybe?" Cem gave me another earnest look, but I only managed a meek smile.

"What movie?" Emir asked.

My stomach squeezed like a stress ball in a giant's grip. This was my opening. "I work for the local film office. We have an American film crew who're interested in using this hotel as a location. It's absolutely perfect. The trouble is…" I glanced down at the remnants of my lunch, gathering courage. "They want to come in next Tuesday, for a recce, and stay here for a few nights. Could we relocate you to another hotel? We'd pay for it, of course."

My heart pounding, I tried to read Emir's blank face.

Cem spoke for him. "We can go somewhere else. We might even fly back to Turkey before then, right?" He eyeballed his brother, urging him to get onboard.

I gave him a grateful smile, although it bothered me that he seemed in such a hurry to leave the country. "Thank you, I—"

"No." Emir straightened his back. "We've booked the entire hotel and paid for a month."

"A month?" Cem howled. "You were planning on keeping me here for a month?"

Emir silenced him with one look and turned to me. "I'm not sure if my brother told you, but it's vital that he keeps to himself, to avoid being recognized. So this arrangement," Emir gestured at the room, "is for maximum privacy. We'd never achieve that in a regular hotel."

I looked around, a bit confused. "We could arrange a very remote Airbnb. There's plenty of choice in Hawke's Bay. You could book into a place in the middle of the bush and never see another soul."

Emir scoffed. "We booked this place through someone I trust. How can I trust a random person on a website?"

With a heavy chest and stinging eyes, I picked up my plate. "Thanks for the lunch." I carried my dishes to the sink and proceeded to wash them, to have a moment to myself. A moment to think.

It shouldn't have hit me so hard, I thought as I turned on the tap, hoping the sound of running water covered my sniffly breaths. I'd spent so much money on those useless clothes, and now I would fail Janie and risk losing my job over this.

How had I messed this up so badly?

# CHAPTER 9

# Cem

I was used to Emir bossing me around. Usually, I removed myself from the situation, pretending I didn't care. This time, watching Aria washing her plate so piously I could only assume she was avoiding us, I cared.

We didn't have to treat her this way. She'd helped me multiple times and tolerated borderline sexual harassment. Not even borderline, I thought with a grimace. I'd been well over the line.

"What's the problem?" I hissed in Turkish, glaring at Emir. "Quit being a dick."

He shot me another one of his looks, a calculating one, then focused his piercing gaze on Aria. "Miss Aria?"

She turned around, quickly wiping the corner of her eye, but I saw the tears. Her distress felt like a gut punch, and I sucked in a quick breath, instinctively leaning forward. "Are you okay?"

"Yeah." Her brave smile didn't fool me.

Emir pulled out a chair next to him and she sat down, still holding a soapy sponge. "Did Cem mention you look like an actress he used to work with, Burcu Yılmaz?"

"It... came up." Aria's hand flew to her mouth and her gaze dipped to my crotch, and that's when I realized the accidental pun.

I fought hard not to laugh but didn't fully succeed. Especially as I noticed her cheeks turning pink.

Emir observed us with suspicion. "We were discussing Cem's image. We need to present a softer side to him. Like when Burcu was still in the picture."

I sighed. "I'll find a date. Let's pack up and—"

Emir held up his hand. "Getting you back to Istanbul to date a random woman will not help. You have a reputation; everyone would assume it to be casual. We'd need multiple dates, shared holidays..." Emir shook his head, face drawn. "There's no time for that. But if you were seen with someone special, someone you have a history with... someone the public wants to see you with. Like Burcu—"

"How's that going to work? No one's seen her in years!"

Emir fired me a weighty look, and I finally understood. We both turned to Aria.

"What?" She whispered, her sponge-holding hand frozen in mid-air.

Emir softened his expression. "You look so much like her. If we were to..." He took the sponge off her hand and set it on the table.

Then he studied her bewildered face, head tilted. "She needs a bit of work, but it's doable. We can cover that thing." He pointed at the freckle under her eye.

Aria stared back in terror, her fingers trailing up her face to cover the mark.

Emir held up his phone, aiming it at Aria as if to film her. "Are you used to being photographed? Ever done any acting?"

Her cheeks flamed pink. "I have a degree in film production and on-screen acting, and I've had some minor roles, but—"

"Wow." Emir raised his eyebrow to me before turning back to her. "If we took a few photos of you two together, we might start a rumor about Cem being back with Burcu."

I felt hot and cold. I could follow his logic, but it didn't feel right. "How could we do that to Burcu?"

Aria said nothing, but her eyes had turned into saucers. Blinking saucers. Her fingers hovered above the mark under her eye, and I wanted to punch Emir.

My brother ignored our reactions and kept his tone calm. "A rumor like that wouldn't hurt Burcu. Quite the opposite. Have you seen what they write about her?"

I'd seen the headlines but couldn't bring myself to read the articles. I already knew they were filled with hearsay and outright lies – dramatic claims about drug use and mental illness, one shocking diagnosis after another. Burcu deserved better.

Aria found her voice. "What if she's photographed doing something else, or seen with someone else when she's supposed to be with Cem?"

Emir shook his head. "She hasn't been photographed doing anything in three years."

Aria's eyebrows shot up and she turned to me for confirmation.

"It's true," I said. "She's been… unwell. Her family keeps her out of the public eye."

Emir managed to make his voice sound almost pleasant. "No one's seen her, not even friends. She's on heavy medication, not able to work. I don't expect her to react in any way."

I watched Aria, half-expecting her to walk out. Who in their right mind would want to be any part of this? I didn't, obviously. It was risky and crazy, and there must have been another way to polish my reputation so that it was wholesome enough for Epic Studios.

"If Epic doesn't want me, I'll take another job. One of the local *dizis*."

Emir massaged his temples, his exhalation heavy. "The local studios pay us in Lira and you know it's nose diving. Inflation is insane. We can't afford to work with them, not with our current outgoings. Epic will pay you in American dollars. It's the only option that makes sense."

I could feel his headache transferring to me. If I didn't get paid in American dollars, Emir wouldn't get paid. Dad wouldn't get his treatments. There was no way out.

# CHAPTER 10

I fought the urge to google 'Turkey inflation', but I didn't need the stats to see how bad it was. I could see it on their faces and feel it in the defeated silence that blanketed us. This wasn't a morally questionable PR ploy we could try for kicks. This was the Hail Mary of all PR campaigns.

I already knew I'd agree to it, even before the words left my mouth. A moment ago, I'd had no leverage, but this plan put me back in the driver's seat. I could see a way forward.

"We have no time to waste." Emir stared at us from under his dark brow. He would make an amazing grim reaper. "We need a nice, secluded location, a nondescript car, clothes for Aria... what else?"

"Clothes," I repeated, tempted to point out that I wasn't actually naked. The green dress I'd chosen this morning was one of my favorites. It was also my only dress, but they didn't need to know that.

"He means we need to dress you to look more like Burcu," Cem explained, handing me his phone.

My gaze fell on a candid photo of him with a long-haired woman, her face nearly hidden from view as she looked away from the camera, leaning on his chest. "Her hair's lighter than mine."

"We can use a hat or a scarf." Cem grabbed the phone from me and found another pic.

As he passed the phone back to me, the light touch of his fingers lingered, raising a trail of goosebumps along my arm. It disoriented me for a second, until my eyes focused on a new photo, a close-up of Cem and Burcu, posing side-by-side in a restaurant, fairy lights twinkling around them.

I brought the screen closer, spreading my fingers to zoom in. So, that's what I'd look like if I were gorgeous? To my huge surprise, I could see the resemblance, like looking at myself through one of those TikTok filters. It was me, yet it wasn't. I noted the smoky eye makeup, plump, rosy lips, and shiny hair that fell across her shoulders like a caramel fountain. The glamour version of me, the one I could have been if I'd ever been discovered. If my acting career had ever taken off.

Blindsided by the pain, my other hand gripped the edge of the kitchen island. "She looks like me. Or I look like her, I mean."

She was the big deal. I was the lookalike.

I'd never thought of myself as incredibly unique. There were plenty of pretty, dark-haired women in the film industry, but nobody had ever looked this much like me. Nobody had made me feel like a carbon copy of someone else. Someone famous.

"Are you okay?" Cem's soft voice brought me back to the present.

I placed his phone on the table, but my eyes didn't let go, studying the golden belt buckle holding up Burcu's high-waisted jeans, perfectly accentuating her tiny, black top. It was one of those revealing corset tops that sat somewhere between a tank top and underwear – an outfit with zero comfort. She was probably wearing icepick heels, too, somewhere outside the tightly framed shot.

"I don't have any clothes like these." My voice was hoarse. "And my waist is not this narrow."

"This was taken on set. Burcu didn't dress like this either, not outside work. Wait." Cem picked up the phone and tapped away until he found what he was looking for – a photo of him and Burcu on the beach. It looked like a selfie, with Burcu holding the camera. She wore a yellow sundress and a woven hat. The combination looked more elegant than anything I owned, but it was a style I could possibly pull off.

"Okay." I nodded slowly. "I can source a dress like that I think." What else was on Emir's list? "Oh, the locations! There are some very secluded spots around here and my car is as boring and nondescript as they come." I turned to Emir. "Are you taking the photos? Or should they look like selfies?"

Cem pointed at the photo on his phone screen. "That was a selfie. Is that what you're thinking, Emir?"

Emir scrutinized the photo. "This is good. Very natural."

"Selfies it is then!" Cem's voice brimmed with excitement.

Emir turned to me. "Don't worry, I'll definitely be there to chaperone this one." He shot a sideways glance at Cem, whose smile withered.

"Thank you." My voice crept up. I couldn't decide if his presence would make me feel safer or more agitated. Either way, it probably wasn't wise to spend time alone with the gorgeous actor whose slightest touch made me shiver from head to toe. No, definitely not wise.

I filled my lungs.

*You have leverage. Use it.*

"And you're happy to relocate to another accommodation on Monday?" I asked brightly. "That's four nights away."

Emir gave me a slow nod. "If you agree to these pictures. We need more than one post. Possibly some video. We can do it all on one day if you bring a few different outfits."

"Like, how many?"

"I don't know. Five or six?"

My eyes widened in horror. That was my entire capsule wardrobe, which was mostly jeans and T-shirts anyway and I'd blown my budget on those clothes I'd bought Cem. I'd have to dig through Mom's closet. If I did that, I'd have to tell her what was going on. And if I told her... no, that was definitely a bad idea. "We're not telling anyone else about this, right?"

"I was about to raise that with you. I don't have any NDAs on me, so we have to trust you." Emir looked at me as if he absolutely didn't. "Have you told anyone else about meeting Cem?"

I grimaced. "My boss at the film office knows there's someone Turkish staying here. No names or anything. She doesn't have any links to Turkey, as far as I know."

"Are you sure?" Emir folded his arms, his face unreadable.

I nibbled at my fingernail, trying to anticipate every possible outcome. Who would Janie talk to?

"Please don't do that," Emir barked, and I dropped my hand. "Burcu would never bite her nails."

"Sorry." My face burned.

Cem laughed. "Relax, both of you. This plan is so nuts nobody would ever suspect it."

I smiled. It was impossible not to smile around him. "I hope you're right. What time should I come tomorrow?"

"As early as you can," Emir said. "We don't want to hit traffic."

It was my turn to laugh. "Don't worry. There's no traffic."

I drove away from the hotel, my heart pounding in my ears. I wasn't even sure why I felt so unsettled, but eventually I had to pull over by the beach road and sit in my car, taking deep breaths.

This is good, I told myself. Now I have a chance to make everything work.

I simply had to find six high fashion outfits, choose the right secluded locations... and then search inside myself for the persona I'd left behind. The one I hadn't toyed with in months. The actress.

I'd spent so much time and energy trying to move on, to become someone who didn't need the camera on their face, who didn't seek the thrill of it. If I stepped into this role of Cem's girlfriend, would I lose the progress I'd made? Had I even made any progress? The stirring in my gut made me wonder.

I didn't miss the endless auditions, moldy student flats and the diet of cheap carbs. I couldn't go back to that. At my new job, I was saving money and building a future. Well, if I stopped splurging on overpriced hoodies. Why hadn't I used Cem's credit card?

As my heart rate gradually slowed down, my thoughts cleared. I needed help, and the only person I could turn to was Janie. She had a wardrobe to die for, and she already knew about Cem, sort of. I picked up my phone, took a deep breath and dialed.

Twenty minutes later, I turned onto Janie's long, sweeping driveway, lined with young lemonwood trees. I finally understood why she preferred working from home. Janie lived in a sprawling country mansion in a picture-perfect setting. I passed a grove of fruit trees, a chicken coop, a duck pond and stables. Behind the main house, I glimpsed a large, productive vegetable garden. Janie was obviously self-sufficient and didn't need to work at all.

I parked along the wide turning bay and headed to the grand entrance. She must have seen me arrive since the door swung open in front of me.

"Welcome!" Janie beamed at me, wearing a kowhaiwhai-patterned apron, her cheeks flushed and blond hair curling around her face. She retreated into the house, beckoning me to follow.

A small Boston Terrier rushed to greet me, jumping about my feet. The dog's energy level and general enthusiasm seemed to perfectly match Janie's. She returned to her cooking and baking and at a glance, I couldn't tell how many things she had underway. Potatoes were boiling and a sauce simmering, while something else baked in the oven. A mixture of smells, both herby and sweet, lingered in the air.

"You seem busy," I observed, getting even more nervous.

Janie picked up a wineglass teetering on the edge of a cutting board and took a swig. "We're hosting a little dinner party and I love cooking. In Auckland, I might go for months without doing this. I could never take a day and plan a menu. I ordered everything. This—" she took another gulp of wine, "is heaven. Even if John will miss it, again. Always in Auckland. He misses our old life more than I do." Sadness fell across her eyes, but she gave me a brazen smile, raising her glass. "Wine?"

I shook my head. "I... have a problem."

Janie halted, her wineglass in mid-air. "I thought so. What is it? How can I help?"

I explained the situation, stressing that I'd had no choice but to agree to this charade. My face grew warmer as I talked, and I'm fairly sure I used the word 'charade' more than once. Janie listened in silence, occasionally checking her pots and pans, sipping her wine. When I moved onto the subject of clothing, she removed a tray of biscuits from the oven.

Janie blew out a breath. "So, you need a few outfits that make you look like this Turkish actress? Can I see some photos of her?"

She didn't sound shocked or disapproving. I tried to move past my own shock at her lack of shock and pulled out my phone. After a bit of searching, I found Burcu under Cem's account (I was now one of his over five million followers) and showed Janie the beach photo with Burcu in the yellow dress. Her eyes nearly popped out. "She's the spitting image of you!"

"I told you we look alike."

"Sure, but people say that all the time. It doesn't usually mean much. But this..." Janie took my phone and paced her kitchen floor. "I can see why they've approached you. This is fantastic! They get some lovely PR and we get the hotel. Well played, Aria! You realize this is an acting gig, right?" She turned to face me, a twinkle in her eye.

I swallowed. "I suppose."

"You have an acting background. This is right up your alley."

"No, not really. I never did anything... big. Not like you. It was a hobby." I tried to look non-committal, but Janie didn't buy it.

"No, I watched your showreel. I searched you... You have a real passion for it, don't you?"

Suddenly, I felt hot all over. "I used to, but I had to move on. If you can't make something a career in seven years, it's time..." I trailed off, staring at the tray of biscuits.

I stared at them for so long Janie eventually handed me one. Her voice was low and warm, like on TV. "Being successful is a... by-product. It may happen if you have passion and skills and the right look, and the right timing and the right role. Everything has to fall into place. There are lots of people with passion and craft and commitment who never get that lucky. It doesn't mean they're not good at what they do."

Her words warmed my heart, but they didn't change my fate. "Well, I guess I'm unlucky, then." I bit into the biscuit. It tasted of almonds.

"But that's no reason to deny your passion or downplay your skills. You're a brilliant actress."

My heart pounded in my throat now, making it hard to swallow. I would have to keep the cookie in my mouth. Which was better anyway, since I had nothing intelligent to say. When applying for my current job, I'd presented myself as someone who only desired to work behind the scenes. She hadn't challenged me back then, and since she'd hired me, I assumed it was the right thing to say.

I finally swallowed and found my voice. "You... you're not bothered by that? I mean, if I miss acting?" My voice wobbled on the last word.

Janie laughed. "Of course not! Most jobs in the film industry are held by people who'd rather act, write or direct. Many of them wouldn't have the chops for it, but it's human to dream big, and we all need jobs to sustain us while we dream."

I wondered if I was the one who didn't have the chops. "But... if it's not happening, shouldn't you move on?"

Janie shrugged. "Some people can, and they do. That's great. Only you know if you're one of those people."

She offered me another biscuit and I took it, feeling elated. "Thank you. I do miss it. I thought I could leave it all behind and be sensible, but it's been harder than I thought. I can't stop thinking, what if I gave up right before my big break? I know it's bullshit, but—"

"We've all heard that story many times, but it's only ever told in hindsight, by someone who made it. Hardly the full picture." Janie's mouth curved into a wistful smile.

"I know!" I blinked away tears, feeling like I'd been given more room to breathe, more than I had in months. "Thank you," I whispered again, thinking of the strange opportunity that had landed in my lap. It wasn't TV or film or even theatre. This was acting for Instagram, on steroids, but it was a role, and I could treat it as such.

Maybe that would make it feel less weird, too. I'd treat it as another acting job. I would prep, do some vocal exercises, get in the right state of mind, dress for the part...

"About the clothing..."

Janie smiled. "Don't worry, I have some wardrobe options..." She turned the knobs on her stove, then led me down a wide corridor adorned with pendant lights to a spacious, earth-toned bedroom. Only one side of the king bed looked like it had been slept in, with a tower of books piled on the nightstand. I didn't know much about her husband, other than that he was filthy rich and seemed to be away a lot. I wondered if they were having problems but couldn't bring myself to ask.

Janie opened a door to a huge walk-in wardrobe and flicked on the light. I gasped at the display of designer bling, so at odds with her earthy country life.

"I keep my farm clothes in another closet," she confessed. "This one's a bit of a… shrine."

After half an hour of fitting and planning, I had a stack of garment bags so thick I couldn't properly fold it over my arm and Janie had to help me haul the outfits to my car.

I thanked her with tears in my eyes, but she only waved her hand. "It's good they're getting some use. Good luck with the job!"

I drove away with my nerves strung but also lighter than I'd felt in months. Janie knew who I was. She understood the struggle. Maybe I could relax with trying to change myself and accept that I'd always have this yearning. Maybe I could even accept that I missed acting so much I would take a job pretending to be a Turkish actress.

When I made it back to my apartment, I knew what I had to do. After a bit of googling, I found the show – *Lucky in Love*, starring Cem Erkam and Burcu Yılmaz – with English subtitles.

I made myself a sandwich and a cup of tea and settled in for the afternoon. After two hours and two more cups of tea, I was hooked.

Emre, the character played by Cem, seemed a lot more reserved and serious than the real Cem, but the scenes between him and Burcu kept me glued to my laptop screen, unable to look away. The way Cem looked at his co-star, the way he circled her like a hyena, cornered her, stood impossibly close, his eyes roaming her body like he wanted to eat her… it both disturbed and excited me. Yet, by the third episode, they'd only kissed once. Still, I found my body reacting to every touch.

Immersed in the story, fortified by my third cup of tea, I tried to imitate Burcu's hand gestures and expressions; her over-the-shoulder death stare, the way she threw her hands in the air in frustration and cupped her face in embarrassment, eyes comically wide when something mortifying happened – at least once every five minutes. Her acting felt a little theatrical, but also fun, fit for romantic comedy.

The real Burcu, the one who hadn't been out in public for years, might have acted very differently, but I decided not to worry about that. That cutesy on-screen persona was the one the viewers remembered and loved. She was the one I needed to bring back.

# CHAPTER 11

# Cem

Grateful to be reunited with my suitcase, I dumped its contents onto my bed, rifling through the pile for the right outfit. It had rained all night and morning, so Emir had asked me to postpone our outing with Aria. We'd rescheduled for 4 p.m., then 5 p.m. and finally 6 p.m. It paid off. The sun had finally appeared, making the street glimmer in the warm evening light.

I popped my head out the open window, inhaling the incredible freshness, my body vibrating. Maybe I was high from too much oxygen. It made me think of all the cigarette smoke and pollution I'd inhaled for years. As much as I craved a good cigar, filling my lungs with pristine air felt amazing, and morally superior.

Obviously, I'd gone through Emir's possessions to see if he'd brought any cigarettes – or whiskey. He'd quit two years ago, but relapsed a few times since, so it was possible. As luck would have it, I found nothing, which allowed me to continue basking in moral superiority. Maybe I would actually quit this time, I thought, applying another nicotine patch.

Seeing the puddles along the beach road, I settled on a pair of sneakers and finally decided to try on the casual slacks Aria had bought. They fit perfectly and, to my surprise, looked rather good. On my Instagram feed, I was mostly seen in a designer suit or shirtless. Maybe a pair of slacks and a hoodie was exactly what I needed to soften my image.

Emir met me in the hallway in jeans, a collar shirt and a suit jacket. "You look like you're on your way to the gym."

I picked at the shoulders of the hoodie to proudly show it off. "Is that a problem?"

Emir raised his brow. "I don't think we're going to the gym."

"No, but Aria bought these clothes for me, so there must be something about... this that she likes, and I need her to be comfortable around me, otherwise we'll never pull this off."

Emir cocked his head, impressed. "That's a... good point."

He made it sound like it was the first one I'd ever made. Jerk.

A knock at the door cut off our brewing argument.

I threw some clothes over my arm and followed Emir downstairs. No way I was leaving my brother alone with Aria. If he didn't trust me with her, it went both ways.

We found her on the doorstep in a pale-yellow sundress and a straw hat. It was on the casual side but suited her so perfectly I couldn't help staring. She perused my outfit and her face melted into a gorgeous smile. "You're... wearing the clothes."

I'd never been happier with my wardrobe choice. "Of course!" I freed my hands by dumping my pile of clothing on Emir's arm and struck a pose, hands on hips. A little exaggerated maybe.

Aria laughed. "Done a bit of modelling, perhaps?"

"You can tell?" I wagged my eyebrows, flicking hair off my face like a true diva.

I would have done anything to keep her laughing, but Emir growled from under the clothing pile. "Can we get moving?"

Aria brushed the front of her dress. "Is this okay? I have fancier outfits in the car, but I didn't want to get them dirty on the way."

"How dirty are we talking about?" I looked at the heap of designer clothing Emir grumpily organized over his other arm.

"Well, it might be a little wet after the rain, but it's a short walk."

"Where are we going?" Emir demanded, as we followed her outside.

Aria smiled. "It's a surprise."

I grinned, glancing at my brother – the control freak who hated surprises.

"Sounds great." I caught Aria's gaze, a fleeting moment of connection I wanted to extend. I wanted to tell her to ignore Emir and his moods. "Shotgun!"

Aria's car was a tiny, grey Toyota Aqua. Cheap and definitely not cheerful.

Emir followed us and took the backseat, where he stewed in silence. Perfect. I could almost pretend he wasn't there.

"How did you get into location scouting?" I asked Aria as she steered down the deserted beach road. On the front seat, the left-hand-side traffic felt more disorienting, and I focused my eyes on her.

Her mouth twitched. "My parents really missed me, and I thought I should try to move back home… so I had to find a job. I think I jumped on this one because I wanted to be in the vicinity of the film industry, even if I couldn't do acting. A shadow career, you know? I know they get a bad rap, but what's the alternative? The world only needs so many waitresses."

"So, you'd rather be an actress?"

She looked startled. "Oh, no. Not anymore. I mean, it's not in the cards for me."

"Why?"

"There are no acting jobs around here. Not that I had that many jobs in Auckland, either. Supporting roles, two or three-line parts, occasional ads."

"That sucks."

"It's okay. I mean, I was done with Auckland. I had to make a change. I was broke. In my thirties with no savings or a career of any kind…"

She covered her mouth, her cheeks turning pink. "I don't mean to sound so pathetic, or ungrateful, but I've thought about this a lot."

"No, it's good," I insisted, hoping to keep her talking. "I like honesty. It's refreshing."

We emerged from the town center and onto a short bridge. The ocean glimmered in the distance. I wanted to keep driving, to learn more about her. Having a conversation with someone who wasn't trying to impress me or use me felt freeing, like I was sixteen again, chatting with my friends on the side of the football field, sharing one cigarette between four boys. My fingers twitched, longing for that smoke.

Aria turned off the main road onto a smaller one.

We wove through bright greenery that looked a lot like rain forest, punctuated by tall rose-tinted rock formations. So different from anything I'd seen in the last few years. I'd spent most of my time on the seashore of Istanbul, surrounded by millions of people, millions of seagulls and very few trees.

In my early twenties, before all the fame, I used to drive to the mountains to camp and fish with friends. I remembered the sense of wilderness, not quite like this but similar, surrounding me from every side, making me feel insignificant, yet more alive. Why had I stopped going?

"Do you go camping a lot?" I asked Aria.

"Not, really. I probably should. There's not much else to do here other than go into the bush or onto the beach."

My gaze landed on a young guy pounding the sidewalk in a sagging sleeveless tee and no shoes. "Why does everyone dress so casually? Are they all on their way to the beach or the... bush?"

She glanced over her shoulder as we drove past the dude and laughed, biting her lip. "It's the Kiwi way. We're very laid back. To the point that if you put too much effort into your appearance, it makes you seem a bit... pretentious." She flicked me a sideways glance, eyes glinting with glee.

"Are you talking about my shiny shirt?"

"No, I mean generally, but also, yes. It was so shiny." Her eyes rounded in mock horror.

I looked down at the gym clothes she'd bought me. "Is that why you bought me these clothes? Would you be embarrassed to be seen with me if I was wearing designer clothes?"

Her face reddened. "No! You just... you said you needed to keep a low profile. Shiny stuff like that really stands out here." Her voice dropped to a husky whisper. "And those clothes I bought you are from a really nice shop. They weren't on sale or anything."

She stared at the road, gripping the steering wheel, her chin jutting defensively.

"And I love them!" I brushed my hands down the front of the hoodie. "They're the most comfortable clothes I've ever owned."

Her mouth tugged into a tiny smile. "That's the upside of being ultra-casual. That, and blending in."

"What about your celebrities?" I frowned. "Isn't anyone allowed to stand out?"

"Sure. They'd have designer gear, but maybe not that shiny unless they're attending a glitzy gala... and we don't have many of those. What we have is the tall poppy syndrome. If anyone gets too high and mighty, they get chopped down. It doesn't matter how famous you are, in New Zealand you're just another bloke. When I was young, the prime minister's home phone number was in the phonebook, and she lived on this totally ordinary street in Auckland. Not even the fanciest suburb."

"That's bizarre. And dangerous." I shook my head at the thought.

"I guess, but she's still alive and well."

I asked more questions, not because I was dying to know about the country. I liked listening to the soft, low purr of her voice. It sounded so mellow, nothing like Burcu's. She didn't try to sound feminine or interesting. It was like witnessing a stream of consciousness, and I wanted to swim in it. I was also tickled by the idea of a society that abhorred hierarchy and formal clothing. A country where nobody was *that* special. Not even me. I found it simultaneously unnerving and energizing.

"So, where you come from, shiny shirts are the norm?" She winked at me. "Or is that only for guys who're peacocking?"

"What is peacocking?"

She gave me a cheeky smile. "It's when guys wear really shiny or colorful clothes to draw the attention of females."

I cringed at the thought but couldn't help laughing. "I don't really choose my own clothing. I wear what I'm asked to wear. The designers send me stuff."

"A reluctant peacock, then?"

"Well…" I pulled a face.

"You like the shiny shirts!"

Watching Aria's shoulders shake as she cracked up, struggling to stay on the road, I realized something. It wasn't her likeness with Burcu that made her fascinating, but everything that set her apart – like that low, slightly throaty voice, her brutal honesty and cheekiness. It reminded me of what I'd once had with mates who knew me and poked fun at me, never worried about offending.

Aria slowed down and turned onto a narrow dirt road, which

soon led to an empty parking area. We got out of the car, and she guided us along a small footpath that wound through the bush. The rain-soaked leaves swiped on the sleeves of my hoodie, and I tried to dodge them to keep dry.

The evening sun filtered through the thick greenery, casting a lacy pattern of light over the path, over Aria's gracefully moving shoulders. She had a presence I associated with actors. It seemed different from Burcu's, more understated and grounded, but she had it. Why would she give up acting? Surely, she could travel to auditions from here. I wanted to ask her more about it.

After a moment, I heard a low rumble. Soon, we arrived at an opening and the sight stole my breath. A tall horsetail waterfall poured down a vertical rock wall, lined on both sides by green ferns and vegetation. At the bottom, a perfectly round, shallow pool churned under the gushing water like a giant bubble bath. As we got closer, the roar of water became so loud we had to raise our voices.

"This is insane!" I joined Aria on the sandy strip by the water. "I can't believe there's nobody else here."

"You said you wanted secluded, and it rained last night, so I thought it might look good." She looked proudly at the gushing water.

I took her hand. She jerked a little but didn't pull away.

"I suppose we're playing a couple now." She looked down at our joined hands, stiff as a rod.

"Are you okay with this?" I moved my hand onto her shoulder. "We should look like we're comfortable around each other."

"Yeah, I know."

She drew a deep breath, and I took a photo of us.

Emir appeared on my other side, frowning at the phone screen. "You look like third cousins meeting for the first time at a family reunion."

I pocketed my phone. "And you look like a hitman circling that family reunion. Maybe you should go away. You're making her nervous."

"It's okay—" Aria began protesting, but I gave her a wide-eyed look, attempting to telepathically transmit the words 'whaddya doing? You have a chance to get rid of his sour face. Take it!' I suspect most of that didn't get across, but my comically high-sailing eyebrows probably did the trick and she changed tack.

"Sorry, Emir. It might be easier without an audience."

"You said you have an acting background." Emir stared back, his eyes hard.

Why did he have to be such a jerk? "This is not a run-of-the-mill acting gig and you know it." I gestured so widely I accidentally flicked his chest. Well, maybe not so accidentally. "There's no script, nothing. We have to make it up as we go."

Aria raised her hand, eyes filled with desperation. "I'm sorry. It's me. I haven't acted in months. I'm out of practice. Right now, I'm struggling to relax, like I'm having an out-of-body experience. And you both assessing me like—"

"Fine. I'll wait in the car. Come back in half an hour. With some usable photos, please." Emir's jaw clenched at the word 'please', as if his body was rejecting such overt politeness.

Aria handed him the car keys. Before slinking away, Emir cast one last look at me, a silent warning. I knew what it meant. He'd noticed the way I looked at her and smelled trouble.

"Is he angry with us?" Aria whispered when my brother was out of earshot.

"Yeah, but he's always angry." I dipped my chin to catch her eye. "What did you mean by the out-of-body experience? Or was that just a fancy line to distract Emir?"

She hid her blushed cheeks behind her hands, then peeked at me through her fingers. "No. I am out of my depth here. You're too gorgeous and none of this is real. I feel like I'm wearing one of those VR headsets and like... holding my breath, waiting to wake up." She dropped her hands and looked me in the eye, for a brief moment allowing me to see it all – embarrassment, disbelief and delight. "I've been trying so hard to be happy with my simple life. I tried to stop dreaming, but it didn't work."

"Why would you try to stop dreaming?"

Her smile was almost too sad to be a smile. "I mean giving up those big, unrealistic dreams that will never come true. Like acting." She cast me an apologetic look. "For me, I mean. I tried for years and I learned a lot, but I never made it like you, and that dream was killing me."

I nodded. I knew the struggle. I'd seen it on the fringes of every production, the supporting actors who only got to pop in for a few seconds of forgettable screen time. I'd tried to ignore their jealousy; pretend I didn't see it.

"Come on, let's get up there. We'll get a better angle on the waterfall." I pointed at a large rock by the pool. Who knew if it made any difference, but I needed to move. I needed to try something.

I jumped on top of the rock and held out my hand, pulling her up with me. I wanted to touch her, and I'd take any excuse. Once on top of the rock, Aria found her footing, standing a good two feet away from me, hugging herself, biting on her lip so hard I feared she would draw blood. Yet, she didn't look away from me, not for a second, and those eyes betrayed her. Eyes the color of Turkish tea.

She wasn't only fighting the attraction between us. She was fighting herself.

"What if it's giving up the dream that's killing you?" I asked. "You should never stop dreaming."

Her sigh was heavy. "What do you dream of?"

I scratched my neck. "Maybe doing my own stunts, working outside of Turkey, but I have an accent, so I doubt Hollywood would want me."

"Oh, they would. Anyone would." She was looking at me with sad sincerity, as if she saw something in me. Something undeniable.

I felt a little squeeze in my chest, so sudden and unexpected I almost mistook it for indigestion, but as the warmth spread through my belly, I knew she'd put it there. How, I wasn't sure. It's not like I hadn't heard comments about my looks or talent. That's all I heard, every time we posted something on social media. I was adored and objectified so much it had become almost meaningless. Almost. Only the stats meant something – the number of likes, the number of comments, the engagement. I'd become simultaneously addicted to and immune to praise.

The warm feeling lingered and I held her gaze, afraid to shatter the moment. "Very few people really see me. When you're successful, people don't really want you. They want what you can do for them."

She looked down, her cheeks blotchy pink. "You mean, like people who want the hotel you're staying in—"

"No. I'm not talking about you. In fact, you're the first person to really see me in a long time. You look at me as if I'm a person, not… an object."

Aria looked up, horrified. "Cem. That's… wow. I can't even imagine." She shook her head, a wild look in her eyes.

I found myself moving closer to her, not to touch, only to feel her breath and the heat of her body, hoping to extend the unsettling yet delicious sensation. The sun sizzled hot on my neck, but the air felt cool, filled with fine mist. Everything smelled like rain and growth. Earth and sky. It didn't feel like anything I'd experienced with Burcu. There was the same desire to kiss her, and take her, but with an unfamiliar level of uncertainty, even fear. I had no script. She could slip out of my hands at any moment.

Aria's hair had curled around her face, the damp strands licking her cheeks. It made her look untamed, and I loved it. If we were going to capture something different, something that hadn't featured on my Instagram in years, this was it. Aria, like this, looking at me as if she couldn't decide whether to kiss me or push me off the rock.

I watched closely for any cracks in her armor, that spark I'd seen hiding right under the surface. If only I could get her to relax.

I raised my hand to swipe a strand of hair from her face, but she recoiled, losing her balance. My heart leapt into my throat as her foot stumbled on the slippery surface, fighting for purchase.

My body reacted faster than my brain, catching her by the waist, like I'd caught many actresses in similar scenes, although I'd never seen any of them flailing their arms like this. Nor had any of their faces ever displayed the terror that registered on Aria's.

She felt light and tense, like touching a live wire. I wanted to hold on to her, keep holding until she softened into my touch, but I had no excuse. Nobody was filming us in slow motion. So, I brought her back upright and reluctantly let go. "This is dangerous. I need you to relax, Aria."

She nodded, panting from shock. "I know. I'm sorry. It just… feels *wrong*. I keep telling myself it's an acting job, but Burcu is not a fictional character. She's a real person." Aria blew a shuddering breath. "I shouldn't have watched your show! Now I'm overthinking it. The way she moves, the way she acts around you…" Her eyes burned.

She'd watched the show?

"How does she act around me?" I carefully helped her off the rock. "You mean when she does that nasty look over her shoulder?"

I spun on the grass, casting a menacing look over my shoulder, imitating Burcu's signature move. I knew I looked ridiculous, and it worked. Aria laughed and copied my move, but with far more conviction.

Her performance was so perfect, including the slight thrust of her chin, that I felt my lungs flattening.

Burcu. It was Burcu.

Aria didn't notice my reaction. She thrust her fists to her sides and shouted 'Oof!' – a reaction I immediately recognized.

"That's perfect!"

Buoyed by my praise, she launched into an animated burst of fake Turkish, her eyes wide, hands gesturing with passion. Her speech had the right intonation and rhythm but made absolutely no sense.

I held my breath, watching her in awe. Almost instinctively, I slipped my hands around her waist, a move that might have followed in the same scene if we'd been on set, going through the rehearsed motions. Her arms pressed against my chest and she lifted her chin, eyes defiant, yet filled with desire and the inner conflict I'd witnessed my co-star pull off to perfection. Was it intentional?

"You said *seviyorum seni*," I said. "It means 'I love you.'"

Her eyes burned. "No! I was talking gibberish. I love how your language sounds."

"Yes, you did," I insisted. "You confessed your love and told me you hate how much you want to kiss me right now."

Her eyes widened for half a second before she called my bluff. "Oh, come on!" She shoved my chest, laughing. She was standing far too close to put any weight behind it, and I held her even tighter.

"Don't stop," I whispered. "Stay in character. Show me what Burcu does when I hold her like this."

"She… freezes," Aria whispered, her mouth a couple of inches from mine. "With her lips parted, like she really wants to kiss you, but she never does. She holds there, waiting for your next move. Why is that?"

Her question threw me, but I didn't ease my grip. "I don't know. I suppose… it's my job to kiss her."

"So, you'd be turned off if a woman made the first move?"

I thought about this. "I'd be surprised. It doesn't happen much, but I'm willing to experience it and let you know." I winked at her, trying to mask my uncertainty.

She was getting under my skin, but I didn't want her to stop.

# CHAPTER 12

Was he daring me to kiss him? Cem's hands tightened around my waist, holding me so close I couldn't think. I held still, listening to my own heartbeat. I felt it everywhere, like distant nightclub music, intensified by the rumble of the waterfall.

I slid my hands around his neck and let my gaze dip to his mouth. Such a perfect pair of lips, framed by a beard I wanted to touch. I wondered how rough it was, how much it would give under my fingers.

*Stop staring.*

I cleared my throat, letting the moment pop like a soap bubble. "Should we take some selfies?"

Cem kept one hand on my back and used the other to frame us and the waterfall on his phone screen. I grabbed the brim of my sunhat and leaned on his chest, forcing every doubt and worry out of my mind.

"Relax," he rumbled into my ear.

I took a deep breath, and that's when it hit me. I wasn't here to impersonate Burcu. Not really. My number one job was to look like I was in love with him and if I was honest with myself, I didn't struggle with that part. As soon as I let my thoughts go there, I felt it. That burning, wild and aching sensation poured through me like the water gushing over those rocks after the rain. Uncontrollable.

I didn't know him. The emotion wasn't real, but it could have fooled me.

His fingers drew circles on my lower back, flooding my body with heat, pumping blood to my core, spreading lower. I inhaled his spicy scent like an addict getting her fix, then lifted my lips toward his ear. I had to stand on my toes to get close enough. "Do you want to go in the water? I'm a bit hot." It wasn't because of the sun, but did it matter?

"I'll go if you go."

I glanced over my shoulder at the pond. It didn't look deep, but it was probably freezing. "Deal."

I hated cold water, but I must have had so many endorphins coursing through me I momentarily forgot. Not giving myself time to back out, I chucked my ballet flats and waded to the middle of the pond, so close to the waterfall I could no longer hear anything else. The roar drowned out my thoughts, making it easier to be.

The freezing water stabbed my feet like a school of tiny knives, but it only came up to my knees. I held out my hand, gesturing for Cem to follow. "Come on!"

I expected him to maybe roll up his pant legs, but he took off his hoodie and T-shirt, then his slacks, folded them and placed them carefully on a small fern. That simple action made my heart squeeze.

He didn't know how much the clothes had cost me. He didn't even know I'd paid for them, so why did he care? Maybe he was meticulous with clothes but based on the way he'd cast his belongings across the hotel room, I doubted that.

Cem didn't wade into the water. He leapt in. I wasn't proud of where my gaze went as he stood before me in his boxer shorts.

"My eyes are up here." Cem pointed at his face, split by a cheeky grin.

I splashed him with as much water as I could scoop with two hands. My sudden move caught him off guard and the freezing water landed squarely on his crotch. A surprisingly high shriek escaped his throat, and I doubled over in a fit of giggles. That fleeting moment was worth everything that came after, or so I thought.

He retaliated immediately, somehow drenching me with a bucket load without an actual bucket. Dear God, it was cold! I shivered inside out, but no way was I backing down.

I ladled more water, aiming higher. Seeing his handsome face dripping wet satisfied my soul. He still looked gorgeous, but definitely less polished.

The murderous growl rising from him made the tiny hairs on my neck stand up. "If anyone asks, you were begging for this."

He edged closer, his resonant voice sending tremors down my spine. Even the bite of the icy water couldn't compete with the effect.

I took a wobbly step backwards, my chest shaking with suppressed laughter, my joy mixing with dread as he approached me, arms out, chest wide. The rumble of the waterfall grew louder as we neared it.

I glanced over my shoulder, scanning for an escape, a way to avoid the high-pressure icy shower, but I was too slow. I also underestimated his willingness to dive in. Within two seconds, Cem trapped me in his arms and pushed us under the waterfall. Thank goodness this was not Niagara. Still, the pressure whipped the hat off my head and hit my neck like a massaging shower head on steroids. The chilly water filled my ears, eyes, and mouth, but before I knew it, we were out, coughing, and laughing.

"That was colder than I thought!" Cem sputtered, wiping his eyebrows.

I fished my poor hat from the water. It must have been made of paper, since it now resembled a pile of wet pulp.

"Should we take more photos looking like drowned river rats?" I asked, peeling strands of soaking wet hair off my face.

I'd meant it as a joke, but as we emerged from the water, he fetched his phone and pulled me against himself, immortalizing our soaked clothes, dripping hair and glistening smiles. I pressed my ear against his ribcage, soaking in his warmth. The evening sun heated my back, trapping me between layers of hot and cold. There was no middle ground. I felt like my soul had been jump-started.

Cem pressed a kiss on my forehead, wrapping his arms around my shivering body. I inhaled his closeness, his familiar scent mixed with earth and sunshine. It took me a few beats to realize he was no longer taking photos. I felt his hands pressing against my lower back, rubbing the cold and clammy skin under my wet dress.

Part of me wanted to stay right there, pretending I hadn't noticed we'd slipped from taking photos to embracing each other for no good reason. But I couldn't.

I reluctantly lifted my chin. "Has it been half an hour? Should we go back?"

Cem took a step back, a little flustered. "I was just warming you up." As soon as his hands left my skin, I missed them so much I ached.

Not good. Not good at all.

He picked up his clothes from the rock. A safe distance away, they were still dry.

"I'm so jealous." I sighed, violently shaking from the cold. I positioned myself in full sun, hoping my dress would dry quickly. I also hoped the light-yellow fabric hadn't become completely see-through.

"Take this." He handed me his hoodie.

Grateful, and shaking from the cold, I pulled it on. Nothing had ever felt so good. Or smelled so good.

Cem glanced at his wet boxer shorts. "Do you mind if I…"

He proceeded to pull off his underwear and I promptly turned around. "Sorry. Go ahead."

I waited until he told me to turn around.

"Ready to go?" Cem gestured at the path, now dressed up, holding a wet pair of boxers.

As soon as he turned around, I inhaled the blessed piece of clothing that stood between myself and hypothermia. What were those spices? Cinnamon? Clove? Sniffing the traces of Cem stored in the fabric of his hoodie, watching his muscled frame traipse ahead of me in the T-shirt and grey slacks I'd chosen, I felt a little less sorry for my bank account. Maybe I'd get my money's worth.

My body warmed up slightly on the way, even if my dress remained damp.

We found Emir sitting at a picnic table, staring at his phone. He looked up, unimpressed. "You went swimming?"

I blushed, but Cem smiled broadly, running his fingers through his damp hair. "It was amazing. Look at these!"

He handed his phone to his brother, who swiped through our photos. I held my breath, bracing for his reaction.

After a moment, Emir passed the phone back to Cem and stood up. "We can work with these." He turned to me. "Do you need to get changed?"

I nodded, dazed, and went to search my car for another outfit. I set the ruined hat to the side, grateful that it had been my own. I hadn't brought a change of underwear, so I selected a slightly longer dress, albeit a tight one, and headed behind a bush to get changed. The foliage didn't offer perfect cover, but I figured if I moved fast, it'd be okay.

I reluctantly pulled off Cem's hoodie, then peeled off my wet dress before quickly slipping into the navy-blue halter neck one. Finally, sighing with relief, I wiggled out of my wet cotton underwear.

When I stepped out from behind the bush, I found Emir sitting in the front seat and Cem standing outside the car. His face had frozen into a strange expression I didn't have time to study before he slipped into the backseat.

I threw my wet underwear in the boot and grabbed my other hat – a wide-brimmed, white and floppy sunhat – and sat behind the wheel. "Where should we go next?"

Emir looked up. "Dinner. Somewhere…"

"Secluded?" I finished for him.

A ghost of a smile grazed his lips. "Yes. Thank you for this. You've been extremely helpful, and we really appreciate it. The photos are good. I think they'll work."

I smiled back, surprised by his words. "That's… great."

Cem remained quiet. I was dying to see his face, but he sat behind me, somehow evading the rear-view mirror, so I started the car.

Driving along the dirt road with the evening sun heating my arms and gorgeous greenery whipping past our windows, life made sense. In my new job, I'd spent weeks canvassing the area for the most picturesque restaurants and other potential filming locations. I could take my pick and I knew exactly where to go.

# CHAPTER 13

I was happy to take the backseat. Not because I enjoyed watching my brother and Aria bonding, but because I preferred to keep my hard-on to myself. Again, it was my own fault. Emir had practically ordered me to wait in the car, but I'd stayed outside, claiming I also needed to get changed. True enough, but I could have done it without craning my neck to catch a glimpse of Aria.

Now I had a sore neck, a raging hard-on, and a mind filled with images of her naked body peeking from behind the leaves. She was turning me into an old-school voyeur.

"You will not sleep with her," Emir had hissed before getting into the car. "We need her on our side."

He had a point. I wasn't on the best terms with my former hook ups, which had caused some PR issues in the past.

Aria turned onto a smaller road that meandered through a vineyard, bringing us to a large building with a weathered, wooden exterior and tall windows. Mature trees shaded the yard. Aria parked alongside two Teslas and led us to the main entrance. A sign above the door featured the word 'winery'.

"Wait." I stopped her at the door. "Can we go in like this?"

I'd changed into a clean shirt (the least shiny one I could find) and a pair of designer jeans, but my hair still hung damp from the impromptu shower. I raked my fingers through it, wondering how bad it looked.

Aria glanced at me, surprised, like she'd never considered this. "I don't think they have a dress code. I'm sure we're fine."

I wish I could have pocketed her carefree shrug. That's how many fucks I wanted to give, but it would never work in Istanbul. My appearance would be scrutinized, everywhere I went.

Aria opened the door, and I launched forward to take it from her. She rolled her eyes, but I caught a brief smile.

The interior had a rustic and cozy vibe, with fairy lights hanging above wooden barn tables arranged around a freestanding fireplace. Two of the tables were occupied by older couples and soft folk music carried in from a distant speaker.

Emir gave Aria an approving nod. "This is perfect."

She glowed at his praise and my gut tightened. Why was he suddenly so charming?

We chose a table overlooking the vineyard, ordered glasses of their flagship Pinot Gris and smoked chicken salads. Aria set her hat on the table and combed her fingers through her hair with a look of deep concentration, slightly wincing in pain as she encountered tangles. I loved that guileless, oblivious expression, so deep in thought. She wasn't performing for anyone. She just was.

The wine arrived immediately, poured by a widely smiling server. Everyone in New Zealand smiled like they were on some powerful, euphoria-inducing drugs.

I took a sip of the wine and decided it contributed to the euphoria. "This is very good."

Aria's face lit up. "This is one of the best wineries in the area and we're spoilt for choice."

Emir pulled his laptop from his bag and set it up on the table.

"Are you posting the photos?" I asked.

"I already did. Checking the stats now."

"That was fast!" Aria stared at him in awe. "Can I see it?"

Emir chuckled. An honest-to-God, good-natured laugh. "About three million people already have, so I don't see why not."

She blushed, pulling her phone out of her little canvas bag.

"Oh, my God!" Her voice was a reverent whisper.

I'd seen the photos, yet I had to take out my own phone to see them again. I had to see what she was seeing.

Emir had gone with the freshly showered look, with water dripping down my face and Aria's hand across her forehead. It obscured her hairstyle but revealed her delicate features --a hint of a smile, eyelids half-closed, lips parted. She looked so much like Burcu that I found it hard to tell the difference, but more than that, I couldn't stop staring at the way she leaned on my chest. She looked at home. Anchored. Like there was nowhere else she'd rather be.

We were faking, but part of me yearned for what I saw in that picture. It wasn't adoration or lust. It was trust. Could I really be that person, the one who inspired trust?

It seemed my audience was lapping it up, with a sharp increase in likes and comments, many of them mentioning Burcu.

Emir had written an obscure description, dropping hints about me and Burcu without mentioning her name or even explicitly stating that we were together. He hadn't mentioned a location, either, but the comment section had exploded with guesses on where we might be vacationing.

"Does this mean people can see us together in public?" My eyes flicked at Aria. "Now that the cat's out of the bag."

Emir's mouth twisted. "It's a bit of a risk, if anyone recognizes you and talks to her in Turkish." He glanced at Aria, whose eyes widened.

"Oh, no. That would be a disaster!"

I couldn't help laughing. "She speaks excellent gibberish with a Turkish accent. You should hear her!"

Emir wasn't amused. Aria gave me a half-hearted smile before her attention returned to the photo, her brows drawn together. "How do you think Burcu will take this?"

I hitched up one shoulder. I'd been deliberately avoiding that question. "I don't know. I stopped trying to contact her years ago after she repeatedly ignored me. She's got my details if she wants to get in touch."

The salads arrived. Aria tucked into her meal, and I followed her example.

Emir ignored his food, busy on his laptop.

When we'd nearly finished our meals, he finally pierced a piece of chicken with his fork, only to be pulled straight back to his screen, eyes widening. "The story is out."

Aria looked up. "What?"

Emir stared at his screen, clicking away. "Three, four, no wait... five stories about Cem and Burcu being back together. There'll be more soon."

"Good stories?" I asked hopefully.

Emir gave me a reassuring nod. "For the most part. There are some questions as to whether this is only a publicity stunt, but once we post a few more pictures—"

"Have they approached Burcu's agent?" I asked.

Emir's fingers tapped on the touchpad, a nervous habit. "I'm sure they're trying, but no one's made a statement on her behalf. Yet."

"What if they deny everything?" Aria seemed visibly tense, cleaning her salad bowl with a piece of bread. I'd never seen anyone finish a meal so thoroughly.

Emir's finger-tapping intensified. "They probably will, but who's going to believe them? People only believe what they want to believe." He shot me a meaningful look, then turned to Aria. "Hopefully, the photos do their job either way and remind people of why they love Cem."

He looked at me like he was trying to remind himself of the same thing. I rewarded them both with a pouty look. "What? I'm super loveable!"

Emir's eyes sharpened, staring at the screen. He turned it to me so I could read. "An email from the Epic Studios' PR lady, asking for details on your romantic getaway. They are thrilled to see you with Burcu and hope you are happy together."

I leaned in to read the email, which sounded like she was desperate for confirmation of some kind. "Wow, they're following us closely. Isn't it early morning over there?"

Emir opened another tab with time zone information. "Yeah, 8 a.m."

"Sounds like she's fishing for more information."

"She'll get some, along with the rest of your fans, as soon as we get some more photos of your romantic getaway." He stretched the words 'romantic getaway' in a mocking way, and I felt a little hurt, because that's exactly what those moments at the waterfall had felt like, and I craved more.

"Should we take a selfie here?" I suggested. "The vineyard backdrop looks amazing."

Aria ran her fingers through her hair. "I need to go to the bathroom to redo my makeup." Her hair had dried into soft waves and her skin glowed.

"You look perfect," I told her, my voice cracking a little.

Emir shot me a sharp glance. "She needs to wear the hat. And add some color to those lips. Burcu would never leave the house like that."

"Absolutely." Aria wiped her mouth on a napkin and left the table.

I watched her walk away, hips swaying in the figure-hugging

blue dress.

Emir slapped the back of my head. "Could you be more obvious?"

I huffed. "What?"

"You're leering. I get that you've been celibate for like... a week, and I know you're a dog, but seriously."

"I'm not leering! And it's been at least a month."

"Whatever. You must direct your sexual energy somewhere else."

"It's not just that. I find her fascinating. There's something about her. Something so... real."

Emir's expression shifted from mildly annoyed to alarmed. "No. No. Don't do this to us. I'm sure seeing her brings back a lot of memories or whatever, but it's *not* real. She's not Burcu."

"I like that she's not Burcu! And didn't you want me to act like I'm a little in love with her, so you get the right kind of photos?"

To his credit, Emir looked a bit taken aback. "You know what I mean. She lives half a world away. You'd never make it work and anyway, we both know how long your relationships last. It's not fair to her."

I sighed. He had me there. "Yeah, fine."

We sipped our wines in silence until Aria returned, her hair combed, and lips fortified with pinkish red. I had to admit I preferred her without the makeup, with her face and hair dripping wet.

She placed the white hat on her head and led us through the back door, onto a terrace overlooking the vineyard.

"I'll take some photos of her first," I suggested, Emir's words ringing in my ears. *Keep your distance.*

Emir took a seat under a sun sail, propping his laptop on his knees, staring at us like a director on set. Maybe it was best if I pretended we were on set. That way, I couldn't let myself get too carried away.

Aria posed dutifully at the edge of the terrace, one hand holding onto her hat. She looked gorgeous and very much like Burcu, but I couldn't see any of the raw vulnerability from the earlier photos. After a while, I showed my phone to Emir.

He browsed the pics, his lip curling with disapproval. "Hm. I think you guys need to do some selfies like before. I'll wait in the car." He sounded resigned, but his gaze held the same warning as before.

After he exited, holding Aria's car keys, I caught the worried look on her face.

I smiled at her. "Don't worry. What he means is, you look amazing, but since that picture of us together got such a good response, we should probably try to do another one of those."

She laughed a little. "He's not big on compliments, is he?"

I shook my head. "Not really his thing." I held her gaze, enjoying the connection between us. Us against Emir. Us against the world.

I reached for her hand. "Let's go."

The vines were young and dainty, only up to my waist, running in orderly rows down the gentle slope. We skipped down the path until the restaurant building became a tiny dollhouse on the hill. I headed to a large oak in the middle, pulling us under its shadow. A soft breeze flapped the leaves and the sun filtered through the low-hanging branches, casting us with flickering polka dots of golden light.

I pinned her against the trunk, my hands on her shoulders. "I want to kiss you." The words poured out like they'd been ready and waiting, only looking for that moment of privacy. I was out of control.

Her eyes widened and lips parted.

"I know it's a bad idea," I added, as if it removed my culpability.

"Why?" She looked confused.

Words stuck in my throat.

Because I don't do relationships? Because I will inevitably hurt you? These were Emir's assumptions, not mine.

I was afraid that if I kissed her, if I let myself dream about something like this, something real, I'd split in half. Part of me would forever stay on this remote island. There was no happy ending, only pain down the road.

But I couldn't tell her that.

I blinked at Cem, trying to process his words.

"You mean, it's not good for the Instagram photo?" I had to ask. If there was a way to misunderstand him, I probably would.

Cem's eyes held mine for a long time, his heavy breath on my face making me dizzy. "I don't care about Instagram. I just want to kiss you, and I know I shouldn't. We can't."

My mouth went dry, and I forced myself to close it. "Okay."

Cem lowered his hands to my waist and his forehead against mine. He trapped me between his muscled torso and the gnarled wood of the tree, my hands flattened against his chest. His hot breath made my lips tingle. I'd never wanted to kiss anyone so badly.

I'd also never been so certain that I shouldn't. He was famous and gorgeous and lived on the other side of the world. Even if he was attracted to me, we didn't have a future. We had an unwritten business agreement and fooling around would risk everyone involved. My brain knew this. Even my body knew this, but it didn't obey. I couldn't take my hands off his hard chest or make any move to save myself.

Cem's hand slid lower on my waist and my back arched. "You probably shouldn't touch me like that." I couldn't hide the huskiness of my voice, or the way my breath seized. His eyes glazed over and darkened, eyelids dipping as he cast a hungry look at my lips.

I'd seen this move on TV, literally. I'd seen Cem doing this and even then, he'd held me captive. I'd considered it a bit exaggerated, played up for the cameras, slowed down for the sake of milking that moment right before the ad break. I'd imagined myself on the receiving end, of course, but I thought I might find it funny. I wouldn't succumb to his charm. I'd laugh.

Now, not so much. His brown eyes had captured every molecule in my body, including brain cells. I couldn't think, let alone laugh.

I watched my hands climb his chest like alien creatures, like they belonged to someone else, someone wild and hungry. Acting on their own, my fingers travelled up and dove into his curls. Thick. Crunchy. How could hair feel so satisfying?

He felt nothing like I'd thought he would when watching him on TV. Close up, I saw the faint scars of teenage acne on his cheeks and spotted two grey hairs in his beard.

I looked for further flaws. Maybe, if my brain got the message that he was only human, I could stop reacting like this and remove myself from this situation.

His lips parted and he leaned closer. Some deep, primal part of my brain argued with itself. If you have a chance to kiss a movie star, take it. Take it for all the insignificant women everywhere. Or don't. Show them they aren't gods. Show them—

The moment our lips touched, my reasoning evaporated. There was only his hot, unyielding mouth on mine. The back of my head made contact with the tree, sending a shock wave all the way to my toes. This was not a gentle, exploring kiss. This was savage.

I felt him testing me, like a wild beast let loose from its cage, searching for boundaries. Where were they? Did I have any? My body responded with fervor. My fists clawed for handfuls of his T-shirt and every zone ever earmarked for pleasure lit up, demanding more. His tongue met mine as if challenged to a duel. His hands roamed up and down my body, grazing my breasts as he shifted even closer, pushing his hardness against my swelling softness.

A gasp fought its way out of my throat. Cem reacted by diving for my neck, sucking so hard I both feared and hoped he would leave a mark. Nothing like this would ever happen to me again. I needed evidence.

This felt nothing like the kisses I'd seen on his TV show. It probably wouldn't have made it past the censorship, even if we were filmed as silhouettes, fifty feet away.

I wondered if anyone could see us from the house, or anywhere else, if he were to take me against this tree trunk. Of course he couldn't. None of this could happen. He'd told me it couldn't happen. Maybe that's what fueled the fire in me. I couldn't back down. I felt reckless, hot, charged. His thumb brushed over my nipple, and I moaned, letting my hands trace down his chest, feeling the waistband of his slacks under the T-shirt hem.

As I slid my hand under the shirt, Cem pulled away, panting, his eyebrows knitted. "God, Aria. You can't do this to me."

I blinked, trying to focus my gaze on him and the weird expression on his face. "Do what?"

He threw out his arms in a dramatic gesture. "This! You can't... let me. I told you we can't. It's too risky."

"What's too risky?"

Cem grimaced. "If you told me to stop, maybe I could. But you..." He ran his fingers through his hair, staring at me in desperation.

Irritation rose like a hot wave. "Why is it my job to stop you?"

He looked at me helplessly, ashamed. "Well, women usually have more restraint."

"Oh, do we now? So, men can't help themselves and are therefore excused?"

"Not excused, but—"

"You're a grown man. Take some responsibility!" I lowered my voice for effect, relieved to feel the rise of hot temper and the confidence it gave me. "If you don't want to kiss me, don't kiss me! I kissed you back because *I wanted to*. Not because I expect anything else from you or expect us to ever do that again. I wanted to kiss you, so I did."

I could tell from the look on his face that no one had ever spoken to him like this. We stood for a moment, inert, staring at each other. This time, it was more like a silent battle. A battle of wills.

Finally, Cem burst into laughter. "You're quite the woman Aria..."

I realized he was looking for my last name. "Dunne," I supplied.

"Aria Dunne," he repeated, tasting my boring name on his exotic tongue. "What's your middle name?"

I frowned. "What do you need that for?"

Cem's smile had a cheeky edge. "I'm curious about you."

I huffed in disbelief. He'd been happy to explore my mouth and body without knowing my last name. Why did he suddenly need to know more about me? I was a nobody.

"Grace," I finally said. "My middle name is Grace."

"Grace," he repeated, like it was the most interesting word to ever pass his lips. "Do you want to know mine?"

I pursed my lips, still emboldened by indignation. "I can google it. Tell me something truly personal. Something the internet doesn't know."

I kept my gaze on him, not giving in an inch. His mouth curved in appreciation. "Aria Grace, you're, not like the rest, are you?" He gazed at the vineyard. "Well, the internet doesn't know I'm up for a big budget action-adventure series that has international distribution. At least not all the details, because they're confidential."

My mouth twisted. "No, but Emir told me that. American dollars, inflation, blah blah. I said, tell me something deeply personal."

A shadow crept into his eyes. "Okay." He drew a breath. "I don't know if I really want it."

"What? The role?"

"Don't tell Emir, but I feel dread when I think about it. It's a good role. A lot of money. But it's so… fake. A fairy tale that paints me as this perfect hero. It's for a younger audience and I'm not sure I'm up to being a role model. Kids are impressionable. It's a lot of responsibility. What if I mess up again? It'll be so much worse."

"So, you're scared you won't be a good role model and the studio is scared you might not be a good role model?" I gave him a rueful smile. "A match made in heaven, then?"

Cem laughed, some of the tension melting away. "Yeah, absolutely."

Watching those emotions flicker across his face – doubt, worry, conflict and amusement – something warm blossomed in my chest. I felt like I was seeing beyond the surface. I craved more.

"You said 'what if I mess up again'. What happened before? Why did you have to come here?"

"You really don't know? That one is all over the internet."

"And I'll be googling it the first chance I get, but I'd rather hear your version first."

Cem hung his head, his foot idly moving around a stick that lay between exposed roots. "My version is probably the least accurate. I was drunk. I don't remember much. I only remember that… sensation. That rush you get when you make a disastrous decision. It's like seeing an imminent train wreck. You know you can't stop it, but the moment before it happens, there's this… weightless feeling. This thrill. Because you actually did it. You set it in motion." He winced at his own words, a sudden flash of panic in his eyes as he lifted them to me. "You think I'm unhinged?"

I smiled, despite myself. "Well, unless you're talking about causing a train wreck, or pushing someone off a cliff..."

"No!" he declared to my relief. "I, um... I dropped my pants and mooned at the paparazzi."

My relief was replaced by exhilarated shock. "You what?"

Cem shook his head, his cheeks deepening in color. "I know. I was drunk and they were getting on my nerves, asking me to do this and do that. Nothing's ever enough for them. You can chop yourself up and hand them the pieces and they'll fight over the bones. Not that I was thinking all that when it... happened. It just happened. Then I found out one of them was hiding in the bushes on the other side of the terrace, and they got..."

"A dick pic?" I finished for him.

"I suppose." Cem bit his lip. "Not the standard kind, though."

"What's a standard dick pic? Which official body standardized that?" I tried to keep from laughing but failed miserably.

Cem stared at me for a moment, then cracked a smile. "Honestly, I have no idea. I've never sent one." His smile turned into a chuckle. "But I always thought they were meant to be... not flaccid. I mean—"

"Don't ask me! I've never received one." I took a deep breath, laughter still bubbling in my stomach. "It sounds like neither of us has lived a full life."

"Well, when you measure it like that." Cem shook his head, wiping his eyes, still shaking from silent laughter. "How did this conversation deteriorate so quickly?"

"I don't know, but I swear I had a point, and it wasn't about dick pics." I tried to compose myself, backtracking to our last non-dick topic. "So, you're worried about being a role model?"

"Yeah." Cem sighed, staring off into the distance. "I've thought about it a lot and… what bothers me most is I don't know why I did it. I've blamed it on the alcohol." He lowered his voice. "But honestly, I wasn't *that* drunk. I could have stopped myself, only I didn't."

I nodded. "And now you're scared it might happen again, even if you never drank another drop."

He bobbed his head silently, sucking on his lower lip. "What if I keep having these random lapses of judgment? What if something even worse happens? I mean, I kissed you, even though I decided I definitely shouldn't." He barked a humorless laugh. "It's fun inside my head, I tell you."

I leaned against the tree trunk, studying his conflicted face. A thought that had been brewing at the back of my mind finally surfaced. "What if it's not totally random? Looking at your life, how your brother manages every second of it, how the press follows you around… you don't get a lot of freedom, do you?"

He frowned. "Well, it's not like I have a bedtime, but there are certain things you have to do to be successful, to have a career."

He seemed a bit irritated, like I'd called him a baby, but I couldn't help pushing it. "My life is nothing like yours, but I still feel those expectations – what my parents want, what my boss wants… Sometimes, I feel it drowns out my own voice and I don't even know what *I* want."

"I know the feeling, but it doesn't excuse public nudity." He gritted his teeth, drawing a reluctant breath, like he'd been scolded by someone I couldn't see.

My laughter fizzled out. I couldn't even imagine how it must have felt to have your one mistake amplified like that, staring back at you from hundreds of websites, and shared by millions. He probably couldn't go anywhere in his country without being reminded of it.

I gathered my courage and made eye contact. "To me, it makes sense that you would struggle with those boundaries. I'm sure you're living a charmed life and you have more than I ever even dreamed of, but you don't have a lot of freedom to make mistakes. The rest of us can have a bad day, embarrass ourselves, and move on. For example, I might avoid the laundromat where I had a public meltdown, but it's only one place—"

"Why did you have a meltdown at a laundromat?" His gaze drilled into mine and I swallowed.

Why did I have to use real-life examples?

"I... it was shortly after I moved to Napier and felt really out of place..." I shook my head, forcing myself to return to that day. "I lost my laundry coin. It dropped between the slats of the steps outside and I couldn't get to it."

"O...kay." He waited for more.

My eyes returned to my hands, keeping watch over the nails I was in danger of ripping off. "I mean, I'd had a hard day. This flat I was supposed to move into cancelled on me because someone they liked better happened to be available after all. I'd driven from Auckland with all my stuff with this amazing house in mind and then I had nothing. Nothing but laundry. So, I went to do my laundry, to have time to think." I looked up, giving my ego the last stab of death. "I'm not saying I had a really good reason to ugly cry in public and I'm also not saying I don't cry at a drop of a hat, because I do."

It was better that he knew the truth. The real me.

He looked at me with a mix of amusement and tenderness. "There's nothing shameful about crying, but are you seriously comparing you weeping in public to me showing my ass to the world?"

"That's my point! I can't make the world notice me do anything, embarrassing or not. I used to think it made me a failure, but maybe it's a blessing."

"Trust me, it is." Cem's hand came up to his beard, lightly brushing it like he couldn't quite commit to a gesture of any kind. "So, you're avoiding the laundromat now?"

I blushed, because my real-life example was both embarrassingly true and absolute bullshit. "No. I actually can't avoid it much at all... See, I cried so hard that this old guy came to ask me what was wrong, and I told him about my day, and he said he owned the vacant apartment above the laundromat and the rent was almost the same as the flat I'd missed out on. So, I took him up on the offer. I don't use the laundromat or sit outside it to relive that moment, but I'm not really avoiding it, either."

"Wow! So, your embarrassing moment actually paid off?" He

stared at me in disbelief. "That does seem a bit unfair."

I nodded vigorously. "It is! I think... if I lived under as much scrutiny as you do, I would rebel too. I thought I wanted success and fame and everything that comes with it, but maybe I didn't want *everything*. Maybe I couldn't handle everything."

Cem's gaze swept to my feet. "There's a lot in my life I didn't sign up for, but... I wasn't born rich. I remember what I had before, what I didn't have. When you're so much luckier than most, it feels really shitty to complain."

I instinctively touched his chin, lifting it up. "You're allowed to complain," I argued, anger welling in my chest, even if I was a bit distracted by the texture of his beard. Rougher than expected. Real.

He caught my two fingers, squeezing them inside his fist. "Trust me. Nobody wants to hear the rich and famous complain."

"Well, you're not that famous around here, and the rich in New Zealand complain all the time. They're like the loudest people group."

Cem huffed in amusement. He let go of my fingers and grabbed my entire hand, leading me back to the path between the vines, toward the restaurant. "I like not being famous around here. You might be right about the freedom. It's pretty amazing."

As we reached the restaurant, I froze. "The photos! We didn't take any photos!"

Cem looked equally shocked. "How did we forget? That's so weird!"

I raised a brow, my cheeks pulsing with heat as my mind returned to the culprit – the kiss. "Is it? I forgot my middle name out there."

"Grace!" Cem yelled victoriously, grinning from ear to ear.

"Thanks."

"Should we go back to that tree? For the sake of photography." Cem's eyes flicked to the vineyard and his lips curved.

My insides sloshed like they'd liquified. In that moment, I knew it with absolute certainty. There couldn't be a second kiss. He might not be able to stop, and since I clearly had zero restraint... I wouldn't survive it.

"Let's grab a couple of pics right here." I gestured at the dreamy view of the vineyard. "We can always say we were waiting for the right lighting conditions."

The sun had dipped closer to the horizon, painting the scenery in its golden glow, offering us exactly that. Perfect lighting. Annoyingly perfect.

Cem lifted his phone and coaxed me to him, closer and closer until I leaned on his chest. His heart pounded against my back, echoing inside my ribcage, distracting me with its beat.

"Kiss me?" He angled the phone to capture both of us in the frame.

Steeling my nerves, I reached to press my lips where his beard tapered off on his cheek, waiting for him to snap the photo, but he turned his head, aligning his lips with mine. I jerked back.

"What is it?" He whipped his head left and right, as if expecting to find the reason for my reaction.

"There's no paparazzi," I said. "But I don't think we should do that again."

"Was it not...good?" His eyes glinted, examining mine. He knew

I couldn't deny it. Even the tree couldn't deny it. The air sizzled between us.

I forced my voice to neutral. "It was satisfactory. A solid eight out of ten."

His face fell momentarily until he noticed the smile hiding behind my eyes. "Eight out of ten? Not even nine? Nine and a half?"

I couldn't stop my grin from bursting out. I lifted my fingers as if counting. "Okay. It was a twelve, but please don't let it go to your head. I'm glad it was a fifteen though, because if you're going to kiss someone only once, it should be a seventeen or higher. And now... lucky me, I have a memory of a kiss that was nineteen out of ten." I whipped up my fingers faster and faster, counting like a deranged preschooler.

Cem didn't laugh. "Memory? You're collecting memories here?" His eyes held confusion, laced with hurt.

He couldn't be hurt, I argued. This was supposed to be funny.

I powered on, committing to my skit. "Yes! The memory of our twenty-five out of ten kiss will keep me warm in my old age when I retire from location scouting to spend time with my... budgies." I shrugged. "I haven't figured out what kind of pets I'll devote my twilight years to, but that thirty out of ten kiss will take the place of honor in my memory palace and I'll guard it—"

"What the fuck are you talking about?" He growled, then coughed up a frustrated laugh, his hands rubbing his temples as if I'd given him a headache. I probably had.

I swallowed the stupid jokes I evidently had an endless supply of and looked for the right words. Words that tasted like chalk.

"I'm saying, you're right, this can't be anything real. So, let's not pretend it is. I know you're from a different universe."

"Aria, we both live on Planet Earth."

"You know what I mean. We have a business arrangement."

"Definitely no pleasure?" His head tilted a little as he examined my face, an unsure smile playing on his lips.

It was such a burning gaze I could barely meet his eyes. I couldn't hide it. I couldn't stop my pupils from dilating or my throat drying up. But I had to rise above it.

I overfilled my lungs, gathering my willpower. "Can we be friends, Cem?"

He paused for a moment like I'd slapped him, then gave me a grave nod, his lips sealed and his gaze avoiding mine, until it finally returned with a new resolve. "Friends, huh?"

Was he hurt?

"Friends," I confirmed, offering him a weak smile.

"With ben—"

"No. No benefits."

After a moment, he smiled back. "Well, don't blame me if you accidentally fall in love with me. I can be a pretty amazing friend."

I rolled my eyes, but my neck blazed as I followed him back to the restaurant. This guy was impossible to turn down. Why did I even try?

# CHAPTER 15

# Cem

I felt like I'd broken out of prison, skulking along the main street of Napier. After a late breakfast, I'd faked a headache and retreated to bed as Emir left for a walk around town to do whatever he considered fun. Probably visit all of Napier's museums. As soon as the door closed behind him, I'd jumped into my shoes and snuck out the back.

Like the world's most awkward detective, I followed him. Seeing him turn left, I went right. My plan wasn't brilliant, but it was good enough for what I needed – a moment of freedom. One moment to pretend I was my own man, travelling solo, minding my own business.

Not that I had anything to prove, at least to Aria. She may have had a point, but she didn't understand my reality.

She'd infiltrated my head, though, her words haunting me as I'd woken at 4 a.m., disoriented and so hungry I'd wandered downstairs to make myself a sandwich. Jet lag seemed to hit me at random times like whiplash.

Napier felt safe. Dressed in the slacks and T-shirt Aria had given me, I blended in. Based on the facial expressions of the few locals I'd passed, no one recognized me. My sense of freedom grew at every step, and I straightened my spine, then eventually slowed my pace to peer through the shop windows. The town center offered an eclectic but limited selection of stores. All the Art Deco style and references made the place feel like a cute little time capsule.

I spent a half hour buying souvenirs; Manuka honey and organic lavender oil for my mom. She appreciated anything that claimed to be good for you and looked expensive. Unlike my father, who appreciated cigars. Or, used to. But he didn't need souvenirs.

After I reached the end of the street, I headed toward the shore and wandered around the Art Deco monuments and flowerbeds, eventually reaching the pebbled beach. My feet sunk in, making it hard to walk fast.

The beach stretched in all directions, as flat as a pancake. I could see thousands of miles to the horizon and hundreds of yards along the blanket of pebbles. Despite the blinding brightness, the open space gave me an otherworldly feeling, like I'd reached the edge of the world and could see a glimpse of the great beyond on the horizon.

Emboldened by my anonymity, I decided to explore a different street while I navigated my way back, heading roughly in the right direction.

I wasn't fainting from hunger, and could have walked back to the hotel, no harm done, but my eyes caught the sign for a Turkish restaurant, and it drew me like a magnet. I peered in through the window. The place seemed empty. A young woman clearing the table had curly, blond hair and English features. If the server wasn't Turkish, I could fly under the radar, only enjoying the cooking.

I popped my head in, inhaling the heavenly scent of meat and spices lingering in the air. A far cry from the Subway sandwiches and protein shakes Emir had been fetching from the nearest corner shops.

As I approached the counter, a man popped up from behind it, as if from nowhere, with a packet of paper napkins. Black hair, black beard, olive skin. His eyes widened at the sight of me.

"Hello!" I pretended to notice something on my phone, letting some hair fall over my face.

He wasn't fooled by my English, or the angle of my face.

"*Cem bey*? Cem Erkam?"

I drew a breath and raised my chin. "*Evet.*"

I had been recognized.

Cold sweat prickled down my neck. Emir would be furious, but he didn't need to know, did he? According to those Instagram posts, I was on holiday, possibly somewhere exotic, with Burcu.

"The delicious smell drew me in," I told him in Turkish and ordered a beef *pide* – a type of oval, wood-fire pizza.

The man showed me to a window table and rushed to fulfil my order. I got the feeling the place didn't really have table service, but

I'd receive it anyway. Thankfully, there were no other customers. I'd wandered in well past lunchtime.

Even if these people talked to the media, they couldn't confirm or deny our story. If I only made it out of here without offending anyone or, most importantly, getting photographed in an uncompromising position, all was probably well.

An older woman appeared, eyes wide, carrying a cup of Turkish tea. She set it in front of me with shaking hands. I thanked her and took a sip. The flavor instantly transported me home, and I closed my eyes, savoring it. When I opened them, I found her still standing by the table.

"Can I help you?" I asked.

"*Cem bey*?" She pulled out her phone, her eyes pleading with me.

My hand went up to shield my face, but instead of trying to photograph me, she showed me my own Instagram feed, her eyes shining with excitement. "I knew you and Burcu were back together, but I never, ever thought I'd see you in our restaurant. It's the happiest day of my life!"

I nodded, trying to keep my smile from slipping.

"Where is she? If we could get a picture of the two of you together at our restaurant, it would mean the world to me!"

I blinked, trying to come up with something believable. "She's resting at the hotel. Jet lag."

The woman nodded, her eyes widening in animated sympathy. "Of course! Bring her for dinner, will you? We'll take good care of you."

I could see the hope and fear alternating on her face as she rubbed her hands on her apron. She reminded me of my mother, back when she'd still cooked for us. Back when we didn't have money.

"I'll… ask her," I promised.

The man, presumably her husband, arrived with the *pide*, sliding it in front of me, sizzling on a hot ceramic plate. I inhaled the mouth-watering smell. This would have been a wonderful place to take Aria. Small, intimate, and unpretentious, with what seemed like excellent food. Too bad they were Turkish.

"That's not Burcu!"

The man's booming voice made my stomach clench. I looked up from my meal and saw the couple standing behind the register, peering at the woman's phone.

"No, they're back together, look! Isn't it sweet?" the woman insisted, but the man shook his head.

"No. I know this girl. Aria. She eats here several times a week. If you worked the counter, you'd see her. I know her mother, too. She looks a lot like her."

A piece of *pide* lodged in my throat and I coughed. The couple looked up, worried. The man crossed the floor to give me a couple of whacks on the back. "It's Aria, isn't it?" he demanded as my coughing settled and I could breathe again.

I sighed. There was no point lying. He'd obviously made up his mind and would tell his version of the story until his dying breath.

"Yes, it's Aria," I said. "But she's shy. She doesn't want people to know it's her, so we let everyone think she's Burcu. Can I trust you to keep our secret? In return, I'll bring her here for dinner and post a photo from your restaurant."

His eyes sharpened with interest, and he nodded. "I haven't introduced myself. My name is Kerim." He offered his hand, and I shook it.

We chatted for a while, cataloguing differences between New Zealand and Turkey. He liked the empty beaches, clean air and water, and the locals who smiled like it was going out of fashion.

When he finally left, promising to treat us to a spectacular dinner, I texted Aria.

**Me:** I did something really stupid. Don't tell Emir. I repeat. Do. Not. Tell. Emir. You have to help me.

**Aria:** Another dick pic? Dude, you're on your own.

**Me:** No. But I have to take you out to dinner tonight. I walked into this Turkish restaurant and turns out they know you. Not just me and Burcu. You.

**Aria:** Kerim's? It's my favourite!

**Me:** You like Turkish food?

**Aria:** And you can't go without it for a week? You had to wander into the only place in town where they might know your face and blow our cover?

**Me:** No, I walked into the one restaurant where you apparently eat several times a week and they know your face, and your mother's face.

Too harsh? I stared at my phone screen, my stomach tightening as three dots danced under my reply.

**Aria:** It's a small town! And yes, I like Turkish food. Is that a crime?

**Me:** No. It's fate. You're going to get oodles of it tonight.

**Aria:** What is this dinner about?

**Me:** To thank Kerim and his lovely wife for keeping our secret. By eating here and posting about it.

**Aria:** As you and Burcu?

**Me:** Yes. Except Kerim knows it's you, so you don't have to pretend all night. Only for that one photo.

**Aria:** So, we're not playing a couple?

**Me:** Are you worried someone else will recognize you?

**Aria:** It's Napier. Everyone knows everyone. It doesn't matter whether there's PDA or not, rumours will spread either way.

**Me:** What's PDA again? Paparazzi, Drugs, Alcohol?

**Aria:** Sounds like a frightening combo, but I meant Public Display of Affection.

**Me:** That's much better! I vote for PDA. Definitely.

I stared at the phone for a while, waiting for a response, my heart pounding in my chest. Had I said too much again? Was she really going to friend zone me for good?

Finally, her reply popped up.

**Aria:** What time?

# CHAPTER 16

This fake relationship business was getting out of hand. I closed the car door and groaned. I'd left the office, barely made it to my car, and I'd already lied twice. First, I'd texted Mom and spun a tale about an upset stomach to get out of the fajitas dinner. Then I'd texted Felix, apologizing for my absence, renewing my promise to grab coffees with him, which was probably another lie. I hated lying.

I negotiated my vehicle into the tiny parking lot behind my building and entered through the back door, climbing the narrow stairs. The constant rumble of the industrial dryers made them shake. Gas and overcooked polyester had become the smell I associated with home.

I opened the door to my tiny, bland flat and threw my handbag on the legless spring mattress I called a futon. This was all I could afford right now, but if I worked hard and stayed the course, I would build myself a better life. Not something 'beyond my wildest dreams', only something better than this, better than the shit hole student flats in Auckland.

I was proud of myself for all the healthy little steps I'd taken, of embracing reality and playing the long game. No more of that almost-sick feeling of being on the cusp of something huge, the constant anticipation that held you in its grasp but never delivered. Those soul-destroying highs and lows were in the past now.

I thought of Cem, the Mediterranean Demi-God, currently wandering around Napier, getting in trouble and dragging me in with him. Meeting him had shaken the foundations of my carefully constructed plan, but it didn't have to completely veer me off course. In fact, I should have anticipated temptations and distractions. Maybe not temptations of his magnitude – this was Napier, after all – but resisting their siren calls was a part of any successful plan. I had to be well prepared.

I opened the window and inhaled the flowery scent of late spring. Or was it the laundry liquid from downstairs? Either way, there was something in the air and it filled me with a strange mix of excitement and fear.

I still had Janie's outfits. One of the three I hadn't worn yet would have to do. I selected an olive-green linen jumpsuit with spaghetti straps that was comfortable and didn't stick out too much in my hometown. Even Burcu had been more casual on occasion. I couldn't wear a bra underneath, but I quite liked the feeling of air moving under the fabric. Paired with studded heels, hoop earrings and a clutch, the combination looked both too dressy for Napier and too casual for Cem's Instagram. Good enough.

At precisely six o'clock, I arrived at Kerim's restaurant and found it closed. That's what the red sign on the door proclaimed, at least. I waited for a moment, peering through the glass window. I raised my hand to knock when Kerim himself appeared to open the door. "Aria! *Hoşgeldiniz!*" He beamed, displaying every tooth in his mouth. He smelled of spices, cigarettes and sweat.

Due to my new nighttime routine of tea and *Aşkta Şanslı*, I immediately recognized the Turkish word for welcome and responded with "*Merhaba!*" Hello.

The look on Kerim's face was priceless. "Burcu?"

"No, it's me, Aria. Had you fooled for a moment, didn't I?"

Kerim shook his head and smiled. "Yes, you did. My wife kept insisting it was the actress, Burcu. I got confused."

Perfect, I thought, following him into the dimly lit, empty restaurant. If I could fool him, maybe I could fool others.

"Why are you closed?" I asked.

"We're open for you only," Kerim announced, leading me behind a carved, wooden room divider I couldn't ever remember seeing.

The restaurant looked different. The tables had been rearranged to create a private dining booth. And there, glowing in candlelight, sporting a moderately shiny, black dress shirt, sat my obsession and nemesis, the dick pic king of Istanbul, Cem Erkam.

He bounced to his feet to help me with my chair, creating an awkward dance with Kerim who'd been trying to do the same thing. "Thank you. I wish I had more than one ass so we could do this twice," I muttered.

"You're so weird." Cem chuckled, sitting down across the table.

"You, too." I smiled back, craning my neck to see the menu usually displayed across two screens above the counter, which were hidden from view by that weird, ornamental room divider. "I really like their chicken kebabs."

"We're not ordering from the menu. Kerim's cooking for us."

"Cooking what?"

Cem shrugged. "I don't know. I'm too scared to ask, but based on the *pide* I had earlier today, I'm sure it's amazing."

"Should we take that photo first before my face eats my makeup? Then we don't have to think about it anymore."

"How does your face eat makeup?" Cem leaned in, his eyes narrowing. "Do you even have makeup on?"

"Do you?" I also leaned forward. "Your eyelashes look too dark and thick to be natural."

"Yet, they are. A gift from God. Like the rest of me." He straightened his shoulders, looking so self-satisfied I wanted to both slap him and run my fingers across those biceps. And triceps. All the ceps, really.

"So, settle this mystery, you gift from God. Where did you learn English? I know Kerim's been here for years, and he still struggles... like, I don't think he knows the word 'onions'. I used to ask him to leave them out, but it never happened, so now I eat them. Turns out, I don't mind them as much as I thought."

Cem studied me with amusement. "Maybe he doesn't like

anyone messing with his recipe. If I asked my grandma to leave out onions, she'd do this."

Cem gestured with his hands, producing a sound that fell between a scoff and yelp of pain, his eyes burning with indignation.

"You guys take food seriously, don't you?"

Cem nodded. "Religiously."

I smiled at the image of his grandmother, then realized what he'd done. "You didn't answer my question. Where did you learn English?"

"I lived in L.A. for two years."

"Really? Hollywood?"

Kerim arrived with two wine glasses and filled them with something red. I took a sip and decided it was wine.

"I didn't get anywhere near Hollywood." Cem spoke in a soft voice. "But I did learn English. Emir made it happen. He saw me in a school play and decided I could be a star. He somehow got dad to pay for the trip, but I had to find work there."

"As a waiter?" I blew a deep sigh.

Cem took a long swig of his wine, making me wait. "As Superman. I went around kids' birthday parties and organized games."

"I did that too! I was a fairy."

He cocked his head. "I can see that. A little woodland creature, barefoot, hair in tangles." The softness in his eyes could have been mistaken for affection.

Warmth engulfed my cheeks, and I huffed in mock frustration. "Excuse me if I don't have a million-dollar sponsorship deal with a shampoo brand."

"You mean like Burcu did? She had to spend so much time using all the treatments to make sure her hair was always super shiny. They'd come and spray it in the middle of our scene. I accidentally inhaled that stuff once. Coughed for hours."

"Her hair *is* always so shiny!"

"The magic of... whatever aerosol-based floor wax it was. You still watching the show?" His probing eyes held me hostage.

I squirmed in my seat. "I call it homework, but in reality, I'm completely hooked. I can't stop."

"I've heard people say that."

"Have you ever watched it again? After all these years I mean."

Cem looked at me blankly. "I never watched it. Not even then."

"Really?"

His voice turned raspy as his gaze roamed out the window. "I lived it, with her. It was my version of our love story. I didn't want the scripted version. I didn't care. I never really cared about the lines they gave us. I learned them, I repeated them, but in my head, the words were meaningless. Doing a scene with Burcu, I could only think of her." He turned to me, and his eyes dipped down to my cleavage, dark and unfocused. "What I wanted to do to her. How I wanted to touch her and make her feel."

I'd entered a full-body blush, nipples so hard they were now the only points of my body touching the front of my loose outfit, like two little army-green tents. "There are online fan groups obsessing over every facet of that storyline and articles analyzing your performance in it. You won an award for your acting! And you're telling me you just rattled out lines and looked at her horny?" My blush intensified as I revealed my rather obsessive internet search history.

Cem took a slow drink, smiling at me like he knew something I didn't. That infuriating smile. "What do you want me to tell you? When someone looks like you... I mean her... well, either of you... staring is the only appropriate response."

His eyes kept heating my skin. My brain resisted his statement, but my body decided the only appropriate response was a full-on arousal, the kind that zeroed straight between my thighs, pulsing like a high voltage device on standby. Current running through, ready to explode. What did that make me? A bomb? A coffee maker? Either way, I was in trouble.

I pressed my clammy palms against my hot legs, drawing a deep breath. Cem's eyes followed my rising and falling chest. I looked down and noticed why. Sitting down, the straps of the jumpsuit had become loose, dropping the neckline dangerously low. I maneuvered my arms behind my back and yanked at the bra-style straps that held the fabric up over my still hard nipples. I may have made them a little too tight.

Cem placed his glass back on the table. "Aria?"

"What?" My voice came out husky.

"I don't want to be your friend. It's not enough."

*What do you want from me?* I screamed inside my head.

"What do you want?" I asked out loud, in a fairly neutral tone, picking up my giant wine glass to hide behind. I was certain he could see my reaction to him, plainly displayed across my face and chest.

"Honestly?"

"I'll probably regret this, but yes." I took a sip of wine, my insides wobbly.

Cem leaned in, lowering his voice so I could barely hear it. "You sure about the honesty? There's a lot I want."

My muscles tensed. "Let's break it down. What do you want right now?"

His voice was a rumbling whisper. "I want to make you come."

I nearly inhaled my Pinot Noir. "You can't say stuff like that!"

To my absolute relief, the food arrived. Kerim's smile was filled with hope and suddenly I remembered what we were here for.

"Let's take the photo now!" I urged Cem as soon as we were alone again.

With the photo done, there'd be no reason to prolong the agony of this evening, as much as the resident masochist in me seemed to enjoy it.

He nodded and picked up his phone, framing me with my steaming plate of something red and creamy. "Don't you need to be in the photo, too?" I asked.

"Shh. Look at the camera and think of how much you want me. Maybe tone it down a little so Instagram doesn't censor it."

I rolled my eyes, despite my hot cheeks. "You're extremely presumptuous." But he'd placed the thought in my head, the thought of his hands on my body, and it circled my poor brain like an ear-wormy jingle. My cheeks burned and lips parted. Then the ridiculousness of the situation hit me, a smile broke through, and he took my picture.

"Absolutely fucking perfect," he muttered, typing for a moment, then slipping his phone away. "Let's eat."

The food was so tasty I wanted to keep eating long after there was no room left in my stomach. Kerim came to ask how we liked it, and we both praised his cooking to high heavens, speaking a medley of English and Turkish.

"It's called the sultan's favorite," Kerim explained. "My version of it."

"Why is this not on your regular menu?" I asked.

"I don't know…" Kerim shrugged, then launched into a Turkish explanation he directed at Cem.

"Apparently, New Zealanders don't really want anything beyond kebab," Cem translated. "Brutes."

He showed Kerim the photo of me he'd posted. The big fat tears I wanted to shed over his food appeared in the restaurant owner's eyes and they hugged. I didn't understand a word, apart from the Turkish 'thank you', but I watched in a daze. How could one Instagram post of me with a plate of food elicit such a response?

"What did you write in that post?" I asked him when Kerim left.

"Nothing much. Kerim is happy about the publicity. His wife is a huge fan of *Aşkta Şanslı*. He's going to get lucky tonight. Unlike me."

He met my eyes, teasing, but a little sad. I couldn't say anything. I couldn't tell him that he was wrong, or right. I couldn't sleep with him. I would never survive the fallout. I would never survive being cast aside by a celebrity – someone who was living *my* dream. I'd moved here to heal, to get away from the constant reminders of my failures. Away from the lukewarm relationships that only reminded me of how insignificant I was. How I always came second.

"Why do you even want me?" I asked. "Is it because you miss Burcu? Or... convenience?"

"What's convenient about you? You live across the planet and keep friend zoning me."

Fair enough.

"And Burcu..." His hot gaze searched my face. "I admit I found it confusing at first. I kept looking at you and seeing her, but not anymore. I only see you. You have this funny way of looking at me, like you're amused and disapproving, but also turned on. Like that!" he exclaimed, pointing at my face.

"Was I drooling?" I touched the side of my mouth, feigning embarrassment that really, deep down, was quite real. Clearly, I wasn't a lady, but at least I had my sarcasm.

Cem laughed until tears sprung from his eyes. "That's what I mean! Burcu would never say that. She'd be coy and cute. She'd do that guarded thing women do, playing hard to get. Hard to read. But you—"

"I get it," I said, my cheeks burning, as I used a piece of flatbread to clear my plate. "I'm a savage." I sucked the last bit of sauce off the bread, closing my eyes to savor the taste. If Turkey had this to offer, maybe I could sneak a visit there and eat my way through the country. I wouldn't tell him anything.

"You're plenty cute, but you don't *act* cute. I like it. It makes me wonder how you'd act if—."

"Stop!" Annoyance heated my chest, momentarily surpassing

the arousal. "I'm way more repressed than you think. If you're looking for some free-spirited foreign fuck buddy, I'm not your girl. I joke when I'm nervous, but I'm not that loose."

He studied me from under drawn eyebrows. "I was going to say I wonder how you'd act if you weren't so scared. I'm not sure what you're afraid of, but you're fighting so hard. You're fighting this thing..." His finger wavered between us.

"There's no 'thing'," I trapped his hand against the table, exasperated. "There's a weird business arrangement and some sexual tension you keep stirring up to watch me squirm. You're gorgeous and sexy and I'm human, so of course there's a reaction. It doesn't mean I want to pursue this. Or that I can." I pulled my hand away from his, securing it in my lap.

Cem's voice lost its smirky edge, turning low and gruff. "Don't be embarrassed. I'm so hard for you, I can't sit comfortably anymore."

I swallowed air and leaned forward, almost gasping as the inseam of my jumpsuit dug into my crotch. Adjusting the straps had definitely made the outfit too tight. I moved a little, testing the sensation. Wow! That was new. I rolled my hips, subtly grinding against the friction, my eyes on Cem. I doubted he could pleasure himself this easily, with his hands on the table, fingers tapping on the knife.

"You have to stop licking your lips." His voice held a warning.

My hand sailed to my mouth, and I smiled. I hadn't even noticed myself doing that. The throbbing between my thighs intensified, but I tried my hardest not to let it show. This was for me, not him. I wouldn't let him use me. I would never let him that close. I'd only enjoy his dirty talk, then take care of myself.

For a minute or two, I felt happy with my self-discipline. I took a couple of deep breaths, staring at the wine I'd nursed half-way through.

I could feel him testing his charm on me, single-minded in his pursuit. He probably didn't hear the word 'no' that often. Did he really want me, even for one night, or was he determined to prove that nobody could resist him? The latter seemed likely – my refusal must have bruised his ego.

Cem scooped my hand across the table, running his thumb around my palm in lazy circles. The motion of it, so firm and deliberate, sent an electric hum through me, a vibration with one destination. My crotch would be soaking wet when I finally stood from the table. Which would be never.

"Aria," he whispered. "I know I've been teasing you, but I can't be the only one feeling... this... this energy between us. Am I?" His thumb never left my palm, rubbing it like he was rubbing...

*Don't go there, Aria.*

I focused on the candle flame to stop my eyes from rolling back. Every word out of his mouth rumbled and resonated and swept against me like a touch.

When I finally looked up, his eyes captured me. The only word I could think of was 'yearning' and it sounded ridiculous, even in my own head. The opaque, darkened glow of arousal was still there, but it was delivered as a package deal with something more unsettling. "Seriously, I'll have to take a cold shower in my jeans. I won't be able to take them off."

"Well, I'm ruining an outfit I borrowed from my boss." My words rushed out breathlessly as heat blasted into my cheeks. I couldn't conduct myself around him. I wasn't safe.

I watched his face morph as my words landed.

I expected him to look smug. Victorious. Predatory. He was playing a dirty game and winning at it. Instead, I saw delight. Maybe even relief.

His mouth stretched into a wide grin. "Really? I'm happy to help you out of it and get it dry cleaned. Or burned."

"Burned sounds fair. I think it's seen too much." My mouth felt so dry I could hardly speak, but I had to smile at his enthusiasm.

"I'm jealous of every piece of clothing touching your skin." I had to look away from his dark gaze. Did he know what this piece of clothing was doing to me?

I used my free hand to drain my wine and stopped him from topping it up. "No, absolutely not. I can barely handle you sober."

"Handle me?" He set down the wine bottle and let go of my hand.

"That's what I'm trying to do. I'm trying to... survive this."

"I'm trying to tell you how I feel, and you're trying to... survive me?" He sounded genuinely hurt, but the sting in my chest was quickly replaced by indignation.

"Tell me how you feel?" I glared at him. "You told me you're hard. It's not exactly a love confession."

"Do you want a love confession? Could you *handle* that?" His voice had a sharp edge, but his eyes met me with such vulnerability I couldn't hold his gaze.

"Probably not." My thick voice stuck in my throat. "I mean, I wouldn't believe you."

"You wouldn't believe me now because it's too soon, or... ever?" His thumb kept flipping the knife, rolling it along the tablecloth.

I inhaled, my head spinning. "Never ever."

"Why?"

"Because you hail from a different universe. Words don't mean the same. Nothing's comparable. There's a whole world around you I'm navigating blind."

He exhaled, letting go of the knife. "I'm navigating it blind, too. Trust me. But I thought we had... something."

Again, I felt guilty and couldn't even explain why. "We do." I fiddled with my fingernails, fighting the urge to rip one of them. If I did, I couldn't be Burcu. I couldn't be anything to him. "Still, we don't know each other very well."

"Yet," he said with conviction.

"Yet," I repeated with apprehension.

Kerim appeared with two chocolate cakes, setting them down with a flourish as his wife quickly cleared our plates. "Hope you enjoyed?"

"*Lezzetli*," I said, recalling the word he'd taught me, and Kerim jolted from excitement. It made me think of a lightning rod doing its job.

Cem's eyes widened as he followed our exchange.

"Are you studying Turkish?" He asked when we were alone again.

"I heard it once and it got stuck in my brain."

I had a good memory, especially when it came to useless trivia, but that wasn't the reason I was picking up Turkish words left and right and repeating them until I had them embedded in long-term memory. Cem didn't need to know how much I thought about him and his culture. He would have definitely taken it the wrong way.

"Once you know enough words, I'll teach you how to put them together."

"So, I'd be speaking Turkish?" I laughed.

"Why not?

I didn't want to say anything. I didn't actually want to argue at all. I loved the sound of Turkish and really wanted to learn more.

The cake tasted delicious, but I tried to eat mine without making too many orgasmic sounds. I had to wrap up this evening before I invited him into my hideous flat above the laundromat. I hadn't covered the bed. A full laundry hamper and a stack of dishes waited for me. In a space that small, you couldn't hide anything, and I didn't want him to see or remember me like that. If he actually liked me, I'd leave him with that memory of unmarred potential. I could be the one that got away, instead of one of the hundreds or thousands of conquests he'd happily forgotten. I really hoped it wasn't in the thousands.

As we said goodbye to Kerim and made our way outside, darkness had fallen. Only the last glow of the day lingered on the horizon, peeking from the end of an alley that led to the beach.

"I'll drive you to the hotel." I pointed at my car. "I've only had that one glass of wine."

"Emir's going to be there," he grumbled, half to himself.

I nodded. That's what I was counting on. He couldn't sneak me to his room, not that I wanted to end up there. Okay, part of me wanted to, of course, and that's exactly why I couldn't put myself in that situation.

"Can I text you?" Cem asked as I parked in front of the hotel entrance. He'd been quiet for the entire five-minute drive.

"Text me?"

"As a friend," he added, scratching his beard. "Mostly. Or fifty-fifty. I'll try my best." He gave me a rueful smile, which then turned beseeching. "I get stir crazy in that empty hotel. I don't know anyone here, and I really like talking to you."

"Okay." The familiar dryness crept up my throat.

He was incredibly forward and sure of himself, yet so sweet. It had to be an act. I knew not to trust sweetness from someone who'd charmed millions of people.

I waited for him to get out of my car when he leaned toward me. My spine stiffened and breath became shallow as he kissed me on both cheeks. His hand rested above my knee, shifting an inch toward my inner thigh like a silent promise. The touch only lasted a second or two, but it ruined me.

Once he'd closed the car door, I drove home as fast as I could. I didn't even wait to get inside. The parking lot was half empty and pitch dark, the street level businesses closed. His scent still lingered in the car. Mentally committing to burning the ill-fated jumpsuit, I rocked against its inseam, finally putting my fingers to work, thinking of Cem's thumb against my skin, repeating his brazen words, faster and faster until my wrist ached, until the throbbing tension unraveled into sweet, shaky relief.

# CHAPTER 17

# Cem

I kicked my running shoes across the hotel lobby and marched up the stairs. It had been four days. I hadn't seen Aria in four days and four nights. I knew she was busy organizing other filming locations for the American production, but I'd hoped she'd still check on me.

I'd scared her off. I'd come on too strong and even though I could tell she liked me, other things weighed more. There was my reputation, my fame, and the distance between our two countries. I knew all the things that stood in the way but refused to consider them. We texted a lot, and it gave me hope.

My phone pinged.

**Aria:** How was the run? If you're desperate for a gym, I can smuggle some free weights to the new Airbnb. I doubt my dad would notice them missing from the back of his garage.

**Me:** Yes, please! But I worry anything that's useful for me would rip your handbag.

**Aria:** No worries. I'll get a giant, fortified handbag. Anything to stop you from doing pull-ups from a chandelier. This Airbnb is historic.

**Me:** I'm hurt. Are you suggesting a chandelier would withstand my workout regimen?

**Aria:** I'm saying it can't. I'm also saying you have to stop treating our priceless Art Deco pieces as your personal gym equipment. It hurts my soul.

**Me:** What about my priceless muscles? Wait, not priceless. But we are talking about millions of dollars here.

**Aria:** I'd insert a face palm emoji but can't find it so imagine me going 'duh' as I roll my eyes.

**Me:** I'm imagining you saying 'ahhhh' with your eyes rolling back. Close enough?

I watched the three dots appearing and disappearing, until they went away for good. Again, I'd scared her off. Duh, indeed. So far, I'd kept the texting pretty tasteful. We'd been talking too frequently to qualify as casual and flirting more than any platonic friends should, but I'd somehow avoided grossly inappropriate stuff. Like dick pics. When she wasn't in the same room, I found it easier to behave myself.

I put my phone away and headed to the shower.

Her texts helped me stay sane, but I still felt increasingly restless. Despite its beauty, Napier was an absolute ghost town. Instead of my usual workouts, I ran along the beach, following up with push-ups on the grass. I didn't hate the weather, or the Art Deco arches and statues, but I needed people. I needed her. Jerking off in the shower was also getting old.

"Emir?" I called, hoping he was back from town with some food.

No answer. He must have still been out. As I ran and trained and stayed away from public places, Emir enjoyed culture, visiting museums and historic buildings. He'd even gone to the aquarium. During his explorations, he'd spotted a couple of Turkish people but hadn't popped into Kerim's.

He'd seen the picture on my Instagram and yelled at me about not being included in the plan, but he had little reason to stay angry. The post had been our most successful yet.

The one post *without* me, I thought with a dose of hurt. Yet, I knew why everyone loved that photo – the same reason I did. Lit by candles, her lips stained with wine, Aria looked at me like no one else existed. Like she trusted me implicitly with her heart and mind and body. No matter how many times I revisited the evening, I couldn't remember seeing that look. She'd only given it to the camera for that brief moment. Had it been an act? A happy accident?

She had a grounding, raw presence that held my attention for much longer than felt natural. I couldn't look away. I could imagine that presence carrying a feature film, but not necessarily getting picked for reality shows or gathering millions of views on TikTok.

Maybe that's why she'd found it so hard to break through. Those channels, often our first steppingstones to fame, weren't built for subtlety. Nobody listened long enough to get to the good part anymore.

I would have missed her, too, I realized, if I hadn't first bumped into her right here, without my phone or other distractions. If she hadn't looked exactly like Burcu. I would have passed her by, like everyone else, and missed out on everything.

I peeled off my sweaty workout clothes as I stepped into my room, reaching a naked state by the time I entered the shower.

With the water gushing and gurgling and eventually turning warm, my mind returned to our dinner and that flood of pleasure and excitement when she admitted exactly how turned-on she was. I'd rushed to the door as she'd still been negotiating the stairs in her heels, giving me a moment to look for evidence. Fortunately, Kerim shared the Turkish obsession with elaborate lighting. Mosaic torches and spotlights lined the entryway, exposing the slight darkening of the olive-green fabric between her legs.

I nearly cheered, then spent the rest of the evening in agony until I got back to the hotel and out of my jeans. Not touching her on the way back had been the hardest thing I'd ever done. I'd given myself a metaphorical medal for pulling my hand away from her thigh and getting out of that car.

I let the water gush down my body and stroked myself, reliving the moment, not even questioning why it excited me so much. She'd been fully clothed, yet I found the combination of her brave, husky admission and that visible stain the hottest thing I could think of, one that made me come so fast I could have categorized my shower as earth friendly.

I toweled myself and checked my phone. Still no reply from Aria. She'd sent us the details of our new accommodation earlier. I browsed back to that message, trying to view the new house on the map. I didn't care about the relocation, but moving house meant I would finally see her again. She was supposed to drive us to the new place that afternoon.

When I heard the knock on the front door, I first thought Emir had forgotten his keys.

I wrapped a towel around my waist and jogged downstairs. As I threw the door wide open, I realized my mistake.

Aria gasped, struggling to keep her balance. She was back in her cut-off jeans shorts, but her hair looked freshly blow waved and her slightly too-short T-shirt bared a slice of tanned midriff that made me swallow hard. She gave my outfit a similar once-over and a smile tugged her mouth. "Is this your go-to outfit at home? Are they designer towels? Do you have shiny ones?"

I took a wide stance, folding my arms. It was one thing to joke over text, quite another to watch her eyes sparkle as she made fun of me. I craved it like I craved a cigarette. Except I craved this more.

"Yes. My number one sponsor is a high-end towel brand, and our agreement specifically states that I need to wear their product to three public appearances each week."

She bought my stupid fib for about one second, after which her face lit up with mirth. "Do you get to choose the color and style? Do they have to be bath towels, or can you go for something lightweight, like a... Turkish towel?" Her gaze roamed down my body and her eyebrows sailed to new heights. I wanted to kiss her silly face so badly I took a tiny step forward without even noticing.

"I can choose from a wide range. Would you like to see me in their brand-new dish towel?" I mimed the tiny size of the imaginary cloth and her face reddened.

*Don't overstep. She'll run.*

I cleared my throat. "What are you doing here so early? I thought we agreed on four o'clock."

"We did, but the producer called again and asked me to check the rooms. I think they're having last-minute jitters." She smiled apologetically.

"Probably good to check. Some rooms have a funny smell."

"Have you been farting in there?" she deadpanned.

An abrupt laugh burst out of me. How could she deliver lines like that with a straight face?

"Obviously, I go around the hotel to fart in different rooms, but there are also other... notes. Musty, like an old cellar."

"I'll follow my nose upstairs then." She pointed at the stairs, and I gestured for her to come in.

On the bottom step, she turned around. "Is the sourpuss around?"

"Emir's fetching our lunch."

Aria froze. "Should we wait?"

"For what?"

"I feel like we need a third wheel, what with you wrapped in a dish towel and all."

Her T-shirt probably posed a bigger risk. It wasn't only short but also loose, shifting like a curtain by an open window as she moved, hiding and revealing, begging for me to keep watch. Was she wearing a bra? I couldn't see any evidence.

"Don't worry, I took care of myself in the shower," I blurted. "Now I can behave for at least ten minutes."

She blew out a breath, her cheeks bulging with air. I felt a little bulging under my towel. So, I lied. My body would not behave, but I would try.

"You're used to getting away with murder, aren't you?" She shook her head, eyebrows drawn, but underneath, I caught the hint of glee she tried to hide. "Anyone else says stuff like that and they get done for sexual harassment."

"What? I was saying I *won't* harass you." I threw out my arms, offering her my most disarming smile.

But she was right. I didn't talk like this on set. I didn't talk like this anywhere. Only with her.

"I don't need to know what you do in the shower, Cem. I can't… It's a bit icky." Her face contorted.

"Icky? I was thinking of you the whole time! It was the best moment of my day. No one's allowed to ruin it. Not even you."

Aria rubbed her face with both hands, groaning. "You have to stop that! I have a job to do, and your brother will be back at any minute. Could you turn it down by about two hundred notches? You're coming on so strong I'm sure every female within a five-mile radius either dropped their panties or called the police. Possibly both."

I took a step closer, testing her, giving her time to back away. Another step. More time. She shifted backwards, ever-so-slightly, but her eyes held mine, lips ajar. I advanced until I had her trapped against the curved wall by the staircase. Her expression eased, the indignation melting away with each breath. She wasn't really mad at me, or even that embarrassed. She was enjoying our little game as much as I was, those sparks jumping between us. Somehow, misbehaving this badly, yet still being invited into her orbit, meant more to me than anything. The sense of freedom I felt around her made my chest expand.

I placed one hand on the wall by her head and leaned in, running my fingers down the side of her face. "I'm sorry. I've missed you."

"It's been four days."

"Four days is too long."

Her gaze swept across my arm. "You still have my phone number," she whispered, eyes wide.

"I've been careful not to wash it off," I confessed.

"But you have my number in your phone."

I bit back a smile. "Did you wash off my pin?"

She blushed, presenting her palm with faint numbers still on it. "I didn't actually use your card, you know?"

"You didn't? Why not?"

"I didn't want to feel like your... servant." She wrinkled her nose, the color on her cheeks deepening.

"You're not my servant!"

"Well, it felt a bit like that, with you pushing your money and gold watch and credit card." She peered down, hiding behind her lashes.

"I'm sorry. I was freaking out and people are usually more helpful if you give them money."

"I don't want your money, Cem." She lifted her chin, eyes burning with conviction.

"What do you want, Aria?"

I stared at her parted lips, plump and glossy. I knew what I wanted. Her chest heaved up and down, nipples erect. No bra. My brain registered this by lighting up every region responsible for being irresponsible. I leaned closer, a breath away from her mouth, waiting.

"I want you, against my better judgment." Her husky, troubled voice set my hand in motion, tracing the outline of her chest. Definitely bare underneath the T-shirt. I slipped my hand under the hem and her breath hitched. I held mine, trailing my fingers along her smooth skin all the way to the curve of her breast. Her lips parted even more, and she sucked in a shallow inhale but didn't move, her hands pressing against the wall behind.

I leaned in and whispered into her ear. "I'll give you anything."

When my lips made it to hers, she opened her mouth, releasing a soft moan. Her tongue met me halfway, like a friend waiting at the doorway, inviting me in. For a moment, nothing else existed. Only tongues. Fire. Pulsing need. But when my hand cupped her breast, she tensed under my touch.

I pulled away but not far, our breaths mixing. "Do you not like that?"

Her mouth twisted. "I like everything you do, Cem, but I can't."

"Why?"

Her voice was soft and desperate. "Because I know you're only chasing me for the sake of it. As soon as you have me, you'll be over me. But I won't be over you."

Her words seized me, and my hand dropped. I stood there, frozen, inches away from her, unable to move. "You think I'll forget you? How could I forget you?"

"I bet you've forgotten a lot of women."

She was right, of course. But I knew this was different. She was different. "I haven't chased many women. I don't usually have to chase."

"Maybe that's why you want me?" She raised an eyebrow. "Humans always want what they can't have."

My heart told me she was wrong, but I had no evidence.

I stepped back and ran my fingers through my damp hair. "That's not fair!"

"Why?"

I huffed in frustration. "Because I can't prove you wrong! Anything I say or do is evidence of me chasing you and wanting what I can't have. I can't prove you wrong unless you... let me. Be with me and I'll show you how much more I want. But you won't, will you?"

"You could try to be my friend," she whispered, her chin jutting forward. "If we never slept together, would you rather be my friend or forget about me?"

I filled my lungs, trying to ignore the tropical vanilla scent of her skin lingering in my nose. "You're killing me, but yes. I'd rather be your friend."

Aria exhaled, bringing her hands to her stomach, brushing down the shirt as if trying to lengthen it. "Good. Prove it. Tell me another fart joke. Something disgusting, please. Or better yet, fart." She stared me dead in the eye. "If you care about me at all, you will let one rip right now."

I couldn't pass gas on command, but I burst out laughing. The force of it shook my body, taking the edge off my sexual frustration. "I love how your mind works. Can I bring you along to my next boring interview?"

"I'm sure it'd be the verbal equivalent of an accidental dick pic," she mused, rolling her eyes.

I sighed. "There is no verbal equivalent."

"Your dick leaves everyone speechless. Got it." She gave me an exaggerated thumbs-up and turned back to the stairs. "I'll evaluate the smell in those rooms and decide if we need to bring in the crime scene cleaners or regular ones."

"Be my guest." I followed on her heels. No way I was missing a second of her company, no matter how much sniffing she had on her to-do list.

Aria started from the back of the corridor, peeking into the smallest room I'd deemed unlivable. Not because of the smell, but because the bed was only a single.

Her eyes rounded in mock horror and she fanned herself. "Oof. That's bad." She crossed the floor and opened a window.

The way she said 'oof' sounded so much like Burcu I had to shake my head to dispel the image. I wondered if she'd watched more of my show. She'd mentioned it once in her text but asking about it felt self-centered. Maybe that show was my true dick pic, the one I'd sent to millions of people, begging for them to notice me and be attracted to me.

So, I was thinking of dick pics as I followed Aria to the next room. That was not great, considering I'd promised to be a friend and evidently had zero filter around her. Being able to speak to someone so candidly gave me such a high I was becoming addicted to it. Addicted to her.

Via text, it had been so much easier to stay friendly and not cross those boundaries, but in person, she was this stunning woman who now only vaguely resembled Burcu.

She smelled different, too. I crept in closer, close enough to inhale her scent. I wasn't really that great with 'notes' and had declined the offer to develop my own cologne. What if it ended up smelling like a two-dollar car fragrance? But right now, covertly sniffing Aria as she sniffed a musty bedroom, I got a vivid image of ice cream. She smelled like a fruity ice cream flavor, mango or persimmon or something, and I fought the urge to lick her. Platonic friends probably didn't do that to each other, at least not without consent.

"Yeah, it's a bit... hmm. But nothing a good breeze won't fix," she declared, opening another window.

"My mom would be horrified. She believes all that ails a human body is in some way connected to cold. Like, cold air, cold floors, cold yogurt..."

Aria cast me an odd look, sitting on the bed and bouncing up and down as if to test its softness. "Cold yogurt?"

"Yeah, basically. If it's cold, it can and will make you ill."

"That's insane. Does she heat up her yogurt?"

I shrugged. "She leaves it on the table, I think."

Aria shook her head, eyes wide. "I mean, my mom is a little weird about drafts, it's an old-people thing. But she doesn't go that far. Is your dad the same way?"

Her tone was casual, but her eyes held a tension that made me wonder how much she'd heard about my father. Had the press found out about his diagnosis?

"He's... weird in other ways," I said evasively, took out my phone and did a google search. Nothing alarming popped up and I sighed with relief.

I felt Aria's hand on my back as she guided me out of the room, back into the corridor. "The rooms will be fine with some airing and cleaning. But I'll warn them anyway, since it sounds like one of the crew members is asthmatic."

"Great." I smiled, pocketing my phone.

On the way along the corridor, Aria peeked into my bedroom. "Will you be ready to go this afternoon? The cleaners aren't going to pack your things for you."

My cheeks heated as I joined her at the doorway, observing the godawful mess of clothes, towels and takeaway containers I'd created in a few days. "I know. I'll pack soon."

Truth be told, I hadn't done my own packing in years. I threw what I wanted on the bed, and it magically got folded, shielded in garment bags and vacuum packed into my suitcase.

"Do you need help?" she asked, and I pressed my lips together to stop myself from saying yes. She wasn't my servant. I thought about how I'd tried to buy her phone, and a flush of shame made me ill. I didn't want to be that guy, not with Aria. She didn't trust me, and I couldn't exactly blame her, but I had to do better.

A knock on the door made us both jump. "It's probably Emir," I said, securing the slipping towel around my waist before I traipsed downstairs.

Aria reached me at the door, grabbing my hand before I could turn the doorknob. "Listen."

We held still, and I heard a faint sound of conversation. It wasn't Emir, or at least he wasn't alone.

Aria gave me a meaningful look. "I suppose this will count as one of your three public towel appearances this week?"

I flashed her a smile that was more a grimace, not sure of what to do. She pressed her ear against the door and listened for a few seconds, her eyes widening.

"Oh, my God," she whispered. "The Americans." Her eyes fell on my towel. "It's the film crew. Are you okay with..."

"Am I okay with meeting American film producers wearing a towel? No!" I hissed.

"Fine. Hide in the kitchen. I'll get rid of them."

I shot her a grateful look and slipped away, just in time, as someone knocked again, and Aria turned the doorknob.

# CHAPTER 18

I took a deep breath, trying to prepare myself for whatever waited on the other side of the door. So far, I'd only sent emails and occasionally answered a phone call. Never once had I received multiple visitors from Hollywood. Did Americans always arrive several hours early?

I plastered on my widest smile as I yanked open the door. "Hello! You must be from Golden Age Pictures? I'm Aria."

A petite woman in her thirties with a perfectly styled short, black hair offered her hand, along with a brilliantly white, big-toothed smile. She would have made an incredible cartoon character. "Aria! Hi, I'm Lindsay. We talked on the phone. I'm so glad we found you! And I'm so sorry we're late. We've been going around in circles, getting lost all over town." Behind her, a group of men and women leaned on various pieces of filming equipment. A minibus with taxi signs pulled away from the curb.

I froze, my brain scrambling to find solid ground. "You're not late. I thought you were arriving tonight at eight."

"Yes! Eight in the morning! Did I not write that in the email? I'm pretty sleep deprived."

A cold feeling crept up my spine. Had I misread the email?

"I'm so sorry. Sounds like there's been a miscommunication. We still have the previous guests in the house, but they're checking out very soon. Then we'll bring the cleaners in and get everything ready for you."

Her face fell. "Oh, f-f-fargh." There was a burst of laughter behind her back, and she shot a look over her shoulder. "I'm not putting a dollar in the jar!" The guys standing behind her exchanged sneers.

Turning back to me, she pushed her palms together as if begging for mercy. "How bad is it? Are there any rooms that are ready to go? We've been travelling for hours, and everyone is exhausted!"

She gestured at her crew members, who smiled at me politely, albeit weakly. I did a quick head count – seven. If some of them shared rooms, they would fit into the unoccupied ones for now. It'd be dusty and musty, but I hadn't spotted any evidence of mice or other wildlife.

"Come in, let's figure this out." I opened the door and let them inside the reception, quickly picking up a pair of trainers strewn across the floor, cursing Cem's careless style. I was sure now that he'd folded his clothing at the waterfall to make a point.

The film crew poured in, erupting in a loud conversation about the historical features of the staircase and how to best hide or replace the ugly reception desk.

"Okay," Lindsay raised her voice to silence the group. "Let's get settled into our rooms and then meet down here in one hour to go over the location."

I hurried past them, blocking the stairs and smiling like my life depended on it. "As I told Lindsay, there's been a wee miscommunication. The previous two guests haven't checked out yet, but I'll make sure they leave within an hour. In the meantime, I'll show you to the vacant rooms and maybe you can share until we get those two rooms cleaned and ready for you?"

"As long as I can take a shower by myself," one of the older guys grumbled.

"Maybe you can take turns?" I suggested, immediately regretting my sharp tone. But seriously, did he have to be such an ass? I wasn't suggesting they shared shower cubicles.

I led them upstairs, pointing out the vacant rooms. The crew members negotiated between themselves on who got what, eventually withdrawing into their respective rooms.

Sighing with relief, I hurried back downstairs. I found both Cem and Emir at the reception desk, discussing something in hushed tones. Cem had discovered another maroon bathrobe to cover himself with, this one even smaller.

The men lifted their heads in unison, targeting me with four chocolate brown eyeballs. I raised my finger to my lips and crossed the floor softly, then ushered them both back into the kitchen so we could talk freely.

"What is going on?" Emir hissed as soon as the door closed.

From somewhere deep inside, I coaxed on a reassuring smile. How did the hospitality workers handle these curveballs? I felt out of my depth. "There was a wee mix-up. I swear they said they were arriving at 8 p.m. not 8 a.m. but it doesn't matter. I have to sort this out." I forced myself to meet Emir's thunderous glare. "I need to take you to the Airbnb early. Or, if it's not ready, we need to go somewhere else for a bit. I'm so sorry."

"That's okay." Cem hopped on a barstool, his tone light. "We can go to the aquarium. Right, Emir?" He winked at his brother.

Emir folded his arms across his chest, towering and glowering over me. "No. We're not going anywhere."

Cem shot him an irritated look. "Dude!"

Emir twined his arms so tightly he could have strangled a small creature. "We can make this… um… transition very difficult for you. Unless you agree to help us."

I rubbed my sweaty forehead, trying to summon the patience of those magical hospitality workers. I was starting to suspect I had none of it. What if my shadow career didn't suit me at all?

Cem's voice vibrated with indignation. "She's been nothing but helpful! She's been—"

"Burcu called."

We both fell silent.

Emir cleared his throat. "Or rather, her publicist did. They said they didn't want to expose us, but they will, unless we agree to take this to the next level."

"The next level?" Cem's eyes bulged.

I was still forming a sentence from the fragments of intelligent thought floating around in my brain.

Emir lowered his voice. "I think they're really struggling financially. Inflation has eaten up most of their wealth and Burcu hasn't been able to work. The rumors have damaged her reputation and she hasn't had many offers, but with the news of your relationship, she's seeing some action again. She could get a sponsorship deal and it sounds like they desperately need one. She's doing better, but she's not ready for public outings quite yet. She wants to pay Aria to be her body double, to date Cem and be seen, photographed, that sort of thing." Emir paused, giving me a long, measured look that made my arm hair stand up. "We need you to come with us to Istanbul."

Silence engulfed the room. All I could hear was my own heavy breath, whooshing in and out like wind in a tunnel.

"But I don't speak Turkish."

Cem grinned. "Say, *teşekkürler.*"

Still frowning, I repeated the Turkish word for 'thank you', lengthening the soft ending the same way he'd done.

Emir's eyebrows shot up. "Wow, but really, you can just keep quiet. Smile and wave."

Panic brewed in my gut. "But I can't up and leave. We're working with this film production…" I gestured at the door and the general direction of the film crew.

Emir frowned. "They've got their locations. What do they need you for?"

He was right. I'd probably be appointed to do other work while the filming got underway. But still, the plan made no sense. The brothers stared at me expectantly, like they'd suggested we go around the block for coffees.

"You're not serious, right?" I uttered, my mind reeling.

Emir's eyebrows drew together. "Of course."

To be fair, I'd never witnessed him joking.

Cem nodded eagerly. "We'll need to get you styled and dressed for the part, but we can do that in Istanbul. Right, Emir?"

A tiny part of me fluttered with excitement. This was something the old me, the struggling actress, would have jumped on. A chance to take a weird job that vaguely resembled acting and most likely led nowhere? Sign me up! I'd played Tinkerbell at birthday parties and dressed up as a sexy elf to serve drinks at a Christmas function. But that was back when I still hung onto the dream. The dream of being discovered.

Now, I had a plan, and I knew what this was: a dangerous distraction.

"No. I appreciate the offer, guys, but I really don't think we should take it that far."

Cem's eyes filled with alarm. "Please, Aria! I don't think so either, but if Burcu blows our cover—"

"Do you really think she would?" I asked. "Emir said she's willing to *pay* me to play her in public. She wouldn't suggest that if she was happy to face the media herself."

"But if they release a statement, even that could really hurt us," Emir pointed out.

"Didn't you say it wouldn't matter?" I tried to recall his actual words. "That as long as we started a rumor, people would believe the photos."

Emir averted my eyes, his face glowing with what almost looked like embarrassment. "I never anticipated they'd latch onto this. If we disappoint them, this could get really ugly. I don't think they'd stop at a simple press release. They would try to expose us, expose you…"

Cem cut into my line of sight, blocking Emir. "Think of it as a fun trip, nothing more. I'll take care of everything. Or Emir will. Either way, you have nothing to worry about. Smile and wave for the cameras and then I'll lead you away before they get to ask you anything. We'll keep the appearances short."

I took a step back, my throat tightening at the sound of his voice. I wanted so badly to agree, but how could I? This would make it so much harder to resist him, and if I couldn't… I'd return in pieces.

"I'd have to get time off work. I don't know…"

I moved back until I was almost leaning against the closed door and that's when it happened. As if in slow motion, the door flew open and the impact sent me across the floor, hitting smack bang in the middle of Cem's chest. He caught me, like he'd done before, his firm touch flushing my insides with warmth. I staggered, filling my flattened lungs as I turned to peer over my shoulder.

Lindsay stood in the doorway, her dark bob swaying, her eyes wide. "I'm so sorry! Did I hit you? I was looking for… well, a kitchen." She cut a glance at the fridge.

"Well, you found it." I tried to smile, extracting myself from

Cem's grip. "Do you need a drink or...?"

"Coffee would be amazing!" She declared, taking a seat at the island.

Was I supposed to serve her?

I cleared my throat. "These are Cem and Emir, from Turkey. They're the guests who're about to leave. Cem's actually an actor." As soon as the words left my lips, I stiffened, glancing at Emir in horror. What had I done?

He didn't seem any angrier than before, but it was hard to tell.

Lindsay's eyes lit up as she studied Cem, her gaze lingering on the deep V of chest muscles peeking from underneath the bathrobe. "Is that right? I feel like I've seen you before. Are you working in Turkey? Your film industry is booming!"

Cem shook her hand, throwing in a charming smile. "You may have seen me in *Aşkta Şanslı*. It was sold overseas as Lucky in Love."

I could tell from Lindsay's expression that she had no clue of what he was talking about but kept nodding enthusiastically. "Of course, of course. Are you here for work?"

"No, on holiday."

"Are you available for work?" Her eyes sharpened, roaming his body. "We're casting an Arab character. It's not a major role, but a meaty one... a mysterious stranger." She smiled, her eyes flashing. "He's a horse breeder who happens upon a gold mining town during the gold rush. We're auditioning a few locals tomorrow if you'd like to pop in."

"Cem has a lead role in a new multi-million-dollar international production," Emir injected. "We need to leave for Istanbul very soon."

Cem smiled at Lindsay, completely ignoring his brother. "That sounds great. Any other roles you're casting? Aria is also an actress. Did you know that?"

"Is she?" Lindsay looked at me with renewed interest, although with far less hunger. "We do have a role you could audition for if you wanted to. We're required to cast a certain number of locals to qualify for the tax rebate." She didn't sound too thrilled about the clause. "Anyone have a pen?"

Cem found one on the kitchen counter and Lindsay wrote down times and dates on the back of two business cards, handing one to Cem, another to me. "Email me and I'll forward you the script. Now, the coffee?"

I accepted the card and dutifully boiled the jug, preparing a batch of plunger coffee.

"So, you're leaving soon? Back to Turkey?" Lindsay asked the men as she drew her phone from her pocket, turning her attention to the screen.

Emir cast me a look that felt like a warning. "No. It's so nice here we might extend our stay. We have this hotel booked for another three weeks."

Dread travelled through my body like a cold breeze as he continued in an ominous tone. "Unless, of course, Aria comes with us to the next location. Then we could be swayed." His dark gaze pinned me in its grip.

The electric jug sputtered as it reached its desired temperature. I imagined steam rising from both of us.

Lindsay turned to me, her brow furled. "What's going on?"

I busied myself with the plunger. "He's joking. I promised to take them to a lovely, historic Airbnb and I will go with them, of course, so they don't get lost."

I snuck a meaningful look at Emir.

"Good," he said. "Yes, I was only joking." His words were so deadpan they made me think of an alien learning human communication.

I mustered a strained laugh. "Most people don't get him, but I think he's hilarious." I winked at Lindsay, lowering my voice. "Some things get lost in translation."

She raised her brow, giving me a knowing nod. I poured her a coffee and watched her shoulders drop as she sighed with relief. Setting milk and sugar on the table, I peered past her to Emir, giving him a curt nod. Fine. He could twist my arm, but it wasn't over yet. Once I got them out of this hotel, they had no leverage.

I'd feel bad going back on my word, but maybe I didn't have to. Maybe they'd change their minds. Crazy ideas tended to peter out on their own. In a couple of days, they'd forget all about this and I'd never see them again.

Except maybe at the audition, my old self whispered, and my hand instinctively touched my pocket. I had a feature film audition, and it was all thanks to Cem. Could I actually go? Janie didn't seem to consider it a problem. Maybe I could work around the film role, if I actually got it, which was highly unlikely.

I wiped the counter and turned to Lindsay. "Do you need anything else? I'll get these guys upstairs to pack their things and drive them to the Airbnb. Then I'll send the cleaners here to get your rooms ready. Is that okay?"

Lindsay drained her coffee and smiled. "Perfect! I'll keep everyone in the production meeting so we're out of the way."

"Great. Call me if you need anything." I flashed her one last smile and directed Cem and Emir outside.

"You made a promise," Emir reminded me on the stairs. "I hope you intend to keep it."

I smiled sweetly. "I hope so, too."

# CHAPTER 19

# Cem

I couldn't read Aria and it made me nervous. She'd seemed on edge ever since we'd left the hotel with our haphazardly packed suitcases, headed for somewhere along the coast, driving through the town center and up a steep residential street.

Aria parked behind a traditional white villa. It didn't look as big as our first location, but as we stepped inside, I could tell someone had painstakingly restored the house and equipped it with modern conveniences.

"This is one of Napier's oldest buildings. It survived the earthquake and fire and was restored."

I glanced at the dark, weathered beams running across the ceiling. "It looks... old."

Emir opened a stiff, squeaky door and peered into the small

kitchen. "Why did they restore this? It's only an old house. Small rooms. Low ceiling. Uneven floor."

Aria glared at him. "It's from the 1800s. It's historical."

"Half of Istanbul is from the 1800s," I explained, to apologize for my brother.

We carried our luggage upstairs, examining the two cozy bedrooms. I touched Aria's arm. "It's perfect. Thank you."

"No worries." She hurried down the narrow, squeaky stairs, worn smooth from centuries of use.

There was a certain charm to old buildings, the connection to history. I loved that about Istanbul, too, as did many of my more artistically inclined friends, renovating 1800s flats in our historic suburbs. I couldn't wait to show Aria around the city.

If we could get her to join us. I had a feeling she was planning to disappear. What if she did? I had her phone number, but no address. Could I find her through her job?

Emir sat on the bed and yanked his laptop out of its bag. "I'll book our flights. We need to get moving. You make sure Aria doesn't split on us. You have more pull with her anyway."

He said the last part begrudgingly, and I couldn't help the smack of satisfaction. Growing up, he'd been better at everything– math, science, playing the guitar, even football... the only thing left for me was being fun. With that came the social life and social skills he'd never really had and pretended not to care about.

"I'll talk to her, but you have to stop the blackmail and scare tactics. They won't work. She's not Burcu. She's different. Stubborn."

"Fine," Emir grumbled, his gaze on the screen.

I ran downstairs, then out the door, and caught Aria on the phone next to her car. It sounded like she was talking to the cleaners. I waited for her to finish the call, my hand up as if waiting for my turn to speak in the classroom.

She lowered the phone and turned to me with arched brows. "Is something wrong?"

I leaned on her car, stopping her from opening the door. "We both know something's wrong." I glanced at the house. "My brother's a dick."

"Is he?" She gave me a level gaze.

"No. I mean he has... blind spots. When he feels threatened, or gets stressed, he acts like a douche bag on a power trip instead of asking for help."

Aria gave me a soft nod, her mouth gently curling up. "You don't say?"

I smiled apologetically, relief flooding my body. "Well, you saw him in action. I'm sorry."

Her expression melted further. "It's okay."

"I know we can't force you to do this. It's a lot to ask, but I don't have a choice. I have to go back. I have to help Burcu. This is the first time she's reached out to us in three years. She must be desperate."

"Hmm." She dipped her chin, eyes downcast. "You really care about her."

"I do, but not romantically. We worked together for a long time. She's the reason the show became so popular. I owe her...

everything." I gave her an earnest look.

Aria nodded, her mouth a straight line. "She sounds very special."

"Not as special as you! But I want to be honest with you. If you decided to help me, you deserve the whole truth. I'm not trying to hire you to be a mute body double."

She frowned. "But that's exactly what you're asking. You need me there, not talking, looking like Burcu."

I sighed, running my fingers through my hair, which had dried into some unexpected tangles. I was talking myself into knots and she saw right through me. "I know it sounds that way, but I wanted to tell you that you're more than that, to me." Seeing her alarmed expression, I added, "A friend. And I could really use one."

Aria exhaled, and I swallowed the bubble of disappointment creeping up my throat. I'd never subscribe to this friendship nonsense, but I would have said anything to keep her with me. I didn't even care about the film role, or my reputation. Caring about that was Emir's job. I only wanted to keep Aria.

If I thought beyond the moments I'd spent lusting after her, she'd also given me some of the least lonely, most real and grounding yet joyful moments I could remember since childhood. I wanted to hang onto them, hang onto her. To keep texting her, talking to her, laughing at her jokes, making her laugh... And of course, I still wanted to do things to her I wouldn't let myself even think about. Not right now. Not here. I couldn't risk her running away.

She glanced away, then shook her head, jingling her car keys between her fingers. "What if you lose the film role? You'd spend a lot of money flying me over there for nothing. Money you could spend on helping Burcu and her family, if they're in trouble."

"If I lose the role, I won't have much money to help Burcu," I argued. "Everyone's counting on me."

"You're everyone's golden ticket, aren't you?" Her eyes glowed with sadness, with a hint of defiance.

"I guess."

I knew what she meant, but I couldn't spin this any other way. This was my life. The price I had to pay. I'd lifted my family out of poverty, and I'd keep them cushioned against inflation so that nobody had anything to worry about. They could disapprove of my lifestyle and blame me for the scandals, but they couldn't deny I brought in the money. That I was good for something.

"You're more than that to me," she said quietly, throwing my own words back at me. Except for the 'friend' part. That tiny omission made my heart leap.

"Are you going to the audition?" I asked.

"I don't know. I haven't emailed Lindsay yet. Maybe she didn't mean it. Maybe she won't send the script."

I wanted to shake her shoulders, but worried I couldn't stop touching her if I started. "You need to work on those trust issues."

# CHAPTER 20

Trust issues. That couldn't be right. I'd never been betrayed or cheated on. Discarded, yes. Exchanged for something better, also yes. But not really betrayed. To betray someone, you had to first commit to them, and people didn't commit to me.

I shook my head at the thought as I leaned against my car. "Things work out... for other people."

"But not you?" Cem cocked his head.

I felt a stirring in my gut, a desire to be more open with him, to see what he could handle if we really were friends. I hadn't seen my Auckland friends in months and felt so alone I would probably end up dating Felix just to have someone to talk to.

I nodded at my car. "Let's go for a drive. I want to show you something."

Cem was sitting in my Toyota before I even made it behind the wheel, grinning at me like a Labrador who'd been promised a walk.

"Aren't you going to ask me where we're going?" I cast him an amused glance as I reversed down the driveway and steered up the road, away from the town center.

"I like surprises."

"In that case, close your eyes."

He did.

I laughed. "Are you sure? It's a twenty-minute drive."

"You don't think I can keep my eyes closed for that long?"

I turned on the radio, searching the channels for something mellow to match my mood. I settled for Ed Sheeran.

"I know this one," Cem exclaimed, humming along.

He had a lightness to him I craved, as if he was buoyed by life where I was getting sucked under. I felt jealous yet elated to be near him. With Cem, I couldn't sink any deeper. He had so much good luck and optimism, almost enough for both of us.

We drove in silence, listening to the music. After ten minutes, I noticed Cem had fallen asleep. I'd heard jet lag lasted 24 hours for each time zone crossed, and coming here from Europe, you crossed half of them. How would I cope with the flights if we went to Istanbul? What if I fell asleep in the middle of one of those public outings? It'd be awful, but not the worst outcome I could imagine.

Maybe I really did have trust issues. I couldn't trust anything to work out and not only relationships. For seven years, I'd made rejection part of my weekly routine. I'd told myself I needed to keep putting myself out there, to develop a thicker skin. And to an extent, it worked. I got used to the turndowns. In the end, I hadn't questioned why I only scored two-line parts, or why my boyfriends wanted to keep things casual, or why I had so many superficial friendships that meant more to me than the other person. I'd accepted that I wasn't the one people committed to or banked on. I was the one they used for a while, so that's what I became good at; being useful. If I didn't expect too much, it hurt less.

I glanced at Cem. The lush, fern-covered scenery created a majestic backdrop behind his sleeping frame, like another movie scene I got to enjoy privately. I wondered if he knew how much he'd already given me. Even if I struggled to receive his attention or believe his words, I felt seen. Like I was worth the effort.

The road climbed up a steep hill, emerging from the bush into full sunshine. Finally, we arrived on top. I parked, waking up Cem.

His whole body jerked, ripped from sleep. He blinked, bewildered. "What happened?"

I only meant to touch his forearm, as casually as possible, but he stretched both arms over his head, yawning, and my hand landed on his thigh. "Sorry, I didn't mean to startle you," I muttered, staring at my hand.

He interlaced his fingers behind his head and cast a downward glance at my hand, waiting for my next move.

I had no next move.

Disengage, my brain told me. It was the only option, but actioning the command seemed to take ages. I hoped time only *seemed* to slow down as my brain worked at triple speed, playing a film of every touch and kiss we'd shared, each memory burning hot on my skin.

Cem lowered his arms, placed his hand over mine and gave it a squeeze. My heart lurched somewhere in my windpipe as his gaze dipped to my lips. I tensed every muscle in my body to stop myself from leaning in.

After a moment, he seemed to sober up. "God, I'm so jet lagged. Where are we?"

"It's a lookout called Te Mata Peak."

The parking lot looked empty. We were alone. I got out of the car, and he followed me up a short flight of stairs, to a rock formation that rose above the fenced mountain top. A blast of wind greeted us, and I held onto my T-shirt. I really should have worn a bra, even if I hated the way they trapped me with their metal wires. Even if I'd chosen to play this dangerous game. To entice him, to tease him, make him work hard at this friend gig, I hadn't had this effect on anyone in a long time, maybe ever, and each look and touch built me up in an intoxicating way.

"This is epic!" Cem shouted, spreading his arms, turning to peer into every direction.

To the West, hills and mountains stretched out to the horizon, a bright green gradually fading into a soft, hazy sage. To the East, Napier, framed by the vast ocean, baked in the sun. It was an ethereal view, one that never ceased to amaze me. Looking over the hills, I felt alone in a world mostly void of people, dominated by nature's giant peaks and valleys. It didn't bother me. Here, my perpetual insignificance became a design feature, not a point of despair.

Cem turned to me. "I can't believe we're alone here! Don't people know about this?"

I chuckled. "They do, but there are not that many people."

Cem sighed. "Tell that to Istanbul."

"A lot of people?" My stomach twisted.

Cem gave me a cautious smile. "I don't want to put you off, but yeah, compared to this, we're like sardines."

We sat on a flat rock, and I wrapped my arms around my body to shield myself from the breeze. It was colder up here. Cem immediately removed his T-shirt and wrapped it around my shoulders.

I stared at the goosebumps covering his bare arms and chest. "Now you're freezing. This is silly. Let's go back to the car."

"I don't want to leave yet."

"Okay, then put this back on." I handed his shirt back to him. "I think I have a blanket in the car."

Cem perked up and dove back into his shirt. I gave him the keys and he ran to the car and back in record time, bringing back the checkered woolen blanket I kept for spontaneous picnic needs. So far, no such needs had emerged.

The blanket would have been big enough to reach over our shoulders, sitting side by side, but he straddled the rock. I sat a little farther away, letting him keep the blanket.

"What are you doing?" He scooted closer and yanked me toward him. "Come here. I have a plan for our survival."

I laughed and relented, leaning against his chest. I pulled my knees to my chest, and he wrapped the blanket around both of us, cocooning me in its woolen embrace. Warmth enveloped me from neck to toes and my body relaxed. As soon as it did, I also felt him, the hardness of his chest and the heartbeat that pounded through two layers of T-shirt fabric, delivering its rhythm straight into my chest. His arms settled around my tightly folded limbs like a husk around a seed. I felt him everywhere. The heaviness of those arms made my heart swell, then flutter in panic.

This was quicksand. I already craved more. More of him.

"I looked you up," he whispered in my ear. "You're a great actress."

My body stiffened, but he tightened his hold, not giving in an inch. "What, you watched my showreel?"

"And anything else I could find. It's only fair. You watched my show."

I grunted. There was nothing I could say. He had the right to watch whatever was freely available online. Like I'd looked up his dick pic, which was disappointingly grainy, taken with a long lens in low lighting.

"What I don't understand is why you're not jumping on this chance to audition for the film. Why you'd rather make coffees and chauffeur people around."

"You make me sound like a butler." I attempted to turn around, to give him a dirty look, but was met by a wall of muscle. Despite my indignation, his stroke-hold sent a delicious hum through my body. I didn't want to escape.

"I'm joking." He murmured into my ear. "There's nothing wrong with what you do, but I can see it's not your true passion."

I relaxed into his grip, filling my lungs with the crisp air. "I don't want to get sucked back into that vortex. That life of constant hoping and wishing and dreaming."

"What's wrong with dreaming?"

My muscles stiffened. "Dreaming is toxic."

"Why?"

A hot stirring rose in my gut. This was it. What I'd been wrestling with and what would eventually make him lose interest. Better I got it out now. "Because... we're taught that dreams come true. That if you follow your dreams and work hard, anything is possible. You can be anything. An astronaut. A movie star. But if you look at the numbers, it doesn't add up. There are billions of us. If everyone dreams of stardom, most of us will fail. Billions of people will fail. Their dreams never come true. So, why do we encourage our kids to dream *big*? I used to hang out with a lot of actors, and I came across hundreds of people who all thought they had what it takes. Every one of them genuinely believed that they would beat the odds and become household names... It's not possible. If everyone's a celebrity, no one's a celebrity."

It was easier to speak without seeing his face. His celebrity face.

After a moment, his soft voice travelled into my ear. "Yeah, but not everyone dreams of that. I didn't, yet it happened."

My irritation boiled over, giving me superhuman strength. I twisted on the bench to eyeball him with all my might. "You're one in a billion! And because you're a celebrity, your story is elevated above millions of ordinary stories like mine. Your story is told by the media, and it becomes a narrative people hang on to, a story about hard work and passion being rewarded by this... unfathomable success." The droplets of my spit landed on Cem's shirt front. "Yet, it's so rare that it doesn't matter. It's an anomaly."

He nodded, a little amused by my outburst. "I know, I'm lucky. No need to burn me to a crisp with your laser eyes."

I scoffed, shivering from the breeze that now hit my exposed back, but I wasn't done. "*Lucky* doesn't even scrape the surface. *Lucky* is winning a gift basket at a town fair. I don't have a word for what you are, but I'm willing to make one up. Super... charmed. Kissed by the gods? Triple Irish?"

Okay, not great, but I narrowed my eyes to drive the point home.

"Fair enough." Cem's agreeable smile began eroding my resolve. "But I'm pretty sure triple Irish is a type of whiskey, so I'm not sure I can claim that."

He waited for me to catch my breath, then gently scooped me back inside the blanket, hugging my shoulder against his chest. The warmth felt heavenly, and I found myself back in that dangerous place, inhaling his spicy, heady scent.

"I'm sorry you haven't found success yet," he murmured.

I tried to shake my head, my muscles still stiff and fighting. "I'm not looking for it anymore and honestly, it feels better that way. That's why I moved to Napier and took this job. It was like someone finally turned on the lights and I saw my odds for what they really were and then I couldn't unsee it."

We sat in silence for a long time.

Finally, Cem spoke. Thoughtfully. Carefully. "I think you're throwing the baby out in the bath."

"I'm what?"

"Did I not say it right? You know when you throw away something important with something that's not."

I laughed until tears sprung from my eyes. "You mean *throwing the baby out with the bathwater*?"

Cem laughed with me. "That makes more sense! But you know what I'm talking about. Those big dreams about what we want to achieve or become... Money, power, influence. It's largely stuff we can't control. That's where luck and chance play a part, but passion is different, I think. It's what you enjoy, what gives you purpose. The one thing that makes you want to get out of bed in the morning. If you follow your passion, you're already living your dream, not dreaming of something that may never happen. That way, you can't really fail. Not unless you lose your passion."

I hated that he was right.

"It's funny," I said. "With our acting class, we used to sign emails with 'living the dream'. It was usually sarcastic. Like, when someone got a job as a barista or paid a fortune for new headshots, but when you put it like that, you're right. So often when I went to my scene group or acted in a student film, there was a high, an incredible feeling of being in the zone, becoming the character, making the story come alive. Even when it was unpaid and didn't lead to anything, I loved those moments. I lived for those moments, and I think that's how I kept going for as long as I did. I told myself one day it would all pay off. I would book my first big job and then I could say I'd paid my dues. All the crap I went through would become my inspiring backstory or whatever."

My face flushed with heat as I thought about how I'd interviewed myself in my own head. How delusional I'd been.

"Why do we have to pay our dues?" Cem asked, sounding like he was somewhere far away. "Isn't that part of the same huge lie you were talking about? Every time someone succeeds, we ask them about their struggles and pen stories of how they overcame horrible things. If they haven't struggled enough, we exaggerate." He looked at me sheepishly. "They've done that to me. There're these sad stories about my childhood in the low-income neighborhood, but it wasn't that bad. It was just… ordinary. I didn't struggle that much. But they're not interested in the parts of me that are ordinary. I'm either the perfect success or the perfect failure. There's nothing in between."

"I, for one, am happy you didn't struggle that much." The words bubbled up without much thought, from somewhere deep within me.

Cem huffed a soft note of laughter. "Most people want me for my fame, or my story, or whatever I can do for them. They don't want me… ordinary or even happy."

I nodded, my throat tight. "Misery sells. But I think it's also because that story of overcoming adversity is part of our narrative of justice. We elevate some people and then we want to believe that they *deserve* to be where they are. And I think successful people want to believe it, too, even more desperately. Because that would mean that the world is a just place – that hard work always pays off and evil gets punished. But it's an illusion. There's an element

of randomness that scares us all. It's not evil or unjust. It's just...
random. You never fully know which movie will succeed and whose
career will take off, and who's going to fall ill or lose everything."

I risked a glance at Cem, my entire body vibrating. I knew I
sounded bitter, but I also felt lighter, like I'd cleaned my closet,
laying everything out on the bed. All the dirt and disappointment,
darkness and despair.

The look in his eyes grounded me. I saw no judgment or shock,
only curiosity and that spark I'd come to love, the one that made
me feel like nothing could ever be that bad. "You don't think God
has his hand in it all?"

I took a deep breath. "Maybe on some level. I used to think
there was more design and pre-determination, or something like
that going on. I believed a lot of things and want to believe... but
it's hard."

A giddy smile spread across his face. "I can't help it. I feel like
this is all meant to be. Us. This place. Even the dick pic, since it
brought me here."

I released a sigh, part of me screaming for that assurance that
emanated from him. "Can I borrow your faith for one day?"

"Aria. The game's not over. You can still win. And then you can
join me feeling incredibly lucky and blessed and like you don't
deserve it. It has its perks, I promise."

A smile burst through, and I raised my hands to my face, hiding
behind spread fingers. "You must think I'm deranged."

"You're a bit cuckoo." He dropped his smile, turning serious. "But
if you don't go to this audition, you're a lot more cuckoo than I

thought. It's not an open casting call. They've already met you and invited you to audition. If you don't go, you'll be the person who threw away the winning lottery ticket. There'll be no sympathy, and you give up your right to complain about the injustice or randomness of life. No more speeches. It'd be a terrible loss." The seriousness cracked and his eyes twinkled with glee. He could have said it mockingly, but his voice held me like an embrace.

I had to laugh. He'd somehow managed to both support my argument and help me off my high horse.

"Thank you."

"So, you'll do it?"

"Only to get you off my back," I grumbled, warmth spreading into my belly. Butterflies, nerves, and all the rest. They were here and I felt more alive than I'd felt in weeks.

CHAPTER 21

# *Cem*

I sucked my lungs full of fresh air, feeling like I'd conquered an untouched world that lay at my feet, expanding in every direction. Up here, nothing could reach me – neither my mistakes, nor the expectations of others.

I pulled Aria closer to me, possibly for the fifteenth time. "Thank you for bringing me here."

I couldn't stop touching her, while she seemed to alternate between fight, flight and delight, like a set of constantly changing traffic lights.

"Am I making you uncomfortable?" I asked, tightening my arms around her. "Say the word and I'll let you go, I promise."

She shook her head and a strand of hair caught between her lips. "No. I appreciate you keeping me warm," she whispered, her voice a little strained.

I leaned over her shoulder to get a glimpse of her face, but she turned just enough to hide from my eyes. Something about that evoked a memory of Burcu, evading my eyes as I coaxed out the story of what had happened. My stomach flipped.

"I've seen guys acting... entitled," I said. "I promised myself I'd never become like that. You know, walking around thinking I'm such a big deal, entitled to everything and everyone, but it's hard." I loosened my grip, holding my breath, trying not to laugh at my accidental pun, because I was hard. I was always hard around her.

"I told you I wanted to be friends and you kissed me on the stairs," she reminded me. I heard the smile in her voice.

"Yeah, okay, but what about my herculean effort not to touch your ass? Does that not count for anything?"

"That's a low bar." Her eye roll was so potent I felt it in my stomach.

"I'm sorry, but as long as I have a little hope, I can't let go." I paused, gathering my willpower as I leaned back to create some distance between us. "If you need me to step back, tell me. I don't want to be an entitled asshole. I never want to make you feel unsafe. Even if I am entitled. And an asshole."

Aria turned around to face me, pink blotches on her cheeks, her eyes shining. She took my hand, interlacing her fingers with mine. "Don't worry. I feel safe with you. I just don't trust myself."

Her flustered words poured like warm liquid down my spine, giving me courage. "Aria. I like you a lot. I haven't felt like this about anyone in a long time. Tell me again, why do we have to be friends? Why can't we just... hop on this train and see where it goes?" I winced at my stupid metaphor.

She blinked, gathering shiny drops on her lashes. "Because my heart can't handle the ride."

# CHAPTER 22

*These uneven, shiny nuggets are all that is left
of him. All that ever mattered to him. This is his
legacy. My heart is broken, and these are the pieces
left behind. Was it all worth it?*

My fingers shaking, I fastened my phone to the hands-free stand, pushed 'record' and stepped back to the mark I'd taped on the floor. The rumble of clothes dryers on the first floor sent a vibration through my body, perfectly humming with the nerves that zinged to life.

I'd read the script several times, sinking deeper and deeper into character, until I felt ready to film myself.

I'd emailed Lindsay the previous night after I'd dropped Cem off at the Airbnb, and to my surprise, received the script within half an hour. After a fitful sleep and a stir-crazy half-day at the office, Janie had sent me home to prep for the audition. Which is what I was now doing. Prepping. And thinking of Cem. But mostly prepping.

I'd devoured the script, my heart immediately drawn to my character Eloise, whose family had lost everything in the late 1800s gold rush. The film had a dual timeline with Eloise's part happening in the 1930s, as she arrives in Napier after the earthquake and discovers the truth about her late grandfather's tumultuous life during the gold rush.

It was a story of the sad legacy of gold prospecting and how greed and wishful thinking cost the old man his great love, and eventually, his life. At the end, Eloise is at a similar crossroads, making a choice between love and a promise of great fortune.

I'd expected a two-line part, but Eloise was the central character. A chunk of the story took place in 1880, played by other actors, but my character was there at the beginning, middle and the end. Her narration, part of which I had to learn for the audition, carried the story. I was auditioning for a lead role, I thought with a fresh wave of panic.

Thank goodness I loved accents and had spent so much time learning the American one. I really needed it now.

Still, the connection I felt to the character soothed my nerves. I had tears in my eyes from the cold read. This story felt made for me.

Yet, I wouldn't have been here, attempting to read for it, if it weren't for Cem. The enormity of what he'd done for me sat on my shoulders like the blanket he'd held around me at the peak. I could still feel the weight of his arms. I only had to close my eyes and the feeling returned like a tidal wave.

I took a deep breath, refocusing my misty eyes on the script, looked up at the camera and spoke my first line. The others followed effortlessly, secured in my memory, but I wasn't satisfied. I did it three more times, until the lines were lodged in my heart and I was happy with the playback. Seeing myself on tape always felt unsettling, but it also gave me confidence. I'd been taping myself for practice for years.

Once dressed and with my hair done, I texted Cem.

**Me:** I'm leaving for the audition. Wish me luck!

**Cem:** You don't need luck. You're amazing.

**Me:** Then I need luck to get chosen from the sea of amazing.

**Cem:** Okay... I wish you the brightest life jacket in the sea of amazing.

**Me:** It does sound like a wonderful place for a swim.

**Cem:** Nail this audition and I'll take you there.

**Me:** Deal.

**Cem:** Sweet. I'll get tickets.

**Me:** Wait. The Sea of Amazing is in Istanbul, isn't it?

**Cem:** I'm getting the Black Sea renamed.

**Me:** Sounds like an upgrade.

**Cem:** You'll love it. Can't wait to show you everything.

**Me:** How long am I staying for? Two years?

**Cem:** We need at least three years to explore the 1800s buildings alone.

**Me:** Why do I feel like that's not a joke?

**Cem:** Because I'm serious. I'm going back and you're coming with me.

I dropped the phone on the bed like a hot potato. He was talking crazy, and I had to push all this nonsense from my mind if I wanted to make it to the audition. In the end, he'd change his mind. Sanity would prevail. All I had to do was wait.

# CHAPTER 23

I stared out the plane window, my head spinning. Everything had happened so fast, like dominoes falling, until I sat here, seatbelt fastened, mask on my face, my heart hammering like I'd ingested a week's worth of caffeine in two hours.

Cem and Emir hid behind masks too, even though the airline seemed relaxed about it. This way, nobody would recognize us before we were ready for our first public outing.

Janie had ensured I could take a week off and keep my job, mainly because there wasn't much going on. So, I hadn't abandoned the plan, and it made me a bit calmer. But I'd gone to the audition, and that part felt like a dream.

I'd floated through the door on a high, not only from the nerves and excitement, but from Cem's encouragement. Traces of his endless faith and buoyancy must have rubbed off on me, filling my chest with an odd sensation like I hadn't come in to audition at all but to play the part that was rightfully mine.

Of course, the feeling evaporated as unexpectedly as it had arrived. By the time I shook Lindsay's hand at the doorway, my latent self-doubts rebounded, tensing every muscle in my body, bracing for her crushing verdict.

"It's a big decision, so we'll review the tapes and have to think about this but thank you so much. We really appreciate your time and talent."

I pulled out my phone, opening the calendar app. If I got the part, the filming would start in a week, right after the trip. I'd be so jet lagged I'd probably mess up my lines, but I'd worry about that later.

After the audition, held in the hotel's dusty sitting room, I'd found Emir waiting for me, an open laptop propped against his chest. 'I need your passport number,' he'd said without preamble.

I could only blame that post-audition, nothing-can-touch-me high. My brain chemistry had been so out of balance, I'd dutifully driven home and fetched my passport. After a couple of hours, I had my flight details, a transit visa for passing through L.A. – and one night to pack my bags.

The next morning, I'd hauled my pitiful carry-on with some underwear and basic toiletries into a taxi and we'd taken the first, short flight in a shaky, little plane from Napier to Auckland, to catch the first long-haul flight to L.A. in the evening.

Emir had spent the first flight talking to Cem about his social media accounts, trying to keep his attention on charts and graphs on his laptop screen as he fidgeted in his seat. I'd caught glimpses of the screen but, unable to follow the Turkish, settled on perusing the airline safety card, imagining various plane crash scenarios. They seemed more calming than what waited for me in Istanbul.

I'd agreed not to pack too many of my own clothes. Apparently, they wouldn't be of any use, other than for sleeping and hiding away in Cem's house. Not that it made much difference since I didn't have many pieces of clothing, and, despite living above a laundromat, hardly any of them were clean.

I'd never travelled this far, on such short notice, or in such luxury. Cem shifted in his aisle seat, his long legs stretched on the footstool that came with the incredible first-class seats I'd only ever passed, salivating, on my way to coach. He'd insisted that I take the window seat, and closed his eyes when the plane was still on the tarmac. He'd already dozed through the safety briefings and now snored softly as the plane rolled down the runway.

The flight attendant with her perfect hair and incredible eyelash extensions tapped his shoulder, urging him to sit up and fasten his seatbelt, well after everyone else had been told to do so via the loudspeaker. Cem woke, stretched his body like a lazy cat, and did as he was told. On his other side, separated by the aisle, sat Emir, glued to his laptop and wearing noise cancelling headphones.

"Did I fall asleep again?" Cem asked, adjusting his mask. His eyes wrinkled in the corners.

I wish I could have seen his smile. "You didn't stay in New Zealand long enough to get over the jet lag."

"Next time." He held my gaze until I had to turn away.

There wouldn't be a next time. Why would he ever return? He hadn't wanted to come here in the first place.

"Did you go to the audition?" I asked. The question had been burning in the back of my mind. I wasn't sure what time he'd been appointed, but I hadn't seen him.

Cem glanced at Emir and lowered his voice. "If Emir asks, I didn't. I told him I was going to the aquarium. I'm not sure he bought it, but he hasn't asked me about it."

My heart leapt like a little dolphin. I wanted to ask him more about the role, but Emir glanced our way, dropping his headphones around his neck and popping a mint. Thank goodness for the general noise levels.

"Well, if he asks, tell him you really liked the penguins," I said, leaning so close my mask brushed his ear.

"They have penguins?" Cem's eyes shone with adoration.

"You like penguins?"

"Who doesn't like penguins? I thought it was fish swimming around in tanks."

"You don't like fish?"

Cem's thick eyelashes caught the warm evening light. I couldn't tell if he was smiling. "Fish are fine, but I prefer penguins. They mate for life."

For once, I felt grateful for the mask covering my hanging mouth. I forced my lips to meet, to stop any snide remarks from escaping. I'd seen his dating history – a series of casual hook-ups. He hadn't been seen with any woman more than once since Burcu.

"Penguins are better than people," I finally concluded. Better than either of us, probably.

My stomach plummeted as the plane gathered speed, rattling along the runway.

Cem leaned closer, raising his voice just enough to be heard over the engines. "I want that."

"What? Penguins?"

"No. Something... someone... for life."

"Aha."

"You don't believe me, but I do."

"Uh-huh."

"I'll show you," he finally said.

The plane lifted off the runway. We were airborne.

He glanced at my fidgeting fingers. "Are you scared of flying?"

I couldn't help it. I'd applied two coats of clear polish in the morning, and now desperately tried to stick to only peeling off nail polish so I wouldn't rip off my actual nails. A problem I knew Burcu didn't have. At least on TV, her nails had shined in glossy perfection. I always noticed other people's nails.

"No. I'm fine with flying. I'm just nervous about all this. I'm scared I'll disappoint you. And Emir. Everyone. I feel like I'm not... qualified for this."

"It's not a job. We're friends, remember? You're helping me."

"But you're paying for everything. You're *investing* in this. What if you don't get what you want?"

Cem stared out the window at the vast whiteness of the clouds we were pushing through. "I don't always get what I want." He turned to look at me, holding still like he wanted to say more. Or maybe he was just thinking.

"I didn't say you do."

We emerged from the clouds and into the blue-to-orange gradient sky, the evening sun streaming through the window. Flying to Los Angeles, we'd be travelling away from the sunset.

Cem turned to meet my gaze. "I can handle disappointment. I can give up things… I haven't smoked in nearly two weeks."

"You smoke?" An odd mix of disgust and relief filled me. I couldn't stand the smell of cigarettes, especially on someone's breath, and had never dated a smoker. If he smoked, it would be easier not to fall for him.

"No. I'm not a smoker anymore. I read it's best to affirm the new identity. So… I used to smoke."

"Does your family smoke?"

"Yeah."

"Is that going to be hard?" My voice came out almost excited. If he lapsed on arrival, it would be so easy to stay away from him. That smell of rotting flesh that secreted from every pore of a smoker after they returned from a cigarette break… I'd experienced it enough times to know how it turned my stomach. I'd be free of my stupid crush and wouldn't get my heart broken. The blessed little cancer sticks would save me.

Cem held my gaze, his eyes filled with light. "It'll be easier with you. You're not a smoker, right?"

"No. Never smoked. Hate the smell." I shuddered.

"Perfect! I'll stay by your side, and you can hold my hand every time I really want a cigarette. I'll replace one craving with another."

A craving? Oh, no.

He took my hand, sending a powerful jolt straight to my heart, and other unmentionable places. Dang it. This was even worse.

I took a steadying breath. "Why did you stop smoking?"

Cem held still, staring at our intertwined fingers. "Our dad was diagnosed with lung cancer. We don't know how bad it is yet, but that sort of influenced my decision."

My heart lurched. "I'm so sorry. That must have been a shock."

"Not really. He's a heavy smoker."

"Were you?"

"Not that bad, but still… It's risky, and he didn't ask me to quit." Even through the mask, I heard the pain in his voice.

"So, you quit because he *didn't* ask you to?"

He tilted his head. "Yeah, I know it sounds messed up and it's not the only reason, but it feels great to take some control, make my own choices."

So much for my quiet hope that he'd made the decision on a whim and would slip into his old habits as soon as we landed in Istanbul. But even if he did… I couldn't help the twinge of despair for him. Deep down, I couldn't wish for anything bad for him, not even if it saved me from getting hurt.

After a while, the dinner trays arrived. Cem ordered two glasses of champagne and placed them both next to my chicken pasta, removing his mask. The joy of seeing his smile hit me so hard I nearly leaned in to touch his face.

I raised one of the champagne glasses. "Are you trying to get me drunk?"

Cem shrugged. "Maybe a little more relaxed."

I sighed and downed the drink. Relaxing wasn't a bad idea. I'd already made my choice, stepping on this plane. I might as well try to enjoy it. Did it matter how short-lived my fake relationship with Cem ended up being? I was making memories I'd hopefully keep forever. I hadn't been kidding about that memory palace. Deep inside my mind, my moments with Cem were categorized, cross-referenced with where on my body I'd felt each touch, each word. Concerningly, those sensations were presenting increasingly in my heart.

The champagne fizzed its way to my head, making it light. I couldn't help staring at him. I'd never get enough of the way those eyes sparkled and his mouth curved. This was my chance to live a fairy tale – taste the life I'd once dreamt of. Maybe it would bring closure. Like meeting a person you'd once pined for.

I dug out my phone and pointed the camera at Cem. He smiled for the photo, then grabbed the phone from me and pulled me in for a selfie. When he handed the phone back, his smile vanished. "You know you can't post anything, right? Emir would flip out."

"That's fine." I filled my lungs to dispel the heat enveloping my neck. "I only want something to remember you by."

Cem snatched my phone back. "I won't give you that." Frowning, he deleted the photos I'd taken.

"Why?"

"People collect memories when they're leaving. When someone's dying. I'm not helping you with that."

I sighed. "We're friends, right? Our lives are worlds apart, but we can be friends on different continents and it's nice to have photos to remember friends." My voice came out in desperate bursts.

I tried to take my phone back, but he kept flipping through my photos, holding it out of my reach. Pictures of the hotel whipped past, and I knew what was coming. Why hadn't I deleted that one—

"What's this?" Cem stared at the photo of him sleeping. "Did you sneak into the hotel when I was sleeping?"

"What, no! That was the night we met." My cheeks blazed. Taking that photo had brought me so much grief. How stupid did I have to be?

"You took a photo after I fell asleep?" He looked at me with unbearable hope and delight, his voice soft.

"I thought I might never see you again," I whispered. "You looked so beautiful."

"Admit it." Cem held up the phone as evidence. "You don't want to be friends any more than I do." His voice was as dark and rich as his eyes fixed on mine. "Besides, as soon as we land in Istanbul, you're my girlfriend. I think it's best you stay in character. There will be people in my house. A lot of eyes on us."

I swallowed a hard lump. "Why? Who do you live with?"

"Emir's place is so far from the city it makes no sense for him to sleep there, most of the time. And my parents use the annex. I had it built for them. I have a cook and a cleaner, but they don't live there.

"Wow. That's a lot of eyeballs. From what Emir said, I thought we'd stay at your house. How's that going to work? Do we tell them what's going on?"

Cem bit his lip, casting an angry look at his brother, who seemed to have fallen asleep. "Emir may have left out some details. We can't tell anyone, it's not safe. I think we have to make it look like you live elsewhere, like Burcu does. We'll probably go to a hotel and only visit my house."

Panic constricted my windpipe. "But... I can't pretend to be Burcu to your parents! It'll take them two seconds to figure out I don't speak Turkish and that'll be that."

Cem scratched his beard, looking away. "We'll come up with a story. I'm sure Emir's already thought of something. We'll tell them you're sick or something. We don't have to stay at the house. It's probably best if we don't."

"Did your family ever meet Burcu in person?"

"No. I never brought her home. We spent most of our time on set or met in town. Mom watched the show, but that's it. Her parents didn't like us together and we didn't get to the 'meet the family' thing. Have you ever brought a boyfriend home?"

"No."

I peeled the foil cover off the uninspiring in-flight meal of chicken and pasta. Squeezing every drop out of the lemon wedge provided, I thought about the last two boyfriends I'd seen almost back-to-back in Auckland before my move. They'd been actors, a professional hazard it seemed, and chasing their own dreams that ranked far higher than me in their lives. The first one, Wes, had gotten a leading role in a reality show, shot to fame and abandoned me for someone even more famous than him. Climbing the ladder.

The second one, Jake, had been as unknown as me, but with huge aspirations. I hadn't been part of his plan, but we looked good together, good enough that a public relationship gave us both a social boost. I may have hoped for more, but I'd settled for less. It was easier to focus on my own dreams. That way, we were two people on parallel paths, and as long as those paths aligned, we could go together. But I knew he wouldn't change his course for me, so I kept mine.

"Tell me about your last boyfriend," Cem urged, seeing me deep in thoughts.

My throat tightened and I rinsed down a mouthful of dry pasta with champagne. I hadn't expected to share personal details. His maybe, but not mine. I wasn't the interesting one.

I understood the physical attraction, sort of. He'd been in a foreign land with no other prospects, and I looked like someone he'd once loved. But if he only wanted to sleep with me, he didn't need to know me. Sexual attraction thrived well on its own without any backstory, probably more so.

"What are we doing, twenty questions?" I joked, clearing my throat.

"I'm going to need more than twenty." He looked at me so sincerely and I had to laugh.

"It's an old parlor game."

"Okay, we can play it later, but first, tell me about your last boyfriend. I want to know why you left him."

"What makes you think *I* left *him*?"

"You seem like the kind to run away."

His words gave me a tiny gut punch.

"Well, I didn't. I told him I was moving back to Napier and taking this job. I asked him what he wanted to do. That was the last time we talked."

Cem studied my face, like trying to read between the lines. "Did you give him that speech about how billions of people fail and dreams are toxic?"

"I love how you sum it up." I pulled a face. "And yes, I may have said something to that effect. It was like an... awakening, you know? Like some people find religion or go organic or something."

"Yeah. Except you decided to throw your passion in the bathwater—"

"You're still not using that phrase right, it's—"

"Don't care. So, you told your boyfriend you were abandoning your dreams because they never come true. Then what happened?"

"Then..." I sighed, forcing the words out of my mouth. "He accused me of shitting on *his* dreams and stormed out."

Cem's face morphed into the picture of glee. "Wow. What a baby. Did you notice how maturely and respectfully *I* reacted to your insane rant?"

I could have slapped his smug face, but I had to practically swallow my bottom lip to stop myself from laughing out loud. I was supposed to be furious here. Furious. "Calling someone's deeply considered worldview 'insane' doesn't exactly convey respect."

"Phish. That's not your worldview. You're throwing a tantrum at the universe. Which you have every right to do."

"I'm not—"

"How bad was it?"

I was getting tired of him cutting me off, but his earnest tone gave me pause.

"Tell me," he prompted again, more gently. "You said you lived in Auckland. Did you sleep under a bridge and eat worms for breakfast?"

I deflated in my seat. "Moldy student flats and a diet of noodles, so essentially, yes. For seven years. I studied acting, then stayed in town for auditions and opportunities. It's the biggest city in New Zealand, with the most TV and film productions. All the major studios are there."

"Why not Hollywood? I saw your showreel. You can do accents."

I hung my head, thinking back to those years. "I never had enough money to even entertain that idea. I was trying to survive on sporadic income. From one rent to the next. Some of my friends had backup careers and they split their time between something like content writing and acting, or insurance brokering and acting. They were probably smarter, but I'd been taught to go all in. Having a fallback career meant you didn't fully believe in yourself. I believed, for years. I repeated all these mantras, praying and manifesting shit that never happened."

"And one day, you just... stopped believing?"

I drew in a sharp breath, my skin prickling under his intense gaze. "Why do you care?"

"Because you're fascinating." He dropped the words like they were obvious.

"That doesn't sound right. Do you mean fastidious? I'm not

that either, except with learning lines." I shook my head, looking out the window. The sun had finally dipped below the horizon, leaving behind a peachy glow.

"Has no one ever told you that?"

"No."

"Has anyone told you it's really hard not to stare at you?"

I threw him a dubious look. "No."

"So, no one's trying to hit on you?"

I thought of my life lately. "Maybe in Auckland, but not in Napier. Except for my old school mate Felix. Sort of. I wouldn't call it that, to be honest. He doesn't flirt so it's more like… courtship." I winced at the thought.

I'd left my mom a message about the trip, asking her to tell everyone else, which I assumed would include Felix. I hadn't even called him to cancel the coffee date, which was vaguely set for next week. I could only hope the perpetual postponements would work as the metaphorical bucket of cold water I'd eventually have to throw on that man. I would never date him, even if I ended up back in Napier, all alone. Which I probably would.

"Someone's courting you?" Cem's voice climbed higher. "Please tell me it's not serious."

I frowned. "It's awkward. He lives next door to my parents and helps them a lot."

"Ouch! So, if you let him down, they'll lose the free handyman?"

I nodded, surprised at how he'd put in words so plainly. That's all it was. Guilt. Not a good motive for dating.

"Apart from Felix, no one really flirts with me in Napier. Only

Kerim. But he's not serious."

Cem leaned back in his seat, a wide smile spreading across his face. "So it's up to us Turks to notice a beautiful woman? Huh."

"I guess it is." I turned to the window, hiding my smile. Beautiful, huh? That word had lost its meaning in Napier. My looks didn't help me with my job. Being beautiful, which I'd never been quite sure I was, had become a waste.

The flight attendant gathered our trays and the lights dimmed, ready for that period of compulsory sleep.

Cem handed me the plastic-wrapped blanket. "You should get some sleep."

He took his own advice, dozing off within minutes, his head lolling against the headrest, elbow docked against mine. The seats were so spacious he had to spread pretty wide to achieve physical contact. I didn't mind and kept my arm against his as I browsed the in-flight entertainment. No Turkish TV shows. I settled on a historical film.

After a boring but oddly pleasant two hours, I fell asleep, too.

Cem woke me two hours before arrival. Despite the luxury seating, I'd slept with my head hanging off my shoulders and pulled a muscle in my neck. I cried in pain, trying to gently move my head and realign my tortured spine. The pinch was so strong I fought nausea.

"Are you okay?" Cem stretched in his seat. "You slept in a really weird position."

"I'll be fine." I massaged my neck, waiting for the cramp to release. It gradually did, but I couldn't shake the full-body, battered and bruised feeling. Was this what long-haul flights were like? I'd never been further than Australia.

"We'll get coffee soon," Cem promised, peering down the hallway. "If that makes you feel better."

"How did you know?" I almost blinked back tears.

The coffee tasted weak, so Cem suggested we drink twice as much, promptly ordering whatever he thought I needed, despite my protests. As we descended through American airspace and touched down on LAX, I couldn't shake the feeling I was being cared for, a dangerous feeling I was quickly getting used to, even dependent on.

"Don't judge LA based on this," Cem said with an apologetic smile as we stepped off the plane and entered a tired-looking, carpeted corridor. "I'll bring you back for a proper visit and show you everything, okay? We'll watch the sunset at Griffith Observatory. Buy ice creams at Santa Monica Pier. We'll walk around the block where I used to live. I promise."

I swallowed, unable to answer. Neither his words, nor his optimism, made any sense.

After a grueling layover of security checks and riding an endless labyrinth of hallways in an airport caddy, we made it to the gate and onto the next plane.

Turkish Airlines.

Listening to the airline staff conversing in Turkish, it finally hit me I was entering a foreign country. A truly foreign land with nothing familiar to guide me. Other than Cem.

The passengers getting on the plane looked a lot more like Cem and Emir. Brown eyes, dark curls and beards. Some of the women wore scarves, guiding kids with gorgeous, dark-fringed, chocolatey eyes. Most of them didn't wear masks, and I stared at their faces as they passed us in first class. I could see the vague resemblance, but none of them looked striking like Cem. They were all ordinary people with ordinary faces.

Everyone seemed to speak Turkish – the flight attendants, passengers, as well as Cem and Emir. One of the flight attendants, an impossibly skinny woman with unnaturally plush lips, fussed with Emir and Cem, talking to them far more than the other passengers. I remained quiet, sitting still as a statue in my window seat, afraid that my English would draw attention of someone who might recognize Cem.

When the plane took off and the noise levels rose, I whispered to him. "Are we a couple now? Am I Burcu?"

# CHAPTER 24

Shit.

I'd expected the flight attendants to recognize me, but one of them must have been a particularly devoted fan. Even with all her duties, she kept her eyes trained on me, casting glances across the aisles. Thankfully, Aria somehow sensed the situation and kept quiet, her face mostly turned away.

I'd been hoping to continue our conversation, but I couldn't risk it. After a while, the first flight attendant must have alerted the others since I noticed their interest in us growing to the point that I could have sworn they'd set up some sort of eavesdropping roster.

Whatever 'twenty questions' was, I wanted to play that with Aria. I needed answers. Each one gave me another glimpse into her mind, like a missing puzzle piece that only made sense in context. I could feel the picture emerging, and I couldn't wait to complete it. Whatever had intrigued me at first, now held me spellbound. She was nothing like anyone else, yet familiar, like I'd known her in another life.

I could follow Aria's logic on how random and uncontrollable life seemed, but I couldn't fully agree with her. And deep down, I didn't think even Aria fully believed her own words. Part of her was screaming for something more. Meaning. Purpose. Anything to believe in.

She was lost and I wasn't helping. I was using her likeness with Burcu to advance my own career. No matter what I said, no matter how I pursued her or how much I liked her, she was doing me a huge favor and getting nothing in return. Why had she agreed to this?

I sat back, trying to clear my head. Maybe it was good we couldn't talk for a while. I needed to think. Because she was right. I had free will, even if I sometimes felt like I was floating through life, pulled on a raft by my brother, my family, the circumstances.

Whatever Emir had planned or organized, I had to take responsibility for this. I was dragging this woman across the world and asking her to play my girlfriend, hold her tongue and hide her true identity. Emir had made up a story of laryngitis and how Burcu had to rest her voice. Doctor's orders. I hadn't even told her that yet. She knew nothing of what was coming, yet she sat quietly with her hands in her lap, no doubt trying hard not to fiddle with her nails, ask sharp questions or make jokes.

Waiting for the flight attendant to finally leave, I squeezed her hand and leaned close to whisper. "Thank you. The flight attendant is watching us. Emir told her you have laryngitis and you can't speak."

"Okay." She nodded; her eyes unreadable.

"Are you okay? I know this sucks. I wanted to talk to you, but we have to be careful. They're all listening. She might try to take a photo."

Her shoulders tensed. "My hair is all wrong. I'm not wearing a hat."

"It's fine tied up like that," I assured her. "No one can tell."

I loved the way strands of her dark hair had escaped the messy bun, floating about her face like they had a mind of their own.

I'd never been a huge fan of Burcu's sleek hairdo. Her hair had been too perfect, too tidy, and constantly fussed over by a legion of people. I wanted to mess it up and turn it into bed hair. Aria's was already there, making it easy for me to imagine myself in bed with her, witnessing those loose strands falling, one by one.

I didn't miss the way she favored her left side, massaging her neck. I waited until the 'fasten seat belts' sign switched off. Knowing she couldn't refuse me with words, I unfastened her seatbelt and turned her sideways in her seat. She tensed for a second but relaxed as soon as my fingers landed on her neck, softly rubbing and loosening the knots under her skin.

The trembly whimper that slipped from her mouth shot straight to my dick, but I kept massaging, ignoring the need building up in my body. I couldn't remember wanting anything, or anyone, this badly. Not since Burcu. I remembered a different hunger from my early career, being desperate for the next role, the recognition and fame and after I had it, that hunger lingered, driving me to the next thing.

Wanting something was healthy. Inhaling Aria's ice cream scent, I felt invigorated. This is what I needed. I needed her to resist me, to force me out of my pampered funk, back to that human state of perpetual desire for more that kept us all moving.

Why didn't my career inspire that desire anymore? Why didn't I want this next role? I knew it mattered to Emir and my family. It was a lot of money. It made sense. But everything paled compared to my desire for Aria, to hear her say those words, to see her give up the fight. I wanted her to resist, yet I lived for that moment of surrender.

Was Aria right? Did I only want what I couldn't have? Would I stop wanting her if she gave in? I couldn't imagine it, but I wasn't particularly reliable. I was the guy mooning at the paparazzi, the one that had to be 'managed'. Sadness invaded my chest, welling and mixing with physical arousal like a cocktail of oil and water.

Aria moaned, further relaxing against my hands. Did she know what she was doing to me? I spread my legs a bit wider but couldn't make more room in my jeans and had to make sure the airline blanket obscured my crotch.

I finished the massage, pushing her back to her own seat. "Okay, you're done."

I turned to my in-flight entertainment and chose an episode of CSI that mentioned something about a decomposing body. Perfect. I needed to rein in my thoughts.

# CHAPTER 25

# Aria

A packed airport bus transported us from the plane to the airport building. I waded through a cloud of cigarette smoke lingering outside as I followed Emir and Cem through a set of glass doors and onto an escalator. My neck and shoulders still tingled from the massage, which wasn't technically possible, hours later.

Not being able to talk freely for that many hours left me feeling lost and tense. Cem's touch had helped, grounding me, momentarily pushing those questions out of my mind. But now my mind burned with all the things I wanted to talk to him about. How could I miss a person I stood right behind?

Once we made it through passport control, the brightly lit arrivals lounge greeted us with a buzz of chaos. Behind the wall of people holding signs with Turkish names, I glimpsed the glass doors leading outside. The exit, finally. It was early morning and still dark outside.

Cem and Emir headed to a short man with a grey uniform, impressive moustache, and a tall cart magically holding all our luggage. He led us outside to a sleek black Mercedes. He'd parked on the sidewalk, crowding the taxi stand with yellow cars trickling through. The driver packed our bags in the boot while Emir opened the back door for me, practically shoving me inside behind the tinted windows. He took the front seat while Cem joined me in the back. Not waiting for a gap in traffic, the driver muscled us off onto the road, somehow miraculously not hitting anything he seemed intent on hitting.

For the next half hour, I held onto my seat, fearing for my life, as the speedometer climbed to new heights. The abundantly lit Istanbul whizzed past as we sped along the motorway. Had it not been for the stupendous speed, the low rumble of Turkish between Emir and Cem might have put me to sleep. I hadn't slept a wink on the second 12-hour flight and now it was supposed to be morning, the start of a new day. The sky brightened outside the window at a terrifying pace, turning into hazy peach, then pale blue. Turkish signs and advertisements flanked the road, stuck on every ramshackle building and overpass, constantly reminding me of my cluelessness.

"This is the Asian side," Cem whispered in my ear as we reached a tall bridge covered in red lights.

"And now we're in Europe," he added as we made it to the other side.

My fourth continent within twenty-four hours, I thought, feeling light-headed.

He continued chatting in Turkish, as if I could understand, probably for the driver's sake.

"*Evet, aşkım*," I replied, like I'd heard Burcu say on TV. Yes, my love.

His eyes widened and I burst out laughing, breaking character.

"You're playing a dangerous game." His throaty whisper tickled my ear. "Now I have this dream of you actually speaking Turkish, and I expect you to make it true."

Were there any limits to what he expected from life? I smiled to myself. One day, Cem would jump off a cliff expecting to fly, and grow wings in mid-air. I'd be there, expecting nothing and still stumbling on a rock somewhere.

The sign-filled suburbia turned into the inner city, with skyscrapers and other glass-covered, architectural showpieces rising against the morning sky. From afar, the Istanbul color palette seemed soft and muted, but as we got closer, the thousands of lights from the shops, apartments and streetlamps amplified, making the city glow like a Christmas ornament. I expected the lights to turn off as the daylight broke, but most of them remained.

I liked listening to the language with its almost Arabic consonants and funny vowels that rang in the back of your mouth, making me want to repeat them. I let my lips and tongue silently imitate the effect, hoping Cem wouldn't notice.

At some point during the drive, the driver rolled down his window and lit a cigarette. Cem said something in a decisive tone, and he put it out, to my huge relief, as I sat behind him, directly in the smoke's path. Although I suspected Cem had done it more for himself. I could see the way his hands twitched as he watched the cigarette dangling from the driver's fingers.

I wondered if he could keep away from the smokes in Turkey. The whole country seemed to be smoking, non-stop. Half of the passengers lit up the second they got off the plane, and the other half after they'd unloaded from the airport bus, greatly easing the queues from thereon.

We got off the main motorway and travelled along the coast. Finally, the driver slowed down, turned onto a narrow driveway on the ocean side and we rolled through automatic gates.

I stared at Cem's house – an imposing piece of modern architecture made of stone and glass, accentuated by lighting that seemed appropriate for a public monument, not a residential building. Decorative iron lanterns balanced the industrial-strength spotlights. Despite the hazy morning light already brightening the scene, every artificial light blazed in full wattage.

The driver opened Cem's door, then mine. I stepped out on wobbly legs, staring at the brightly lit doorway.

"*Hoşgeldiniz*. Welcome!" Cem smiled proudly, his hand pressing lightly on my back as he guided me to the door.

It magically opened as we got closer, and I only noticed the small apron-wearing woman behind it when she repeated Cem's greeting. "*Hoşgeldiniz.*"

I tried to respond, but she stepped to one side like a shadow, and Cem led me into a wide entrance hall. He took off his shoes and I followed his example.

"Here." He handed me a pair of fluffy slippers and found a similar pair for himself and Emir. "Our mother will freak out if I let your feet get cold, especially when we tell her you have a sore throat."

He led me to a vast lounge filled with velvety furniture in the shades of deep green, warm grey and brushed chrome, lit even more abundantly than the exterior. Emir trailed in behind us, directing the driver upstairs with the bags.

A sweet, orangey scent lingered in the air. Behind a wall of glass panels serving as the fourth wall, an Olympic-size swimming pool reflected the outdoor lights. I could hardly count the number of light sources in the room, the absolute opulence of it making my chest glow. Or maybe it was him.

I felt Cem's hand on my waist, his closeness invading my senses, his presence stronger here than any other space we'd been before. He'd become one with the room, surrounding me like its walls, bathing me in its lights.

I was about to ask him if I could follow the driver to wherever he was taking my bag, when an older woman floated through one of the doorways, her dark hair in a loose bun and ample floral silk billowing around her arms. She headed straight to Emir, who kissed the back of her hand, then pressed it against his forehead. Cem was next, performing the same elaborate greeting. When she turned to me, every muscle in my body seized. Was I supposed to do the same? What if that greeting was only for family members? From the words they exchanged, I picked out one familiar one I'd heard on Cem's show. *Annem.* Mother.

I shot Cem a quick smile, my heart hammering in my throat. He gave me a subtle nod, subtly lifting his hand. So, kissing then? Turning my deer-in-headlights smile at Cem's mother, I followed the odd kissing ritual, getting a lungful of sweet, fruity perfume.

After the greeting, she held onto my shoulders and said something that sounded like a question. I smiled, trying to look like I understood, but thankfully Cem stepped in to speak for me. I recognized the name of *Burcu*. He gestured at my throat, and I smiled apologetically as if to confirm the diagnosis.

As Cem's mother focused back on her son, I pulled my phone out of my pocket. During the taxi ride, I'd figured out my New Zealand SIM card didn't work over here, but if Cem's house had wi-fi, I could at least get online and use a translator app – very discreetly, of course.

I clicked on the strongest network that popped up and handed my phone to Emir. He glanced at the empty field and quickly typed in the password. I was online. The app loaded, and as their mother turned back to me with raised eyebrows, her words appeared in English on my screen.

"Will you join us for breakfast?"

I dropped the phone lower to hide it from her view and shook my head. I was dying to find a bedroom, lock the door and collapse on any level surface. A floor would do.

Despite my gestures, she took me by the elbow and led me to a large dining room, chatting in a friendly tone. The long table was laden with food. Baskets of flatbread and colorful bowls filled with dips and sauces in a range of colors, and a large pan of something mushy and red that reminded me of Kerim's incredible meal.

A burly man with a greying beard and sickly pallor sat at the end of the table, beckoning me closer with a scowl that immediately made me think of Emir. What was I supposed to do with his hand or other body parts?

Before I had time to escalate into a full-scale panic, Emir cut in front of me and kissed his father the same way he'd kissed his mother. Relieved for the demonstration, I crossed the floor like a newborn deer and greeted him the same way. He reeked of cigarettes.

Cem held back, hovering at the doorway. Everyone swiveled to stare at him. Silence filled the room, thick and fast, as the two men glared each other. Finally, Cem's father nodded, and Cem crossed the floor. I watched their strained greeting, relieved when everyone started speaking again. It made my own silence seem less pronounced, as if I was merely within the listening phase of a conversation.

Cem's father seated me right next to him. Cem rushed to take the chair on the other side as Emir seated himself across the table. How could I digest anything with eyes tracking my every move?

I felt Cem's fingers curl around my left hand under the table. The small woman I'd met at the door appeared again, pouring tea into tulip-shaped glasses. Cem picked his glass up by the rim and raised it to his lips, taking a long sip.

I imitated his movements, filling my mouth with the strong, sweet and aromatic drink, a taste I'd forever associate with the man who held my hand. Ever since we'd left New Zealand, he hadn't gone for more than a few minutes without touching me in some way.

Cem's father began filling his plate and everyone else followed, serving me with dedication until my plate was bursting. With no hope of following the conversation, I decided I might as well eat my way through Turkey.

# CHAPTER 26

# Cem

I'd never been so grateful for a language barrier. Even though my father thought the woman sitting next to me understood Turkish, he didn't hold his tongue.

"You have no idea what we've been through because of you," he muttered as soon as he'd got one sip of tea. "I've lost a lot of business."

"They'll come back when they see him with Burcu," my mother cooed, nodding at Aria. "After the wedding."

Wedding? I swallowed but didn't say anything.

My father rolled his eyes. "The point was for you to stay out of the limelight, not to fly your girlfriend over there and create new headlines!"

Emir held up a finger. "But they're good headlines. Epic Studios hasn't dropped him yet. They're watching and waiting. Silence doesn't help. We need good publicity, fast."

"I saw the story about you dating," my mom chimed in, her eyes sparkling. "A beautiful picture."

"And right underneath, there was the other story, the one everyone still talks about." Dad sucked in a labored breath.

"It'll fade away." mom waved her hand. "Give it time."

"Only God knows how much time I have," Dad grumbled.

It was because of my money that he'd likely cling to life. I'd paid for the regular CT scans that detected the cancer. He couldn't blame me for smoking, either.

"Did you get the test results?" I asked, keeping my tone even.

"It's not small cell and it hasn't spread," my mom announced with her unbeatable optimism.

"So, it's curable?"

My father harrumphed as if he had no trust in any of that.

"There's a good chance," mom said.

"There's a chance," Dad corrected.

Was he annoyed that his deathly diagnosis wasn't that deadly after all? He'd been leaning into those dramatic statements ever since the CT scans showed a mass, making me feel responsible. Why did I always feel responsible?

"So, with a positive attitude, you'll live to a hundred." I flashed him a chipper smile.

There was more than a handful of sarcasm, but Mom smiled enthusiastically. "Yes! I've been telling him that. He's been so grumpy since your... you know."

"Since cousin Burak sent him a picture of my ass he found on the internet?"

"*Allah, Allah!* We don't have to talk that way at the table!" Mom cast a horrified look at Aria, who'd focused her energies on tasting different jams.

Fortunately, Mom interpreted her disinterest as tactfulness. "See! She's pretending she doesn't hear us."

"She knows about the pictures." I looked my mom in the eye. "Everybody does."

"You made sure of that," Dad scoffed.

My gut sizzled. "What do you mean? I didn't take the photos or post them everywhere."

"You chose to parade yourself all over the place. I gave you a job at my store, a way to earn an honest living. Maybe it's not that glamorous, selling antiques... but it's a respectable job. You *chose* to become a celebrity. And that way, everything you do is everybody's business. That's your choice." He drew a breath and tried to stifle his cough into a napkin, producing a muffled bark that somehow sounded worse than a cough.

I sighed, not wanting to process his words. Emir averted my eyes. I knew my brother didn't want the antiques gig, either –inheriting a dusty pile of old stuff that didn't sell, and he was the firstborn, poised to take over the ownership whereas I would have been running errands.

"I can't undo it even if I wanted to. Once everyone knows who you are—"

"Then you behave accordingly and keep your pants on!" He

coughed into his napkin again.

"*Allah, Allah!*" Mom shook her head.

My cheeks flamed, but I bit my tongue for mom's sake. She looked like she might well die of shame and worry if I kept provoking him.

She would have been so relieved to find out our guest didn't understand a word of Turkish. She might have even wanted to know the amazing woman that Aria really was. But I felt Emir's menacing eyes on me, demanding that I stick to the script.

My father folded his napkin and resumed eating. Despite the scathing words, I could see his mouth twitching behind his dark beard – a tell I'd known since childhood of doubts entering his mind. Everyone knew my acting income had kept the antique shop from going under. Dad didn't wish for me to work in his shop. He felt sorry for himself for whatever comments our busybody neighbors and extended family had made about my photos.

Staring at his hunched frame, my anger fizzled out, replaced by shame. I didn't want to cause my family pain, yet here I was, the crux of the worst scandal they'd ever been part of.

Yet, as I leaned into the shame, I noticed a sense of distance. There was nothing I could do to fix my mistake or argue it away. I had to accept the blame and the fallout.

I almost felt grateful for failing. Failing so spectacularly that I could look at my life like it wasn't mine, but a farce played by actors. For years, I'd tried so hard to make things okay, showering them with gifts, as if to make up for Dad's disappointment, or for my absence as the overwhelming production schedule ate up my weeks.

I'd never even considered the alternative – accepting Dad's disappointment as one of life's mysterious constants and living on my own terms.

I'd done the worst, yet here we still sat around the same dining table, my mother's fingers wrapped around her evil eye pendant as she read my father's moods, and my father staring back at us, his eyebrows drawn together into one dark and angry ridge. The weather in my house never changed.

I could see them both gearing up with reframed arguments and held up my hand. "I'm sorry. I should have considered my fame and I didn't. I'm glad you sent me to New Zealand. It was the right thing to do."

That shut them up. The silence that fell over the table was so palpable even Aria perked up. She whipped her head from side to side, trying to figure out why everyone was staring at me with their mouths open.

Then I noticed her gaze lowering down to her lap and I shifted a little closer to see what she was looking at. I saw the lines of text on her phone screen. The translator! She'd been translating our conversation.

# CHAPTER 27

My app only caught baffling snippets of dialogue.

*Gee, change your attitude.*

*…treated and prolonged its lifespan.*

*Put himself on the agenda.*

*…send me to New Zealand. Gee!*

Lost in translation, I shifted my focus back to eating, something I usually excelled at. But it turned out my appetite was no match for Turkish hospitality.

I ate until I felt like I would split at the seams. Every time I made some headway, Cem's mom offered me more and my tea glass got refilled. Finally, I took a hint from Cem and placed my teaspoon over my glass. The tea stopped flowing.

As my stomach got heavier, my head became lighter, lolling

about on my shoulders. Jet lag and a full stomach were a powerful combination.

Right when I thought I would pass out, Cem helped me up, said something to his family and escorted me out of the room.

"I'm sorry," he whispered as we got out of earshot. "You get to rest now, I promise."

"That's okay." I leaned half of my weight against his chest as we walked.

"Do I need to carry you?"

Ugh. I wanted him to carry me. From now on, I'd dream about being carried by him. *Thank you for this new craving.*

"Gee," I muttered.

"Gee?"

"It's what you said a lot at the table, according to the translator. It was like a word you repeat... *Allah*?"

Cem chuckled. "*Allah, Allah.* It's like... oh my God, or my goodness."

"Or geeee..." I stretched the word, dissolving into such tired, uncontrollable giggles I nearly lost my footing and Cem had to steer me toward the stairs.

"I'll add it to my everyday vocabulary if it makes you that happy."

He took me up a curved staircase to another sitting room, which opened out to a wide balcony overlooking the marina. I counted at least three luxury yachts. A steady stream of dog walkers and joggers pounded the concrete walkway. So many people, everywhere. Across the strip of ocean, in the distance, the city continued.

"Is that the Asian side?" I asked, blinking against the daylight. My brain disagreed with the time of day, yet the light felt hazy and soft, not like the daylight back home. Filtered through layers of smoke, maybe.

"Yes. That's the bridge we drove across." He pointed to my right. "And here's the bedroom."

He opened the door and I gasped. The room was the size of my entire apartment back home. I peeked into the massive marble ensuite, gaping at the freestanding bathtub and two showers, then let my gaze roam across the king bed with a studded velvet headboard and embroidered cushions arranged across a silky, terracotta bed spread. The colors of spices. Curcumin. Chili. Cinnamon. Ginger. Everything in Cem's house brought tastes on my tongue. Including him.

"What's behind there?" I pointed at another door by the bed.

"A closet."

Cem dutifully opened the door and I peered into the generous walk-in wardrobe filled with suits, shirts and pants.

"It's the temple of shiny shirts!" I grinned, brushing the smooth fabrics.

Cem grabbed me by the wrist. "Stop it! You'll make them greasy." His glare lacked commitment, but his tight grip delivered the message. Maybe not the right message, but the sheer force of it shot right to my core.

"It's not my fault your breakfast was half finger food," I grumbled, walking into the ensuite to wash my hands.

"You didn't like it?"

I stepped out of the bathroom and found him looking concerned. I smiled. "I loved it." I couldn't lie to him.

"Good." Cem walked me to the bed and sat me down. I sunk into the soft mattress and couldn't resist falling on my back. So soft. "This is the world's most comfortable bed."

I closed my eyes and let out a deep sigh. The exhaustion was trying to pull me under but being able to speak freely and be myself felt as heavenly as the bed and part of me wanted to fight a moment longer, to stay with him.

Cem threw himself on the bed next to me. "It cost a fortune. Worth it, though."

He turned to look at me and I met his gaze, sleepy and victorious. He'd done it. He'd got me into his bed. Probably not in the way he'd envisioned, but it was the kind of bed that inspired commitment. If any of my ex-boyfriends had slept on something like this, I would have quietly moved in. Locked *them* out, maybe, but I would have kept the bed.

I rolled over, relishing how my shoulder sank in without the crunchy rearranging of bones my own mattress delivered. "Can I stay here for the rest of this trip?" I mumbled into a maroon cushion.

"Only if I get to do the same."

"Deal. I wouldn't even notice you there." I drew a deep, luxurious breath and released it, sinking deeper into the soft fabric.

"I wish I could say the same." He rolled over to his side with his elbow propped, head leaning on hand. Poised to stare at me. I felt his other hand on my forearm, sending a flurry of confused signals that fought with the ones entailing sleep.

I closed my eyes, my exhaustion mixing with giddiness. I already knew I'd give in, eventually. I'd let him peel away my defenses, one by one, along with my clothing, no matter how unceremoniously he'd dump me after I'd carried out my wordless human prop duties in this strange land.

I surrender, I thought to myself. And that was the last thing I remembered.

CHAPTER 28

I woke up, rather unpleasantly, to Emir's stern face hovering over me.

"*Allah, Allah!* Don't sneak up like that!" I sandwiched my head between the pillows to block him out.

"We need to get you out of here."

Aria stirred next to me. After a moment, her head popped up from behind a throw pillow. She'd been hiding behind them. Why did I have so many throw pillows? Damn interior designers.

"What are you talking about?" she asked.

Emir switched to English. "We have to move you somewhere more private before Mom gets too involved. I caught her rewatching *Aşkta Şanslı*. She wants to contact Burcu's family and invite them over. I told her Burcu has a doctor's appointment and Cem has to visit Ankara."

"So, where're we going?" Aria blinked and rubbed her eyes.

"I made a reservation in Bursa tonight."

"Where's Bursa?" Aria asked, scrambling out of bed, smoothing her slacks and T-shirt, which were in no danger of getting wrinkled. In fact, the only piece of clothing I'd seen on her that probably required ironing was the funny green jumpsuit that would forever squat in my brain.

Emir's voice scratched my nerves. "Bursa is far enough that it's quiet, but not too far, since you're coming back for the weekend. We need to do a public outing on Saturday. I've got it all planned."

I sat up, rubbing my eyes, then my entire face, trying to regain some level of functionality. Unlike Aria's, my designer shirt had deep creases from sleeping. Wearing shiny clothes felt more natural in Istanbul but missed the comfort of the outfit Aria had bought me. I missed the freedom of New Zealand.

Emir pointed at our suitcases, still upright and unopened by the door. "You need to pack light. And get changed."

Everything he said made sense, but his presence bugged me. Especially the way he'd walked in without knocking, as if there couldn't possibly be any reason for privacy. Was it because he trusted me to stick with the plan, or because he was an ass? I could never really tell.

I shook my head, following Aria's example of opening my suitcase on the bed. She grabbed her toothbrush and retreated to the bathroom to brush her teeth. Again, I followed her example, letting Emir stand there, shifting his weight from side to side, looking increasingly annoyed.

With a minty fresh mouth, I returned to my suitcase and took out Mom's presents, handing them to Emir. "Can you deliver these?"

Aria joined us and picked up the bottle of honey I was holding, her eyes huge. "This is UMF twenty-five!"

"What does that mean?"

"It's like the rarest superfood on the planet."

I shrugged. "I picked those up for my mom."

Her forehead wrinkled. "This stuff fights bacteria. Like, serious, antibiotic-resistant bacteria. This level of purity would be ridiculously expensive."

I couldn't remember how much I'd paid for it. I probably hadn't considered that at all. I felt Emir's eyes on my back but fought the urge to turn around.

"What do you mean by ridiculously expensive?" My brother asked, an edge to his voice.

"Well, Cem knows. He bought it." Aria stared at me in confusion.

"I... didn't look at the prices." I heaved the rest of my suitcase contents on the bed for the cleaners to deal with. It was probably dirty anyway. "What are we talking about, thousands?"

Aria blushed, handing the honey to Emir. "No, like a hundred dollars, but we're talking about two hundred grams of honey, so I think it's ridiculous."

I let out a sigh of relief and noticed Emir doing the same. "Yeah, absolutely. I wish I could have you explain the health benefits to Mom. She'd be over the moon."

As soon as I said it, I felt the pain. Why wasn't she here as her amazing self, as a guest of honor? My mother would love her. She'd be shocked I was seeing someone who lived so far away, but she'd probably double down on trying to win her over, to make sure she loved our country and never left. We could double team her. I turned to Emir, who read my mind.

"Don't even think about telling her," he hissed. "If Mom finds out, everyone finds out."

My mother couldn't keep secrets, not even the small, fun ones. She ruined every surprise party, looking like the cat who got the cream. It only took a couple of clever questions from someone like Emir, who hated surprises, to bring it all out. Still, I couldn't help my flare of anger.

"Get out." I pointed at the door, indicating that either he move or I'd remove him. "We'll pack up and shower and meet you outside."

Emir took the gifts and left, and I locked the door behind him, enjoying the definitive 'click' of the bolt sliding into its slot.

"What's wrong? Why are you so angry?" Aria asked, taking a step forward.

"I just... wish things were different." I sighed, looking at her tiny suitcase on the bed. She'd already closed it, after removing a box of chocolates. I took her hands in mine and held tight, drawing strength from the touch. "I'm so happy you're here, but I never considered how weird it would feel. I wish you were here as yourself. You deserve better than this."

She peered at me through her lashes. "I don't deserve anything. I haven't done anything yet. Let's go with the plan, see if I can actually help you, and if anyone believes I'm Burcu... and if I manage to be of some use, then you can buy me a present." She grinned and my heart squeezed.

"Deal."

"But no hundred-dollar honey."

"Okay."

"Or anything else that costs like crazy, especially if it tastes or works the same as the ten-dollar alternative. You know those really expensive pens rich people gift to each other?"

I laughed at her expression. I had a couple of the ones she was talking about at the back of my closet.

She gave me a hint of a smile, but her brows drew together. "I've never understood that. Because you can't use a pen like that, not unless it's to sign a contract on world peace. So, in the end, you get less use out of it than from a regular pen. What's the point?"

She looked so adorably indignant I couldn't resist. "Well, I've used my diamond-studded Montblanc to sign a few arms and stomachs. And a boob, once. It was... smooth."

"The pen or the boob?" She glared at me.

"Um, both."

She shook her head. "You're an ass."

I wrapped my hands around her lower back, bringing her closer. "I know. I can tell that you love me, though. Admit it."

She shook her head again. Slowly. Deliberately. But her fingers played with the buttons of my shirt and her breath turned shallow. I could feel her arousal. She held back, but her body craved mine like I craved her. Neither of us could hide it.

I glanced at the locked door. We were alone. I'd never had her like this, at my mercy. A hurricane of thoughts whirled through my mind, images of what I could do, how she might react. Aria, within my grasp.

Before I knew it, my mouth was on hers, tasting the sweet, minty flavor. She kissed me back, but her spine tightened under my hands.

I pulled back an inch and held my breath, our lips almost touching, breath mixing in hot, minty gusts. If she didn't want me, I had to back down. I had to. This was like staring at a piece of chocolate cake on the table. If you couldn't eat it, you didn't bring it into the house to torture yourself. What was I doing?

"Cem," she whispered. "I'm not strong enough to resist you."

"Why do you have to resist me?" I stole another kiss and retreated again, but not far.

"Because you'll break my heart." She lifted her eyes at me, and I saw it all. The fear. The longing.

I wanted to fix it. I desperately wanted to change everything that stood in our way, but I couldn't. My life wasn't mine. I felt like a zoo animal, finally becoming aware of my captivity. I wanted to smash every wall.

"I probably will," I said, reluctantly letting go of her. "I don't want to, but... You're right. I come with baggage."

I glanced at our suitcases; her tiny carry-on dwarfed by my 30-inch titanium luggage. It seemed to perfectly illustrate my point.

Aria followed my gaze. "The size of my suitcase in no way correlates with my emotional baggage. I travel light because I don't own anything worth dragging across the world."

"I don't care about the stuff. You know that, right? I care about you."

"Yet, you'll break my heart."

"I'm trying to be honest. I come with all this mess. It's... complicated. My life is complicated. You said you wanted to stop chasing those dreams. I made fun of you, and I still think you're overreacting... looking at life through this twisted lens. But so am I. We all are."

I wedged my hands into my pockets. I wouldn't touch her again. She deserved better. Better than anything I could give her. "Maybe I don't agree with your thinking, but I understand. You want off the rollercoaster. Higher highs and lower lows. It's tiring. And now I've roped you into my crap. As soon as we arrived, I knew this was wrong. This is not how I wanted to introduce you to my family, my country. I want you to be here as... you. As mine." I swallowed, the lump of regret in my throat ballooning like dough.

"We can't."

"I know. Maybe it's all too messy to ever work out, and maybe that means I'll break your heart, whether I want to or not. But you should know one thing."

She stared at me, still like a statue. "What?"

"Mine will break, too."

I watched her chest rise and fall as she studied my eyes, unsure. I waited a long time, observing her face, a woman at war with herself. Finally, she spoke. "Okay, then."

"Okay, what?"

She took a step closer, placing her hands on my chest. "Let's break our hearts."

I couldn't take my eyes off hers. They held me like a single flame in a dark room. Full of courage and hunger.

For a second, I hesitated. This wasn't enough, but I couldn't back down. Not with that mango-vanilla scent blurring my thoughts and those gusts of heavy breath escaping through her parted lips. Guileless. Surrendering. She'd captured me in the web of my own making and all I could do was claim her.

Her fingers tightened around my shirt fabric. There was no fight. No games. Only need. The delectable, hot sensation of her lips melting against mine, her tongue tasting me, instantly zapping every part of my body to attention. All I could think of was that fire between us and how it would swallow me whole.

"Aria," I gasped, pushing her backwards until I had her pinned against the wall, deliciously trapped between the plaster board and my hard cock. "I can't stop. You have to stop me."

"Don't you dare stop," she hissed, eyes blazing.

I peeled off her T-shirt, exposing a white, lacy bra. It probably had a clasp of sorts, but I couldn't be bothered looking for one. It was a cheap and sorry piece of cloth, and I wanted something better for her. With one brisk motion, I ripped the thing in half. The sound it gave matched my mood. Savage. Hungry. Frustrated.

# CHAPTER 29

The sound of my bra tearing should have brought me back to reality, but I must have left my brain on one of the other continents. Later, I'd examine the reasons, the black box of Aria's poor decision making, because I knew I wouldn't stop him. Not now, not ever.

"You don't have a monopoly on misbehaving." I curled my fingers through the gap between his shirt buttons.

Yanking my hands apart, I sent the buttons flying, exposing those movie star abs I hadn't seen nearly enough of. His shiny shirt probably cost ten times as much as my bra, but he didn't seem to mind, grinning at me like he wanted me to destroy more than his shirt.

Freed from clothing, my skin pebbled and nipples pinched. His gaze fell on them, so delightfully drunken that I swear I felt it on my skin before he touched me, like a crackle of electricity before the zap. When his mouth closed on the peak of one breast, the sharp sensation stole my breath.

Had I really forgotten how it felt, or had it never really felt like this? Every suck turned into a starburst that travelled through me as if carried by one single nerve, delivering the sensation straight to the bundle between my legs. I'd never felt so wired and connected, so driven by need.

"Cem. Oh my God, Cem." My voice escaped as a breathy whisper and my back arched against the wall as his hands found my hips, thumbs sinking into the soft hollow inside my pelvic bones.

Pinned between him and the wall, almost suspended in air by his strong grip, took my excitement to another level. What I thought I knew about sex was that I preferred comfort and familiarity. I could only come when on top, on my own terms. But every touch from Cem took me further from the familiar territory and to my surprise, my body was there for it.

"So fucking hot." His breath blazed against my skin as his mouth trailed up to my face. "There's nothing hotter than a woman who's turned on. There's nothing hotter than... you." He nuzzled into my neck to draw a deep breath like he was trying to inhale me. That sound sent more shivers through me, and my muscles seized as his hand slid under the waistband of my slacks, discovering a pair of soaked panties.

I stifled a yelp as his fingers brushed me. Well, almost stifled. Encouraged by my sounds, he kissed my neck as his fingers worked between my thighs with a mix of skill and desperate fervor. I wanted him closer, all over my skin, but I was wearing twenty hours of airplane cabin.

"I need a shower," I panted. "Come with me?"

He smirked and grabbed me from behind my knees. I clung around his neck as he carried me to the bathroom. I'm being carried by Cem, my brain catalogued, the details so blurry I doubted I'd remember much of it later. Only the overwhelming sensation. The desire vibrating through me.

He turned on the shower as we undressed, then guided me under the stream. The water caressed my feverish skin and I closed my eyes, letting the layers of travel wash away.

When I opened my eyes, my stomach flipped. Cem stood in front of me, fully naked. Fully... large. Without thinking, my fingers wrapped around him, feeling the warm pulse under the taut, wet skin. So beautiful I wanted to cry. He growled at my touch and stood under the showerhead, shielding me like an umbrella, his dark curls straightening as they soaked. "Oh, God. Aria."

I gave him a couple of strong strokes, enjoying the feeling of power, until he removed my hand and pushed me against the patterned, blue tile. Cool, but not cold. The mixture of hot and cold made me think of the waterfall. Cem's mouth explored mine, our tongues swirling as his fingers slipped between my legs. My lungs flattened as he pushed deeper, the palm of his hand rubbing against my swollen flesh. The sound of running water and his hungry kiss muffled my cry.

"Before you break my heart," I rasped. "Will you make me come?"

His voice rumbled through me. "I'll do anything. I told you."

That's when I knew why I'd brought him here. "I don't want you to be with me like you are with… everyone else. I want you to remember me." At least we weren't in bed, I thought.

His brown eyes tracked mine, full of need and something else. "I won't have to remember. I'll keep you so you can remind me every day." The tenderness in his voice made my heart squeeze.

I had to focus on the physical sensation. "Please, Cem."

I laid my hand on his shoulder, guiding him lower. He didn't resist, trailing his tongue all the way to where I needed it. There it was. What I craved. The moment his mouth landed on me, my arms spread wide along the wet tile and all thoughts vanished. "Yes!"

I expected him to get bored and move on to something else, but Cem ate me like he hadn't been fed in weeks, with long, deliberate strokes and little licks.

"Don't stop," I uttered, on the cusp of losing it.

I'd take this souvenir. The movie star orgasm. My legs shook from the effort of holding myself upright. They'd give in, I knew it, but I needed this. The pressure built in my belly, and everything pooled down. Everything in me zeroed in on that point of contact. Fire and ice. Lava and hundred-dollar honey. All pouring through me, uncontrollably. I was officially a lost cause. If this was a free sample, I was already hooked on whatever he was selling, for life.

"Come, Aria," he grunted, applying more pressure.

My vision burst with thousands of stars and my body arched against the cool tiles. I unraveled, crying out louder than I ever intended, my body taking over, pulsing with waves of pleasure until my knees buckled and he caught me.

"That was amazing." I felt his smile against my skin. "But please don't pass out. I need you."

I hung from his neck until I found balance, my feet against the floor, the delicious sensations still throbbing between my legs, making every cell vibrate.

He needed me.

I didn't have a routine. I didn't offer blowjobs for birthday presents or rewards for housework. I'd never really wanted to. But now I needed to see him to lose control, just like me.

I crouched down and closed my mouth around him.

Cem. Cem. His name filled my mind as he filled my mouth, hard and perfect. I tightened my fists around his thick shaft and moved, listening to his heavy gasps rising above the sound of the shower. He was mine. In this moment, he was mine and couldn't think of anyone or anything else.

He mumbled something in Turkish, a ramble of throaty consonants that sounded dirtier than anything I could imagine in English. His fingers sunk into my wet hair, and I understood. More. Faster. I matched my pace with his breath, feeling a delicious pull in the bottom of my belly as I sensed him getting closer.

He made a funny sound when he came, something between pain and pleasure. I held on for as long as I could, then I discreetly spit into the drain, hoping he wasn't offended. I wasn't a professional.

My arms started to shiver so I stood and stepped under the shower. Cem leaned against the wall, eyes closed. Finally, he ran his hand over his face and opened them. "Well, that was new."

"What, a blow job in the shower?"

He laughed. "I don't mean that. Although, it was the first time in this shower."

I wiped the water from my eyes to see him clearly. "I thought you'd tried everything."

"Why would you think that?"

"I don't know. Access?"

"You think I've done every woman I've had access to, in every location I've had access to?" He looked blurry behind the water droplets, but I detected the hurt in his voice.

I tried to lighten my tone. "Yeah, nah. That'd be in the millions, right?"

"Are you flattering me or judging me?" He stared at me, water dripping down from his beard, the hard angles of his muscles gleaming under the shower mist, looking so bloody perfect. Yet, I had to look deeper, at the human beneath.

I sighed. "I think I'm... misjudging you."

He nodded, his gaze dipping down at my feet.

"I'm sorry," I added quietly.

Feeling like I wanted to hide, I turned to search the in-built shelves for shampoo. He pushed himself off the wall, picked up a pink bottle and handed it to me.

"Thank you," I muttered, shampooing my hair. The pink stuff smelled amazing.

He shifted behind me, running his fingers through my wet hair until the shampoo rinsed out, his touch unbearably gentle. Reverent, slow strokes that made me tremble like an internal earthquake. More intimate than anything we'd just done. My heart lurched and I took a deep breath.

"Why haven't you done this before?" I asked. "Your bathroom is practically built for... um... steamy encounters." I found the pair for the pink bottle that said conditioner and moved onto that. "Let me guess," I continued breathlessly. "They all spread their legs before they ever make it here?"

I had to be crass. I had to shake the weird mood his soft touch had spread down my back, its sticky tendrils sneaking into my heart.

I heard his heavy exhale as he let go of my hair and grabbed a bottle of shower gel. I busied myself with applying and rinsing the conditioner. When I risked another glance at him, I caught him leaning languidly on the wall, looking like a Mediterranean god covered in suds, his eyes all dark thunder. "I never brought anyone up here."

Blood whooshed in my ears. I stepped out of the shower and found a towel on a shelf. In fact, I found fifteen towels, all stacked so neatly they must have been measured with a ruler. With shaking hands, I pulled down the remaining fourteen with my one, scattering them across the floor.

"I'm sorry." I kneeled down to gather them, feeling naked for the first time since I'd discarded my pants on the bathroom floor.

"Stop, Aria. It's fine." Cem dropped a towel on my shoulders and crouched next to me, his skin still soapy and slick.

I could have an affair with him, collect memories and make this special for me. *For me*. But it couldn't be special for him. I'd remain a tiny blip on his radar. He wouldn't remember me.

I had convinced myself of that, and it let me off the hook. I couldn't really break his heart. Not in a million years.

"Are you okay?" He rubbed the towel against my skin like he'd rescued me from drowning.

"Yeah, nah. I just find it hard to believe. That I'd be... the first one. I'm never—"

"You're the one and only." He kissed my neck, then my ear, his hot breath flowing straight into my heart. "And there are so many firsts I want to experience with you. If I can stop you from running away. If I can somehow stop you from... dismissing us."

I heard the pain in his voice, but I couldn't believe it. He was an actor. A great actor.

"I've seen a lot of pictures of you with gorgeous women. Are you telling me you don't sleep with them?"

He chuckled. "I'm not celibate, but I've never brought anyone home. Why would I? They'd bump into my parents, and you've seen where that leads. I'd be meeting their parents and so on."

"And you don't want to get serious," I finished for him, resuming my towel-folding. I couldn't get them as neat and tidy as they'd been, no matter what I tried.

When I restarted the folding for the third time, Cem yanked the towel from me.

"You know what I think?" he said, expertly folding the towel and sliding it on the shelf. "I think you're hellbent on misjudging me because then you'll have an excuse not to take this seriously."

His words stung a little, but I still had a half a leg to stand on.

"I don't believe everything I read online, but it doesn't look like you've been serious with anyone. They call you a playboy."

Cem's eyebrows sailed up. "I don't want to get serious with the wrong person. Do you? How about that neighbor who butlers for your parents? Do you want to get serious with him?"

"No," I admitted. "But I'm not sleeping with him, either."

He stood up and heaved the rest of the towels into a laundry basket. "You might, one day. When you're lonely enough. Or maybe you're stronger than me, I don't know. I'm weak. What we did…" He peered over his shoulder at our crime scene. "I've thought about that… about so many things I wanted to do to you… since the moment we met. I thought if I had sex with you, I could think clearly for a second."

I got up, too, wrapping the towel tighter around myself, watching those incredible muscles flex as he rinsed himself under the shower.

He turned off the water and grabbed the towel he'd just neatly folded, securing it around his waist.

"Did it work?" I asked. "Can you think clearly right now?"

His eyes glimmered with an emotion I couldn't quite interpret. "All I can think is that I want more, but I won't."

"Won't what?"

"I won't touch you again until you say it."

"Say what?" My gut wobbled and I hugged myself to stop from visibly shaking.

He closed the distance between us and placed his lips on mine, giving me a long, deliberate kiss. Heat rushed through me, sending more blood to where half of it was still residing, making me throb. What was he doing to me?

Finally, he released my mouth, like blowing out a candle, leaving me a puddle of liquid stearin. "Tell me we have something real. That it's not all in my head, Aria." The demand in his voice, the sheer will it carried, was almost enough to bend reality. Almost.

Had I continued standing right there, within the atmosphere of warmth and faith that radiated from him like hot shower steam, I would have told him anything. I would have said anything to stay.

But reality had a way of pounding through.

"It's been forty minutes! The driver's waiting!" Emir's booming voice effortlessly cut through two doors. Even his door-knocking sounded fist-based.

"He sounds pissed off," I whispered.

Cem shrugged. "When does he not?"

"What if he finds out about us?"

"What is there to find out?" Cem shot me a demanding look, which quickly turned into a pout.

"I don't know." I hugged the towel tighter around myself. I'd already fallen for him, hard, but how could I tell him when I didn't see a future. I couldn't imagine a reality where the two of us ever shared a life, a home, or even a country. I could fall for him all I wanted, but it didn't magically change reality.

"I've never wanted anyone like this, Cem. But you know, as well as I do, that we can't... build on this."

"Why?"

"Because I'm here to do a job, and I still intend to do it. I won't let you throw away your career."

"I don't care—"

"Yes, you do!" I stared him down, flames in my belly. "I've never had a chance like the one you have. If you throw this away, I'll be mad at you forever."

"Forever, huh?"

"Yep." I huffed.

"You'd give me forever?" His mouth curved into an adorable smirk.

"Get ready!" I ordered, rushing into the bedroom.

My heart would shatter into a million pieces, but I wouldn't let him fail. Not because of me.

Cem followed me, still distractingly naked. "I'll get ready, but we're not going with Emir's stupid plan. We're going with mine."

# CHAPTER 30

When the lights of Istanbul faded and darkness engulfed our car, I sighed with relief. Convincing Emir to stay back had taken every ounce of my charm (and restraint) but he'd finally agreed to let us drive to Bursa without him. I'd slipped Tarik, my driver, the new address and he'd simply nodded. He knew where his paycheck came from.

"What's in Bursa?" Aria asked, fiddling with the hem of her shirt. She'd dressed in a pair of jean shorts and a loose tee, exactly as I remembered her from our first meeting, fresh and sexy in that half-accidental way. Except, now I'd seen under that shirt, and no amount of loose-fitting cotton could distract me from the curve of her chest. I knew what was underneath, and I was desperate for more.

"We're not going to Bursa. I'm taking you to my boat and Tarik won't tell a soul, right?"

Tarik recognized his name and gave me a quick glance, most likely wondering what I was on about. He didn't speak much English, which was probably for the best. I'd already sworn him to secrecy.

I laced my fingers with Aria's, tightening my fist. I wanted to steal her away, if only for two nights. I craved more time with her, on my own terms. Surely it made no difference to Emir where we went, as long as we didn't stay in my house and kept out of sight. Especially if he didn't know about it.

My boat wasn't huge, but it was well equipped. Most importantly, it was moored at a small marina by the Black Sea, well outside of the city. My father had planned on taking it on a longer cruise during the summer. Maybe he still was. But he'd never been that outdoorsy and being ill, he'd most likely opt for a cruise ship with food and entertainment. I wasn't big on sailing, either, but I wanted to take Aria to somewhere that was mine. My lair. Not a random hotel Emir had picked for maximum privacy.

The paparazzi knew the location of the boat, which is why Emir would have never suggested it, but as we arrived at the dark and quiet marina, I felt good about my decision. I trusted Tarik and I hadn't noticed anyone following us.

"Where are we?" Aria asked as we unloaded our bags on the footpath near the dock.

I gestured at the dark ocean. "Behold, the Sea of Amazing."

Her eyes lit up. "Are we going sailing?"

"No, sorry. I think that might be too noticeable, but we can hide on the boat, here in the marina. Tarik will bring us some supplies."

Aria's face brightened. "I love that! Much better than a hotel."

My chest glowed from her approval, as I led her down the dock to my solar-powered, long-range cruiser. Its fifty-foot frame was dwarfed by a Russian oligarch's yacht. I'd always hated the floating money bag, but now it almost worked as a privacy screen, hiding my boat in its shadow.

Tarik had driven away to buy us food. I hoped he wouldn't attract any attention – or call Emir.

"It's a yacht!" Aria stared at the boat in reverence.

I had to double-check she wasn't looking at the oligarch's vessel. "Nope. That one's a yacht." I pointed at the monstrosity.

Aria glanced at it, then turned back to my boat. "Is it really yours?"

I lowered my voice. "No, we're going to break in. How good are you with locks?"

The fleeting shock on her face was so rewarding I didn't regret my stupid joke, not even after she punched me in the arm. My insides hummed and a stupid grin hung on my face. I knew she could take it as well as she could dish it out. Like hanging out with a friend, being myself. The thought startled me. Had I really never been myself with a woman before?

I helped Aria onboard and lifted our bags on the deck, producing the key from my jeans pocket. As I opened the door, countless fragmented memories flooded my mind. This is where I'd brought my dates. I remembered the cocktail of emotions on the doorstep

– the awkwardness, expectations, desire, the pinch of shame.

This time felt different, though. The desire was there, stronger than ever, but I didn't feel like I was doing anything wrong. I wasn't playing a game of saying-the-right-thing-to-get-her-naked. I didn't have an exit strategy. I only wanted to get her inside and keep her.

I smiled when I noticed Aria removing her sneakers at the doorway.

To be safe, I didn't turn on any lights and we relied on the distant glow of the marina and the full moon to fumble our way inside.

The interior had been cleaned since the last party. A faint scent of lemon lingered in the air. Must have been my mother. I spotted one of her romance novels on the coffee table. Aria picked it up, tilted it toward the light and smiled at the passionately embracing couple on the cover.

"It's not mine."

"There's no shame in reading romance."

"Of course not, but it's still not mine, so don't ask me if it's any good. My mom comes here to read. Or to hide from dad and us, I'm not sure." Leaving the bags by the hull stairs, I led us through the boat to the kitchen and dining area, flicking on a small light. The kitchen gave to the ocean side, extending out to a deck shielded by the neighboring yacht. Nobody would see us if we spent time on that side, even during the day.

The cupboards were bare, but I found a bottle of champagne in the fridge. "Sorry, there's no food until Tarik comes back, but we can always start with this."

Aria sat at the dining table, leaning her elbows against it. The full moon behind the angled windows gave her a silvery silhouette. "Sure. Although my head's already spinning. Must be the jet lag."

"Must be." I poured two glasses. "My head's been spinning since I met you, but I've also had non-stop jet lag, so it's hard to say." I kept my smile cheeky, despite everything welling inside.

"Ah, that's a shame, isn't it? It would have been quite romantic, otherwise. I've never made anyone's head spin."

She was joking in her usual style, but I couldn't help the burst of emotion fighting out of me. I handed her the champagne glass and sat across the table. How could I make her see? "You make me dizzy all the time, Aria. Maybe that's why I had to bring you here. I can't stand sharing you with the world, with Emir and his plans... my family, the paparazzi... Can we forget about them all? Can we pretend I brought you to Istanbul just to be with me?"

I pushed my glass to the side and grabbed her hands across the table.

Her smile was tinged with pain. "Oh God, Cem. What are you doing to me?"

"What am I doing to you?"

"You're seducing me, and it's not fair. You're making me feel things I can't afford to feel."

"Why not? We don't have to break each other's hearts. Not really." I needed her to believe me, to help me believe my own words.

"Cem. We're hiding on your boat to even be together. These are stolen moments." She tilted her head, her eyes welling. "Don't get me wrong, I love being with you. I can't resist you but don't give me false hope. I can't handle it."

A teardrop in the corner of her eye caught moonlight and my chest contracted. I let her take another swig of her champagne before I pulled her up to stand and held her close, moving us a couple of steps so I could reach the remote control for the sound system. I flipped through radio stations until I found a mellow song, keeping the volume so low it wouldn't be heard from the outside. I swayed us to the music, gently leading us right under the angled window and the starry sky behind it.

"Have you noticed?" I asked.

"Noticed what?"

"That we had sex and I'm not losing interest in you. In fact, I've never wanted you more."

She pulled away to look at me, her eyes comically huge. "*Allah, Allah!* There's not enough evidence. Wanting more sex doesn't prove anything."

"What does?"

She made a small, sad sound. "I don't know."

"I'll bring you the proof. You'll see." I bent down to taste her lips. I wouldn't go any further, I promised myself, not until she told me what I needed to hear. That we did have a future, one that we could claim. Somewhere, beyond all the chaos surrounding us, she'd be mine.

She matched my hunger with fire, dipping her head back as her tongue met mine. I momentarily forgot my 2-second-old promise and lifted her onto the edge of the table, leaning against her. A ragged moan released from her mouth, harmonizing with my own guttural sounds. I couldn't control myself around her, and that's why I really shouldn't have made any promises. My hands were getting ahead of my brain, and her shower-fresh scent, mixed with something not-so-innocent, probably releasing from both of our skins, already had me achingly hard.

She shifted against my cock and smiled. Victorious. Teasing. Losing the last of my cool, I ripped off her T-shirt. Its seam gave a tearing sound.

"Are you going to destroy all my clothes?" she asked, panting.

I shut her up with my mouth, our tongues now dancing like our feet had, too close and desperate to properly move. I didn't want any distance between us. My mouth trailed down her neck and reached her bra. Another simple cotton piece. Before I could decide what to do with it, she unhooked it from the back and tossed it to the floor. "It's my last one. No caveman moves, please."

I smiled, finding the perfect peaks of her breasts, sucking and licking like she was an ice cream melting in the sun. She moaned, opening her knees wider, and I touched her. I thought I was teasing her, but it was likely the other way around.

"I want you, Cem. Now, please."

"Aria," I whispered, gathering what was left of my resolve. "I'm desperate for you, but I need you to say it."

# CHAPTER 31

# Aria

My entire body throbbed, slick and hot, and he pulled away, shooting me that sad and determined look I'd seen before. The one I had no response to. No solution. Because of course I loved him. I'd always love him. I'd never been this hopelessly and utterly owned by someone.

Yet I knew this love couldn't be counted on. It was the kind that flew away and left you devastated. People who were destined for greater things always took off to greater heights, leaving me behind.

"Don't stop," I pleaded as the throb between my thighs turned into an ache. "I need you."

"Let's go," he said, taking my hand.

I hopped off the table and followed him through the boat to

where our bags sat next to the stairs leading to the second level. I trailed behind as he carried our luggage to the small bedroom on top. Behind it, through an open doorway, I saw the cockpit. "Isn't the bedroom usually below the deck?"

"If it was, we'd miss out on the stars." He pointed at the large skylight above the bed.

The freakishly bright full moon I'd noticed earlier had climbed higher, casting its glow on the white sheets. I threw myself across the bed to take in the view. For all the big city light pollution, the stars still winked at me, sprinkled around that cheesy moon. "Which one of us is going to turn into a werewolf, do you think?"

Cem stretched out next to me, his hands behind his head. "I'm already transitioning."

I laughed, rolling over to my side, head propped by an elbow. "Please, expand."

"Heightened sense of smell. Craving for meat. A hard-on."

I giggled. "I don't think that's a symptom. And I have that too."

"You're killing me, Aria!" He groaned. "I might have to take a cold shower. Unless you're willing to admit the depth of your feelings for me."

I opened my suitcase to find a T-shirt. I could feel his eyes following my every move, his breath shallow.

I hid inside the loosest shirt I owned, one that was good for one thing only – sleeping in comfort. "Feelings are overrated, anyway." I yawned, letting my head sink into the soft pillow. "What if we did fall in love and moved in together and then you found out I'm always behind with my laundry? Or I found out you put empty milk containers back in the fridge? What if all the petty things of daily life eventually eat away at us until there's nothing left?"

His bubbly laugh shook the bed. "I love your optimism."

"I'm a realist," I argued. "I don't think the glass is half full or half empty. It's at 50 percent capacity."

"No! You think the glass is fully empty and possibly so cracked it can't hold any liquid." He cast me a smug smile.

I whipped a pillow at his face. "And you think the glass may spontaneously overflow, right? Because life is full of miracles."

"Why not?" He laughed, returning the pillow by whacking it onto my stomach, then rolled over to land directly on top of it, pinning me between the soft layers, his face an inch from mine.

Oh. The pressure.

His brown eyes bore into mine, making my heart thump in my throat. "You being here is a miracle." He bent down to kiss my nose. "Besides, I pay other people to deal with milk and laundry."

"What a charmed life." My nose tingled. I couldn't stop smiling.

"We can have any kind of life we want. Anything you want."

"Would you give it all up to do laundry and buy milk with me?" The words tumbled out before I could catch them. Examine them. Cancel them. Because they held a truth I had to hide.

Cem frowned. "Is that what you want?"

I shook my head. "It's a theoretical question. Nobody would give up what you have. The money. The opportunities... Of course not."

He froze for a moment, his forehead wrinkled, staring at something to my side, then rolled back onto his side of the bed, releasing a deep sigh that turned into a yawn. I yawned, too.

"I'm sorry. I think the jet lag is catching up with me again."

"Me, too."

I didn't remember falling asleep, but it must have happened quickly. Werewolves and laundry piles featured in a restless dream that lingered when I woke up to the brilliant sunshine. Midday sunshine. This jet lag was going to be a killer.

Sleeping under a skylight felt a lot like sleeping outside, except for the lack of wind. I climbed out from underneath a blanket I didn't remember covering myself with, noting Cem's muscular arm strewn across my pillow. I'd been sleeping on his arm.

I left him sleeping and tiptoed downstairs. Tarik must have sneaked in while we slept since the fridge was stocked with every grocery item imaginable. I popped two slices of bread in the toaster and fried a couple of eggs.

I eyed the Turkish tea kettle, which looked like two kettles stacked on top of each other. I'd already failed at making him tea and didn't want to relive the embarrassment, so I turned my attention to the fancy coffee maker. The digital screen guided me through endless steps: Empty the drip tray – water tank almost empty – insufficient beans, until it relented and produced a small espresso. By the time I finished making the second one, Cem appeared, his bed hair brushing the doorframe as he entered the kitchen in his boxer shorts.

"Put some clothes on or I'll have to ogle you," I warned, handing him the coffee.

"Ogle away." A gorgeous grin lit up his face as he stared at me over the rim of his coffee, muscles on his torso rippling as he swallowed.

"Do you even drink coffee?" I asked. "I don't know how to use the tea kettle."

"I'll show you one day." His eyes still on me, he took a sip of the coffee and winced. "Any chance you have those sugar packets in your pocket?"

I glanced at my oversized T-shirt. "What pocket?"

My eyes followed the tensing and flexing of his muscles as he shifted, forgetting to blink. I took a sip of my coffee, but edged a little closer, letting my other hand brush across his six-pack (or was it an eight-pack?), right down to that V-shape above his waistband. He'd turned up in boxer shorts – how could I help myself? "Did I mention I ogle with my fingers?"

His abs shook with laughter. "Am I allowed to do that, too, because I'd happily ogle you out of that shirt?"

I took a deep breath, again trying to memorize the vision in front of me. One day, I'd be married to someone like Felix, trying to fatten him up enough so his ribcage didn't show, and I'd need this image. I needed the memory of this moment, as vivid as possible. I closed my eyes.

"You don't need your eyes for ogling?" He asked.

"Nah. I've burned the image of you on to my hard drive, permanently. Thank you, sir." I removed my hand and opened my eyes. "Eggs on toast?"

"Yes, please!" Cem grabbed the plates and we sat at the table.

We ate in silence, his eyes hardly straying from me, serious and probing. My cheeks warmed under his gaze, even though I didn't understand why he had to stare at me like that. Finally, he swallowed the last piece and spoke in a soft voice. "Why do you look at me like that? Like you're saying goodbye?"

"I'm not saying goodbye. I made you breakfast." I pushed a crumb around my plate with my fingernail. I wasn't used to how my nails felt when they were longer, the sound they made. It wasn't me.

"You look at me with that... wistful sadness and I hate it."

"Wistful sadness? I think you have been reading your mom's romance novels."

He didn't laugh. Instead, he stared at me with such intensity my insides flipped, and face flushed with warmth. "No jokes, Aria. Please. Tell me the truth."

I forced myself to hold his gaze, even if it felt like I was staring directly into the sun. "Are *you* going to tell me the truth?"

"Let's make a pact. From now on, we'll tell the truth, God's honest truth, no matter what."

"God's honest truth," I repeated. "That sounds high and mighty."

He exhaled. "I know my English is weird. Can we move past that?"

I swallowed my guilt. "Your English is amazing. Phenomenal. I didn't mean it like—"

"The truth, Aria."

My mouth was so dry I could hardly coax my tongue to work. "Fine. I'm falling for you. Free falling. And I'm scared."

"Why?"

"Because I'll hit the ground."

"If you fall, I'll catch you. You know that." His smile was gentle, with a hint of cheekiness.

"You are skilled at that, aren't you? It's like a *dizi* trick, isn't it? Something they teach at acting class in Turkey?"

"Not really. You must stand in the right spot and have fast reflexes."

He got up and pulled me up to stand. "Come on, I'll show you." He positioned me right next to him, facing the other way. "Fall backwards."

"What? Right here?" My body seized. "Is this like one of those trust exercises?"

"What is this, a corporate retreat? No! We're doing a scene."

"Okay." I rolled my eyes, took a deep breath, and fell backwards.

I didn't expect it to feel like a big deal. It was essentially the same as throwing myself on the bed or couch. Vertical to horizontal. Humans did it multiple times a day.

But as I fell, time slowed. Reaching the tipping point of losing my balance, my stomach bottomed out and my heart soared. I sensed a glimpse of something beautiful, something I couldn't quite touch. And then, I landed in his arms, and he brought me back against his chest like I weighed nothing.

I remembered the feeling of his arms, but I'd never thrown myself on him like this, without a fight. The warm sensation spreading through my body was so sweet and lovely it made me choke up. For a moment, I'd shed myself of the doubt and worry, my constant companions, entering a moment of sweet amnesia.

"I'll always catch you, Aria," he whispered, smiling. "If you let me."

It was so cheesy and yet so sweet that I could barely speak. "Cem..."

He lifted my chin and found my trembling lips. "Are you okay?"

I smiled through a film of tears. "I'm still scared, but if you must know, I'm madly in love with you."

He grinned victoriously, cupping my face in his hands. "That's my girl."

My in-breath made my entire body wobble, but I fought out the words quickly before he could kiss me and turn my brain to mush. "Your turn, Cem! God's honest truth."

I held my breath as he looked at me for a long time, his lips twitching. I imagined words arranging behind them like guests at a surprise party. "I fell for you a long time ago. Before you friend-zoned me, before you even agreed to play Burcu."

I shook my head, rejecting the idea. "You didn't even know me then. You still don't."

"Sometimes, if you have a little faith, you can sense it. Like a premonition. The essence of someone."

"The essence?"

"Is that not the right word? I felt like I knew you already, and then everything I learned was mere detail. Fascinating detail. You're honest and funny and clever and a little crazy, and you make me feel like I'm more than a marketable face and a body. Like I'm someone you could trust. Not a monkey in a circus but a... real man." His voice broke and I felt a tug in my heart, my insides swirling like flood waters. I still felt his hand on my waist, holding me up, steadying me. I pressed my hands against his bare chest, feeling his heartbeat under my palms. A real heart.

"I trust you, Cem. And I hate the idea of anyone treating you like a... human resource." I winced. "But it doesn't mean you're in love with me. Maybe you miss being seen as a person and not as a celebrity. That makes sense."

He pinned me with a look that made my body freeze to the spot I was standing on. "I know how I feel, and you can't rationalize it away. I love that you hold me to a higher standard, but it's not just that. It's you. Every new thing I learn about you makes me want to learn the next thing."

"But what if it's not good? Like... I bite my nails." I trailed my index finger along my bottom lip. It felt so much longer than I remembered. Unreal. Like all of this.

"I know." He smiled.

"I hate doing laundry."

"I figured." His eyes did a little half roll.

"I'm terrible at parallel parking."

"Tarik is great at it. So what?"

I shook my head, disappointed with my petty, drain-circling thoughts. I wanted to shake them off and gobble up his affection, whatever it was, however short-lived.

Cem rescued my nails by wrapping his hand around mine and bringing it down. He stepped a little closer, enveloping me in his warm, intoxicating scent. "You don't love someone because you know everything about them, and you haven't discovered any major faults. That's why you'd love a toaster, maybe. Not a person."

I blinked, forgetting to breathe. "Why do you love somebody, then? What makes us fall in love?"

"I'm probably the last person you should ask. I know nothing about love. I only know that if I think about you leaving… if I think about losing you, it hurts. It physically hurts."

I swallowed against the stickiness in my throat. I'd run out of arguments and in their place, I found only warmth. Terrible, overwhelming, paralyzing warmth. Oh, how I wanted this to be true, like a dream I never wanted to wake up from.

Cem's eyes implored mine. "If I'm completely honest, I've had a lot of doubts about… myself. If I could really be worth your trust. And every time I see that doubt in your eyes, it's like you're driving that knife a little deeper."

My chest felt like it might burst. I had to deflect. "God, you're dramatic." I tried to smile but couldn't resist placing a gentle kiss between his hard pecs. My wobbly voice betrayed me. "I think you're more of a man than you know. Maybe you haven't needed all those resources yet. With your charmed life and all."

He grabbed me by the arms and flashed me an infuriating grin. "You're insufferable. I'm expressing my emotions, trying to be romantic… and you're making fun of me."

I cocked my head, blinking away the moisture that had gathered in my eyes, and matched his smile. "Is it a Turkish thing, being so emotional?"

"Maybe. But choose wisely. Emir won't give you much."

"I believe you." My next blink gathered a ripe teardrop,

launching it down my cheek.

Cem's finger caught it halfway down. "No more jokes, then?"

"I'm all out."

We stared at each other, the air sizzling between us. "How lucky are we?" His eyes sparkled. "Two people falling for each other, at the same time?"

I knew I had a half-witted smile on my face, but I didn't care. Because he was right. I felt lucky. For the first time in months, I didn't want to be anybody else. I didn't want to be anywhere else.

When his mouth claimed mine, I felt even luckier.

Without another word, Cem took my hand and led me back upstairs. I'm not sure how we ended up on the bed, but we did. This time, my brain barely registered the change from vertical to horizontal, as if I'd decoupled myself from gravity.

Seagulls flew overhead, shrieking behind the window as they went. Cem rolled over me, trapping me between his flexed arms. My body called for his, swelling and pulsing in anticipation, yet deliciously peaceful. Knowing that he felt something for me, something he considered real, even if only in this moment, made my chest glow. I was someone. I was known. I was seen.

I gasped as he relaxed one arm, letting some of his weight fall on me. His fingers traced my skin, all the way down, curling inside the waistband of my shorts. I'd slept in them, the zipper and buttons sinking their red marks into my stomach.

Cem unbuttoned and unzipped me, freeing me from the stiff denim and revealing my uninspired cotton underwear. He rubbed circles over them, intolerably slowly. "As long as we're being honest, seeing you come in my shower is the hottest thing I've ever witnessed. I don't think I'll ever be able to take a shower without picturing that."

He brought his face inches from mine, blocking the blue sky above. Dark curls fell down, brushing my cheeks, and his brown eyes had a shine on them that tightened my throat. "I feel free with you," he said. "Like my life is... mine, you know? This moment is all mine. All ours."

I knew. "It is yours, Cem. And I'm yours, too."

In that moment, I wanted him inside me more than I wanted an orgasm. I wanted to see him lose it, see the fine lines on his forehead smooth and all the tension evaporate. But it also felt final, like the moment of no return. I wasn't fooling around with the movie star. I was his conquest.

His mouth grazed my ear on its way to my neck and his fingers kept teasing me through my underwear, then slipped underneath again, getting closer and closer. For a moment, I couldn't think at all, only close my eyes and watch the fireworks as his touch built up a tsunami of pleasure within me. A strand of his hair fell across my face and filled my nose with his spicy scent. The scent of Istanbul.

He'd made it through my defenses, layer by layer. Every touch that fired up my body sent a secondary ache to my heart. The beauty of his full attention, the perfection of that fleeting moment, made me ache as the pleasure mounted and finally took over. I whimpered. Something about more, or yes. Or something else incoherent.

"Aria, can I?"

I cracked my eyelids. "What?"

The sound of the condom wrapper sobered me up a little and I understood. "Yes!" *What a funny question.*

He filled me, almost to the edge of pain, and pulled me up so I sat in his lap, achingly full, beautifully anchored, throbbing like I was coming apart at the seams.

"Let me see you." He held my face in his hands, kissing my cheek right below my left eye. The liver spot, I thought. My makeup must have worn off. I would have been embarrassed, but there was room for only one thing in my mind – the pleasure radiating from my core. Only a little more friction.

He slid his fingers under my bottom, reaching further than I'd expected, applying pressure as he bucked his hips, thrusting a bit deeper. Once. Twice. My mouth opened but no sound emerged.

I'd never come even close to this position, not that I could remember trying. I couldn't remember anyone else, like my mind had been wiped clean. It shouldn't feel this good, my brain insisted, but my body knew better, rocking against him until the pleasure reached its peak. I dug my nails into his lower back as my insides coiled and uncoiled and the universe rearranged itself. I was vaguely aware of the sounds he made as he came, pulsing inside me. Hugging me.

Eventually, the waves turned into gentle laps and he pulled away, discarding the condom. I crawled under the covers, but the lull of satisfaction eluded me. When Cem's arm slid around my waist, I shivered. "I'm still a bit turned on," I confessed. "I don't know how that's possible."

His eyes sparkled. "Give me a minute." The bed rocked as he rolled over onto his side. Or maybe the whole boat did.

I laughed. "You can't be ready to go again in a minute."

"No, but this guy is." He touched my lower back with something.

When he turned it on, I knew. "A vibrator?" I turned around to look at the little silver bullet in his hand.

My fingers flew up to my face as my gut twisted. "How many women do you bring in here?"

He smiled evasively. "Some."

"And you've used that with…" I swallowed, trying to rearrange my thoughts. Was I overreacting?

"No. This is brand new. I always throw them away with the condoms, to be honest. I ordered a few."

He went back to open the bedside drawer and picked up two unboxed ones. I stared at them.

Cem turned off the vibrator and put it away with the boxes, then pushed me back on the bed, burying his face in my neck. "What's this about?"

I had no answer, but I couldn't help the hollow feeling in my belly. I'd always known I was one of many, but I'd chosen not to think about it.

"Tell me about those women." My voice cracked, but I forced myself to look at him. The truth couldn't be worse than what I was imagining. Could it?

He gave me a pained look. "What do you want to know? They were mostly women I worked with. I met a couple of them at a nightclub. They were attractive and willing. Some liked vibrators."

"Did they sleep here?" I let my head sink into the pillow, trying to imagine the Turkish ladies lying in my place, gazing at the sky. Gazing at him. Speaking fluent Turkish.

I waited for the sting of jealousy, but it never arrived. I only felt the distance between us, like he'd retreated behind a glass. A cloudy TV screen.

"Yes. It was usually late, and we fell asleep. Then I called them a cab in the morning."

"No breakfast?"

"I don't usually keep breakfast foods around. They'd go bad."

I nodded against the pillow. "So, one-night stands? You have a routine of one-night stands?"

"A routine?" He frowned at me. "You make it sound like flossing. And I'm not doing it anymore."

"It's okay if you are. I'm not judging you." *You're not really mine to judge.*

"Why not? I'm with you, Aria. It's not okay if I sleep with someone else. How could it be okay?"

I shrugged. "I don't know. It just is."

"What about you? I'd lose my shit if—"

"I can't even think of someone else, Cem. I can't remember their names. Nobody else exists."

"Yet you think it's okay for me to sleep around?"

"I'm saying I'd love you anyway. I read this article about you that described you as a committed bachelor."

"And that's why you think I can't be faithful?" The hurt in his voice made my eyes burn.

"No, Cem. I think you're amazing—"

"Then make me promise I'll never use those vibrators with anyone else. Carve your name on my wall, Aria. Be jealous." He gestured at the wall behind us.

I shook my head with a smile. "You don't really want that."

"It's better than you looking at me like that. Like I could never be someone real for you."

My chest filled with heat. "That's not fair! I've given you everything I have. I've abandoned my plan and followed you across the world. I know we joked about breaking each other's hearts, but it's true. I'll split in half when…I have to go."

"You don't have to go anywhere! Whatever happens with this Burcu thing, we'll figure it out. Just stay with me, please."

The burning in his eyes was likely matched by the one I felt behind mine. I heaved a breath, and my body shook from desperation. "How, Cem? I don't fit into your life. I'm not here as myself. That would ruin everything."

His expression softened, and he brushed a strand of hair behind my ear. "I know how it looks, and I hate it. I should have thought about that before I asked you to come. I wanted you with me, at any price. It wasn't right."

"It's okay." I fought tears. "I wanted to be with you, too. I'll pay any price."

"I don't want you to! Fight for us, Aria. Fight for me."

I nodded, but looked away, because deep down, I knew I wouldn't fight. To fight, I'd have to believe we belonged together. I'd have to believe I deserved to be with a movie star that millions of women wanted. When, in reality, I hadn't been worth the fight for anyone.

Cem's words continued to pour over me in hot waves. "And you believe me when I tell you that there's no one else, right? I never had sex with someone that I was in love with. Only you."

"Not even Burcu?"

He paused for a moment, looking conflicted.

"God's honest truth," I reminded him. I'd flinched at the term, thinking I'd never be able to say it with a straight face, but he'd obliterated my sarcasm. I had nothing left.

"The truth is… I measure by a different stick now. I thought I loved Burcu, but it feels like nothing compared to how I feel about you."

I sniffed. He was so certain, so full of optimism. I wanted him to be right. I wanted him to be happy. But… "I've never felt like this either, but it doesn't mean everything will magically work out. Words are cheap, Cem."

He sat up. "I'm trying to take action. You'll see." Swinging his legs over the edge of the bed, he stood up and opened his suitcase, dumping a pile of shirts and pants on the bed.

His phone buzzed on the shelf above the bed, moving closer to the edge until it fell onto the sheets. I saw Emir's name, then Cem picked it up.

As he talked, the atmosphere in the room shifted. I could feel it, like an icy wind on the cusp of winter. Our time was coming to an end.

# Cem

I held her hand all the way to Galata. We spent most of the drive idling in traffic, waiting for another car or motorbike or someone pushing a wooden cart along cobblestones to get out of our way. Istanbul had never felt so crowded. Or ancient.

Emir had called and ordered us to get back a day earlier than planned. Apparently, the stylist he wanted wasn't available on Saturday. I'd told him to cancel the whole thing, but he'd dangled a carrot, telling me the studio was ready to sign. They only needed to see more of us in the media. One public outing as a doting couple, and my best-paid role yet would be black on white. Enough money to fund everything I wanted. A break from acting. Freedom to travel. I'd take a year off to hang out in New Zealand.

Aria insisted that we follow through. I think she felt like she owed us something, not just me, but Emir. I loved that about her, that sense of duty, always wanting to do the right thing but this didn't feel right.

We packed up and drove back, picking up Emir from my house in Bebek, then headed to Galata. If my brother suspected we'd veered from the Bursa plan, he didn't say anything.

Tarik stopped in front of a slow-moving cart, rolled down his window and yelled at the old man to get out of the way. Aria's eyes widened. She had a lot to learn about my city, if I could get her to stay.

"I told you half of Istanbul is from the 1800s. You love that, don't you? Crumbling old places?" I nudged her arm, pointing at the end of a steep, narrow cobblestone street giving to Galata tower. "That used to be a prison."

Her eyes rounded. "That's too pretty to be a prison."

"It wasn't originally built for that, but..." My throat tightened. "Anything can become a prison, I suppose."

She lifted her gaze, peering right through me. "It doesn't matter how gorgeous it is if you can't leave."

I drew a sharp breath, trying to stop my thumbs from fidgeting. "There was a guy called Çelebi, an Ottoman scientist and inventor who lived in the 1600s. Apparently, he made himself a pair of wooden wings, jumped off the roof of Galata tower and flew all the way to the Asian side."

"For real?"

I smiled at her stunned expression. "Probably not, but I like to think so."

"Me too." She craned her neck as the tower disappeared behind the street corner.

I stared out the window, squeezing her hand. I needed her. She elevated every mundane moment that otherwise passed me by, used me, discarded me. With Aria, time slowed down and details came into focus. Looking at Istanbul through her eyes, its color and vibrancy filled my senses.

The last of the evening sun gilded the sky behind the rooftops. This city was my beautiful prison, a tower where I resided above everyone else. Alone. Disconnected. A pawn in everyone else's game, with no control of my own destiny.

I tightened my grip on her hand until she yelped.

"I'm sorry," I whispered, easing my hold. "I was imagining myself on the roof, about to fall."

"You'd never fall. You'd fly."

The husky conviction in her voice drew my eyes back to her, catching the sunset's glow on her face. I imagined myself gliding across the Bosphorus Strait and beyond.

I leaned in to kiss her, instinctively, but she glanced at Emir on the front seat, shaking her head. "What?" I whispered.

"He doesn't know, does he?"

I shrugged. "Does it matter?"

I could tell it mattered to her. She was here to save my career and fulfil any expectations my asshole brother had placed on her. I sighed, leaning back in my seat, my eyes still on her like a security camera pointed at the safe. Always watching.

The car stopped in front of a building I vaguely remembered.

I'd been here for a party or gathering of sorts years ago. "Wait. Who's the stylist?" I asked Emir.

"I arranged someone you used to work with on *Aşkta Şanslı*. Made her sign an NDA. There are not that many people we can trust."

"Who? Deniz? Melis?"

"Melis." He sounded surprised, like I couldn't possibly remember the names of people who dressed me and did my hair and makeup for eighteen months.

"You'll love Melis," I assured Aria. "She's an artist."

"A costume designer," Emir corrected.

"And an artist. She creates digital paintings," I corrected back with a flash of annoyance.

"Whatever," Emir grumbled in Turkish. "As long as she can make this girl look the part." He hooked a thumb over his shoulder at Aria without bothering to turn. "Looking like Burcu is not enough. She has to look like hot, successful Burcu, not... homely Burcu."

I had to hold down my fists to stop myself from sucker punching him from the back seat.

CHAPTER 33

# Aria

I couldn't take my eyes off the medley of colors and shapes flickering past the window. Modern and historic, polished and derelict, decorative and sleek. Istanbul had it all, sometimes within the same building. The sheer amount of color and chaos of human life made me want to slow down, so I'd have enough time to stare at everything. Compared to Istanbul, Napier felt like an empty theme park. Boring.

In this neighborhood, nothing seemed sacred. One could simply drill a hole and pull a bunch of uncovered cables through the wall of a 200-year-old building – such as the one we'd now stopped in front of. Emir got out of the car and opened the door for me. Cem strapped a mask on his face and followed us.

Racks of gaudy souvenir socks camouflaged the building

entrance. I didn't notice the open doorway behind them until Cem pushed past the socks and disappeared inside. We trailed behind him into an arched hallway of crumbling brick, lit by yellow torches. Red velvet couches and a red fridge flanked the wall and a lone cat ambled down the well-worn stone steps.

Cem headed to the stairs, taking us up three stories. One side of the staircase was open, revealing the smallest inner courtyard I'd ever seen, with nothing but grass and rubbish on the bottom. A few windows dotted along the walls offered the neighbors clear views of each other's bedrooms. Everything looked original, but in a rather creepy way.

We reached a heavy-looking door with iron bars, and Cem knocked. After a moment, footsteps echoed on the other side and the door creaked open.

Light from the apartment flooded the dim stairwell and gave a golden halo to a small woman of my age who beamed at us. "*Cem bey! Hoşgeldiniz!*"

That's as far as I could follow, before the conversation became a happy flow of foreign babble. Melis had dark curls and a round face and wore a beautifully tailored pantsuit with a low-cut silk top. Its wild pattern gave off an artistic vibe and perfectly matched the mood of the apartment.

Turkish rugs and chandeliers dominated the hallway. We left our shoes at the door but weren't offered slippers. Faint cigarette smoke, mixed with something sweet, lingered in the air. As in Cem's house, various wall and ceiling lamps, all lit, filled my vision, but here, the decor was a mix of historic and eclectic. I could have studied the overload of colors, patterns and art for hours, but hearing my name, I tried to refocus.

"*Allah, Allah!* It's Burcu! But not." Melis stared at me for a moment in stunned silence, then gave me a delighted smile. "So nice to meet you, Aria! I'm Melis." She leaned in to kiss my cheeks and gave me a hug.

I returned her warm greeting somewhat awkwardly. "You, too! Thank you for... whatever you're doing for us."

"Oh, you thank me later. If it works out!" She let out a bubbly laugh and guided us into the living room. Another huge chandelier hung from the ceiling and a long, plush, orange couch ran along two walls. Right in the middle stood a clothing rack bursting with bold colors. Scary colors.

Emir dropped onto the couch, pulling his laptop from the bag he always carried. "You have an hour before the hairdresser gets here. You need to find something for Soho House," he told Melis.

"It's a high-end restaurant. Requires membership," Cem explained without a hint of enthusiasm.

I nodded in terror, and he took my hand. He'd been holding my hand almost nonstop, probably enough to qualify as clingy. But as soon as he let go, I missed his strong, warm grasp. Maybe I was the clingy one.

"Relax," he whispered. "We'll get through this, and then..." He looked over his shoulder at Emir, his face conflicted.

I knew he wanted to look beyond this, imagining a future where everything was different. But if we succeeded and he got the role, I couldn't see myself fitting into his plan, no matter how much he wanted to believe so. Still, I'd be part of his journey and that had to be enough.

Melis gave us a meaningful look, grabbed the clothing rack and wheeled it out the door, gesturing for me to follow. "We'll be in the bedroom. *Görüşürüz.*"

I gave Cem a quick smile before I slipped away. This was it. I would transform into Burcu and take the deception to the next level.

The bedroom delivered another explosion of color with a deep red bedspread and a matching art print with wild, intertwined flower shapes in place of a headboard. "Is it yours?" I pointed at the artwork. "It's beautiful."

Melis's eyes brightened. "I was supposed to sell it, but I couldn't. So, I sold the headboard." Her laugh was a little sad.

She had a resilient, no-nonsense air about her I instantly liked.

I glanced at the skimpy dresses, staring at me in yellow, gold and the kind of green they keyed out in movies. The kind of dresses that needed silicon straps to stay on hangers. I'd watched enough of Cem's TV show to know that Burcu was a size or two smaller than me. "I'm not sure I can fit into any of these. Can you show me the one that's the most... forgiving?"

Melis laughed. "These are not for comfort. Think of it like wearing a piece of art. You become part of the creation." She gestured wildly with her hand, like painting something on a canvas.

I swallowed, resigning to my fate.

After half an hour of grueling fitting room work, I'd lightly destroyed one dress and discarded two that neither of us could zip up. Feeling like the Christmas ham, I accepted the next option – the golden evening gown with an incredibly deep V neckline. "Is the idea to show my bellybutton?" I asked.

"Shush." Melis waved her finger. "It's not that bad. We'll add some tape."

"What, to extend the material?"

She rolled her eyes. "No, to keep it from slipping."

I sighed. "If all else fails, maybe you can cover me with the tape?"

She shook her head and released a deep sigh. "I need to make some tea," she announced and left me with the dress.

"Sorry, I'm very tired," I mumbled at her receding back. I'd lost all control over my behavior. The jet lag had returned, making it hard to stand upright. I kept eyeing the bed, wishing I could keel over, but I was also hungry, and a restaurant had been mentioned. Although, it was probably a pretentious establishment with tiny portions.

To my immense relief, the golden dress fit. It wasn't as short as the others, but the deep neckline meant I couldn't wear a bra.

Hearing Melis re-entering the room, I stepped out from behind the clothing rack, my only privacy screen, channeling all that was left of my inner goddess.

"Bravo! We found it!" Melis set down the tea glass with a clatter, clapped her hands and leapt in to adjust my waist and shoulders.

I gently closed my eyes as she fussed over me, attaching pieces of tape that felt cool and strange against my skin. Unlike the previous contenders, this dress let me breathe, but I felt naked.

Once I'd been armed with matching, spiky heels and a tiny

golden clutch, Melis grabbed me by the elbow. "Let's get this signed off before the hairdresser arrives."

"Do I still have to take this off when she does my hair?" The thought of undressing and dressing one more time made my legs shake.

"No, we'll throw a towel over you. I think it's best you get used to this dress and maybe practice walking in those heels?"

How did she know I'd struggle?

I took a teetering step, yawning so widely my jaw clicked. Melis held onto my arm to keep me upright. "Look at you! You're exhausted. Cem better make this up to you!"

I managed a meek smile. "It's okay. He flew me to Istanbul."

"But he's paying you, right?"

I shook my head a little too hard and felt woozy. "No, I'm helping out as a friend, that's all."

"A friend?" Melis stopped us at the doorway and lowered her voice, giving me a stern look. "He looks at you like…" She frowned. "We have a saying; *the eyes are the mirror of the heart.*"

"The eyes are the windows to the soul?"

"Windows? That's funny. I can see it in his eyes," she whispered.

"See what?"

"He looks at you like nobody else exists. Like he looked at Burcu. It's like being back on set. Nobody could take their eyes off Cem and Burcu. You don't often see that kind of chemistry. It was magical, even when the cameras weren't rolling."

I felt a confusing mix of joy and hollow fear. They'd been so perfect, Burcu and Cem. So perfectly matched. Nobody would ever say that about Cem and me. We were so unlikely. So odd.

Melis marched me into the living room. I gathered the last bit of my energy and did a careful twirl to show off the golden gown.

Not careful enough. As I shifted my balance back on two feet, my heel landed on the edge of the rug and I wobbled, waving my arms like I was about to take flight.

Cem stood up, but I managed to regain my balance before he reached me. Thank God. I didn't need another 'catching the falling girl' incident, this time with an audience. Although my flailing had probably looked bad enough. I noticed Emir frowning at me, the crease between his eyes so deep it could have held spare change. Cem escorted me to the couch, and I collapsed on the orange velvet, mortified.

"I'm sorry. I'm so tired, I think it's affecting my balance."

Cem yawned, which made me yawn. "I know. It's the jet lag. We have a hotel room booked, but Emir thinks we should do this one outing first."

Emir cleared his throat. "I heard a couple of big names are out at Soho so the paps are already there. We're all tired but it's the perfect opportunity." His thumb moved over his phone screen as he stared at something.

There was a knock on the door. Melis, who was handing me the steaming glass of tea I'd left in the bedroom, straightened up. "The hairdresser is here."

I took a shaky sip of tea, letting the strong flavor revive me as much as it could. Cem's hand rested against my lower back, his thumb idly stroking the shiny fabric. Tingling warmth pooled between my thighs and my heart crept to my throat. I liked his touch too much. It didn't only feel good – it meant something, and that thought made it hard to breathe. I tried to bring my focus back to the tea. I'd make it through this day. Possibly with my heart and body in shatters, but I'd make it through.

"*Merhaba!*"

The low, gruff voice at the doorway caught my attention. The hairdresser – a man probably in his forties – took a wide stance, heaving his wheelie bag, which looked a lot like an airline carry-on, between his spread legs, leaning on it like a rockstar posing with a guitar. With long, messy curls and rolled up sleeves exposing inked, veiny arms, he looked nothing like any hairdresser I'd ever seen.

Cem acknowledged his presence by standing up and shaking his hand. They spoke for a moment in Turkish, occasionally gesturing at me, never smiling. Although I couldn't understand a word, I sensed an odd level of animosity, as if they were sizing each other up.

Eventually, the hairdresser shrunk back, throwing one last defiant look at Cem before he turned to me with a smile. "Aria? My name is Savaş. Please, come." The words came out slowly, with great effort and a thick accent.

I glanced at Cem, almost instinctively. He nodded, but followed us to the dining room, where Melis had cleared space around the table and set one chair in the middle for me.

"How long will this take?" I asked, turning to Cem, who'd positioned himself at the doorway, leaning on the frame. "Maybe you can take a nap while he fixes my hair. Then at least one of us will look alive."

His eyelids dipped at the mention of sleep, and he pushed himself upright. "Maybe," he said begrudgingly, casting one last look at Savaş before he left.

The hairdresser ignored him, digging through his bag for supplies. As he walked to the sink, Melis stepped in. "Did you see that?" she whispered.

"You mean that murder-y look? What's going on?"

Melis smiled. "I knew it! He's jealous."

"Who? Cem?"

"It's a Turkish thing. Men are very protective. Territorial. It can be a little... overbearing. It means you're not just friends." She stared at me all starry-eyed with a beaming smile.

I shook my head in disbelief. "I live in New Zealand. None of this is... real." I drew a breath, trying to discard the strange feeling. "So, you used to work with Cem?"

Melis shrugged. "I was only the wardrobe girl. A nobody. But he was always nice to me. That's Cem. We were all a little in love with him. If he ever looked at me like that—" Melis glanced over her shoulder at the direction Cem had gone. "I'd faint. Seriously. Cem Erkam. He's just..." Her eyes burned with a level of devotion I would have reserved for someone immortal, or someone with particularly useful superpowers.

"Do you know Burcu?" I asked, trying to focus on the job at hand. "Can you give me any tips on how she would move or gesture? I've only seen her in that TV show. I don't even know what she looks like right now. There are no recent pictures online."

Melis looked surprised. "I saw her last week. I brought her some clothing samples. She's lost a bit of weight, but you're right, no one's seen her, so it doesn't matter. Her hair is the same, but I think Savaş will take care of that for you."

I stood up, perching my hands on my hips. "But how does she stand? Does she move her hands when she speaks? I'm so nervous about this."

Melis cocked her head, examining me with her lips pursed. "Too... masculine."

I dropped my arms to my sides.

"Too awkward. Burcu would always hold something." She handed me the clutch I'd placed on the table. I wrapped my fingers around it and tried to relax my shoulders.

"That's perfect. I can see why Cem looks at you like that. There's so much Burcu. Love like that never goes away."

I nodded, a lump swelling in my throat. To my relief, the hairdresser returned, guided me back into my seat and dressed me in a sleeved cover that reminded me of a hospital gown. Melis brought me a new glass of tea and left me with him, taking another tray with two tea glasses to Cem and Emir.

I twisted my fingers into a knot, wishing I had my phone, or even a magazine. My nails, hidden under the black cape, were in danger again.

Savaş didn't speak much English. Answering even a simple question seemed to cause him so much stress I gave up and closed my eyes, trying to stay sufficiently awake so I wouldn't fall over.

I shouldn't have worried about staying awake. Savaş wasn't

the gentle type. In fact, I'd never been in so much pain at the hairdressers. For some inexplicable reason, applying highlights started with rigorous back combing. After the foils were in place, he told me to wait there and left the room – probably for a cigarette break, based on his unmistakable smoker's smell.

Upon his return, he walked me into the bathroom to rinse my hair with the help of a portable hairdressing sink and the shower head. I grit my teeth as he tugged at my locks and massaged my scalp so hard, I felt like my head was in a vise. The pain didn't course through me entirely without pleasure but delivered a confusing mixture of sensations. I wondered if he was punishing me for something Cem had said or showcasing what kind of lover he'd be. A hair-yanker, definitely. Fast and rough.

I sighed with relief when he finally took me back to the kitchen for blow drying, but my comfort was short-lived. The cloud of tangles created by the back combing had to be undone, so Savaş (or Savage, as I now called him in my head) put his veiny arms to work, applying more strength than he would have needed for pulling dandelion roots.

When my hair was finally finished, I had tears in my eyes.

"What is wrong?" He asked me. "It looks very... amazing. *Çok güzel.*"

He removed my cape and swiveled my chair, which didn't really swivel but scraped against the floor, and walked me to the floor-to-ceiling mirror in the hallway. I gasped.

Approaching my golden reflection felt like an out-of-body experience. The woman in the mirror wasn't me. With her golden dress and sun-kissed ombre waves, she belonged to Burcu's Instagram feed. I studied myself as if from the outside, floating over my own shoulder like a lost little ghost.

I wiped the moisture from the corner of my eye and smiled. "Thank you. It looks beautiful."

Savaş grabbed my shoulders, maybe to straighten my spine, or to show how much strength he held in his fingertips, and that's when I saw Cem. He appeared in the mirror, by my side. Savaş anticipated his move, stepping out of the way just in time to avoid a collision.

"Are you crying?" Cem dabbed his thumb on the corner of my eye.

"No. Just… emotional, I guess," I whispered, peeking over my shoulder to see that Savaş had gone. I saw him through the dining room doorway, packing his gear.

"Why? What happened? Do you want to cancel this? I'll talk to Emir—"

"No! It's nothing like that. He was a bit rough with my hair, but it doesn't hurt anymore, and it looks great, right?"

I swiped a glossy lock over my shoulder, but catching the look on his face, my hand froze mid-motion.

"He hurt you?" Cem exhaled the words without moving his jaw, a vein on his temple ticking.

Sensing where this was going, I locked my hands around his arm. I couldn't physically stop him, but maybe, if I applied my entire body weight, I could slow him down. "I get that this is some kind of Turkish alpha male thing, but can you reel it in? You're scaring me."

Cem frowned. "I can't let anyone hurt you. It's on me."

"It's really not! They don't know we're… together. I'm supposed to be your fake girlfriend."

His frown deepened, tinged with confusion. "No! I mean, okay… But I don't like this."

Cem released a breath, and his shoulders dropped half an inch. "I don't trust him. I only agreed to Melis… but Emir said she can't color hair. She'll do your makeup, though."

Makeup? I'd slapped on some foundation and mascara before leaving the boat, naively thinking that would be enough.

"Great." I smiled, covering my surprise. "That means Savaş is done, and he'll be leaving. We can forget about him." I stroked my hands down his solid arm, telling myself I was only trying to stop a violent clash of the veiny arms and veiny temples, not working up another lady boner. But yes, I was thinking about the explosive strength residing within those muscles and tendons and veins… Maybe I had a thing for veins?

Or, more alarmingly, I had a thing for Cem and his possessive caveman jealousy.

As if on cue, Savaş wheeled his luggage past us, giving Cem a thunderous look on his way out. Melis wobbled behind him, carrying the portable wash basin he'd used in the bathroom.

"Let me help you." Cem launched forward, trying to take it off her, but she shook her head, scurrying out of his reach. "No need. I'll be back soon."

Melis closed the door behind them, clearly as concerned as I was about creating distance between the two guys.

"See? He's gone." I waved at the door.

Cem's shoulders dropped a bit more and he followed me back to the dining room. "I'm so tired," he groaned as he collapsed in a chair, and I joined him in a particularly face-stretching yawn.

Five minutes later, Melis found us both resting against the dining table like two blackout drunks. "*Allah, Allah!*"

I pushed myself upright. "Sorry. Is it time for makeup?"

Melis slammed a giant toolbox on the table and opened it. I peered in at the wide array of brushes and products. "Wow. Did you do this on *Aşkta Şanslı*?"

"Only as a backup. I borrowed this kit from a colleague. But I'm good."

I smiled. "Of course."

I followed her instructions, turning left and right, closing my eyes, then staring at the ceiling, wondering what she was doing to me, while Cem slept against the uncomfortably hard glass top table. I kept my voice low, happy to see him getting some rest. When I saw Melis pull out a pair of eyelash extensions, I cheered to myself. Cem would get a bit more sleep. In fact, I wasn't going to wake him up at all. I'd let Emir be the bad guy – he was so good at it.

As I suspected, Emir marched in on Melis powdering my forehead. "Time to go." He brushed down the wrinkled dress shirt he must have slept in and covered it up by buttoning his jacket. His hair stuck out on the side.

I exchanged a quick look with Melis, who moved in with a bottle of hairspray and styled it to perfection, despite his protests.

Cem woke up to the commotion and got up, too. His hair looked even messier, but Melis returned to powdering my face, even though I was certain none of my actual skin was still visible or causing any concern.

Finally, she stepped aside, and I made it up on my spiky heels, swaying like Felix. Thinking of him made me oddly homesick. I imagined myself sitting in a cafe with my triple shot flat white, comfortable in my own jeans and sneakers, being myself. I had to shake the image. Not today.

I found my balance, grabbed the hairspray, and approached Cem. "Your hair's a bit…"

From the corner of my eye, I saw Melis's eyes widen in reverence as I touched his curls, straightening out the tangles he'd created. She'd done the same to Emir, yet her response told me this was completely different. I was touching Cem, the immortal creature they idolized but didn't consider the same species. Maybe Burcu could have fixed his hair, but not me – another 'nobody'.

Cem didn't seem to mind. Before I could pull my hand back, he caught my wrist. "You look exactly like Burcu." He frowned.

"That's good, right?"

"I guess."

He took my hand and Emir guided us to the door. Melis hugged me goodbye. "*Görüşürüz*. We'll meet again."

"Thank you! *Teşekkürler*." I smiled proudly as my brain unearthed the right word, which I hopefully pronounced correctly.

Melis's smile grew wider. "Perfect! You're ready."

I didn't feel ready, but it didn't matter. It was time to step out in public. Time to smile and wave.

CHAPTER 34

"Soho House." Emir told Tarik when we all dashed into the car.

"*Yok!*" I cried, louder than I'd intended. "Not there."

"What do you mean?" Emir turned around on the front seat and peered at me like I'd lost my mind. We were speaking Turkish, but he still lowered his voice. "It's exclusive, which means it's safer. You'll pose for some photos on the steps going in."

It all made sense, but I was feeling more than a little antagonistic. "I want to be by the sea." I tapped Tarik on the shoulder. "Take us to Villa Bosphorus."

He started driving, but glanced at Emir, conflicted.

My brother's shoulders crept toward his ears. "It's too open. I don't like it. I already tipped off a couple of reporters about Soho.

They're good ones, the ones who didn't write about your... you know. They've earned this."

"I don't owe anyone anything for *not* exploiting me at my weakest moment! Fuck that!"

Emir scoffed. "What's your solution then? Random strangers taking photos of you as you eat? We are doing this to get you photographed."

He was right, but I felt irritation swirling in my gut like a swarm of bees and couldn't stop. "The pics will be unflattering either way, but at least we get to look at the ocean. And I'm sure the paps are more than happy to drive if you tip them off again."

"But we haven't made a reservation—"

"Then make one!" I shot back. "You're supposed to be my manager, not my... parole officer."

Silence fell between us and Tarik drove around Beyoglu, turning left, then left again, until we circled back to our starting point.

I exhaled a deep sigh. "Okay, I'm sorry. I know you're trying to save my career, but you've made all of my decisions lately. Let me make this one." It wasn't strictly true. We'd gone to the boat, after all, but I didn't particularly care about semantics.

Emir growled. "Villa Bosphorus," he said to Tarik, then turned his attention to his phone, probably to reorganize everything he'd anal-retentively put together.

Despite his frustration, I felt vindicated.

"What was that about?" Aria whispered as Tarik steered us toward the bridge.

Melis had given her a long, sleek trench coat which she'd

gratefully wrapped around her shiny dress. Her face was made up to look like a porcelain doll, flawless and ethereal, but her eyes met me openly, the true mirrors of her heart. I wanted to wipe off the layers of cosmetics and reveal her freckle, the sign of the real Aria, the one I wanted.

"Just... me flying across the strait." I gestured at the bridge rising ahead of us and made a face. She smiled – a smile that hit me square in the chest and gave me energy. With her by my side, I could handle anything, even the guilt over my childish tantrums. Why did I have to act like a spoilt brat, especially in her presence? Did it really matter where we ate?

But driving across the bridge, the city lights flickering against the deep indigo sky, I felt an inkling of freedom.

# CHAPTER 35

My stomach gurgled from nerves and hunger as we drove down the narrow cobblestone streets, turning left and right so many times I lost any sense of direction. The nightly Istanbul burned bright with lights glowing from every shop window, streetlamps and overhead fairy lights illuminating colorful mosaics on the walls. Teetering piles of oranges and pomegranates framed the entrances of little shops and eateries. The entire city was alight and alive, making my insides hum like someone plucked on invisible strings.

"This is unreal." I muttered to myself.

Emir was still with us, as was the driver, who seemed like quite the hot head, leaning on his horn and using expressive hand gestures, many of them involving his thumb.

Cem plucked my hand out of my lap. I braced for the bone-crunching squeeze he'd delivered earlier, but he kept his touch light. "It'll be over soon."

I nodded, my chest tightening, because as much as I felt out of my element, I didn't want this to be over. I didn't want to let go of him; I didn't even mind him re-stacking the bones in my hand as long as he kept holding it. Holding me.

The view from the bridge stole my breath. In the distance, the city lights turned into clusters of pin pricks, revealing the expansive scale of human inhabitation. I didn't understand the words, but I knew Cem had fought Emir to bring me here instead of the private club. Pretending to be Burcu like this, out in the open, terrified me, but I saw the elation on his face and steeled my nerves. I'd do this for him. All those years of acting training had to be good for something.

I focused my thoughts on Burcu and everything I knew about her. How she walked and laughed and gestured. How she touched Cem. If I was to be her, I would have to think and feel like her.

I leaned into Cem, lowering my voice so it wouldn't be heard from the front seat. "What did Burcu want most in life? What did she care about?"

Cem looked out the window, silent for a moment. "She cared about everybody else. Her family and friends. Animals. Strangers. Other people's opinions."

"Opinions?"

Cem's thumb brushed mine. "She worried about what anyone said about her, even online. It's not healthy, especially if you're famous. That brings out the haters. Burcu read everything and took it to heart. Someone said she ran funny and she spent hours practicing running for a five-second shot. She wanted to make sure nobody had anything bad to say about her. That's not possible."

I sighed. I could feel her burden. Poor Burcu had been after perfection.

"What about in her private life?"

"What private life?" Cem's voice rose in frustration. "She was always on display. Always. Except when we were alone. I could make her relax, and I loved it. I loved that I could free her, for a moment, but being with me... that turned out to be her biggest mistake." I felt his pain, moving like low-lying fog under his words.

"Why?"

"She was worried about her reputation. It's different here. Turkey is conservative. And being with me..." Cem paused for a second, his gaze roaming out the window, voice catching in his throat. "I know she regretted it, right after. I would have married her, but she'd made up her mind and I never saw her again."

I held my breath until I felt dizzy. "You slept with her and she... vanished?"

Cem made a gruff noise, still staring out the window. "Everyone kept telling me it had nothing to do with me, but to this day, I don't know. I hear a lot of bullshit and I've become more aware of that lately." He turned to me, his eyes catching the light from the streetlamps. "Thanks to you."

"Thanks to me?"

"When I met you, I saw something. Like, a glimpse outside the Matrix, you know? What the world looks like outside of the bubble.

It's brutal. But everything you say, how you see me… it's like I'm finally looking into a mirror that doesn't distort."

I sighed, exaggeratedly. "In other words, I make you feel bad about yourself. I'm the human equivalent of harsh overhead lighting in shopping mall fitting rooms."

He burst out in laughter and the infectious rumble of it hummed straight to my core. I'd never tire of that sound of pure delight.

"Do you always get rose-tinted lightbulbs?" I asked, thinking of the first time I'd heard about him.

"What?"

"Before you arrived at the hotel, I bumped into the janitor, and he said he had to change the lightbulbs before you arrived."

"Seriously?" Cem stared at me like I'd lost my mind.

"I thought it was your request, but now I'm thinking that was probably…" I nodded at the front seat, my voice barely above whisper.

Cem nodded, averting my eyes. "He's big on lighting and photography, but I never thought he'd go that far."

He shook his head, staring out the window. When he finally turned back to me, I saw tears in his eyes. I couldn't tell if they were from laughter or something else. "You make me feel alive, Aria. Real. I want real. It's worth more than a thousand beautiful lies. Even if it sometimes hurts. Please don't change."

I looked straight into his pleading eyes. "I promise I'll never become one of your star-struck fan girls, even if your fame and fortune freaks me out a little."

It was a promise to me rather than to him. He'd likely grow

tired of my honesty and stupid jokes, and retreat into his bubble of comfortable lies. Who wouldn't?

I stared at my fingernails, which Melis had filed smooth and covered with gold-tinted polish. They helped me imagine myself as Burcu, channeling absolute control, chasing perfection. Always alert, always on, never sloppy like Aria, that crazy Kiwi.

The familiar buzz of performance returned, energizing every cell in my body. I'd missed acting so much. I'd gone without it like on life support, alive but not kicking. Not really here.

Tarik turned into a narrow alleyway and stopped short of hitting a wall. He opened the door for Cem, who in turn opened my door and helped me onto the uneven stone pavement. I aimed my heels carefully, avoiding any obvious wobbles until we reached a heavy, paneled door.

A staunch maître 'd greeted us at the door, passing us to a waiter who had an air of authority. He led us through the restaurant of exposed brick, gilded mirrors and intricate lighting, to an elevated terrace with expansive ocean views. The European side of Istanbul glimmered across the strait, and the bridge connecting the two sides glowed against the inky sky in festive lighting.

The waiter showed us to a far-off table by the balustrade. I noticed heads turning as we crossed the terrace but kept my eyes on the table. The night felt warm, warmer than I'd expected, and I let Cem help me out of my coat. When I took the seat he offered, I noticed the terrace heaters radiating like giant, floating fireplaces on either side of us.

Cem sat across the table, placing his elbows on the white cloth as he leaned in to smile at me. The waiter stared at him, either shocked at his table manners or starstruck, I couldn't tell. I heard the faint rustle of the other diners turning on their seats and the low murmur of their commentary. The air bristled with tension. It was probably a blessing I didn't speak Turkish.

I held my tongue, terrified to blow our cover. From the corner of my eye, I saw someone raising their phone to take a photo. Someone else stood up from a table behind Cem, moving closer to for a better shot. Would they actually let us eat? Bathing in the blissful warmth from the heaters, I felt my spine relax and eyelids dip, but the steady supply of adrenaline kept me upright.

I held a gracious smile and gazed adoringly at Cem as he rattled off what I hoped was our dinner order in Turkish. The waiter nodded and left.

When we were finally alone, I leaned closer and whispered. "It's probably too late to tell you I hate squid."

Cem looked amused. "I didn't order squid."

"I mean, I love squid. They are beautiful, super intelligent animals and I don't want to eat them."

"You're not a vegetarian... are you?" He flicked a nervous glance at the restaurant.

I shook my head. "I'd make a terrible one, with all the chicken I eat."

"So, chickens are not intelligent?"

I shrugged, enjoying the sparkle in his eyes. "Not so much."

"What about fish?"

"Absolute morons."

We both laughed, although I tried to do it without snorting. I was quite sure Burcu would never stoop so low.

Cem held my eyes. "I don't want to do this. I want to be with you, not Burcu. Let's stop this. Let's tell everyone." He implored me with his eyes, then looked around as if envisioning the scene that would unfold.

I shook my head, placing my hand firmly over his. "No, Cem. No."

I couldn't betray the promise I'd made to Emir. I couldn't be complicit in Cem losing that role, or the architect of another scandal.

I pinned him with a serious look. "Smile and wave, remember? Like those penguins in that movie."

The creatures that mated for life. How did they manage that?

I scanned the terrace. "By the way, if anyone gets too close, you need to switch to Turkish. I'll just... nod."

Cem sighed, light behind his eyes dimming. "Fine."

# CHAPTER 36

# *Cem*

The waiter returned with a bottle of raki. I caught the flash of suspicion behind Aria's perfectly composed veneer. As he filled our glasses with the cloudy liquid, he leaned in and whispered. "It's really good to see you together. I hope you don't mind me saying, *Cem bey*, my mother will be delighted. She's been praying for this ever since *Aşkta Şanslı* was cancelled. *Cem bey* with Burcu... She always says you were made for each other. I hope you don't mind."

"I don't mind, thank you. We're very happy," I responded politely.

I was lying. I minded so much my skin sizzled.

Aria beamed at him, and he blushed, stumbling backwards as he exited toward the kitchen. He'd bought our relationship. Not that I cared. I craved to see it all blow up, but not in a way that implicated Aria. I couldn't blame her for wanting to escape my own life.

We raised our glasses, but our celebration was premature. A young woman in a black cocktail dress approached our table. I saw the gleam in her eyes before she opened her mouth – that crazy, burning look that preceded trouble.

"*Cem bey*?" She played with her perfectly styled hair. "I can't believe it's you!"

Ignoring Aria, she offered her arm for me to sign.

"I don't have a pen."

"I do!" She produced one from her clutch.

I signed the woman's arm and bid her farewell, but she took out her phone.

"One photo of you two," she cooed, acknowledging Aria for the first time.

We posed for the photo, leaning across the table to get closer to each other.

"I can't believe you two are back together! So perfect!" She turned to Aria with an inquisitive look.

Aria responded with a regal smile, so perfectly timed that I could have sworn she'd understood every word. But I could tell our eager fan wasn't convinced.

Her gaze lingered on her for a long time, like a lion stalking its prey. "It's such a shame about those articles... I can see they're not true. You look so healthy and vibrant. You've put on weight. What would you say to all those people spreading lies?"

Aria tensed, probably reacting to the woman's viper-like smile. She held her pleasant expression, glancing at me for help.

I shot the woman a warning look. "This is highly inappropriate. We're not here to give interviews. We're having dinner."

"My apologies." The woman smiled and stepped backwards, not missing a beat.

I'd all but lost my fake smile when she finally moved on. She didn't go far, though. I could still see her at a nearby table, tapping on her phone, keeping watch.

I felt a little ill. Her fangirl act had started off pitch perfect, but I'd immediately recognized that honeyed tone of prying for a scoop. Who was she? A gossip journalist? An influencer?

She had a glass of water in front of her. A laptop peeked out of the giant handbag she'd lifted on the seat next to her. The man sharing her table didn't seem like her partner, at least not in the romantic sense. He sat back in his chair, smoking and browsing his phone, displaying no jealousy or bother over her interest in us.

Our food arrived – sea bass with salads. It was a stroke of luck I hadn't ordered the squid the place was famous for.

"Everything okay?" The waiter asked.

He must have witnessed the photograph session.

I assured him everything was fine. Demanding they remove another customer would cause a scene and not the scene I wanted to cause.

We ate in silence, trying to ignore the long looks from our fellow diners. The food tasted as good as I'd hoped for, and I watched Aria's face, trying to determine whether she liked it. I couldn't read her face; not like I was used to. She'd slipped back into character, mostly staring at the twinkling city lights or batting her lashes at me, her face a mask of politeness.

I felt like throwing my dinner into the ocean. I wanted my Aria, not this Burcu-like doll who smiled and nodded and ate like a bird. Yet, I couldn't stop staring at her, my gaze dipping to her deep cleavage, then returning to her perfectly controlled expression, studying every detail. Strangers might have been fooled, but I could see the difference. Simmering under the act, Aria had so much more life in her, a cheeky, fighting spirit I'd never seen in Burcu. She was unruly in the best way possible.

By the time we finished our meal, I cancelled the desserts and messaged Emir. I felt utterly exhausted, and the unnerving woman hadn't stopped watching us. She'd ordered a coffee she hadn't touched, too busy browsing her phone. Whatever she was cooking up, I didn't want to eat it.

I left a wad of money on the table and gestured for Aria to get up. She must have been reading my mind as she glanced at the suspicious woman, grabbed her clutch and jacket and fell in step with me. We beelined through the restaurant and into the car waiting outside.

"Drive," I told Tarik.

"You're on Twitter," Emir said as the car revved down the alley. "Hashtag *CemCucu*. Well done. I think we could still swing by the Soho House to get you photographed over there. Drinks at the bar, something like that."

I groaned. "But... jet lag!"

"We'll keep it short. I booked you a hotel room a little outside of town, but we need to be discreet about it. I promised Burcu's family that we wouldn't get any pics that might impact her reputation. They were worried."

Aria's eyes narrowed. "How would us booking into a hotel impact her reputation?"

I sighed. "It implies we're sleeping together. Makes her look… easy. People are quick to judge."

"Let me get this straight. You show your ass to the world and that puts a *dent* in your reputation. She is seen booking into a hotel with her boyfriend and that's enough to ruin hers?"

I winced, my shoulders creeping up as I considered this.

Aria stared at me with her eyes flaming. "Double standards!"

"Totally agree." I meant it, but I couldn't help smiling at her outrage.

"But we posted pictures from New Zealand! What do they think we did over there? Sleep in different hotels?"

"We kept the location vague," Emir reminded. "I know there were some theories, but some fans still like to believe Burcu is a virgin."

"Wow. Maybe we should have brought Emir along as the third wheel." Aria nodded at my brother.

I made a face. Not seeing my brother's permanent frown had been the highlight of our dinner.

"I can join you for the drinks," Emir offered.

Before I could protest, Tarik swerved, taking a sharp left. I didn't mind being thrown against Aria, my cheek planted right between her breasts, but Tarik's words ruined my pleasure. "*Takip ediliyoruz.* We're being followed."

Emir gave instructions as we drove around in circles, trying to lose the tail. No luck. The black SUV was right behind us.

"Is someone following us?" Aria asked. It amazed me how much she picked up without translation.

"Probably the paparazzi. What should we do?" I asked Emir. "They'll follow us to Soho. If it's the bloodthirsty paps, they'll keep following us, even after the drinks."

I saw the tightness in Emir's shoulders. "Could be the guys who published the rumor about your drug addiction and used that same, pixelated... um, penis shot for God knows how many—"

"Yeah, okay!" I didn't need to revisit that memory.

"If we'd stuck to my plan, none of this would have happened." Emir's voice brimmed with annoyance.

"Well, it happened," I barked. "What do we do?"

"I can't shake these guys." Tarik cast us a pained look, speeding down the bridge, bright lights flashing past.

Istanbul traffic was always bad. With so many cars on the roads, many of them driving erratically, even a skilled driver would struggle. Whoever chased us wasn't subtle about it, willing to run red lights and cut in line.

I rubbed my forehead. "We'll figure something out."

Aria squeezed my arm. "If I was Burcu and we were out on a date, where would you take me? Back home?"

"I guess."

"So, take me to Burcu's house."

"What do you mean? I don't even know where she lives."

"I bet the paparazzi does. And Melis. Ask her," Aria stared at me, her brow raised. "If you drive me there, you'll give them nothing unsavory to report."

"She's right." Emir was already on the phone.

A few minutes later, he rattled off the instructions to Burcu's house. "Melis had her personal phone number and address. Burcu is expecting us."

Hearing the new directions, Tarik did a U-turn. Despite the tooting of horns and screeching of brakes, no metal made contact. For a second, I thought we may have lost the SUV, but it copied Tarik's move, scaling the concrete berm between the lanes.

"Oh, my God!" Aria panted, her face white. She brought her nails to her lips, but turned her hand at the last minute, sinking her teeth into her knuckles. It must have been so hard to stop biting your nails. The thought made me crave a cigarette so much I nearly stole one from Tarik's pocket.

"It's okay." I tapped our driver's shoulder. "Let them follow us."

I leaned back in the seat, clasping Aria's hand. Tarik slowed down and she released her teeth from her fist, swiping her lipstick onto her cheek on the way down. I should have said something, but I kind of liked that small crack in her armor.

When we reached Burcu's address, North of Bebek, a pair of decorative cast iron gates opened for us, then closed quickly, leaving the SUV outside.

We peered through the back window as the paparazzi pulled on the curb.

"Do you think they'll wait out there?" Aria asked.

A muscle on Emir's jaw twitched. "They might. They're expecting Cem to drop you off and drive home."

This was not how I'd envisioned the night going. Forcing myself into action, I got out of the car and opened the door for Aria. Emir joined us. The photographer had made it to the gate and the bright camera flashes lit up the footpath like a lightning storm as we approached the entrance.

I spotted a cracked wall panel and a sad ceramic pot with no plant. The grass looked scraggly. So, it was true. They were in financial trouble. Burcu would have never settled for anything other than perfection. Otherwise, the house looked like a recent build. They were probably doing everything they could to hang onto it.

The front door opened, and I braced myself. I wasn't ready for this.

# CHAPTER 37

My first instinct was to hide behind Cem's back. Behind anything, really. When the door opened, I knew I'd been right. One should never meet their doppelgänger. Nothing invites comparison like two nearly identical people.

A woman in a sheeny wrap top and high-waisted jeans stepped into the light of the iron lanterns framing her front door. A shy smile wavered on her lips and within seconds, my brain registered half-a-dozen differences – all of them in her favor. She was at least two sizes smaller, with an impossibly tiny waist and narrow hips. Her neck appeared longer and more graceful, her eyelashes thicker. I could tell she wasn't wearing as much makeup as me yet looked more striking. Whatever star quality was, she exuded it. I could imitate her all I liked, but I could never carry myself with such regal elegance.

I stared at Cem, wondering what was going through his mind, seeing the woman who'd vanished after sleeping with him. He hadn't had much of a closure, I realized. Was he really over Burcu? How could he possibly be?

Cem and Emir greeted Burcu with kisses. Her melodic voice was as soft as a whisper. I listened to their Turkish chatter, shrinking into the background, until Cem brought me forward and switched to English. "This is Aria. I told you about her."

Burcu nodded, her face pleasant but unreadable. "Nice to meet you. Your dress is beautiful." Her English had a funny lilt.

"Thank you," I matched my volume to theirs.

Burcu looked over her shoulder. "My father is out with my brothers… *tavla*."

"Backgammon," Cem translated.

"Yes! And my mother went to bed and told the servants to go away. She has a headache." Burcu tapped her own forehead. "But I think it's good we don't tell them, yes?"

"Probably better that way," Emir confirmed. "Thank you for letting us hide here. We won't be long. We're hoping the paparazzi lose interest and leave."

Burcu glanced at the gate, which thankfully didn't offer a direct view to the entrance. "They think Cem drove me home after a date?"

We all nodded, and she stepped aside to let us in. "Please come inside, but please keep your voices down."

I followed the Erkam brothers into the brightly lit hallway, taking off my pointy, golden heels with great relief. My body had decided to cut off circulation to my pinkie toes, turning them into white nuggets, which I was happy to hide inside Burcu's guest slippers. I wobbled behind everyone else, searching for balance, desperate for the night to be over.

Burcu led us into an opulently decorated sitting room bursting with tasseled cushions, rugs and wall hangings. The palette of red and gold was set against a creamy wallpaper and the chandelier looked heavy enough to kill. If this family was in financial trouble, it wasn't immediately obvious.

We took seats across the endless, luxurious couch and Burcu excused herself, saying something to Emir who followed her.

"She's going to make tea," Cem explained.

Tea, again?

"But it's late and we arrived unannounced," I argued.

Cem leaned back against the plush couch. "It's a matter of hospitality."

"She looks amazing." I glanced at the direction Burcu had exited.

Cem's eyebrows lifted as he gazed at the doorway. "She looks like she's doing better. That's good."

I swallowed, zipping my mouth. There was no point digging a deeper hole for myself. If I could see the difference between us, Cem could see it. I wanted him to tell me I looked just as beautiful and not like the peasant version of a goddess, but it wasn't true, and I also despised insecure bullshit like that. I would not let those words pass my lips. I would not compete with this incredible woman, even if I'd been forced into a situation of rivalry.

I focused my eyes on a candle holder that sat on the coffee table. A flickering flame danced inside, making the star-patterned mosaic twinkle.

Cem scooted closer to me, placing his hand on the small of my back. The touch made my heart ache. It could have reassured me, if it weren't for the very abrupt way that he detached from me as Burcu and Emir re-entered the room, carrying trays of tea and snacks.

Burcu must have started laying out treats the moment she got off the phone with Emir. The presentation looked as flawless as the caramel waves falling on her shoulders. I accepted my tea with a thank you. Turkish was coming a little easier.

The meal of fish and vegetables had been as light as air and seeing the array of nuts, seeds and dried fruit on the platter, I snuck a handful onto my saucer.

With everyone served, Burcu took a seat next to Emir, facing me and Cem. "You look a lot like me," she stated approvingly, slightly cocking her head as her eyes examined me. "How much do you weigh?"

I nearly inhaled my tea. "Pardon me?"

Burcu stared back, oblivious to my discomfort. "I mean, how many kilograms?"

I glanced at Cem, but he didn't seem particularly outraged. Why wasn't anyone defending me?

"I'm not sure," I finally uttered, placing the cashew nut I'd been about to eat back on the saucer.

"I'm fifty-five kilos," Burcu announced with a smile. "Two kilos lighter than I was during the filming of *Aşkta Şanslı*. But if you're heavier, that's okay. Once I'm ready to go public again, people will think I lost some weight." She beamed, taking a tiny sip of her tea. "I can't wait to get back to my old life."

She released a deep sigh, her smile wavering between hope and desperation.

"I love this candle holder."

I wasn't sure why I said it. Maybe to steer everyone's attention away from my weight.

Burcu smiled. "You do? It's yours!"

I shook my head. "Oh, no. I didn't mean—"

"Let me get something to wrap it up." She stood, turning to Cem and Emir. "So, what's the plan? My father would not want anyone to write about us..." She paused, as if looking for the word, then shot me an apologetic look and continued in Turkish.

Emir raised his hand. "Don't worry. If we go first, the paparazzi will follow us. Then we'll send another car to pick up Aria."

A cold shiver ran down my neck. I pivoted on the couch to face Cem, pleading with my eyes.

*Don't leave me here with her. Please.*

I couldn't catch his gaze. Cem stared at Burcu, deep in thought.

Burcu smiled. "Sounds like a good plan. Maybe it's best if she gets changed into something less... golden?" She turned to me. "I can lend you some black clothes."

I nodded. That's what I needed – another fitting room experience with a piece of clothing I couldn't zip up or squeeze into. Sensing that I had little choice, I finished my tea and followed Burcu down a long hallway, into a bedroom with a giant walk-in closet. She laid some black pants and shirts on the bed. "Choose what you like. You can redo your makeup in the bathroom."

As she left the room, I caught my reflection in the full-length mirror and gasped. My lipstick had smeared on the left side of my mouth, creating a joker-like effect.

That's what I was. Except I was all out of jokes.

Utterly humiliated, I rushed into the bathroom. This is why I never wore lipstick. I could get done up for a role, but in real life, I could never maintain a flawless appearance. I prayed that the mishap had taken place after all those photos at the restaurant.

I located a box of cotton pads among Burcu's massive selection of toiletries and wiped off the lipstick. For a moment, I thought about reapplying it – Melis had slipped a touch-up kit into my clutch – but what was the point? I couldn't compete with perfection.

# CHAPTER 38

I had nearly fallen asleep on Burcu's couch when she reappeared in front of me.

"Alya is getting changed." She smiled, refilling my tea.

"Aria," I corrected, and she gave a carefree shrug.

Emir, who seemed equally exhausted, pushed himself upright and exchanged a look with Burcu. It could have been him politely acknowledging her presence, but something about that look bothered me.

"I'll order Aria's ride." Emir stretched, picking up his laptop.

Burcu waited for me to take a sip of tea, then gestured for me to get up. "Can I talk to you, Cem? It won't take long."

I yawned but got up and followed her through the dining area, onto a deck overlooking the swimming pool.

"It's good to see you," I said as we settled into a pair of sun loungers by the water.

Burcu's smile held like a still photo. "I'm feeling a lot better. I'm on new medication and it's making a difference."

I studied her, trying to remember what we'd once had, how I'd felt about her. She was as beautiful as ever, yet she felt like a stranger. There was no spark of recognition in my heart, no light behind her eyes pulling me in. They gazed back at me like two evil eye beads, glassy and impenetrable. I wondered if it was the medication or the illness, or maybe both.

"You seem... different," I said diplomatically.

"I think I'm ready to return to work. You know my family needs money. I really appreciate your help with finding this body double and bringing her here. It's a great start. I thought I'd take her off your hands and use her for a few jobs myself, but seeing you together, I feel..." She lowered her voice, her eye contact unnerving. "I'm ready, Cem. You can send her away and we can continue together. You and me."

Her smile radiated confidence, her posture straight as a rod, her neck elongated. Like a swan. An elegant, ferocious, territorial swan. I'd seen swans fighting. They fought to kill. Maybe that's what had changed. I couldn't see a hint of her old anxiety, that ever-present uncertainty that made the corners of her eyes twitch and her forehead wrinkle. They were replaced by a strange, calm composure. Two huge, unblinking eyes boring into mine.

Burcu brought her chair closer to mine, leaning in. A cloying floral fragrance filled my nose, tickling the back of my throat. Had she always worn this much perfume?

"We were once the number one couple in this city. We can do it again. Nobody else will stand a chance. We can revive both our careers. We can take our pick of the brand ambassador deals. There's a perfume brand I really want."

Was it the one currently teasing a sneeze out of me? I forced a smile, leaning as far back in my chair as I could. "Are you proposing a fake relationship?"

Burcu's face fell. "Cem! It's always been real between us, you know that!" She looked hurt, which felt like an improvement. A sign of humanity. "I'm offering you a chance to stop this fake relationship nonsense and have something real."

I bit my lip to stop from scoffing out loud. I couldn't even see the real person behind her composed veneer. But she kept staring at me, unyielding. My fingers fidgeted. I'd never craved a cigarette as much as I did right then. What did non-smokers do with their hands?

"We haven't seen each other in three years." I tried to sound patient, waiting for her to realize the insanity of her words. There was no 'us'. Our relationship had ended a long time ago. She'd ended it.

"I know. I wish we hadn't lost all that time, but I know you still think of me." Her eyes searched mine like she was reading the small print on a contract.

"How do you know that?"

Her eyes rounded. "Come on, Cem! You haven't had any serious girlfriends and you're hanging out with my body double."

My chest burned, spitting out angry words. "She's a person. Her name is Aria."

Burcu's brow knitted. "Of course she's a person. You know I don't treat my staff poorly. I know everyone by name. I pay them well. What are you saying?"

"I'm saying she's not a staff member. She's a... friend. She didn't have to do anything for me but she's helping both of us."

Burcu nodded slowly. "I see. She's a friend. I can only hope you're still paying her."

"Why?"

She gave a reproaching look. "I can see she's a little in love with you. Can't blame her, Cem, that's what happens to most of us, but it's not fair to lead her on. Pay her what she's worth. That way she won't feel quite as used."

My jaw tightened. "I'm not using her."

"She's a fish out of water. She doesn't belong." Burcu shrugged her dainty shoulders as if apologizing for the sad facts neither of us could change.

That's how it was in the Turkish TV industry. We dated our own kind, because no one else knew what it was like. If I worked in this town, Burcu would make a great ally. She spoke the language and knew the game inside out.

The night air was warm and muggy, but a shiver ran down my spine. Sitting here, listening to her, I felt like I'd tried on my old life, a shrunken jacket that didn't allow me to move my arms, or breathe. I fought to fill my lungs, my chest tightening. I couldn't go back to this.

But what did I want instead? What did I want, apart from Aria?

"I talked to Emir." Burcu lifted her chin, peering at me from underneath those perfect eyelashes. "He agrees that the two of us make sense. You can't continue with that replacement out there. It's only a matter of time before you're found out. She doesn't speak a word of Turkish. She's fat. I don't mind. She carries her weight really well. But you know the press will comment on it. Do you want her to hear that? You know how our country is about weight. The foreigners will never understand, they're so sensitive. The faster you send her home, the faster we can get back on track. Nobody needs to know about this arrangement. I'm sure you don't want to drag her into the middle of a scandal."

I sighed, because that's exactly what I'd been about to do during our dinner. Aria had stopped me. I rubbed my temples. "I'm trying to put the latest scandal behind me."

She patted my knee. "I know. I can't believe how much you get away with." She rolled her eyes affectionately.

"Double standards," I muttered, thinking of Aria. I needed her fighting spirit. I needed her.

I made a move to get up, but Burcu held her hand on my knee.

"I have something for you." She dipped her other hand into a box on a nearby table, and handed me an individually wrapped cigar, a cutter and a lighter. It was the brand we'd smoked together, the celebration cigar after wrapping up an episode.

And there it was, staring at me like a long-lost friend. "I... quit smoking."

She laughed, slapping my arm. "You did not!"

"I did. It's been a couple of weeks, I think." I glanced up at the starry sky, trying to count the days. They seemed to blend together.

"Then you've definitely earned one. For old times' sake. Or maybe there's something else we used to do that we could pick up again?" She bit her lip and batted her lashes, her fingers sliding from my arm onto my thigh.

My hands acted before my brain even caught up, unwrapping and cutting the cigar as if on autopilot. Holding the silver lighter, toasting the end of it, giving it a quick blow. I told myself I was prepping it for her, giving her hands something else to do, so she'd stop touching me, but before I knew it, I'd taken a long drag without even offering it to her first. Not a puff. A drag.

Damn this woman. She'd caught me at my weakest moment.

Giggling, Burcu took the cigar from me. "Looks like you really needed it."

Puffing on the cigar didn't seem to deter her from touching me. She was getting braver, much braver than she'd been three years ago. "I'd do anything for you. You know that, right?"

Her gaze dipped between my legs. The smoke burned my lungs and the familiar buzz travelled through my body. This wasn't the right way to smoke a cigar, inhaling it for a quick nicotine hit. But I hadn't changed my patch for a while and... I didn't have an excuse, only pathetic weakness.

The pleasure of smoking mixed with intense shame, making me nauseous. I thought about my father and the path he was walking. The treatments. The pain. The uncertainty. He expected me to follow him – live like him and die like him. Despite my protests and tantrums, here I was, following.

I handed Burcu the cigar, leaning back into the chair. I had to get out of here.

My heart had permanently lodged in my throat, and it wasn't coming down. I stared at the two of them, perfectly lit by warm torches and framed against the pool, mirroring the night sky. I was watching a scene in *Aşkta Şanslı*. The only thing I'd never seen on TV was smoking. I watched Cem inhale his cigar like he was sucking poison out of a wound and felt sick to my stomach.

This is what I'd hoped – that he'd start smoking again and I'd find him repulsive. But in that moment, I only felt pain. Pain over their closeness, her manicured hand on his thigh, the faint Turkish words they shared, the swirl of smoke rising to the sky, circling them like a protective shield, closing out the world.

I didn't belong here, but these two did. They belonged to the world of glitz and glamour, romancing the screen, loved by millions.

The waistband of Burcu's black tights dug into my stomach, signaling how poorly I fit into this world. I was an intruder, the obstacle standing in the way of Cem's success, derailing his life.

I retreated into the hallway on shaky legs and kept stumbling backwards, not in control of my movements, until I reached the living room and bumped into Emir.

"Do you want me to book you an earlier flight?" he asked, holding up his phone. "There's one leaving tonight."

"To...night?" I stammered, leaning on the wall for support, a sharp ache piercing my chest. "You don't need my help anymore?"

Emir lifted a shoulder. "I'm sure Cem would love to have you around, but I don't think it's fair to you if Burcu is willing to take over. That's easier for everyone, isn't it?"

Burcu was willing to take over?

"Of course." My mouth tasted like old batteries. "When's the flight?"

Emir grimaced as he tapped on his phone. "This one is in two hours. We'll have to get Cem out of here and make a move. I can get your luggage delivered straight to the airport. Istanbul Airport is closer than Sabiha Gokcen where we arrived. How's that?"

"That's... very efficient." I stared in awe, every muscle clenched, as he typed away.

So, this was how it all ended, with a stomach-turning fall, like being kicked out of an airplane and falling and falling, waiting to hit the ground. I definitely hadn't brought a parachute. Not even an umbrella. I'd hopped on this ride with no plan on how to get back down safely.

"Done," Emir announced. "I've emailed you the new ticket."

"Thank you."

"Tarik will take Cem and me home as planned, and I've ordered you a taxi. It'll be waiting outside on the curb. Once the paparazzi has gone, hop in. Another driver will meet you at the airport check-in with your luggage."

"How do I find him?"

"I told him to meet you at Turkish Airlines check-in. He has your name and will hold up a sign. You won't miss him, and you'll probably recognize your suitcase."

I nodded, trying to memorize these details I didn't even want to think about. I'd been in Istanbul for two days. Two days, and already it was over.

"Here's some money for your troubles. I hope it's enough. We're both grateful for your help and discretion." Emir handed me an envelope, which I didn't open. I would have handed it back, but that's when Cem and Burcu joined us, trailed by a cloud of cigar smoke.

Later, I realized that's exactly what I should have done – I should have thrown the money at Emir's face. Maybe then, things would have been different. But I stood rigid like a statue, barely able to breathe.

"We need to go," Emir told Cem, guiding him toward the front door.

"Yeah, okay."

Cem gave me a wide berth, a sheepish smile on his face. Was he trying to hide the fact he'd been smoking? I would have smelled him from a mile away, but at that moment, I hardly cared. I just wanted him to look at me. I followed them to the door, my eyes fixed on him as he put his shoes on. Did he know about the new plan? Had he agreed to it?

I took a step closer, but Cem retreated out the door. "You have a ride?" He asked me across the threshold.

"Yes," I said flatly, "don't worry about me."

"Okay. I'll see you later." He lifted his hand in greeting, a warm smile on his face, and that's when I knew.

He had no idea.

I should have screamed. I should have run after him.

Later, I reimagined the situation so many times, with so many different outcomes, but then, I did what I'd been doing all night. I smiled and waved.

I must have looked miserable, holding back tears, but Cem had already disappeared into the dark night.

Burcu handed me an open gift box. I stared down at the candle holder. "It was so lovely to meet you," she said, offering me a pair of ballet flats, a far more comfortable alternative to the golden heels waiting for me at the door.

"Thank you." I focused on breathing in and out. In and out.

Breath became my singular focus, the only way to keep myself together. To not dissolve onto the floor.

In. Out. Out of this house. Into that taxi. Onboard that plane. Somewhere private where I could fall apart.

# CHAPTER 40

# Cem

"You did what?" I shouted, raising my white-knuckled fists.

Emir shrunk back, probably regretting his decision to join me in the back seat. "I asked her if she wanted to take an earlier flight and she said yes. Burcu told me she's willing to take over. It was the logical choice." He blinked in confusion.

The nightly Istanbul traffic flickered past, a blur of colorful lights as Tarik drove us away from Burcu's house. I wanted to throw up. My brother had casually swapped the woman I loved for a soulless lookalike, acting as if it was no big deal.

Of course. He didn't know.

"You didn't even let me say goodbye. I know you're a heartless robot, but—"

"Call her. She's probably still at the airport." Emir pointed at the phone in my hand.

"No. We have to drive there. Now."

"Why?" Emir's forehead creased. "She's a lovely girl and she was helpful, but she won't think less of you if you're not there to see her off. I paid her well and she was happy to go."

"What do you mean, happy?" My heart pounded in my chest. "Did she say she was happy... to go?"

Emir shrugged. "She didn't argue."

No, it wasn't true, I told myself. Aria wasn't happy to leave me. She couldn't be. I tapped Tarik's shoulder. "Take us to the airport, now!"

Tarik turned to Emir, who shook his head.

"Fine!" I shouted. "Stop the car and I'll get a taxi."

"Istanbul Airport," Emir told Tarik, then turned to me. "And you tell me what's going on."

"He's in love with the New Zealand woman," Tarik said quietly, his berating eyes flashing at us on the rear-view mirror. "You're all business, you don't notice, but it's obvious."

Emir glared at me. "You're in love with the New Zealand woman? The heavier version of Burcu?"

I sighed, cursing the Turkish habit of openly commenting on everyone's weight.

"She's perfect. And yes, I love her. I don't want to do fake dating anymore. I don't care what the studio's expecting or what anyone else thinks. I want Aria."

Emir leaned his face into his hand, groaning. "You could have told me that!"

"I was going to. I didn't know you'd send her away behind my back."

"We talked about this, remember? That you shouldn't get involved with her. I figured you wouldn't listen, but I thought at most you'd sleep with her once. Not fall in love."

I rubbed my forehead. "I didn't mean to."

"You know she lives in New Zealand, right? And you live and work here."

"What if I didn't?"

"What do you mean? You have a chance at a global film career. Nobody throws that away."

I huffed. "You sound like Aria."

"Clearly, she's a smart girl. She wants the best for you."

"But—"

"Don't be stupid, Cem. This is not the storyline of some vapid *dizi*. Love doesn't conquer all. Not things like this."

I clamped my mouth shut. My brother would never understand.

"Excuse me, but what time is her flight?" Tarik gestured at the sea of red brake lights ahead of us. Traffic ground to a halt.

"Eleven-thirty." Emir looked at his watch. "In half an hour."

"I'm sorry, *Cem bey*, but if that flight leaves on time, we'll never make it." Tarik's voice carried a level of compassion my brother wasn't capable of.

"Fine." I released a sigh so heavy my soul may have escaped with it. "Let's go home."

Emir's shoulders dropped in relief. If only he'd known that was the moment I saw my cage and everything it was made of, every bar holding me back, standing in the way of my freedom. And I was ready to break it all down.

## CHAPTER 41

When someone pounded on the front door, I'd been crying for three days, two of them within the confines of my stuffy apartment. I dragged myself out of bed, pushing away Kerim's takeaway containers, glancing at Burcu's candle holder with its burned-out tea light. My flat had transformed into a wallowing central.

I paused at the door, then dashed into the bathroom to examine my face. Swollen eyes, messy hair, dried food on my tank top. I tried to scrape it off with my last remaining fingernail.

Who was at the door, anyway? I hadn't ordered anything or told anyone I'd returned. That had been my only solace upon landing in Napier – four days of wallowing in peace before anyone expected me to join the living. I didn't have to answer phone calls or explain my puffy, red face.

Another knock. The hope I'd tried my hardest to extinguish hit me like whiplash, whispering Cem's name. I so desperately wanted it to be him, I didn't even care about how horrid I looked, or what my apartment smelled like. Okay, I cared a little, but I had no time to fix anything. He'd have to take me as I was.

A third knock. I drew a deep breath, shivering from head to toe, and yanked the door open.

Felix.

The gust of air from my swinging door made him sway so hard he stumbled backwards, nearly losing his footing.

My stomach dropped and eyes welled. How long would I keep torturing myself?

Felix stared at me in shock. "Are you okay?"

I rubbed my eyes, turning away. "Um… sure. Allergies."

"You don't even react to that privet hedge at the back of your parent's house, it's—"

"Fine. It's not allergies." I spun on my heel to face him again. "What do you want?"

Felix took a half a step back, baffled by my tone. "I came to pick you up for coffee. You said Tuesday?"

"Did I?" I blinked, trying to rearrange the chaotic timeline of the last couple of weeks. "Didn't my mom tell you that I went… overseas?"

"Overseas? When?" His eyes widened.

Mom hadn't told him? Maybe they weren't quite that buddy-buddy, Felix and my parents. I found the thought somehow comforting.

"So, you wanna go?" Felix asked, tilting his head toward the stairs.

I let out a sad chuckle. "You want to take this girl out for a coffee?" I pointed at my kebab-sauce-adorned top.

He stared back, clueless. "That's why I'm here."

To Felix's credit, he didn't seem to notice much difference in me. And, he wasn't leaving, just swaying at my doorway, waiting for an answer.

"Okay." I sighed. "Give me a minute."

A cup of coffee wouldn't kill me. I'd have to leave the house eventually. I'd have to stop watching *Aşkta Şanslı* and replaying every word Cem had ever said to me. I had to get out of my memory palace and let those memories cool down. Maybe after a while they wouldn't hurt so much.

After five minutes, I'd washed my face, thrown on a slightly cleaner T-shirt and sat in Felix's van, heading downtown.

"Where did you go?" he asked. "Australia?"

"Istanbul."

"Istanbul, Turkey?"

"Is there another Istanbul?"

"You seem angry."

I shrugged. Maybe I was. It felt better to be angry than sad. At least anger came with some energy, as did coffee. I'd count both of those as tiny victories.

"I'm trying to get over something. Someone." I looked out the window, avoiding his eyes.

"Ah, okay."

I braced myself for a follow-up question, but Felix drove on in silence.

Napier looked the same as always. Beautiful, sleepy, empty. Without Cem, my town felt like an empty shell. Nothing here made me feel alive. Nothing captured my heart.

Felix parked outside the cafe, and I cringed. We were only one block from my office.

"Wait. Is there anywhere else we can go? This is so close to work, and I haven't told my boss I'm back—"

"But I told you about this cafe. This is the…"

He looked so forlorn that I gave up. "Don't sweat it. It's fine."

I climbed out of the van and Felix escorted me to a corner table. We ordered flat whites, and he insisted on sharing a piece of carrot cake. The coffee was strong, I had to admit.

"So, you're getting over someone?" Felix asked, his eyes regarding me with cautious curiosity.

I gathered my thoughts to answer, when I heard Janie's bright voice. "Aria! You're back already!"

Of course. We'd arrived for the morning coffee break and here she was, as if on cue.

I turned around, trying to arrange my features into a smile. "Hi, Janie! Yes, I'm back."

I must have looked rather distraught since her face immediately fell. "What happened?"

Janie took a seat next to me, ignoring Felix. "Tell me!"

I dropped the fake smile, meeting her concerned eyes. "I… I had to leave early. They didn't need me anymore. The actress I was impersonating took over the role herself. Who better to play her than herself, right?" I shot for a bright tone, and I tried to smile again, but my mouth didn't cooperate.

"Oh, Aria! He broke your heart, didn't he? The bastard! That beautiful bastard."

"Who's a beautiful bastard?" Felix asked.

Janie waved a dismissive hand at my date, took me by the elbow and walked me out of the cafe. "Bye!" she called from the door.

I could only imagine Felix's expression, but I didn't have the energy to care. The pain had momentarily taken over my body, demanding all my resources.

Janie kept escorting me until we got to the office entrance. "Pete's not here, don't worry."

She walked me to the couch, plonking me down. "I'll make you some tea."

I burst into tears. "Not tea."

Oh, God. I was triggered by tea now? How had I turned into this scorching hot mess? I heaved in breaths between wailing sobs, sounding like a toddler having a meltdown.

"What's wrong?" Janie sat next to me, throwing her arm over my shoulder, waited for me to calm down and listened as I told her the whole sorry saga, sniffling and wiping my nose on my T-shirt sleeve until she fetched me a roll of toilet paper.

When I finished, Janie blew out a sigh. "That was quite the story."

I looked at her over my wad of toilet paper. "I don't know how to pull myself together. I know I have to, but I ... miss him so much."

"Of course you do." She rubbed my arm. "Can you call him?

Email him?"

I shook my head, spraying snotty tears over my arms. "No. I don't want to stand in the way of his dreams. He'll be huge, I know it. He'll go to Hollywood."

Janie nodded. "Maybe. Sounds like he has the talent, the looks and the opportunity."

"Exactly. He needs to go for it. I'd never forgive myself if I blew it for him, but it still hurts. Letting go hurts."

Janie stared past me, deep in thought. "Has he let go, though? Do you think? It sounds like it wasn't his decision. And it sounds like maybe he's looking for a new direction in life."

I scoffed. "He's not looking to buy a farm and keep chickens. No offence."

"None taken." Janie smiled. "But he might be looking for something... different. Celebrity life isn't the perfect fit for everyone. It's exhausting. Not a great foundation for lasting relationships, either."

Despite my self-centered wallowing, I detected the pain in her voice. "Did it affect your marriage? Is that why you quit?"

Janie sighed. "I thought it would help us, getting away from it all, but I don't think we were on the same page. Maybe there wasn't anything left to save."

"I'm sorry," I sniffled, feeling horrible. "Here I am, crying over a two-week relationship. A *fake* relationship."

"But yours is a fresh pain. I've done my crying." She smiled her usual bright smile, like nothing could ever touch her. I couldn't imagine Janie even crying. How did she look? Did she snot all over the place and sound like a dying whale?

"And it doesn't sound fake, what you went through. It sounds quite real. So passionate. I've forgotten what that feels like." She released a wistful sigh. "Has he tried to contact you?"

I shook my head. "He must be prepping for the new role already."

My phone rang, startling us both. Unknown number.

I took a deep breath before I answered.

"Aria Dunne?" A female voice chirped in my ear.

"Yes."

"I'm calling about the role. When would you be available for a fitting? We have a few costumes to finish."

It took several beats before I recognized Lindsay's voice and remembered the audition.

"Lindsay? What? Have I... Did you..." I couldn't find the words.

"Did you get my message?" Lindsay asked. "I sent you the updated script and the shooting schedule. We start the day after tomorrow."

I flashed a panicky look at Janie, who smiled encouragingly, leaning in to hear both sides of the conversation. I hadn't checked my email in a couple of days, after compulsively clicking on the refresh button for 24 hours. I'd had to cut myself off before I lost my mind. Cem had my number. He'd call if he wanted to.

"Yes, of course. Thank you. Thank you."

I promised Lindsay I'd show up at the hotel early in the morning, then ended the call as quickly as I could without being impolite. Any longer, and I would have sniffed.

Shaking from the suspended sniffles, I turned to Janie. "They cast me. The role is mine."

She jumped to her feet, clapping her hands. "That's amazing! I've always said the best way to work through the pain is to work through the pain."

"Work through the pain," I repeated.

What else could I do?

# CHAPTER 42

I sat in front of a three-paneled dressing mirror, examining the 1930s dropped-waist dress and head scarf that transformed me into Eloise – the woman who had to make a choice between love and a great fortune.

I felt her pain.

I preferred her pain.

For the past week, I'd lived through the 1800s gold rush and the tumultuous 1930s. I'd journeyed with my character as she witnessed the ugly things in her family's past. It was a pain I could handle. The faux pain played for the cameras. The other pain, I'd locked away. Over the days, the tears had dried, other than for the scenes I needed them for. The joy of bringing the story to life, of doing what I loved to the best of my ability, gave me strength.

I hadn't heard a word from Cem, but I suddenly had a lot of lines to learn and no time to think about him. Well, no. I still thought about him, almost constantly, but I didn't have time to google him, searching for the headlines about his new role and international stardom. Maybe that was for the best. As much as I wanted to see his career rise to new heights, every photo of him made me ache. I'd never been more grateful to have a job to do, a job that required my full attention and pulled me into a completely different, imaginary world.

After a week of outdoor shoots, we were back at the hotel. Stepping back into the pink building brought back a flood of memories, but I tried to brush them aside and focus on the job.

This was my chance, the one I'd waited for my whole life. And it was all because of Cem. I couldn't be angry at him. He'd given me more than I'd ever thought possible. He'd made me believe. He'd made me dream, but I didn't dream of international stardom. I dreamed of him. That was the price I paid – the fresh stab of disappointment every time I didn't find him behind the door, or around the corner.

It hurt, but also amazed me. Because that hope I nursed and pain I felt wouldn't have been possible without a dash of faith. Part of me now trusted a higher power that didn't hate me. I believed that good things could happen, that I could be lucky or even blessed. Life felt a little less random. A little less bleak.

"You're up in five," Lindsay called from the doorway. "Have you checked the changes? Are you ready?"

With a small crew, her producer role seemed very hands-on.

I lifted my script. "Yes, I did a read-through. Good to go."

Lindsay's eyes glinted. "By the way, Ali's role got recast. I'll take you to meet him now. Don't worry. It's a short scene with two lines, you'll have a chance to rehearse the other scenes later. He's very experienced."

My heartbeat kicked up a notch. "What happened to Petros?"

I'd already run lines with the quiet, slightly wooden Armenian guy. He didn't exactly match the character description, but he'd done a solid job.

Lindsay waved her hand. "Petros is fine, but Lars wants to go a different direction with this."

I was still getting used to the fast-moving, ever-evolving nature of this film production. I could only hope our director shared more than his first name with Lars von Trier. I'd never heard of a character being recast after rehearsals, unless they did something like… my thoughts ran away before I could catch them, and I tried to mentally wipe Cem's famous dick pic from my mind.

"We're still shooting in order, right?" My stomach twisted.

Lindsay winked with a knowing smile. "Yes, don't worry. No intimacy today. Just scene five, as per your call sheet."

I gave her a wobbly nod. The love story was only a subplot that emerged alongside other adventures, but I hadn't played an intimate scene in ages. I hadn't touched another man since…

It's only a bit of kissing, I told myself. No big deal.

I gathered the script and my water bottle and stepped out of the hotel room doubling as my dressing room. It wasn't the one Cem had stayed in. I wasn't a masochist. Still, everything around here reminded me of him, so much that I had to fix my eyes on my squeaking 1930s leather shoes. Left. Right. Left. Right. Don't look. Don't think.

I followed Lindsay downstairs, through the reception area cleared for filming and into the sitting room that had turned into a production dump with gear, drink bottles and scripts lying on every surface.

And there, in the far corner of the crammed room, sunken into a mauve velvet Art Deco chair, bent over a script, was Cem.

"I believe you two know each other?" Lindsay beamed at me, pointing at him across the room. "He asked me to keep it a surprise."

I stared, unable to reply. Cem looked up, but not at me. His eyes were trained on Harriet, our assistant director, who stood by his chair with a stern expression. It looked like he was asking something. Harriet shook her head, annoyed.

Lindsay touched my arm. "You guys don't need introductions, right? I have to check on the set." She swiveled and swept away, her shoulder catching on the light curtain, which fell like a veil over her head.

I snuck a little closer to Cem and Harriet to hear them over the chatter and footsteps.

"That's too bad, ba-d," Harriet said. "There's a 'd' at the end. When you say it, it sounds like bet or bat."

"That's too bad," Cem read again, emphasizing the 'd', maybe a little too hard.

Harriet frowned. "Yes, that's the sound but try to say it naturally.

I mean, it's okay to have an accent but we shouldn't need subtitles."

Cem nodded. "I'm sorry. I'll keep practicing."

"You do that." Harriet left the room, wearing the expression I'd become familiar with, the one that said, 'where's the next fire?'.

On the way, she shoulder-tapped two camera ops who followed her outside. The others had left, probably to set up the scene. We were alone.

Dozens of thoughts burst into my mind, fighting for attention. I couldn't breathe. I couldn't move. What was he doing here? Was he really acting in this film? Why? What had happened in Istanbul?

Above all, I had a strange sensation I was witnessing a miracle – an immortal being choosing a mortal life. He'd become one of us, sitting in a crammed room, dressed in what looked like a pair of dungarees, his dark curls trapped under a vintage flat cap, humbly learning a two-line scene, struggling with the word 'bad'. None of it made any sense.

I took a step forward, as silently as possible.

"You can come closer, Aria. I won't bite. At least not too hard." He looked up from his script, a fleeting smile crossing his lips.

"What are you doing here?" I shuffled my feet, suddenly self-conscious over the 1930s dress with a giant bow hanging around my neck. My hair was pinned under the scarf and my lips were painted crimson. I wasn't myself.

"Waiting for you." He got up and met me at the doorway, where my vintage shoes had evidently been nailed to the floor.

I could have sworn the air vibrated, distorting my vision as he got closer. It didn't help that he'd really been dressed as a 1930s farmhand in a beige undershirt and dirty dungarees. "Your clothes have no shine." My mouth felt drier than sandpaper.

He laughed. "Is it working for you? I brought my 'mana' shirt as well, for when I'm not acting. Although I think that one should have some shine to it. I looked up the meaning." His eyes sparkled. "But if you prefer me like this, I'll dress up like a horse breeder for the rest of my days."

I shook my head, as if to dispel the image. "It's so weird. Like it's you... but not you. I have so many questions."

"Ask."

"Why are you here?"

He looked at me for a long time, his expression wavering between amusement and sadness. "Do you have to ask?"

"Don't tell me you threw away that role! After all we went through."

*After all I went through.*

His eyes hardened. "It was mine to throw away."

Anger flashed inside me like an explosion, blurring my vision. I shoved his chest with all my strength. "No, it wasn't!"

He didn't budge, but as I went for another hit, he caught my wrists, locking me on to him.

"Aria," he whispered.

Powerful cries shook my body. "Nobody throws away an opportunity like that! I can't be responsible—."

I felt his hot breath on my forehead. "You're not. It's my life. My mistakes. My choices."

"But you chose her. The beautiful, skinny one. I'm the ugly, fat copy." The words sputtered like hot bubbles from a boiling jug.

Cem squeezed my wrists. "No, I didn't and I'm sorry about what Burcu said. Turkish people are weird. We comment on everyone's weight, but it's not mean spirited, it's a cultural thing. You're perfect. I wouldn't change a thing."

"But I saw you out there, smoking together. She was touching you... it looked so right. Like you belonged together."

Cem winced. "Is that why you left?"

I gave him a wobbly nod. "I didn't want to make it awkward for you if you wanted to go with her. For your career and everything. You guys make sense. Unlike us." I'd been repeating that line, willing myself to believe it.

He shook his head. "I don't care what it looks like. Nothing makes sense without you."

"But Emir said—"

"I fired him."

"You did what?" I looked up, blinking away hot tears, my breath escaping in shuddering bursts.

Cem smiled. "I'm managing myself now. It feels good."

The exasperation in my chest spilled over and words flew out. "I was just getting over you!" I bit my lower lip. It tasted like lipstick, then blood. "I've tried so hard."

He let go of my wrists but pulled me to his chest. "Don't try so hard."

I banged his chest with powerless fists that bounced off the hard muscle. He held me tighter.

"You broke my heart," I whispered into his dungarees. They

smelled vaguely of hay. So not like him. But he pressed me against his warm chest, I detected his familiar scent, and it shot straight to my heart. Istanbul.

"And you broke mine," he whispered into my hair. "We did what we set out to do, but I couldn't let you go."

My whole body shook as he squeezed me to his chest, my insides rearranging themselves and the world once again turning upside down. He was here. He was real. He was holding me.

Harriet appeared behind us. "First positions!"

I wiped my eyes, sucked in several deep breaths and we followed her to the reception area where our characters had their first scene together, one where Eloise tells Ali that the hotel has no vacancies and graciously turns him down as a romantic prospect.

I gathered all my strength and waited for the makeup artist to reapply the lipstick I'd eaten, staring at my short but somewhat tidy nails. I couldn't let Cem's presence distract me. Maybe he had so many opportunities he could throw them away like candy wrappers, but I only had this one shot. I couldn't risk blowing it.

But when I glanced at Cem, I noticed he looked serious. His attention on the director, he went over his lines, blocking the scene with the camera. I was the one standing behind the desk with minimal stage direction. I clung to the edge of the wooden tabletop, an antique piece of furniture the set designer had sourced from somewhere.

My nerves vibrated like I was hovering on a knife's edge. Would he distract me? Would I blow this scene?

As we took the first positions, I witnessed another miracle.

Before my eyes, Cem transformed into someone else. I felt like I watched his ego shrink, revealing an awkward vulnerability that held me spellbound. Cem was no longer Cem. He'd turned into a poor horse breeder looking for a room in a fully booked town. He took off his hat as he approached the desk, casting me a look I'd never seen before. With every movement and gesture, he handed over his authority, elevating me, supporting the role I was meant to play.

We had a script. I knew the story. Yet, I felt like we were improvising. Dancing. He was leading me into the spotlight and stepping into the shadows. My world had flipped on its axis. Fire coursed through every fiber of my being, and I let the moment sweep me away.

After the first take, the director gave me a thumbs-up and asked Cem to play his part even more awkwardly. He did. I relaxed further, inserting a bit of playfulness into my own performance, shooting down his advances with grace and a hint of amusement.

When Lars called 'cut' on the fifth take and announced he was happy to move on, I released a deep sigh. My body flooded with a strange mix of endorphins and nerves. I'd played a scene with Cem and nailed it.

"Tea?" Cem called across the room, pointing at the kitchen. "We have a bit of time, right?" Gone was the awkwardness of his performance. His smile shone with familiar confidence, lighting up the room.

"Yes, absolutely," Lindsay responded with a huge smile, then turned to me, lowering her voice. "What's his deal? Is he single?"

My response erupted loud, fast and unfiltered. "No, he's not."

Lindsay raised her hands, taking a step back. "I see. Apologies."

My heart pounding, I followed Cem into the kitchen. He was mine. Mine. Lindsay would regret the day she tried to make a move on my Cem.

I found him filling the electric jug and surged in front of him, looking straight into those deep brown eyes, placing my hands on the chest of his ridiculous dungarees. "What are you doing to me, Cem? I just went crazy jealous bitch over you. I basically told Lindsay to back off."

His mouth curved into a victorious smile as he flicked on the jug and slid his hands around my waist. "Thank you. That woman scares me."

My heart pounded and my palms felt sticky with sweat. "I can't believe you're here. I thought you'd forget about me."

He shook his head, tightening his hold on me. "Never."

Overcome by emotion, my head fell on his chest, and I squeezed my eyelids. "I tried so hard to forget you."

"You can't. I live inside your memory palace, Aria. I moved in with all my stuff."

"You did!" I laughed shakily. "It's strewn across the floor and the bed. You're the messiest guy I know."

He held me so tight I could barely breathe. I felt him draw a ragged breath, his body shuddering. "When you left... I never knew anything could hurt so much." His voice was thick and throaty.

Remorse strangled my throat. "I'm so sorry. I should have fought for us. I thought I was doing the right thing. I thought I was the only one getting hurt."

"Why would you think that?"

"Because I thought you were somehow… divine. Bullet proof."

He grabbed my shoulders, raw pain behind his eyes. "I'm a guy who's in love with you. You can hurt me so easily it's not funny."

"I'm sorry, Cem." I forced myself to meet his burning gaze. "I thought I knew what you wanted. Or needed."

"Just like Emir." He heaved a sigh, leaning his forehead against mine. "I'm so tired of it."

"What did he say when you turned down the role?"

"Not much. I think he's still processing it. Figuring out what to do without that big paycheck."

I glanced at the door, wondering if the other crew members were holding back on using the kitchen to give us privacy. Cem buried his face into my hair, kissing me behind the ear.

"What about your dad's treatment?" I asked, trying to focus. I could easily lose myself in his arms.

"I sold my boat," he murmured, inhaling me.

"Seriously? Why?" I tried to pull away to catch his eye, but he held me too tight.

"Because I needed the money, and that was the most expensive, useless thing I owned."

"It's not useless."

He finally met my gaze, eyes full of fire. "Well, I used it as a place to hook up, and I don't want to do that anymore."

He stood so close that his presence filled my every sense, warmth spreading down my limbs with each breath I drew, with each lungful of his scent. I had to take a step back, to get to the end of my burning questions.

"So, you're not going to be a committed bachelor anymore?"

He threw out his arms, eyes blazing. "What does that even mean? Who commits to being a bachelor? Seriously?"

"I don't know. It'd make a weird ceremony."

Cem burst into laughter. "God, I missed you!" He caught my hand, his gaze flicking at the ceiling. "Wanna come to my room? I booked the same one as last time. It's got a fancy Art Deco chair you like. If you could sit in it naked, that would really make my day."

"Are you suggesting we destroy a piece of antique furniture by having sex on it?"

"I'll order a replacement. My dad's antique shop has about ten of those."

Again, he closed the distance between us, stroking his hands down my arms, giving me shivers. But I had a job to do.

I took a step back, glancing at the door. "We can't leave. They're setting up the next shot. I don't want to get fired."

"Don't worry. You're looking at the executive producer." He jerked a thumb at himself and grinned.

My stomach flip flopped so hard it hurt. "You invested in this film?" I almost couldn't look at him. "Did they hire me because—"

Cem's eyes circled the room. "No! They hired you... way before. I think." He wasn't even a little convincing.

Pain of the realization seared through me. "Please don't tell me..."

I tried to turn away, but Cem grabbed my hand, his eyes searching for mine, desperate. "Aria. Come on. It's not like that. They loved you, but they were considering someone else they thought was more bankable... So, I suggested I'll make an investment to balance the scales. I didn't think you should lose out to someone who got hired because of their fame. I helped them make the decision they *wanted* to make. You know Lars. He's either crazy or genius or both. He's not someone who compromises his artistic vision for a bit of cash. It doesn't matter how you got the part. It matters how you play it."

I'd thought of this as my big break. The one I'd earned. But had I really?

"So, it was you?" I blinked back tears, my throat so tight I could hardly speak. "You did this for me?"

He brushed his fingers down the side of my face, catching a wayward tear. "You promised I could buy you a present. Would you rather have a hundred-dollar jar of honey?"

I looked down at my vintage shoes, trying to gather my thoughts. They'd scattered like rabbits after a gunshot. What did this mean? Did his revelation cancel out everything I was proud of, everything I had worked for? Was part of me still so hung up on the idea of earning my success, that I couldn't accept the possibility of luck, blessing or even a bit of help?

I looked out the window. "Back in Auckland, when I dreamed about this, when I imagined myself finally getting that lead role... I thought I'd never let myself become one of those obnoxious jerks who thought they worked harder and were more talented than everyone else, so they deserved it… I promised myself I'd never think like that. I thought I'd be happy. Grateful. I'd count my lucky stars—"

"Count me!" Cem cupped my face, his brown eyes burning holes in mine.

"What?"

"I'm your lucky star, Aria. Count me." His eyes glowed.

I don't know whether it was his creative grasp of the English language, or that slightly frenzied, earnest delivery, but it made sense.

"You are a star," I admitted, a smile hovering on my lips, a ray of hope piercing the dark cloud swelling inside.

"And I'm lucky."

"Triple Irish." A dreamy smile seized my lips. Then a thought hit me. "But what about you? How can you go from leading roles to… this?"

Cem's eyes widened. "What are you talking about? I get to act with you!" He touched my chin, gently bringing my face closer to his. "Besides, it's only the beginning. I have to learn to pronounce words like 'bad' and then I can go for bigger English-speaking roles." He rolled his eyes animatedly.

I couldn't hold back my shaky laugh. "That'll be fun. Want me to teach you?"

Cem trailed his hands down my back, anchoring my hips to his. "Will you teach naked?"

"*Allah, Allah!*" I protested, but let him pull me against him, enjoying the erection I felt through his dungarees. I inhaled his scent, the familiar spice and musk, but no tobacco. "You didn't start smoking again?"

"Gee! No, I didn't. How many more questions do you have?" His hands roamed my body, lighting up little fires all over the place.

I could barely concentrate, but I had to put my mind at ease. "Umm... Do you want to stay in New Zealand?"

"I'll stay wherever you are."

My heart ached. "But I love Istanbul!"

He released a sigh of relief. "Then I might take you back. But I'll have to marry you first."

"What?"

"It's a Turkish thing. We can't risk your reputation..."

My face burned. "Cem! You can't joke about something like that!"

"I'm not joking." He flicked his fingers and a ring appeared, like a magic trick. "You're the one always joking. Us Turks take this stuff seriously. Weddings and formalities. Family gatherings and all that."

I stared at the antique gold band, my mind reeling, body paralyzed. "You'd take me back there as... myself?"

"Yes! You, Aria. I want you. I wanted you from the start."

"But what about the press?"

Cem's cheeks flared. "They kind of already know. I told them I'm going to New Zealand to propose to Aria Grace Dunne."

"What?" My eyes were in danger of falling out of my head.

He grimaced. "It was premature, I know. But they were talking about me and Burcu and I... flipped out. I didn't think."

I stared at him, then the ring, then him again. "Well, that's the verbal equivalent of a dick pic."

He snort-laughed, nearly dropping the ring. "You're right!" He wiped his eyes, his expression turning serious. "You're famous in Turkey now. Are you mad at me?"

I slowly shook my head. "No. I'm just… digesting this."

He took a step closer. "I know I'll keep making mistakes, and I probably should have a manager, or a babysitter but I want to be better. I want you to hold me accountable. Expect more from me, like you do. Don't coddle me. I'm going to do everything to be worth your trust."

I played with the button of his dirty dungarees, marveling at his transformation. He was still Cem, but he was also just a man. I could imagine myself with him. I could imagine a life. He wasn't here to sweep me away to a fairy tale. He'd stepped out his bubble and joined me at the bottom of the world. Anyone with money could throw it around for effect, but Cem had rearranged his life to make room for me. He'd chosen to have less so that we could have a life together.

"It's not going to be easy. Starting over. Buying milk. Doing laundry." I studied his eyes, searching for the shadow of doubt, but I only saw determination.

"You're worth it, Aria." His eyes glistened and voice cracked. "You're worth everything. If you'll have me?"

I looked into his eyes and my heart did somersaults. I finally believed. "You're brave, you know? Even braver than I thought."

His face morphed into a cheeky smile. "I said, don't coddle me.

God's honest truth, remember?"

I slid my hands around his neck, my heart so full it was about to explode.

"God's honest truth…" My finger played with the curls in his neck. "I'm all yours, Cem. And I want you to kiss me so hard I forget how to breathe."

"I can do that."

And he did.

*Bitirildi* (The End)

# Thank you!

In 2022, my little family set off on an insane adventure. After two years of covid lockdowns in New Zealand, we decided to drag the kids to Finland, to get acquainted with their roots. This involved months of camper van life, a tour of the post-pandemic Europe suffering from a heat wave, and later, quite by chance (or divine intervention), a four-month house-sitting gig near Helsinki, complete with a rather hyper dog. Although exciting and invigorating, it was also the most draining year of my adult life and I'm still processing everything that happened. Not least because I genuinely didn't know, upon leaving New Zealand, if I'd ever come back to live here.

(I did. Still here and I love it.)

But I brought with me one memory that doesn't come with complicated emotions, one that remains untainted and magical – the four days I spent in Istanbul with my husband. We ditched the kids with their grandparents and set off towards a modest Airbnb I'd picked based on no reviews (I'm brave/stupid).

As we arrived, late at night, we found the door unlocked and the flat both empty and obviously occupied, with personal belongings everywhere  TV on. With our phones not working on Turkish soil, we logged into the Airbnb wifi and managed to contact the host.

She told us to wait in the lobby and after a while, a young man who didn't speak a word of English, appeared and escorted us down the road to an alternative accommodation –a 1800s building complete with an arched stone lobby, three bedrooms, sea views and multiple chandeliers (even in the bathroom). This was my first taste of Turkish hospitality and opulence, and I soon learned more as we explored the city and talked to some wonderful people.

I've been watching Turkish TV shows ever since I accidentally discovered Erkenci Kus when looking for character inspiration for my previous book, *Night and Day*. Can Yaman's bedroom eyes instantly passed every language barrier, and I soon discovered there were many other, equally swoon-worthy candidates. I loved the way the *dizis* slowed down to give us those long looks and precious moments, much like a book would. I fell in love with the unashamedly romantic storytelling, to the point that a regular Hollywood romcom felt crass in comparison. But watching has never been enough for me. When I'm moved, I have to create.

However, when you live in a vehicle with two children, trying to earn enough money designing book covers to pay for petrol, worrying about where to park at night, there's little time (or space) for writing. This book only exists because of Hannu and Kate Kuusi, who took their six kids to Thailand and invited us to stay in their gigantic, fully equipped house, rent-free. My oldest got into a local school and we lived a borrowed life, frequently losing each other in the bowels of their mansion. I even got to know some school mums and pretended to be one of them. It was fun. And most of all, it lowered my daily stress levels to a manageable level so that I could once again write and create. Within one year, I experienced two vastly different lifestyles, to the point that I felt at home in both settings. An enlightening experience, to say the least.

I'm also grateful to our Turkish babysitter Kardelen Cakir, who graciously answered my countless questions and brainstormed important things like names of imaginary Turkish people and TV shows. I'm beyond grateful to Aida Kohen, an insightful artist I met in Istanbul, who helped me understand the Turkish culture and mentality. Obviously, I latched on to her and bothered her with a long video call later on.

I'm grateful to my wonderful beta readers, Erin Branscom, Charlotte Skye, Geniene Sadler and Polly Meek. Your feedback was invaluable! I'm also grateful to my editor Rachel Collins and proofreader Roxana Coumans, for helping me make this book shine as brightly as Cem's shirts. Thank you to Jen Morris for, again, helping me shape up the dreaded book blurb. And, special thanks to my trusted ARC readers Jenny Avery and Luna Day, for catching some remaining errors. I'm sure some are still hiding in there for those interested in a literary Easter egg hunt.

Lastly, I'm grateful for this opportunity to write and share my stories with you. I don't know if I could tolerate reality without medication if I didn't have this escape. Writing is one of God's greatest gifts. Do it. Share it. Add your voice to the mix. I'm doing it, and I didn't even grow up speaking English. If I can do it, you can do it.

# About the author

Enni Amanda is a graphic designer moonlighting as a rom-com author, or maybe it's the other way around. In 2006, she and her husband moved from Finland to New Zealand and fell in love with the gorgeous islands and their laid-back people. They spent eight years traveling between the two rather inconveniently located countries, studying filmmaking and running a film festival. Through all the filmmaking, Enni discovered a passion for screenwriting, which eventually led to writing books (a slippery slope). Her heart-warming, funny stories explore real-life issues like identity, found family, and the housing crisis. These days, she lives in the Waikato, close to the rolling hills of the Shire, raising two cute, rambunctious boys while writing away and ignoring housework.

# Thank you for reading!

If you enjoyed this book, please tell your friends
and leave a review on your favorite retailer website!
Referrals and reviews help unknown indie authors like
me get discovered.

To find out about my upcoming books,
sign up for my newsletter at
**enniamanda.com**

www.ingramcontent.com/pod-product-compliance
Lightning Source LLC
Chambersburg PA
CBHW011028190726
48290CB00011B/2750